W0254561

A POET FOR EVERY DAY OF THE YEAR

Also edited by Allie Esiri
from Macmillan Children's Books

A Poem for Every Night of the Year
A Poem for Every Day of the Year
Shakespeare for Every Day of the Year

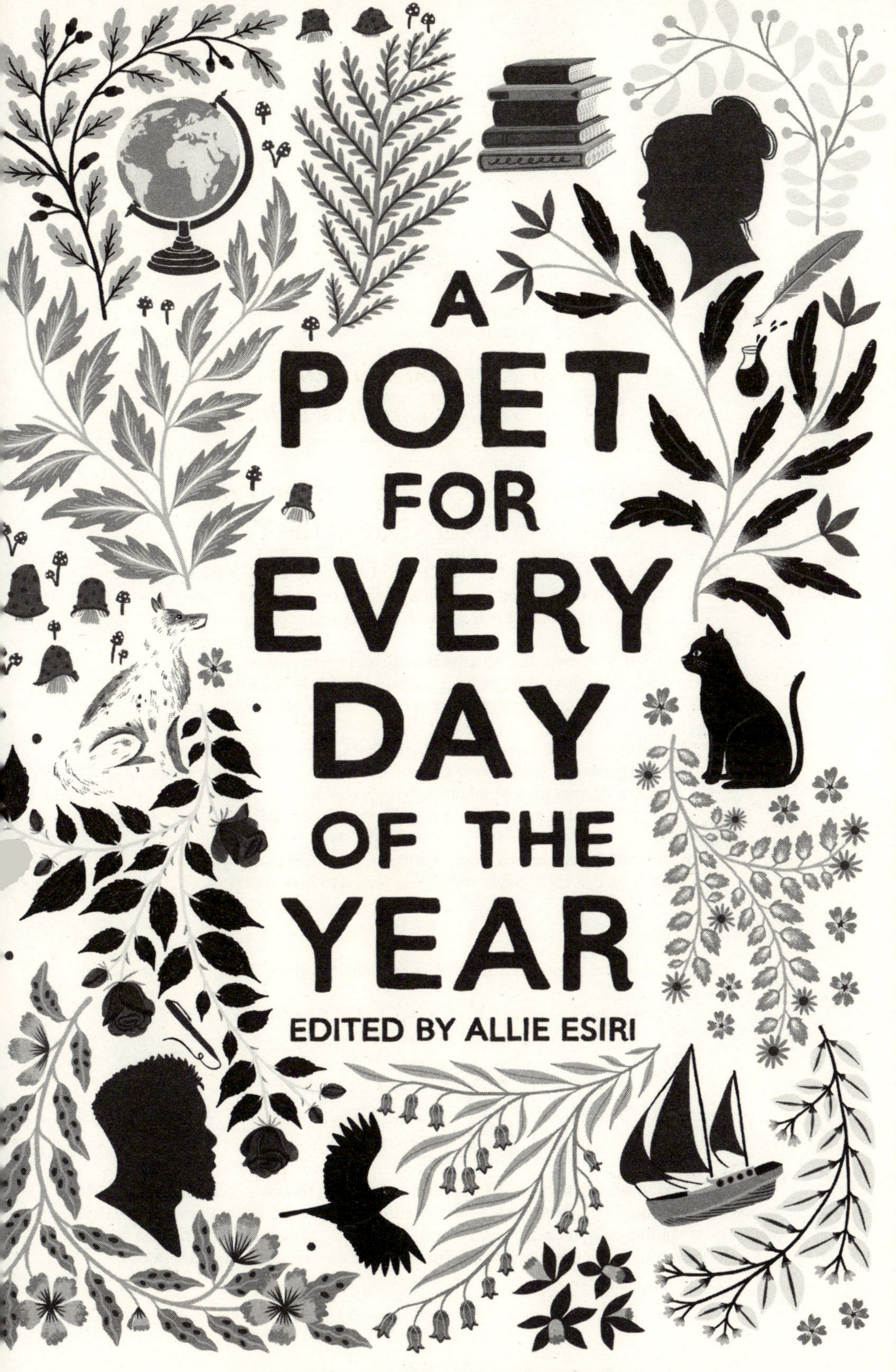

MACMILLAN CHILDREN'S BOOKS

Published 2021 by Macmillan Children's Books
an imprint of Pan Macmillan
The Smithson, 6 Briset Street, London EC1M 5NR
EU representative: Macmillan Publishers Ireland Ltd, 1st Floor,
The Liffey Trust Centre, 117–126 Sheriff Street Upper
Dublin 1, D01 YC43
Associated companies throughout the world
www.panmacmillan.com

ISBN 978-1-5290-5482-8

3 5 7 9 8 6 4

A CIP catalogue record for this book is available from the British Library.

Printed and bound by CPI Group (UK) Ltd, Croydon CR0 4YY
Typeset by The Dimpse

for Helen McCrory —
phenomenal actress and
phenomenal friend

Contents

February

March

April

May

June

July

August

September

October

November

December

Introduction

Writing in his 1821 essay 'The Defence of Poetry', the Romantic poet Percy Shelley famously declared that 'Poets are the unacknowledged legislators of the world'. A bold statement, it captures the rather paradoxical nature of the poet – at once a figure who has the potential to shape the world irrevocably with just a handful of well-chosen words, and one who is also perpetually overlooked and under-appreciated by society at large.

This new anthology seeks to shed light on the place and influence poets hold in the world – as forces of change and witnesses of history; as chroniclers of the everyday and architects of transcendent and escapist images – and to make sure that their genius is very much appreciated. Within the pages of this book you will discover an array of some of the most beautiful, uplifting, challenging, poignant, tragic, inspiring and comforting poems ever written by 366 different poets – one for each day of the (leap) year.

Poetry at its best has always, from Homer in Ancient Greece to contemporary greats such as Kae Tempest and Simon Armitage, enabled us to see different worlds, or rather, our own world differently. And yet so many similar collections of verse have focused almost entirely on white, western male writers, creating an even more unacknowledged class among the already unacknowledged exceptional women, LGBTQIA+ and minority poets. But with a whole calendar to fill, it has been a pleasure and a privilege to include a huge range of writers from across the globe and time, going as far back as 2000 BC. Sitting alongside canonical titans such as Chaucer, Shakespeare and Wordsworth are lesser known names such as Enheduanna and Charlotte Mew. Next to traditional sonnets, ballads, and heroic couplets you'll find curious and idiosyncratic forms such as cinquains, haikus, clerihews, calligrams and prose poems. No one writer or form dominates the book as each day offers something a little different.

But unlike my previous anthologies, which were built around the idea of offering A Poem for Every... the focus here is as much on the writers as their works. Each poet will be introduced to you through a short paragraph that will give you a snapshot of their life story, their place in literary history and other pieces of illuminating context, as well as some amusing anecdotes that you won't find in a textbook, like the time Byron called a certain other Romantic poet, 'Turdsworth'. I want these poems to transport you from the Roman forum to the Harlem Renaissance, from a Chinese tea ceremony to a summer cricket match.

You'll see that poets from seemingly incomparable backgrounds have written on the same themes, and have shared experiences sometimes millennia apart. They are constantly in dialogue with one another, and not just in the expected combinations. Here you will see how the modernist Ezra Pound was indebted to the ancient wisdom of Li Bai; how Ireland's W. B. Yeats would inform Chinua Achebe's poetry in Nigeria, and how contemporary performance and slam poets are continuing in a rich tradition of oral poetry that extends back to a time before official records and literacy.

Sometimes the connections between poets are more than purely literary. In these pages you will find husbands and wives, secret lovers, sons and daughters, neighbours and friends, siblings and brothers in arms. Occasionally poets will be united by how they lived – sometimes as noble courtiers, more frequently as penniless paupers – or how they died, often, unhappy and unrecognized.

Much of this book is dedicated to the promotion of those who have been unfairly all but forgotten. But conversely, it's also important to address the complex reputations of some of our most beloved writers. How do we go about reconciling the fact that so many writers who were so rich in talent were so inexcusably poor in their treatment of others? Readers, scholars and critics have found racism, religious bigotry, misogyny, intolerance and cruelty in countless poets – does this diminish the brilliance of their writing?

It is a difficult, sensitive issue with no easy answer, but maybe we can turn to the poets themselves for guidance. W. H. Auden – seemingly one of the good guys, who helped a woman escape from Nazi Germany through a marriage of convenience – once argued for the separation of the artist from their work in his poetic elegy for W. B. Yeats, saying, 'The death of the poet was kept from his poems.' Allen Ginsberg similarly made a case for cherishing the work not the person when he said, 'Poets are damned . . . but see with the eyes of angels.' As such, these individuals are included in this book on the basis that their works are undeniably influential and can still speak to us, still move us in isolation of their author's deeds.

But this book also seeks to celebrate all the progress that has been made. Poetry today is less an elitist circle, more an ever-growing community that's enriched by a plurality of writers who are giving a voice to the historically voiceless and lending an ear to those too often left unheard. I'm so proud to have put together an inclusive book that strives to be representative of, and relatable to, readers of all backgrounds.

As you go through the year you will see that many key cultural events and historical anniversaries, from Holocaust Memorial Day, to International Women's Day to UK Black History Month – as well as various national holidays and independence days – are commemorated with poets and poems relevant to those dates, which ask us to reflect on the past and consider how much more we still need to do in the fight for equality in future. At other times you will find runs of poems on a similar theme:

love around Valentine's Day, the War Poets near Armistice Day, nature coming into bloom in spring.

In addition to these poems and poets chosen to tie in with specific dates, are a whole host of entries that are simply there for their own sake. There are nonsense poems to entertain, satires to amuse, epics to beguile, nature verses to soothe and romances to melt even the iciest hearts.

A collection of such infinite variety fittingly has no set way of being read. You can make it a daily habit – a poem in the morning to invigorate the mind, or every evening to calm the soul – or approach it as a treasure trove of poetic gems to dip into whenever you want. 366 poets are waiting for you within these pages. All they need, dear reader, is you, as in the words of Walt Whitman, 'To have great poets, there must be great audiences.'

Allie Esiri

January

1 January ✶ *from* New Year's Morning ✶ Helen Hunt Jackson

15 October 1830 – 12 August 1885

The little town of Amherst, Massachusetts, can lay a strong claim to be one of the most literary locations in the United States. Not only is it the home of the great Emily Dickinson (see 4 December), but that also of her fellow poet, and childhood friend, Helen Hunt Jackson. Although she had a great many poems published to critical acclaim in her later years, Jackson's legacy is perhaps tied more closely to her political writing. The Indian Rights Association was created as a result of her influential essay, *A Century of Dishonor,* which detailed the wrongs and injustices committed against Native Americans by federal officers. Her zeal for life stayed with her until her final days, as reported by Dickinson in a letter she wrote to Jackson's husband about their last correspondence: '"Dear friend, can you walk?", were the last words that I wrote her. "I can fly" – her immortal (soaring) reply.'

Each morn is New Year's morn come true,
Morn of a festival to keep.

All nights are sacred nights to make
Confession and resolve and prayer;
All days are sacred days to wake
New gladness in the sunny air.
Only a night from old to new;
Only a sleep from night to morn.
The new is but the old come true;
Each sunrise sees a new year born.

2 January ✶ The Uncertainty of the Poet ✶ Wendy Cope

Born 1945

Wendy Cope began her professional career working as a primary school teacher before becoming a poet. Her work reveals a rare comic ability, and dazzles with irony, wit, and perfectly executed parody. Cope's books have been bestsellers, and they have also proven popular with critics who've called her 'a jet-age Tennyson' – for her common touch and perfect pitch – and compared her to Byron for her technically accomplished and wide-ranging work. This typically playful poem is in response to the 1913 painting *The Uncertainty of the Poet* by the godfather of Surrealism, Giorgio de Chirico.

I am a poet.
I am very fond of bananas.

I am bananas.
I am very fond of a poet.

I am a poet of bananas.
I am very fond,

A fond poet of 'I am, I am' –
Very bananas,

Fond of 'Am I bananas,
Am I?' – a very poet.

Bananas of a poet!
Am I fond? Am I very?

Poet bananas! I am.
I am fond of a 'very'.

I am of very fond bananas.
Am I a poet?

3 January ✶ When We Two Parted ✶ George Gordon, Lord Byron

22 January 1788 – 19 April 1824

One of Lord Byron's many claims to fame (or infamy) is that he was the first modern celebrity. A bestselling writer of his day, he was a kind of poster boy for the Romantic movement, along with his contemporaries and friends, Mary and Percy Shelley, and John Keats. Aristocratic, rebellious, handsome and, according to the writer Lady Caroline Lamb, 'mad, bad and dangerous to know', he was revered almost as much for his libertine lifestyle as he was for his brooding, bohemian poems. Indeed, his work was so popular that his poetry was even pirated. You could fill an entire book with tales of Byron's various anti-authoritarian escapades, from his later decision to go and fight in the Greek War of Independence to the time he kept a bear at Trinity College, Cambridge, after he was told that dogs were not allowed. He even attempted to get the bear enrolled as a student.

When we two parted
  In silence and tears,
Half broken-hearted
  To sever for years,
Pale grew thy cheek and cold,
  Colder thy kiss;
Truly that hour foretold
  Sorrow to this.

The dew of the morning
  Sunk chill on my brow—
It felt like the warning
  Of what I feel now.
Thy vows are all broken,
  And light is thy fame;
I hear thy name spoken,
  And share in its shame.

They name thee before me,
  A knell to mine ear;
A shudder comes o'er me—
  Why wert thou so dear?
They know not I knew thee,
  Who knew thee too well—
Long, long shall I rue thee,
  Too deeply to tell.

In secret we met—
  In silence I grieve,
That thy heart could forget,
  Thy spirit deceive.
If I should meet thee
  After long years,
How should I greet thee?—
  With silence and tears.

4 January ✶ Poetry ✶ Eleanor Farjeon

13 February 1881 – 5 June 1965

Eleanor Farjeon's artistic career was almost fated, growing up with a novelist father and composer brother. She spent her adult life in illustrious literary circles with friends such as D. H. Lawrence, Robert Frost and Edward Thomas. Her most famous work is the hymn 'Morning has Broken', which was set to an old Gaelic tune and then transformed into a hit song in the 1970s by the English singer-songwriter Yusuf Islam, known then as Cat Stevens. Farjeon wrote fiction and non-fiction for both children and adults, and there is a prestigious yearly award for children's literature that bears her name.

What is Poetry? Who knows?
Not a rose, but the scent of a rose;
Not a sky, but the light in the sky;
Not the fly, but the gleam of the fly;
Not the sea, but the sound of the sea;
Not myself, but what makes me
See, hear, and feel something that prose
Cannot: and what it is, who knows?

5 January ✶ BC:AD ✶ U. A. Fanthorpe

22 July 1929 – 28 April 2009

U. A. Fanthorpe is a poet who serves to show that it's never too late to become a writer. After working as an English teacher at a girls' college – and then later as a hospital receptionist – she finally had her poems published shortly before turning fifty. A fan of T. S. Eliot and W. H. Auden, she wrote on Englishness, art, nature and her Quaker background (as seen in this poem for Epiphany). Few have been better able to summarize the centrality of poetry in our lives than Fanthorpe in these lines from an interview: 'Poetry is important because it reaches the places that other kinds of writing can't reach . . . [It] has all the voices – wit, sincerity, pastiche, tragedy, delight, and most importantly it's with us from the start of our lives to the end.'

This was the moment when Before
Turned into After, and the future's
Uninvented timekeepers presented arms.

This was the moment when nothing
Happened. Only dull peace
Sprawled boringly over the earth.

This was the moment when even energetic Romans
Could find nothing better to do
Than counting heads in remote provinces.

And this was the moment
When a few farm workers and three
Members of an obscure Persian sect

Walked haphazard by starlight straight
Into the kingdom of heaven.

6 January ✶ Epiphany at Saint Mary and All Saints ✶ Geoffrey Hill

18 June 1932 – 30 June 2016

Geoffrey Hill is one of the UK's most highly regarded post-war poets. The only child of a police constable, he studied English at Oxford before going on to forge a fruitful career in academia, teaching at universities in England and the US. Towards the end of his life, he was given both the prestigious post of Professor of Poetry at Oxford and a knighthood. A poet of dizzying learning and intelligence, he was lauded by critics and seen as the ingenious inheritor of Eliot's status, without becoming a public literary celebrity. Perhaps his lack of wider recognition is due to the fact that he believed poetry could, and should, be difficult, since human beings are difficult.

The wise men, vulnerable in ageing plaster,
are borne as gifts
to be set down among the other treasures
in their familial strangeness, mystery's toys.

Below the church the Stour slovens
through its narrow cut.
On service roads the lights cast amber salt
slatted with a thin rain doubling as snow.

Showings are not unknown: a six-winged seraph
somewhere impends—it is the geste of invention,
not the creative but the creator spirit.
The night air sings a colder spell to come.

7 January ✶ The Garden Year ✶ Sara Coleridge

23 December 1802 – 3 May 1852

The name is a bit of a giveaway, but Sara Coleridge hails from a very literary family. The daughter of the early Romantic poet Samuel Taylor Coleridge, she was born in the Lake District, and grew up under the influence of her father, her uncle, the Poet Laureate Robert Southey, and a neighbour by the name of William Wordsworth. Sara was an editor of her father's work, and in her own right a translator, a novelist – best known for the fairy tale *Phantasmion* – and a poet who wrote verses for children, such as the one below.

January brings the snow,
Makes our feet and fingers glow.

February brings the rain,
Thaws the frozen lake again.

March brings breezes, loud and shrill,
To stir the dancing daffodil.

April brings the primrose sweet,
Scatters daisies at our feet.

May brings flocks of pretty lambs
Skipping by their fleecy dams.

June brings tulips, lilies, roses,
Fills the children's hands with posies.

Hot July brings cooling showers,
Apricots, and gillyflowers.

August brings the sheaves of corn,
Then the harvest home is borne.

Warm September brings the fruit;
Sportsmen then begin to shoot.

Fresh October brings the pheasant;
Then to gather nuts is pleasant.

Dull November brings the blast;
Then the leaves are whirling fast.

Chill December brings the sleet,
Blazing fire, and Christmas treat.

8 January ✶ Light Snow-Fall After Frost ✶ Thomas Hardy

2 June 1840 – 11 January 1928

Thomas Hardy is primarily known to most readers as a novelist, the author of such classics as *Tess of the d'Urbervilles* and *Jude the Obscure*. But in fact he considered himself to be first and foremost a poet, and he wrote over a thousand poems. Hardy grew up in the rural county of Dorset, which provided him with the inspiration for many of the rustic characters and settings that define his work. His keen ear for the musicality of language came perhaps from his violin-playing father, while a love of literature was imbued in him by his mother. His long life spanned from the early Victorian period to the 1920s, and so he can be seen as a literary bridge between the late Romantics and the wave of modernist talents (Virginia Woolf, Ezra Pound, W. B. Yeats) with whom he was friends. A master of various styles of prose and verse, he adapted his own writing throughout his career to reflect the changing world around him.

On the flat road a man at last appears:
How much his whitening hairs
Owe to the settling snow's mute anchorage,
And how much to a life's rough pilgrimage,
One cannot certify.

The frost is on the wane,
And cobwebs hanging close outside the pane
Pose as festoons of thick white worsted there,
Of their pale presence no eye being aware
Till the rime made them plain.

A second man comes by;
His ruddy beard brings fire to the pallid scene:
His coat is faded green;
Hence seems it that his mien
Wears something of the dye
Of the berried holm-trees that he passes nigh.

The snow-feathers so gently swoop that though
But half an hour ago
The road was brown, and now is starkly white,
A watcher would have failed defining quite
When it transformed it so.

9 January ✶ Snow ✶ Adelaide Crapsey

9 September 1878 – 8 October 1914

The American poet Adelaide Crapsey is responsible for creating a unique kind of cinquain (a poem composed of five lines and twenty-two syllables, a variation of the haiku). Growing up in New York, she benefited from a liberal education which gave young women a stronger than usual start at the turn of the century. She also lived in Britain, France and Rome – taking inspiration with her along the way – before becoming a teacher. Her life was unfortunately troubled by chronic illness, but even in her final years, which she spent in a sanatorium, Crapsey was writing and inventing new poetic forms which linked old traditions to modernist approaches.

Look up . . .
From bleakening hills
Blows down the light, first breath
Of wintry wind . . . look up, and scent
The snow!

10 January ✶ The Birch Tree ✶ Sergei Yesenin, translated by K. M. W. Klara

3 October 1895 – 28 December 1925

Sergei Yesenin, like Byron before him, developed a notorious reputation in his native Russia as a flamboyant 'hooligan' poet. Born to a peasant family, he moved to Moscow at seventeen, and was a literary voice of the Revolutionary period. He became disillusioned with the revolution when he saw that his beloved countryside would be sacrificed for the purpose of industrialization. He helped to start the Imaginist movement (a distant relative to the Imagist movement of Ezra Pound), which focused on poetry defined by striking images. 'The Birch Tree' is still part of the Russian school curriculum.

Under my window
Tucked in the snow
White birch retired
Clad in silver glow.

On the fluffy branches
Snowy-trim with silver-tinge
Melted around catkins
Forming white fringe.

Like golden fires
Snow-flakes blazed
While birch stood still
Asleep, or amazed.

Meanwhile, lazily
Strolling around,
Dawn threw more 'silver'
On the twigs (and ground).

11 January ✶ On Change of Weathers ✶ Francis Quarles

c. 8 May 1592 – 8 September 1644

It's a wonder that Francis Quarles had any time to devote to poetry, given that he and his wife had an incredible eighteen children. But he enjoyed much success with his work, especially during the early part of the English Civil War. For a time he also held the title of the Chronologer of the City of London, a post previously taken by the great writers Ben Jonson and Thomas Middleton. His most popular work was an anthology of symbols, with complementary mottoes and verses, which he called *Emblems*. Quarles managed to survive both the plague and the sword, but when he eventually did die, he left his family in relative poverty.

And were it for thy profit, to obtain
All *Sunshine?* No vicissitude of *Rain?*
Think'st thou, that thy laborious *Plough* requires
Not Winter *frosts,* as well as Summer *fires?*
There must be both: Sometimes these hearts of ours
Must have the sweet, the seasonable Show'rs
Of Tears; Sometimes the Frost of chill *despair*
Makes our desired *sunshine* seeme more *fair;*
Weathers that most oppose to Flesh and Blood,
Are such as help to make our *Harvest* good.
We may not choose, great *God;* It is thy *Task:*
We know not what to *have;* nor how to *ask*.

12 January ✶ A Song for England ✶ Andrew Salkey

30 January 1928 – 28 April 1995

Andrew Salkey was born in Panama, but brought up in Jamaica by his mother and grandparents while his father stayed put. The fact that he didn't meet his father until 1960 perhaps explains why so much of his poetry was about maternal relationships, although this poem is about the less-than-delightful English weather. He was a leading light of the *Caribbean Voices* programme (on BBC Radio) and the Caribbean Artists Movement. In his later years he relocated to Amherst, Massachusetts, to teach poetry, giving the town yet another literary connection.

An' a so de rain a-fall
An' a so de snow a-rain

An' a so de fog a-fall
An' a so de sun a-fail

An' a so de seasons mix
An' a so de bag-o-tricks

But a so me understan'
De misery o' de Englishman.

13 January ✶ After the Winter ✶ Claude McKay

15 September 1889 – 22 May 1948

Festus Claudius McKay grew up in Jamaica before winning a stipend to study in New York City in 1914. A prominent figure associated with the New York-based Harlem Renaissance, he wrote with pride about his African heritage, the struggles of living in a racist American society, and his experiences of rural life in Jamaica. In addition to being a poet, he also worked as a constable in the Jamaican capital of Kingston.

Some day, when trees have shed their leaves
    And against the morning's white
The shivering birds beneath the eaves
    Have sheltered for the night,
We'll turn our faces southward, love,
    Toward the summer isle
Where bamboos spire the shafted grove
    And wide-mouthed orchids smile.

And we will seek the quiet hill
    Where towers the cotton tree,
And leaps the laughing crystal rill,
    And works the droning bee.
And we will build a cottage there
    Beside an open glade,
With black-ribbed blue-bells blowing near,
    And ferns that never fade.

14 January ✶ We Real Cool ✶ Gwendolyn Brooks

7 June 1917 – 3 December 2000

If U. A. Fanthorpe proved that you can never be too old to become a poet, then Gwendolyn Brooks showed that there's no such thing as being too young either. Encouraged by her parents, Brooks published her first poem when she was just thirteen, kick-starting a remarkable career that saw her become the first Black author to win the Pulitzer Prize for Poetry in 1950. She described her poems as non-compromising in their pursuit of meaning and addressing social issues. Her political engagement later saw her work for the leading American Civil Rights organization known as the NAACP (National Association for the Advancement of Colored People).

The Pool Players.
Seven at the Golden Shovel.

We real cool. We
Left school. We

Lurk late. We
Strike straight. We

Sing sin. We
Thin gin. We

Jazz June. We
Die soon.

15 January ✶ Still I Rise ✶ Maya Angelou

4 April 1928 – 28 May 2014

Who better to recognize on Martin Luther King, Jr.'s birthday than Maya Angelou, whose work did so much to champion Black experiences and female empowerment? As a young woman, she worked for Martin Luther King, Jr. and Malcolm X, before going on to become a modern icon of the Civil Rights movement in her own right. The ultimate Renaissance woman, she was also the first Black female Hollywood director, and a prodigious poet and author: her autobiographical *I Know Why the Caged Bird Sings* is perhaps one of the best known and most beloved books of modern times. Although often commenting on political issues close to her, she spoke to what is unique and powerful in every one of us, while emphasizing the compassionate strength of the human spirit which pulses through us all. In 1993, she was asked to read a poem at the inauguration of President Bill Clinton, and in 2010 she was awarded the Presidential Medal of Freedom by President Barack Obama.

You may write me down in history
With your bitter, twisted lies,
You may trod me in the very dirt
But still, like dust, I'll rise.

Does my sassiness upset you?
Why are you beset with gloom?
'Cause I walk like I've got oil wells
Pumping in my living room.

Just like moons and like suns,
With the certainty of tides,
Just like hopes springing high,
Still I'll rise.

Did you want to see me broken?
Bowed head and lowered eyes?
Shoulders falling down like teardrops,
Weakened by my soulful cries?

Does my haughtiness offend you?
Don't you take it awful hard
'Cause I laugh like I've got gold mines
Diggin' in my own backyard.

You may shoot me with your words,
You may cut me with your eyes,
You may kill me with your hatefulness,
But still, like air, I'll rise.

Does my sexiness upset you?
Does it come as a surprise
That I dance like I've got diamonds
At the meeting of my thighs?

Out of the huts of history's shame
I rise
Up from a past that's rooted in pain
I rise
I'm a black ocean, leaping and wide,
Welling and swelling I bear in the tide.

Leaving behind nights of terror and fear
I rise
Into a daybreak that's wondrously clear
I rise
Bringing the gifts that my ancestors gave,
I am the dream and the hope of the slave.
I rise
I rise
I rise.

16 January ✶ Ancestors ✶ Nikita Gill

Born 1987

Nikita Gill had her first story, a non-fiction piece about her grandfather, published in a newspaper at the age of twelve. Raised in India, she studied, and now lives, in England. She is a pioneer for sharing poetry visually on social media and an unwavering supporter of poetry, no matter the platform used to deliver it. She has garnered hundreds of thousands of followers for her inspirational, compassionate poetry.

Your ancestors did not survive
everything that nearly ended them
for you to shrink yourself
to make someone else
comfortable.

This sacrifice is your warcry, be loud,
be everything and make them proud.

17 January ✶ January ✶ Joseph Coelho

Joseph Coelho is an award-winning children's author, performance poet and playwright. He writes about communities and families, and cleverly observes the wonder of the everyday. This January poem is based on an Irish legend from the seventeenth century.

There is a legend of two murmurations of starlings warring above the City of Cork in Ireland in the 1600s – starlings have never been known to war in flocks but they certainly do fight.

They were the Rorschach of the winter months,
the folding of sky-shadows,
of air-shoals pirouetting into the January nip,
swarms riding frosted winds,
silently testing the sky with their ink-magic.

Not ready for the tentacle gathering
that rose from the east
the heat of spring starlings
cloaked in oil slicks
needle beaked
and strong of claw.

The clash of murmurs
was whispered
in a rain of birds
as flightless feathers fell
in the war of winds.

Winter flew into spring,
black storms colliding with hot nights.
The murmurations twisted through one another
winter desperate to stay,
spring determined to arrive.

The people watch as feathers cloak them
farmers clutching hopeful seeds
children gazing with eager fingers
on buttoned jackets.
Which swarm will win this war?

But the birds that come with the sun
are always victorious – the winter flock is tired
their wings have beaten cold into existence
it is time for them to leave.

Beaten and flight-sore the winter murmuration
rides its ribbon away
as spring's flock swoops into longer days
and brighter skies,
as farmers test the warmth of soil
and children release that first coat button.

18 January ✶ Us Two ✶ A. A. Milne

18 January 1882 – 31 January 1956

A. A. Milne is the author of the beloved storybooks about the teddy bear with a big heart (and little brain), Winnie-the-Pooh, and wonderful collections of light verse, all of which he wrote for his son Christopher Robin. Despite studying Maths at the University of Cambridge, he decided to pursue literature professionally, finding success writing for the magazine *Punch* and a number of plays. Outside of his work, he's known to have played in a literary superstar cricket team that included J. M. Barrie (Peter Pan), Arthur Conan Doyle (Sherlock Holmes) and P. G. Wodehouse (Jeeves and Wooster) – you'd think their team-talk banter would have been of a rather more literary nature than you'd normally hear on a cricket field!

Wherever I am, there's always Pooh,
There's always Pooh and Me.
Whatever I do, he wants to do,
'Where are you going today?' says Pooh:
'Well, that's very odd 'cos I was too.
Let's go together,' says Pooh, says he.
'Let's go together,' says Pooh.

'What's twice eleven?' I said to Pooh.
('Twice what?' said Pooh to Me.)
'I *think* it ought to be twenty-two.'
'Just what I think myself,' said Pooh.
'It wasn't an easy sum to do,
But that's what it is,' said Pooh, said he.
'That's what it is,' said Pooh.

'Let's look for dragons,' I said to Pooh.
'Yes, let's,' said Pooh to Me.
We crossed the river and found a few –
'Yes, those are dragons all right,' said Pooh.
'As soon as I saw their beaks I knew.
That's what they are,' said Pooh, said he.
'That's what they are,' said Pooh.

'Let's frighten the dragons,' I said to Pooh.
'That's right,' said Pooh to Me.
'I'm not afraid,' I said to Pooh,
And I held his paw and I shouted 'Shoo!
Silly old dragons!' – and off they flew.
'I wasn't afraid,' said Pooh, said he,
'I'm *never* afraid with you.'

So wherever I am, there's always Pooh,
There's always Pooh and Me.
'What would I do?' I said to Pooh,
'If it wasn't for you,' and Pooh said: 'True,
It isn't much fun for One, but Two
Can stick together,' says Pooh, says he.
'That's how it is,' says Pooh.

19 January ✶ You Must Never Bath in an Irish Stew ✶ Spike Milligan

16 April 1918 – 27 February 2002

Born Terence Alan Milligan, to an Irish father and English mother, Spike Milligan was a brilliant comedian – he was a member of the Goons, a comedy troupe that was a forerunner to Monty Python – and the creator of sublimely ridiculous poems. His irrepressible energy and penchant for silliness made him notoriously difficult to work with. Indeed his agent told a story of a time when he spent an entire meeting pretending to be a jellyfish. A writer both of long-form memoirs and pithy one-liners ('I thought I'd begin by reading a poem by Shakespeare, but then I thought, "Why should I? He never reads any of mine".'), he was adored by children and appealed to the inner child within his adult fans. His absurd sense of humour remained with him until the very end: the epitaph on his gravestone includes the phrase *'Dúirt mé leat go raibh mé breoite',* Gaelic for 'I told you I was ill'.

You must never bath in an Irish Stew
It's a most illogical thing to do
But should you persist against my reasoning
Don't fail to add the appropriate seasoning.

20 January ✶ Only Snow ✶ Allan Ahlberg

Born 1938

Allan Ahlberg is best known for his many lively, rhyming picture books (there are over a hundred, including *Each Peach Pear Plum*, *The Jolly Postman* and *Peepo!*), many of which were lovingly illustrated by his late wife, Janet. He has devoted his career to writing books that invite children to discover and share in the joy of reading. Ahlberg himself has said that he was such an avid reader as a child that he joined three libraries so that he could take out twelve books at once.

Outside, the sky was almost brown.
The clouds were hanging low.
Then all of a sudden it happened:
The air was full of snow.

The children rushed to the windows.
The teacher let them go,
Though she teased them for their foolishness.
After all, it was only snow.

It was only snow that was falling,
Only out of the sky,
Only unto the turning earth
Before the blink of an eye.

What else could it do from up there,
But fall in the usual way?
It was only weather, really.
What else could you say?

The teacher sat at her desk
Putting ticks in a little row,
While the children stared through steamy glass
At the only snow.

21 January ✶ Winter-Time ✶
Robert Louis Stevenson

13 November 1850 – 3 December 1894

Another writer who found solace in reading was Robert Louis Stevenson, the author of novels including *Treasure Island*, *Kidnapped* and *Strange Case of Dr Jekyll and Mr Hyde*, and some of the very best poems ever written for children. Brought up in Edinburgh, his schooling was sporadic due to chronic illnesses, but he had a nurse who regularly read to him; he touchingly later dedicated his collection, *A Child's Garden of Verses*, to her. Like so many poets before, and since, Stevenson was a rebel at university, where his outrageous outfits saw him given the nickname 'Velvet Jacket'. Despite qualifying to practise as a barrister (after eschewing the family business of engineering), Stevenson refused to give up on his childhood dream of becoming a writer, and devoted his life to literature to such an extent that he always carried two books in his pocket wherever he went – 'one to read, one to write in'.

Late lies the wintry sun a-bed,
A frosty, fiery sleepy-head;
Blinks but an hour or two; and then,
A blood-red orange, sets again.

Before the stars have left the skies,
At morning in the dark I rise;
And shivering in my nakedness,
By the cold candle, bathe and dress.

Close by the jolly fire I sit
To warm my frozen bones a bit;
Or with a reindeer-sled, explore
The colder countries round the door.

When to go out, my nurse doth wrap
Me in my comforter and cap;
The cold wind burns my face, and blows
Its frosty pepper up my nose.

Black are my steps on silver sod;
Thick blows my frosty breath abroad;
And tree and house, and hill and lake,
Are frosted like a wedding-cake.

22 January ✶ I Am the Song ✶ Charles Causley

24 August 1917 – 4 November 2003

'If I didn't write poetry I think I'd explode,' said Charles Causley, who turned to literature as a means of escaping from, and making sense of, the traumas that defined his early life – his father's death from long-standing injuries from the First World War, and his own experiences in the navy in the Second World War. As such, many of his poems focus on childhood, and they share a preoccupation with the loss of innocence in the face of suffering with those of William Blake. His simple, unadorned style made him accessible to readers of all ages and backgrounds, but without diminishing his reputation in literary circles – Philip Larkin, Seamus Heaney and Ted Hughes all ranked among his admirers. He is proudly celebrated to this day by his native Cornish community, who hold an annual Charles Causley Festival.

I am the song that sings the bird.
I am the leaf that grows the land.
I am the tide that moves the moon.
I am the stream that halts the sand.
I am the cloud that drives the storm.
I am the earth that lights the sun.
I am the fire that strikes the stone.
I am the clay that shapes the hand.
I am the word that speaks the man.

23 January ✶ Nature Table ✶ Fleur Adcock

Born 1934

Fleur Adcock was born in New Zealand and migrated between her home country and England throughout her childhood. She has worked as a librarian, and as a translator of Latin and Romanian poetry, but is now better known for her own writing. Her award-winning poems take everyday subjects and issues of identity, and lace them with a beguiling blend of irony, fantasy and darkness.

The tadpoles won't keep still in the aquarium;
Ben's tried seven times to count them –
thirty-two, thirty-three, wriggle, wriggle –
all right, he's got better things to do.

Heidi stares into the tank, wearing
a snail on her knuckle like a ring.
She can see purple clouds in the water,
a sky for the tadpoles in their world.

Matthew's drawing a worm. Yesterday
he put one down Elizabeth's neck.
But these are safely locked in the wormery
eating their mud; he's tried that too.

Laura sways with her nose in a daffodil,
drunk on pollen, her eyes tight shut.
The whole inside of her head is filling
with a slow hum of fizzy yellow.

Tom squashes his nose against the window.
He hopes it may look like a snail's belly
to the thrush outside. But is not attacked:
the thrush is happy on the bird-table.

The wind ruffles a chaffinch's crest
and gives the sparrows frilly grey knickers
as they squabble over their seeds and bread.
The sun swings in and out of clouds.

Ben's constructing a wigwam of leaves
for the snails. Heidi whispers to the tadpoles
'Promise you won't start eating each other!'
Matthew's rather hoping they will.

A wash of sun sluices the window,
bleaches Tom's hair blonder, separates
Laura from her daffodil with a sneeze,
and sends the tadpoles briefly frantic;

until the clouds flop down again
grey as wet canvas. The wind quickens,
birds go flying, window-glass rattles,
pellets of hail are among the birdseed.

24 January ✶ Slithering Silver ✶ Liz Brownlee

Born 1958

A children's poet and a UK National Poetry Day ambassador, Liz Brownlee fuses visual and aural techniques to create uniquely immersive poetry. Her work tackles many subjects, from notable women to the animals at the local zoo in her hometown of Bristol, and she experiments with form, as seen in this ingenious shape poem.

A shiny, slimy trail unravels behind each tiny snail tail's travels, without fail it's long and winding, though only one footprint's left behind him . . .

25 January ✶ A Red, Red Rose ✶ Robert Burns

25 January 1759 – 21 July 1796

Like millions of teenage boys around the world, Robert Burns turned to poetry as a means of impressing a girl. Unlike most teenage boys, however, Burns went on to become one of the most famous British writers and the national poet of Scotland. Born in Alloway in South West Scotland to a humble tenant-farming family, Burns grew up in a small rural community. But even when he swapped the trowel for the pen in his youth, he never forgot his roots. He wrote his poems in the local vernacular and gathered up and recorded the traditional songs of his lowland Scots dialect. His books of comic, romantic and broadly relatable verse enjoyed stratospheric success in Edinburgh, then in London, and then the world over, from China to Russia, where his attention to inequalities faced by the working classes was greatly admired. Indeed, his egalitarian worldview is perhaps best outlined in this quotation: 'The Honest man, though e'er sae poor, / Is king o' men for a' that.' In Scotland, 25 January is recognized as Burns Night, when people raise a toast and have a feast in honour of his life and work.

O my Luve is like a red, red rose
  That's newly sprung in June;
O my Luve is like the melody
  That's sweetly played in tune.

So fair art thou, my bonnie lass,
  So deep in luve am I;
And I will luve thee still, my dear,
  Till a' the seas gang dry.

Till a' the seas gang dry, my dear,
  And the rocks melt wi' the sun;
I will love thee still, my dear,
  While the sands o' life shall run.

And fare thee weel, my only luve!
  And fare thee weel awhile!
And I will come again, my luve,
  Though it were ten thousand mile.

26 January ✶ Spiritual Song of the Aborigine ✶ Hyllus Maris

25 December 1933 – 4 August 1986

26 January is a controversial date in Australia. A national day marking the country's supposed founding, it is seen to eradicate the history of the Aboriginal people who were living on the land for millennia before it was colonized, and this poem addresses the controversial notion that Australia was ever 'founded'. It was written by Hyllus Maris, a poet, social worker and key figure in the Aboriginal rights movement who co-founded the National Council of Aboriginal and Island Women.

I am a child of the Dreamtime People
Part of the land, like the gnarled gumtree
I am the river, softly singing
Chanting our songs on my way to the sea
My spirit is the dust-devils
Mirages, that dance on the plain
I'm the snow, the wind and the falling rain
I'm part of the rocks and the red desert earth
Red as the blood that flows in my veins
I am eagle, crow and snake that glides
Through the rainforest that clings to the mountainside
I awakened here when the earth was new
There was emu, wombat, kangaroo
No other man of a different hue
I am this land
And this land is me
I am Australia.

27 January ✶ If This Is A Man ✶ Primo Levi

31 July 1919 – 11 April 1987

The Jewish Italian writer Primo Levi is best known for his harrowing account of his first-hand experience of the Holocaust, *If This Is A Man,* which starts with this poem. Born in Turin, Levi began his studies before the fascists in Italy banned Jews from state education, and he completed his degree in chemistry with the help of a fearless professor. Work was hard to come by, though, and he could only gain employment using forged documents. He joined an Italian resistance group in 1943, before being arrested and sent to Auschwitz – he was one of the few Italians who survived the Nazi concentration camp, which was liberated in 1945. He returned to Turin and wrote the book that chronicled his horrifying ordeal, with the vow never to forget. It went largely unread until 1958, when a second edition and translations were published, and it now stands alongside *The Diary of Anne Frank* as one of the most important pieces of Holocaust literature.

You who live safe
In your warm houses,
You who find, returning in the evening,
Hot food and friendly faces:
    Consider if this is a man
    Who works in the mud
    Who does not know peace
    Who fights for a scrap of bread
    Who dies because of a yes or a no.
    Consider if this is a woman,
    Without hair and without name
    With no more strength to remember,
    Her eyes empty and her womb cold
    Like a frog in the winter.
Meditate that this came about:

I commend these words to you.
Carve them in your hearts
At home, in the street,
Going to bed, rising;
Repeat them to your children,
    Or may your house fall apart,
    May illness impede you,
    May your children turn their faces from you.

28 January ✶ Anne Frank Huis ✶ Andrew Motion

Born 1952

The Poet Laureate between 1999 and 2009, Andrew Motion was the first to hold the position for a finite time, and so the first, as he put it, to be able to say 'I *was* Poet Laureate' (excluding John Dryden, who was ignominiously fired). He was taught by W. H. Auden as a student at Oxford, and while teaching at Hull became close to Philip Larkin, whose biography he went on to write. During his time as Poet Laureate he co-founded the Poetry Archive – an organization that produces, acquires and preserves recordings of poets reading their own work. Of his own poetry he has said, 'I want my writing to be as clear as water. I want readers to see all the way through its surfaces into the swamp.'

Even now, after twice her lifetime of grief
and anger in the very place, whoever comes
to climb these narrow stairs, discovers how
the bookcase slides aside, then walks through
shadow into sunlit room, can never help

but break her secrecy again. Just listening
is a kind of guilt: the Westerkirk repeats
itself outside, as if all time worked round
towards her fear, and made each stroke
die down on guarded streets. Imagine it –

four years of whispering, and loneliness,
and plotting, day by day, the Allied line
in Europe with a yellow chalk. What hope
she had for ordinary love and interest
survives her here, displayed above the bed

as pictures of her family; some actors;
fashions chosen by Princess Elizabeth.
And those who stoop to see them find
not only patience missing its reward,
but one enduring wish for chances

like my own: to leave as simply
as I do, and walk at ease
up dusty tree-lined avenues, or watch
a silent barge come clear of bridges
settling their reflections in the blue canal.

29 January ✶ Persephone ✶ Michael Longley

Born 1939

A Belfast poet, with a classics degree from Trinity College Dublin, Longley is a leading light in Northern Irish poetry. Like Robert Burns, he claims to have written his first poem as a teenager 'in order to impress a girlfriend'. Since then he has tackled some rather more serious subjects, from the Troubles in Belfast to love, grief and nature. Of poetry he has said, 'Though the poet's first duty must be to his imagination, he has other obligations – and not just as a citizen. He would be inhuman if he did not respond to tragic events in his own community, and a poor artist if he did not seek to endorse that response imaginatively.'

I

I see as through a skylight in my brain
The mole strew its buildings in the rain,

The swallows turn above their broken home
And all my acres in delirium.

II

Straitjacketed by cold and numskulled
Now sleep the welladjusted and the skilled –

The bat folds its wing like a winter leaf,
The squirrel in its hollow holds aloof.

III

The weasel and ferret, the stoat and fox
Move hand in glove across the equinox.

I can tell how softly their footsteps go –
Their footsteps borrow silence from the snow.

30 January ✶ Lot's Wife ✶ Anna Akhmatova, translated by Stanley Kunitz

23 June 1889 – 5 March 1966

Anna Akhmatova was born Anna Andreevna Gorenko to a noble family in Odessa, in what is now Ukraine. But when she announced that she was going to be a poet, her father insisted that she change her name, so as not to bring the family into disrepute. One of the most celebrated writers in twentieth-century Russian literature, she is revered by many for her body of work which tells of the people's suffering under Stalin. Although her books were banned under the Soviet regime, her income halted and her status reduced to that of a 'non-person', she chose to remain in her homeland, insisting that poets can only sustain art in their native country.

And the just man trailed God's shining agent,
over a black mountain, in his giant track,
while a restless voice kept harrying his woman:
'It's not too late, you can still look back

at the red towers of your native Sodom,
the square where once you sang, the spinning-shed,
at the empty windows set in the tall house
where sons and daughters blessed your marriage-bed.'

A single glance: a sudden dart of pain
stitching her eyes before she made a sound . . .
Her body flaked into transparent salt,
and her swift legs rooted to the ground.

Who will grieve for this woman? Does she not seem
too insignificant for our concern?
Yet in my heart I never will deny her,
who suffered death because she chose to turn.

31 January ✶ Eurydice (Orpheus) ✶ Imogen Russell Williams

Born 1982

Imogen Russell Williams is a champion of children's literature, writing for the *Guardian* and the *Times Literary Supplement,* amongst other print and broadcast outlets. In addition to her work in journalism, she is the author of highly regarded non-fiction books and poetry.

Here in the soft black ash I found some bone
in fragments: femur, little finger, rib
and strung together music of my own
for the first time.

Halt as a child's first footsteps, thud and plink,
a tonking tune like birdscratch on the air –
a blunt cascade, the overflowing brink
of a mud dam.

The music of my husband hales down suns.
He gets out his guitar, and plucks; extracts
with the strings' fall, the sweet note-runs,
his listeners' guts.

He had the heart from me. Of course he did –
when Orpheus plays for you, you will be played.
His lyre coiled me round. The serpent slid
up to my waist.

But now it seems I have come to prefer
my own halt limping music. With a chord
(strange, dissonant, dissolving in a blur)
I turn his head.

February

1 February ✶ St Brigid and the Baker ✶ Tony Mitton

Born 1951

Tony Mitton was born in the Libyan capital of Tripoli and spent his childhood moving between countries and continents due to his father's military postings. Like many poets writing today, he started his working life as a primary school teacher. He began writing poems as a teenager, but it was only after discovering he could amuse his own children with his writing that he decided to pursue it professionally. Of poetry he has said, 'It can help us to see the magical in the ordinary.' This poem commemorates the ancient Celtic festival of St Brigid's Day, which marks (perhaps prematurely) the arrival of spring on 1 February each year.

As Brigid was walking
the old narrow track
she passed by a baker
with bread in his sack.

She put out a hand
from the fold of her cloak,
and these are the words
she softly spoke:

'Please give me a loaf
for my sisters and me,
and we'll share it tonight
as we sit to our tea.'

But the baker, he muttered
and shook a mean head.
'If you want to eat, sister,
then bake your own bread.'

She looks in his eyes then,
but all that she found
was a stare that was hard
as the stones on the ground.

So Brigid passed quietly
along the hard track
as the bread turned to stone
on the baker's back.

2 February ✶ On the Birth of a Son ✶
Su Shi, translated by Arthur Waley

8 January 1037 – 24 August 1101

The Chinese New Year usually takes place in early February, so here is a run of the country's greatest poets. This eleventh-century writer of the Song Dynasty was clearly versatile: he worked as a calligrapher, poet and painter, and even served as a public official. But after opposing reforms by the ruler Wang Anshi (himself a poet), Su was banished to Hubei. Clearly not one to bear a grudge, Su continued to exchange poetry with Wang during his exile. His masterful poetry combines spontaneity and a razor-sharp sense of humour, often directed at politicians. It's easy to see why Wang wasn't best pleased with Su after reading the poem below . . .

Families when a child is born
Hope it will turn out intelligent.
I, through intelligence,
Having wrecked my whole life,
Only hope that the baby will prove
Ignorant and stupid.
Then he'll be happy all his days
And grow into a Cabinet Minister.

3 February ✶ Two Poems ✶ Tu Fu, translated by Wai-lim Yip

712 – 770

Continuing our run marking the Chinese New Year is Tu Fu (sometimes known as Du Fu), a writer considered, alongside his Tang Dynasty contemporary Li Po (who follows tomorrow), to be the greatest Chinese poet. Indeed, despite his work being well over a thousand years old, his writing dating to roughly the same period as *Beowulf,* Chinese schoolchildren learn his poems by heart to this day. He would no doubt be surprised at how posterity has lauded his achievements; after all, he spent most of his life seeking, and ultimately failing, to succeed in the upper levels of government before dying in relative poverty. Despite enduring a difficult life, Tu Fu is best known for his beautiful, uplifting poetry about nature.

1

Lingering sun: rivers and mountains brighten.
Spring winds: flowers and grass give out scent.
Soil thaws and swallows fly.
On the warm sand sleeping, drake and duck.

2

Jade river: birds are dazzling white and whiter.
Green mountains: flowers seem to flame.
This spring: look! is going.
What day is the day of return?

4 February ✶ Addressed Humorously to Tu Fu ✶ Li Po, translated by Shigeyoshi Obata

701 – 762

Rounding off our trilogy of Chinese poems is this piece by Li Po, a contemporary of Tu Fu's who enjoyed a similar level of acclaim. Writing over a thousand years before the likes of William Wordsworth and Lord Byron, Li Po could be seen as a poet of the Romantic tradition, both in the way that he drew inspiration from immersing himself in nature and in his revolutionary spirit (he was once arrested for treason). This poem, addressed to Tu Fu, is a funny and revealing reminder of the toll poetry can take on those who devote their lives to it.

Here! is this you on the top of Fan-ko Mountain,
Wearing a huge hat in the noon-day sun?
How thin, how wretchedly thin, you have grown!
You must have been suffering from poetry again.

5 February ✶ The Exaltation of Inanna ✶ Enheduanna

2285 – 2250 BC

The ancient poet Enheduanna – a Sumerian high priestess who lived in what is now southern Iraq – deserves more recognition than she currently has, given that she is the earliest named writer in the history of humankind. She was principally associated with the deity Inanna, who had her hands rather full as the goddess of beauty, love, desire, war, justice, and political power. These themes saturate Enheduanna's verse, and they continue to suffuse poetry in many different and often volatile combinations, 4,300 years down the line.

True goddess fit for divine powers, your splendid utterances
  are magnificent.

Deep-hearted, good woman with a radiant heart,
I will enumerate your divine powers for you!

I, Enheduanna, the *en* priestess, entered my holy *jipar* in
  your service.
I carried the ritual basket, and intoned the song of joy,
But funeral offerings were brought, as if I had never lived
  there.

I approached the light, but the light was scorching hot to me.
I approached that shade, but I was covered with a storm.
My honeyed mouth became venomous.
My ability to soothe moods vanished.

Suen, tell An about Lugalane and my fate!
Man An undo it for me! As soon as you tell An about it, An will release me.

The woman will take the destiny away from Lugalane; foreign lands and flood lie at her feet.
The woman too is exalted, and can make cities tremble.
Step forward, so that she will cool her heart for me.

I, Enheduanna, will recite a prayer to you.
To you, holy Inanna,
I shall give free vent to my tears like sweet beer!

6 February ✶ Snowdrop Time ✶ Mary Webb

25 March 1881 – 8 October 1927

Mary Webb may well have grown up with poetic genius (and genes) running through her veins, as her mother Sarah Alice Scott was distantly related to the great novelist and poet Walter Scott. But it was her father, a teacher called George Edward Meredith (not to be confused with the Victorian poet George Meredith), who is thought to have imbued her with an enduring passion for literature and for the Shropshire countryside where she grew up. Webb initially began writing to entertain her five younger siblings, before finding success, and a wider audience with her 1924 novel *Precious Bane*. Her legacy was given a boost by Prime Minister Stanley Baldwin, who hailed her as a neglected genius.

> Ah, hush! Tread softly through the rime,
> For there will be a blackbird singing, or a thrush.
> Like coloured beads the elmbuds flush:
> All the trees dream of leaves and flowers and light.
> And see! The northern bank is much more white
> Than frosty grass, for now is snowdrop time.

7 February ✶ February Twilight ✶ Sara Teasdale

8 August 1884 – 29 January 1933

Sara Teasdale's rise from budding writer to professional poet was a rather smooth and seamless process – her first poem was printed in a newspaper in 1907 and her first book of poetry was published just months later. And unlike many poets, she was very successful in her lifetime, winning the Pulitzer for poetry (then called the Columbia Poetry prize) in 1918. But sadly she enjoyed none of this ease and fulfilment in her personal life. Her marriage to the businessman Ernst Filsinger in 1914 (after she'd turned down a proposal from the poet Vachel Lindsay) was one marked by distance and disappointment, and it ended in divorce in 1929. Her mental and physical health disintegrated, leading to her early death in 1933. However, her reputation as a writer of well-crafted and lyrical poems goes undiminished.

I stood beside a hill
   Smooth with new-laid snow.
A single star looked out
   From the cold evening glow.

There was no other creature
   That saw what I could see –
I stood and watched the evening star
   As long as it watched me.

8 February ✶ The Peace of Wild Things ✶ Wendell Berry

Born 1934

A committed environmentalist, Wendell Berry has looked after a farm in his native Kentucky for much of his life. Whether writing poetry, stories or essays, his work exhorts us to value and honour nature. This poem summarizes the appeal of farming and the way in which it brings people closer to the joys and reassurances offered by the pastoral world.

When despair for the world grows in me
and I wake in the night at the least sound
in fear of what my life and my children's lives may be,
I go and lie down where the wood drake
rests in his beauty on the water, and the great heron feeds.
I come into the peace of wild things
who do not tax their lives with forethought
of grief. I come into the presence of still water.
And I feel above me the day-blind stars
waiting with their light. For a time
I rest in the grace of the world, and am free.

9 February ✶ i carry your heart with me(i carry it in ✶ E. E. Cummings

14 October 1894 – 3 September 1962

The American poet E. E. Cummings is known as one of the twentieth century's most innovative writers. His experimental approach saw him break grammatical rules and place words in unusual arrangements on the page. This eschewal of linguistic tradition aligns him with other modernists – such as Ezra Pound – who felt that new modes of literary expression could revitalize a world still reeling from the then unprecedented devastation of the Great War. As a pacifist, Cummings served in the ambulance service on the French/German border, and he and his colleagues amused themselves by encoding rude meanings in their letters home to baffle the French censors. This playful, satirical streak pervades much of his work, but he also wrote a great many romantic verses. This poem begins a run of love poetry in the lead-up to Valentine's Day.

i carry your heart with me(i carry it in
my heart)i am never without it(anywhere
i go you go,my dear;and whatever is done
by only me is your doing,my darling)
                                                      i fear
no fate(for you are my fate,my sweet)i want
no world(for beautiful you are my world,my true)
and it's you are whatever a moon has always meant
and whatever a sun will always sing is you

here is the deepest secret nobody knows
(here is the root of the root and the bud of the bud
and the sky of the sky of a tree called life;which grows
higher than soul can hope or mind can hide)
and this is the wonder that's keeping the stars apart

i carry your heart(i carry it in my heart)

10 February ✶ It Is Here ✶ Harold Pinter

10 October 1930 – 24 December 2008

Harold Pinter is almost synonymous with twentieth-century British theatre – to the point that there is an actual theatre in London that bears his name. In addition to a long and garlanded career as a playwright, which was capped with a Nobel Prize for Literature in 2005, Pinter was also a screenwriter, actor, director, political activist and poet. And his singular voice has seen him join the ranks of writers, such as Franz Kafka and George Orwell, who have had an adjective made out of their name: 'Pinteresque', in his case. This term usually applies to a slightly-longer-than-comfortable pause in a play when the dialogue gives way to a heavy silence that is shot through with an indefinable sense of threat or danger, despite the conversation being undramatic or even trivial. But Pinter himself dismissed the adjectival use of his name in this way, stating, 'What I write is what I write.' This love poem was written for his second wife, the historian Antonia Fraser.

(for A)

What sound was that?

I turn away, into the shaking room.

What was that sound that came in on the dark?
What is this maze of light it leaves us in?
What is this stance we take,
To turn away and then turn back?
What did we hear?

It was the breath we took when we first met.

Listen. It is here.

11 February ✶ Three Lies and One Truth about the Moon ✶ Henry Normal

Born 1956

Not too many poets can claim to have toured with a band or written award-winning TV. But Henry Normal has done both, having appeared alongside the indie rockers Pulp and co-created the hit comedy *The Royle Family.* He now works predominantly as a poet and has founded two poetry festivals. His hometown of Nottingham has garlanded him with many distinctions, from honorary doctorates to having a local beer created in his name.

1. The moon only exists at night, and occasionally during the day, in summer

2. No one has ever landed on the moon, and the Russian President knows this but promised his mum he wouldn't say anything

3. The moon is a hollow spaceship inhabited by nazi rabbits that turn men into werewolves

4. If my heart was as big as the moon I couldn't love you more

12 February ✶ I Wanna Be Yours ✶ John Cooper Clarke

Born 1949

Another rock'n'roll performance poet, John Cooper Clarke is a true 'people's poet', having emerged from the UK punk movement of the 1970s. He set his words to music, made hit records, and appeared as the opening act for bands including The Clash before he headlined his own gigs with an impressive roster of supporting acts: Duran Duran, New Order and Joy Division. Still hugely influential in the worlds of poetry and music, his poem 'I Wanna Be Yours' was adapted into a song that appeared on the Arctic Monkeys' 2013 chart-topping album *AM*. The group's frontman Alex Turner revealed that hearing Cooper Clarke's poem in an English lesson at school inspired him to become a lyricist.

I wanna be your vacuum cleaner
Breathing in your dust
I wanna be your Ford Cortina
I will never rust
If you like your coffee hot
Let me be your coffee pot
You call the shots
I wanna be yours

I wanna be your raincoat
For those frequent rainy days
I wanna be your dreamboat
When you want to sail away
Let me be your teddy bear
Take me with you anywhere
I don't care
I wanna be yours

I wanna be your electric meter
I will not run out
I wanna be the electric heater
You'll get cold without
I wanna be your setting lotion
Hold your hair in deep devotion
Deep as the deep Atlantic ocean
That's how deep is my devotion

13 February ✶ At a Dinner Party ✶ Amy Levy

10 November 1861 – 10 September 1889

Amy Levy was a feminist trailblazer, novelist, essayist and poet who was only the second Jewish woman to attend Cambridge University. Though her life was short, it was filled with remarkable achievements and insights into the social issues of her day. Levy's writing was revered by Oscar Wilde, among others, and she developed friendships with fellow forward-thinkers and 'emancipated women' such as Eleanor Marx. Her poems were open and lucid about her experiences of anti-Semitism and mental health struggles, and some expressed love for another woman – then still a taboo. This poem gives a snapshot of a blossoming secret love.

With fruit and flowers the board is decked,
  The wine and laughter flow;
I'll not complain—could one expect
  So dull a world to know?

You look across the fruit and flowers,
  My glance your glances find.—
It is our secret, only ours,
  Since all the world is blind.

14 February ✶ The Lover Writes a One-Word Poem ✶ Gavin Ewart

4 February 1916 – 25 October 1995

A disciple of the modernists Ezra Pound and T. S. Eliot, Gavin Ewart had his first book published before he was twenty-three. His development as a poet was halted by his active service during the Second World War, but was thankfully rejuvenated in the 1960s. Although today he's not as renowned as his contemporaries, Ewart enjoyed the status of a literary celebrity during his lifetime, prompting his peer Philip Larkin to say: 'The most remarkable phenomenon of the English poetic scene during the last ten years has been the advent, or perhaps I should say the irruption of, Gavin Ewart.' This one-word love poem chosen for Valentine's Day arguably expresses the lover's overwhelming adoration of his partner better than many much wordier verses.

You!

15 February ✶ A Very Valentine ✶ Gertrude Stein

3 February 1874 – 27 July 1946

Although her own work was never stratospherically successful and is still largely overlooked, it is fair to say that behind almost every great artist and writer of the early twentieth century stood Gertrude Stein. Her Paris home became a new kind of 'salon' in the 1920s where the best and brightest avant-garde painters, poets and novelists would come to gain insight from her keen critical eye – and learn from one another. Ernest Hemingway, James Joyce, F. Scott Fitzgerald, Henri Matisse and Pablo Picasso were just some of the names associated with Stein, who regularly hosted the kinds of get-togethers that sound like they were conceived by someone playing a game of 'dream dinner party'. She remains immortalized in her portrait painted by Picasso.

Very fine is my valentine.
Very fine and very mine.
Very mine is my valentine very mine and very fine.
Very fine is my valentine and mine, very fine very mine and mine is my valentine.

16 February ✶ The Owl and the Pussy-Cat ✶ Edward Lear

12 May 1812 – 29 January 1888

A pioneer of nonsense poetry, Edward Lear started out as a visual artist. Despite enduring some very trying circumstances growing up – he was one of a scarcely believable twenty-one children, received no formal education and suffered from poor health – he went on to become a well-regarded illustrator, especially of birds and wildlife. He was championed in his endeavours for many years by the Earl of Derby, for whose grandchildren Lear wrote his first book of nonsense verse. Along with Lewis Carroll, he eventually helped shape the burgeoning English traditions of the absurd, and he is also recognized for popularizing the limerick in Victorian England. The brilliance of Lear's whimsical verse lies in the fact that it can be enjoyed on any number of levels; his poetry is that of the all-too-rare kind that is read at both nursery school and university.

I

The Owl and the Pussy-cat went to sea
  In a beautiful pea-green boat,
They took some honey, and plenty of money,
  Wrapped up in a five-pound note.
The Owl looked up to the stars above,
  And sang to a small guitar,
'O lovely Pussy! O Pussy, my love,
  What a beautiful Pussy you are,
    You are,
    You are!
What a beautiful Pussy you are!'

II

Pussy said to the Owl, 'You elegant fowl!
  How charmingly sweet you sing!
O let us be married! too long we have tarried:
  But what shall we do for a ring?'
They sailed away, for a year and a day,
  To the land where the Bong-Tree grows
And there in a wood a Piggy-wig stood
  With a ring at the end of his nose,
        His nose,
        His nose,
  With a ring at the end of his nose.

III

'Dear Pig, are you willing to sell for one shilling
  Your ring?' Said the Piggy, 'I will.'
So they took it away, and were married next day
  By the Turkey who lives on the hill.
They dined on mince, and slices of quince,
  Which they ate with a runcible spoon;
And hand in hand, on the edge of the sand,
  They danced by the light of the moon,
        The moon,
        The moon,
They danced by the light of the moon.

17 February ✶ The Bargain ✶ Sir Philip Sidney

30 November 1554 – 17 October 1586

Most eighteen-year-olds today have barely left home, but when Philip Sidney was that age, he was not only a Member of Parliament, but an envoy sent to France to try to broker a marriage for Elizabeth I. His career as a courtier was unsuccessful, and on his return to court, he was left largely on the sidelines. This gave him more time to focus on his writing – much to the benefit of future poets such as Shakespeare, who were greatly influenced by Sidney's innovations with the Petrarchan sonnet. His masterpiece was the lengthy prose text *Arcadia*, which brought new life to the medieval tradition of the chivalric romance. And there could truly be no better person to write of noble doings than Sidney, who prided himself on his gentlemanliness to the point that he refused to have his work published in his lifetime as to make money from it would be improper. The best tribute to his honourable character comes from the moments before his death in a military campaign against the Spanish in the Netherlands; while dying he offered his water to a nearby wounded soldier declaring: 'Thy necessity is yet greater than mine.' He was rewarded with a burial at St Paul's Cathedral and a beautiful elegy by his friend Edmund Spenser.

My true love hath my heart, and I have his,
   By just exchange one for another given:
I hold his dear, and mine he cannot miss,
   There never was a better bargain driven:
         My true love hath my heart, and I have his.

His heart in me keeps him and me in one,
   My heart in him his thoughts and senses guides:
He loves my heart, for once it was his own,
   I cherish his because in me it bides:
         My true love hath my heart, and I have his.

18 February ✶ Love is like a Dizziness ✶ James Hogg

9 December 1770 – 21 November 1835

James Hogg can stake a claim to be the second coming of the Scottish Bard, Robert Burns. And it's not because he said that they shared a birthday. Like Burns, Hogg had hardly any formal education, having grown up on a farm, and like Burns he was greatly influenced by local folk stories – his grandfather was said to be the last man to speak to fairies. Even after he had been discovered by Walter Scott, and his stories and poems published by the *Edinburgh Magazine,* he continued to help on the family farm. He became known as the 'Ettrick Shepherd' in reference to his home village, but his work and his legacy extended far beyond rural Scotland. Today he is remembered for his stirring love poetry, and is recognized as an influential member of the Romantic movement, which was spearheaded by his friends Wordsworth and Southey.

O, love, love, love!
Love is like a dizziness;
It winna let a puir body
Gang about his biziness!

19 February ✶ 'Love like a juggler comes to play his prize' ✶ Lady Mary Wroth

18 October 1587 – c. 1652

Like Enheduanna (see 5 February), Mary Wroth deserves to be much better known for her historic poetic achievement: she was the first Englishwoman to publish a full sonnet sequence, at a time when the few women who were lucky enough to have an education concentrated predominantly on translation. Admired by the poet-playwrights Ben Jonson and George Chapman, Wroth also had strong family ties to the world of letters as the niece of poets Sir Philip and Mary Sidney. In fact, she was so well connected that in 1600 there is a record of Queen Elizabeth I visiting her family home and commending young Mary for her dancing.

Love like a juggler comes to play his prize,
  And all minds draw his wonders to admire,
  To see how cunningly he (wanting eyes)
  Can yet deceive the best sight of desire.

The wanton child, how he can fain his fire
  So prettily, as none sees his disguise,
  How finely do his tricks; while we fools hire
  The badge, and office of his tyrannies.

For in the end such juggling doth he make,
  As he our hearts instead of eyes doth take;
  For men can only by their flights abuse

The sight with nimble, and delightful skill,
  But if he play, his gain is our lost will,
  Yet childlike we cannot his sports refuse.

20 February ✶ Mad Girl's Love Song ✶ Sylvia Plath

27 October 1932 – 11 February 1963

Sylvia Plath had a short yet remarkably intense life in the public eye, beginning when her first poem was published at just nine years old. A gifted student, she won a scholarship to come over from America to study at Cambridge, where she fell into a whirlwind romance with English poet Ted Hughes. They married after just four months, but their relationship was a largely tempestuous affair that exacerbated the fragility of Plath's mental health – a struggle which she once heartbreakingly described as follows: 'It is as if my life were magically run by two electric currents: joyous positive and despairing negative – whichever is running at the moment dominates my life, floods it.' Her poetry is defined by this compelling balance between beauty and darkness, compassion and cynicism, but her affliction would eventually claim her life. Today she is perhaps best known for her semi-autobiographical novel *The Bell Jar*. This villanelle (a type of poem with repetition of the first and third lines from the first stanza), written for *Granta* magazine in 1953, serves as a fitting reminder that Plath was a master of verse as well as prose.

'I shut my eyes and all the world drops dead;
I lift my lids and all is born again.
(I think I made you up inside my head.)

The stars go waltzing out in blue and red,
And arbitrary blackness gallops in:
I shut my eyes and all the world drops dead.

I dreamed that you bewitched me into bed
And sung me moon-struck, kissed me quite insane.
(I think I made you up inside my head.)

God topples from the sky, hell's fires fade:
Exit seraphim and Satan's men:
I shut my eyes and all the world drops dead.

I fancied you'd return the way you said,
But I grow old and I forget your name.
(I think I made you up inside my head.)

I should have loved a thunderbird instead;
At least when spring comes they roar back again.
I shut my eyes and all the world drops dead.
(I think I made you up inside my head.)'

21 February ✶ A Declaration of Need ✶ John Hegley

Born 1953

John Hegley was once described as 'awesomely mundane' by the *Independent,* which may sound like a damning criticism, but is in fact glowing praise for a poet who writes with wit and playfulness about everyday objects such as potatoes and glasses. His unique brand of comic poems and songs has seen him perform everywhere from schools to prisons, the British Library to Glastonbury Festival. He's a major figure in the comedy world and on the poetry circuit.

I need you like a novel needs a plot.
I need you like the greedy need a lot.
I need you like a hovel needs a certain level of
 grottiness to qualify.
I need you like acne cream needs spottiness.
Like a calendar needs a week.
Like a colander needs a leek.
Like people need to seek out what life on Mars is.
Like hospitals need vases.
I need you.
I need you like a zoo needs a giraffe.
I need you like a psycho needs a path.
I need you like King Arthur needs a table
that was more than just a table for one.
I need you like a kiwi needs a fruit.
I need you like a wee wee needs a route out of the body.
I need you like Noddy needed little ears,
just for the contrast.
I need you like bone needs marrow.
I need you like straight needs narrow.

I need you like the broadest bean needs something else
    on the plate
before it can participate
in what you might describe as a decent meal.
I need you like a cappuccino needs froth.
I need you like a candle needs a moth
if it's going to burn its wings off.

22 February ✶ A Bicycle Built for Two ✶
Carolyn Wells

18 June 1862 – 26 March 1942

Carolyn Wells may have been nearing forty by the time her writing career took off, but she more than made up for lost time as the author of some 170 titles. Her work includes detective stories, humorous articles for satirical magazines, many of which were illustrated by the leading cartoonists of her age, and children's poetry.

There was an ambitious young eel
Who determined to ride on a wheel;
    But try as he might,
    He couldn't ride right,
In spite of his ardor and zeal.

If he sat on the saddle to ride
His tail only pedalled one side;
    And I'm sure you'll admit
    That an eel couldn't sit
On a bicycle saddle astride.

Or if he hung over the top,
He could go, but he never could stop;
    For of course it is clear
    He had no way to steer,
And under the wheel he would flop.

His neighbor, observing the fun,
Said, 'I think that the thing can be done,
    If you'll listen to me,
    You'll quickly agree
That two heads are better than one.

‘And this is my project, old chap,
Around our two waists I will wrap
    This beautiful belt
    Of bottle-green felt
And fasten it firm with a strap.’

This done, with a dignified mien
The two squirmed up on the machine,
    And rode gayly away,
    Or at least, so they say,
Who witnessed the wonderful scene

23 February ✶ O Tell me the Truth About Love ✶ W. H. Auden

21 February 1907 – 29 September 1973

W. H. Auden is one of the first names that would come up in any discussion of the twentieth century's greatest poet. A Pulitzer Prize winner, he followed and built on the modernist style developed by the likes of T. S. Eliot, who helped him publish his first book, and wrote on everything from love to grief and politics to art with clarity, irony and not a drop of sentimentality. He emigrated from England to the US in anticipation of the outbreak of the Second World War, but not before helping a German woman – the actress, and daughter of Thomas Mann, Erika Mann – escape from the Nazis through a marriage of convenience. He returned to England in his later years to teach poetry at Oxford, but his critical and popular reputation was not truly cemented until the years after his death. Indeed, sales of his works suddenly spiked in the mid-1990s after his poems were featured in the hit films *Four Weddings and a Funeral* and *Before Sunrise*.

Some say that love's a little boy,
And some say it's a bird,
Some say it makes the world go round,
And some say that's absurd,
And when I asked the man next-door,
Who looked as if he knew,
His wife got very cross indeed,
And said it wouldn't do.

Does it look like a pair of pyjamas,
  Or the ham in a temperance hotel?
Does its odour remind one of llamas,
  Or has it a comforting smell?
Is it prickly to touch as a hedge is,
  Or soft as eiderdown fluff?
Is it sharp or quite smooth at the edges?
  O tell me the truth about love.

Our history books refer to it
In cryptic little notes,
It's quite a common topic on
The Transatlantic boats;
I've found the subject mentioned in
Accounts of suicides,
And even seen it scribbled on
The backs of railway-guides.

Does it howl like a hungry Alsatian,
  Or boom like a military band?
Could one give a first-rate imitation
  On a saw or a Steinway Grand?
Is its singing at parties a riot?
  Does it only like Classical stuff?
Will it stop when one wants to be quiet?
  O tell me the truth about love.

I looked inside the summer-house;
It wasn't over there:
I tried the Thames at Maidenhead,
And Brighton's bracing air.
I don't know what the blackbird sang,
Or what the tulip said;
But it wasn't in the chicken-run,
Or underneath the bed.

Can it pull extraordinary faces?
   Is it usually sick on a swing?
Does it spend all its time at the races,
   Or fiddling with pieces of string?
Has it views of its own about money?
   Does it think Patriotism enough?
Are its stories vulgar but funny?
   O tell me the truth about love.

When it comes, will it come without warning
   Just as I'm picking my nose?
Will it knock on my door in the morning,
   Or tread in the bus on my toes?
Will it come like a change in the weather?
   Will its greeting be courteous or rough?
Will it alter my life altogether?
   O tell me the truth about love.

24 February ✶ The Donkey ✶ Theodore Roethke

25 May 1908 – 1 August 1963

The Michigan-born Theodore Roethke spent many an hour in the greenhouses belonging to his German immigrant father's successful floral business, and much of his work reveals an affection for the natural world. Roethke endured a difficult adolescence following the death of his father, a period which he would return to frequently in his reflective poetry. That said, many of his poems, such as this one, reveal that he also cultivated a keen sense of humour and an occasionally playful, absurd streak in his writing. He won the Pulitzer Prize for his extraordinary collection *The Waking* and he was also a devoted and very popular poetry professor. A meticulous and exacting master of his craft, it is thought that he only published about 3 per cent of the lines he composed in his two hundred notebooks.

I had a Donkey, that was all right,
But he always wanted to fly my Kite;
Every time I let him, the String would bust.
Your Donkey is better behaved, I trust.

25 February ✶ Approximately ✶ Yannis Ritsos, translated by Nikos Stangos

1 May 1909 – 11 November 1990

For Yannis Ritsos, poetry was more than a profession or a craft – it was a form of salvation from the financial hardships, illness and loss that blighted his early life. His poems – written in clear and simple language designed to foster solidarity among readers and listeners – told of his personal tragedies and his hopes for a better world for working-class people under communist rule. His activism led him to become a member of the Greek resistance during the country's occupation by the Germans during the Second World War, but he found himself exiled after the war when the communist movement was outlawed. He was placed under house arrest on returning years later, and his books were frequently banned as they were seen as a threat. Twice nominated for the Nobel Prize, Ritsos's non-political work was also highly regarded for its sensuousness and mysterious allure.

He picks up in his hands things that don't match – a stone,
a broken roof-tile, two burned matches,
the rusty nail from the wall opposite,
the leaf that came in through the window, the drops
dropping from the watered flower pots, that bit of straw
the wind blew in your hair yesterday – he takes them
and he builds, in his backyard, approximately a tree.
Poetry is in this 'approximately'. Can you see it?

26 February ✶ 'To . . .' ✶ Alexander Pushkin

6 June 1799 – 10 February 1837

Pushkin, like his British counterpart Lord Byron, was an aristocratic maverick whose satirical eye and anti-establishment attitude made him as adored by readers as it made him reviled by Russian high society. His first poems were not printed right away, as they largely made fun of important political figures of the day, but as soon as he published a popular mock-epic poem in 1820, he was exiled from St Petersburg. While banished, he continued to produce the work which has now cemented his place as one of Russia's greatest literary stars, but his troubles with the Russian court were not over. He married the beautiful Natalia Goncharova, who attracted the eye of the tsar himself, and Pushkin, a desperately volatile soul to the end, was killed in a duel with another of her suitors.

I still recall the wondrous moment:
When you appeared before my sight
As though a brief and fleeting omen,
Pure phantom in enchanting light.
In sorrow, when I felt unwell,
Caught in the bustle, in a daze,
I fell under your voice's spell
And dreamt the features of your face.
Years passed and gales had dispelled
My former hopes, and in those days,
I lost your voice's sacred spell,
The holy features of your face.
Detained in darkness, isolation,
My days began to drag in strife.
Without faith and inspiration,
Without tears, and love and life.
My soul attained its waking moment:
You re-appeared before my sight,

As though a brief and fleeting omen,
Pure phantom in enchanting light.
And now, my heart, with fascination,
Beats rapidly and finds revived
Devout faith and inspiration,
And tender tears and love and life.

27 February ✶ Wynken, Blynken and Nod ✶ Eugene Field

2 September 1850 – 4 November 1895

Eugene Field grew up on the periphery of history as the son of the attorney who represented Dred Scott, an enslaved man who sued for his freedom in the Supreme Court in 1857 – a case that some argue sparked the American Civil War. His own work was not as weighty, but it certainly brought joy to thousands of people. He began his career writing humorous articles, poems and stories for a local newspaper column called 'Funny Fancies' that was syndicated across America. Unlike many poets, he enjoyed a happy marriage to his childhood sweetheart with whom he had eight children. Many of his poems were written for them, and Field was something of a big kid himself, known for pulling pranks; he even claimed to his friends that he had two birthdays. You can't help but suspect he might have got on rather well with Spike Milligan (see 19 January).

Wynken, Blynken, and Nod one night
  Sailed off in a wooden shoe,—
Sailed on a river of crystal light
  Into a sea of dew.
'Where are you going, and what do you wish?'
  The old moon asked the three.
'We have come to fish for the herring-fish
  That live in this beautiful sea;
  Nets of silver and gold have we,'
        Said Wynken,
        Blynken,
        And Nod.

The old moon laughed and sang a song,
  As they rocked in the wooden shoe;
And the wind that sped them all night long
  Ruffled the waves of dew;
The little stars were the herring-fish
  That lived in the beautiful sea.
'Now cast your nets wherever you wish,—
  Never afraid are we!'
  So cried the stars to the fishermen three,
      Wynken,
      Blynken,
      And Nod.

All night long their nets they threw
  To the stars in the twinkling foam,—
Then down from the skies came the wooden shoe,
  Bringing the fishermen home:
'Twas all so pretty a sail, it seemed
  As if it could not be;
And some folk thought 'twas a dream they'd dreamed
  Of sailing that beautiful sea;
  But I shall name you the fishermen three:
      Wynken,
      Blynken,
      And Nod.

Wynken and Blynken are two little eyes,
  And Nod is a little head,
And the wooden shoe that sailed the skies
  Is a wee one's trundle-bed;
So shut your eyes while Mother sings
  Of wonderful sights that be,
And you shall see the beautiful things
  As you rock in the misty sea
  Where the old shoe rocked the fishermen three:—
      Wynken,
      Blynken,
      And Nod.

28 February ✶ ‘I so liked Spring . . .’ ✶ Charlotte Mew

15 November 1869 – 24 March 1928

Charlotte Mew once refused to provide biographical information, but we now know a little bit more about her than some of her contemporaries did. She was born in Bloomsbury, which would become the heart of London’s literary society, as the eldest daughter of seven children. And although she began publishing her poems at the age of twenty, she would have to wait two more decades before her literary reputation took hold with the release of her 1912 poem ‘The Farmer’s Bride’. After that, she was unofficially inducted into London’s cultural circles where she stood out for her diminutive stature and for wearing tailored men’s suits. She was widely admired by leading writers from Thomas Hardy to Walter de la Mare, and Virginia Woolf went so far as to call Mew ‘the greatest living poetess’.

I so liked Spring last year
Because you were here; –
The thrushes too –
Because it was these you so liked to hear –
I so liked you.

This year’s a different thing, –
I’ll not think of you.
But I’ll like the Spring because it is simply Spring
As the thrushes do.

29 February ✶ A Leap-Year Romance ✶
Marion Bernstein

1846–1906

Glaswegians may want to claim her as one of their own, but the Victorian poet Marion Bernstein was in fact born and raised in East London before moving to Scotland's second city. It was here though that Bernstein made her living as a music teacher and as a writer of poems that drew from scenes of Glasgow life. A forthright, radical social commentator and proto-feminist, Bernstein wrote with moral conviction and charisma, and her oeuvre of some 200 poems (most of which were printed in local papers) merits more recognition than it has received to date. This charming poem about a boy who's too shy to propose to his loved one plays on the old leap year tradition that sees women subvert conventions and ask for their partner's hand in marriage. Today of course women don't have to wait until 29 February comes around again!

Young William loved fair Rosalie,
Who dwelt upon the banks of Dee,
And quite as much in love was she,
But William loved so timidly.
He looked, and sighed, but nought said he.
Things went on thus for years just three–
The fourth year leap-year chanced to be,
And, tired of his timidity,
'How very shy you are,' said she,
I'm sure you're not a bit like me!
I wish that we could change, for we
Are quite unsuited thus to be.
You'd be a gentler girl than me,
And I'd not fail in bravery
If I were you, and you were me,
How very different things would be!

I would go down on bended knee,
And say, 'Miss, will you marry me?'
And you'd say 'yes' undoubtedly,
And then how happy we should be!'
Young William stared at Rosalie,
As most men would, it seems to me,
And how it chanced I ne'er could see,
Or whether she proposed, or he,
But, 'tis a fact well known to me,
The middle of last February
Young William wedded Rosalie.

March

1 March ✶ Welsh Incident ✶ Robert Graves

24 July 1895 – 7 December 1985

Robert Graves may have been born in London as the son of an Irish poet, but he's also an honorary Welshman, having served with the Royal Welsh Fusiliers in the First World War and later written this excellent poem about the country – chosen for St David's Day. He is today best remembered for his collection of war poems and for his books, the autobiographical *Goodbye to All That*, and the novel *I, Claudius* about the Roman emperor. But despite his success as a novelist, it was always a love of poetry which guided his work and life; he once said: 'Since the age of fifteen poetry has been my ruling passion and I have never intentionally undertaken any task or formed any relationship that seemed inconsistent with poetic principles.' Unlike his modernist contemporaries, however, he was a staunch literary traditionalist – interested in myths and folklore – and claimed that 'experimental work has no future'.

But that was nothing to what things came out
From the sea-caves of Criccieth yonder.'
'What were they? Mermaids? dragons? ghosts?'
'Nothing at all of any things like that.'
'What were they, then?'
'All sorts of queer things,
Things never seen or heard or written about,
Very strange, un-Welsh, utterly peculiar
Things. Oh, solid enough they seemed to touch,
Had anyone dared it. Marvellous creation,
All various shapes and sizes, and no sizes,
All new, each perfectly unlike his neighbour,
Though all came moving slowly out together.'
'Describe just one of them.'
'I am unable.'
'What were their colours?'

'Mostly nameless colours,
Colours you'd like to see; but one was puce
Or perhaps more like crimson, but not purplish.
Some had no colour.'
'Tell me, had they legs?'
'Not a leg or foot among them that I saw.'
'But did these things come out in any order?'
What o'clock was it? What was the day of the week?
Who else was present? How was the weather?'
'I was coming to that. It was half-past three
On Easter Tuesday last. The sun was shining.
The Harlech Silver Band played Marchog Jesu
On thirty-seven shimmering instruments,
Collecting for Caernarvon's (Fever) Hospital Fund.
The populations of Pwllheli, Criccieth,
Portmadoc, Borth, Tremadoc, Penrhyndeudraeth,
Were all assembled. Criccieth's mayor addressed them
First in good Welsh and then in fluent English,
Twisting his fingers in his chain of office,
Welcoming the things. They came out on the sand,
Not keeping time to the band, moving seaward
Silently at a snail's pace. But at last
The most odd, indescribable thing of all
Which hardly one man there could see for wonder
Did something recognizably a something.'
'Well, what?'
'It made a noise.'
'A frightening noise?'
'No, no.'
'A musical noise? A noise of scuffling?'
'No, but a very loud, respectable noise –
Like groaning to oneself on Sunday morning
In Chapel, close before the second psalm.'
'What did the mayor do?'
'I was coming to that.'

2 March ✶ The Crow and the Fox ✶
Jean de La Fontaine

8 July 1621 – 13 April 1695

Jean de La Fontaine was a seventeenth-century fable writer, or fabulist, and one of the most continuously popular French poets from the pre-Revolutionary period. In his early years, La Fontaine briefly attended a seminary before going on to study law – a fitting background for an author of allegorical moral parables about common human foibles. He is best known for his masterpiece, *Fables*, published in twelve volumes over almost thirty years. In these books, La Fontaine collected 239 tales from ancient sources such as Aesop and Horace – as well as various medieval French, Italian and even Persian writers – and retold them in free verse, usually with a wickedly funny, cynical tone. Initially intended for adult readers, the stories eventually became set-texts at French schools. La Fontaine's enduring legacy has seen him commemorated on stamps and coins in his home country, and his influence can clearly be felt in the fables of today – not least in stories by the likes of Julia Donaldson, which similarly revolve around shrewd animals outwitting others.

A master crow, perched on a tree one day,
Was holding in his beak a piece of cheese.
A master fox, by th' odor drawn that way,
Spake unto him in words like these:
'Good-morning, my Lord Crow!
How well you look, how handsome you do grow!
Upon my honor, if your note
Bears a resemblance to your coat,
You are the phœnix of the dwellers in these woods.'
At these words does the crow exceedingly rejoice;
And, to display his beauteous voice,
He opens a wide beak, lets fall his stolen goods.

The fox seized on't, and said, 'My dear good sir,
Learn you that every flatterer
Lives at the expense of him who hears him out.
This lesson is well worth some cheese, no doubt.'
The crow, ashamed, and much in pain,
Swore, but a little late, they'd not catch him again.

3 March ✶ The Mouse and the Lion ✶
Julia Donaldson

Born 1948

If you browsed the bookshelves of any nursery in Britain you would almost certainly find at least one, if not several, books by Julia Donaldson. Donaldson began her career writing songs for children's television – one of these, 'A Squash and a Squeeze', was turned into a picture book, sparking a prolific and hugely successful career as an author of children's literature. She was named the Children's Laureate between 2011 and 2013. While she is undoubtedly most renowned for her books, Donaldson has written wonderful poems such as this one, which is more than a little reminiscent of her bestseller, *The Gruffalo*.

In the hottest sun of the longest day
A lion lay down for a doze.
A little brown mouse pattered out to play.
He danced on the whiskery nose.
Pit-a-pat, pit-a-pat, pit-a-pat, pit-a-pat,
He danced on the whiskery nose.

The lion awoke with a sneeze, 'A-choo!'
He picked up the mouse in his paw.
'And who may I venture to ask are you?'
He said with a terrible roar.
Grr, grrr, grrrrr, GRRRRRR,
He said with a terrible roar.

'I'll save your life if you'll let me go.'
The mouse's voice shook as he spoke.
The lion laughed loudly, 'Oh ho ho ho.
I'll let you go free for your joke.'
Oho, oho, ohohohoho,
I'll let you go free for your joke.

As chance would have it, the following week
The lion was caught in a net
When all of a sudden he heard a squeak:
'Well met, noble lion, well met.'
Squeak, squeak, squeak, squeak.
Well met, noble lion, well met.

The little mouse nibbled and gnawed and bit
Till the lion was finally free.
'It's nothing, dear lion, don't mention it:
I'm repaying your kindness to me.'
Nibbly, nibbly, nibbly, nibble,
Repaying your kindness to me.

'For one of the lessons which mice must learn
From their whiskery father and mother
Is the famous old saying that one good turn
Always deserves another.'
Pit-a-pat, grrr, ohoho, squeak!
Always deserves another.

4 March ✶ The End of the World ✶ Giles Andreae (as Purple Ronnie)

Born 1966

Giles Andreae started his career working in advertising and writing greetings cards which featured a series of very funny poems alongside cartoons of his stickman character, Purple Ronnie. He has gone on to create other hugely successful characters such as the philosopher/poet Edward Monkton and many award-winning picture books, including one of the bestselling children's books of all time, *Giraffes Can't Dance.*

I hope that I'm there at the end of the world,
When everyone stands in a queue,
And says all the wickedest things that they've done
And the bad things they've wanted to do.

Naughty folks' heads will cave in and explode,
And goo will spurt out of their brains;
Their tummies will tangle and turn inside out
And their bottoms will burst into flames.

But people like me who've been lovely and kind
Will rocket straight up to the sky,
And watch the whole rumpus from big squashy beds
With loads of ice cream and fudge pie.

And angels will cuddle and stroke us,
And say how fantastic we are;
And how, out of all of the people they've met,
We're the smashingly fabbest by far.

5 March ✶ Lavender's Blue ✶ Anon.

Many poems appear in anthologies anonymously, without an author credited. This is often due to the millennia-old tradition of oral poetry whereby verse would be passed down from generation to generation, often changing with each rendition, without a word being written down. Instead these poems would be kept alive by a balladeer reciting poems in the town square, a minstrel at a banquet, a traveller round a campfire or a parent singing lullabies. Even today when we hear playground rhymes, football chants or sea shanties we rarely know who came up with the lines. But sometimes 'Anon.' entries are a sign of the sad truth that many great writers were discarded from literary history, either by accident or design. As Virginia Woolf puts it in her masterpiece *A Room of One's Own*: 'I would venture to guess that Anon., who wrote so many poems without signing them, was often a woman.' This little run of Anon. poems leading up to International Women's Day is intended as a tribute to all those brilliant, nameless women.

Lavender's blue, dilly dilly, lavender's green,
When I am king, dilly dilly, you shall be queen;
Call up your men, dilly, dilly, set them to work,
Some to the plough, dilly dilly, some to the cart;
Some to make hay, dilly dilly, some to thresh corn,
Whilst you and I, dilly dilly, keep ourselves warm.

6 March ✶ Bobby Shaftoe ✶ Anon.

Here is another example of a traditional poem without a known author. This one is often sung, but that doesn't make it any less of a poem. In fact, in many languages the word for poem and song is the same, and the word 'lyric' literally refers to a poem accompanied by a lyre. This poem can be performed as a sea shanty or as a nursery rhyme, and like many of those there's a hidden meaning to be found here that would likely go over the heads of the children singing it. In this case it's the story of a woman longing for the return of her beloved.

Bobby Shaftoe's gone to sea,
Silver buckles on his knee;
He'll come back and marry me,
Bonny Bobby Shaftoe.

Bobby Shaftoe's bright and fair,
Combing down his yellow hair,
He's my ain for evermair,
Bonny Bobby Shaftoe.

Bobby Shaftoe's tall and slim,
Always dressed so neat and trim,
The ladies they all keek at him,
Bonny Bobby Shaftoe.

Bobby Shaftoe's getten a bairn
For to dandle in his arm;
In his arm and on his knee,
Bonny Bobby Shaftoe.

7 March ✶ The Bold Pedlar and Robinhood ✶ Anon.

Another form of poetry that is part of the anonymous oral tradition of storytelling is the ballad. Ballads were usually driven by a strong, stirring narrative, and would most likely have been set to music for people to dance to – the word derives from the Latin *ballare,* meaning 'to dance'. Ballads would typically be composed of four-line stanzas and have a simple rhyme scheme to make them easy to remember and pass on. This one is probably from the eighteenth century and is about a pedlar who comes across the famous outlaw Robinhood.

There chanced to be a Pedlar bold,
   A Pedlar bold he chanced to be,
He put his pack all on his back,
   And so merrily trudged o'er the lee.

By chance he met two troublesome men,
   Two troublesome men they chanced to be,
The one of them was bold Robinhood,
   And the other was little John so free.

Oh, Pedlar, Pedlar, what is in thy pack,
   Come speedily and tell to me,
I've several suits of the gay green silks,
   And silken bow strings by two of three.

If you have several suits of the gay green silk
   And silken bow strings 'twas three,
Then it's by my body, cries little John
   One half your pack shall belong to me.

Oh nay, oh nay, says the Pedlar bold,
Oh nay, oh my that never can be,
For there's never a man from fair Nottingham,
Can take one half my pack from me.

Then the Pedlar pull'd off his pack,
And put it a little below his knee,
Saying if you do move me one perch from this
My pack and all shall gang with thee.

Then little John he drew his sword,
The Pedlar by his pack did stand,
They fought until they both did sweat,
Till he cry'd Pedlar pray hold your hand.

Then Robinhood he was standing by,
And he did laugh most heartily,
Saying I could find a man of a smaller seal
Could thrash the Pedlar and also thee.

Go you try master, says little John,
Go you try master most speedily,
Or by my body, says little John,
I am sure this night you will know.

Then Robinhood he drew his sword,
And the Pedlar by his pack did stand,
They fought until the blood in streams did flow
Till he cry'd, Pedlar, pray hold your hand.

Oh, Pedlar, Pedlar, what is thy name,
Come speedily and tell to me,
Name my name I ne'er will tell,
Till I both your names you have told to me

The one of us is bold Robinhood,
  And the other little John so free,
Now says the Pedlar it lays to my goodwill,
  Whether my name I chase to tell to thee.

I am Gamble Gold of the gay green woods,
  And travell'd far beyond the sea,
For killing a man in my father's land,
  And from my country was forced to flee.

If you are Gamble Gold of the gay green woods
  And travell'd far beyond the sea,
You are my mother's own sister's son,
  What nearer cousins then can we be.

They sheathed their swords with friendly words
  So merrily did they agree,
They went to a tavern and there they dined
  And cracked bottles most merrily.

8 March ✶ The Socialist and the Suffragist ✶ Charlotte Perkins Gilman

3 July 1860 – 17 August 1935

On International Women's Day we recognize the pioneering brilliance of the American writer, publisher and activist Charlotte Perkins Gilman. The author of the groundbreaking 1892 feminist short story *The Yellow Wallpaper*, she tackled issues such as post-natal depression and female subjugation in an era in which such discussions were unheard of in the public arena. And as both the suffragist and socialist movements began to gain traction in the early twentieth century, Gilman wrote a number of poems to help rally these often-linked political causes. A progressive outlier in her personal life as well as in her professional output, Gilman separated from her husband – after years of marriage and motherhood took too much of a toll on her mental health – despite it being rare for women to be able to take that kind of decision at the time. While she may not be quite as well-known as her great-aunt Harriet Beecher Stowe (author of *Uncle Tom's Cabin*), Gilman was rediscovered by the feminist movement in the 1960s and has since been read more widely.

Said the Socialist to the Suffragist:
'My cause is greater than yours!
You only work for a Special Class,
We work for the gain of the General Mass,
Which every good ensures!'

Said the Suffragist to the Socialist:
'You underrate my Cause!
While women remain a Subject Class,
You never can move the General Mass,
With your Economic Laws!'

Said the Socialist to the Suffragist:
'You misinterpret facts!
There is no room for doubt or schism
In Economic Determinism –
It governs all our acts!'

Said the Suffragist to the Socialist:
'You men will always find
That this old world will never move
More swiftly in its ancient groove
While women stay behind!'

'A lifted world lifts women up,'
The Socialist explained.
'You cannot lift the world at all
While half of it is kept so small,'
The Suffragist maintained.

The world awoke, and tartly spoke:
'Your work is all the same:
Work together or work apart,
Work, each of you, with all your heart –
Just get into the game!'

9 March ✶ The Rights of Woman ✶ Anna Letitia Barbauld

20 June 1743 – 9 March 1825

Continuing a run of extraordinary (if overlooked) women writers, is this poem by Anna Letitia Barbauld. In a time when professional female writers were anomalies, Barbauld forged a career that spanned decades and saw her become one of the leading progressive voices in Britain. She was a persistent and committed political activist, advocating religious freedom and hastening the eventual abolition of slavery in England with devastating poetic epistles to William Wilberforce and other influential figures. The Romantics Wordsworth and Coleridge initially praised, but then dismissed her work, which is likely to have contributed to her relative obscurity. Nor did it help that she wrote a scathing satire, '1811', on the demise of the British Empire during the Napoleonic Wars, which saw her slip further from favour. However, no amount of criticism received from her contemporaries can dim her enduring brilliance, such as in this poem where she can be found introducing nuance and restraint to the divisive issue of the day.

Yes, injured Woman! rise, assert thy right!
Woman! too long degraded, scorned, oppressed;
O born to rule in partial Law's despite,
Resume thy native empire o'er the breast!

Go forth arrayed in panoply divine,
That angel pureness which admits no stain;
Go, bid proud Man his boasted rule resign,
And kiss the golden sceptre of thy reign.

Go, gird thyself with grace, collect thy store
Of bright artillery glancing from afar;
Soft melting tones thy thundering cannon's roar,
Blushes and fears thy magazine of war.

Thy rights are empire: urge no meaner claim—
Felt, not defined, and if debated, lost;
Like sacred mysteries which, withheld from fame,
Shunning discussion, are revered the most.

Try all that wit and art suggest to bend
Of thy imperial foe the stubborn knee;
Make treacherous Man thy subject, not thy friend;
Thou mayst command, but never canst be free.

Awe the licentious and restrain the rude;
Soften the sullen, clear the cloudy brow:
Be, more than princes' gifts thy favours sued –
She hazards all, who will the least allow.

But hope not, courted idol of mankind,
On this proud eminence secure to stay;
Subduing and subdued, thou soon shalt find
Thy coldness soften, and thy pride give way.

Then, then, abandon each ambitious thought;
Conquest or rule thy heart shall feebly move,
In Nature's school, by her soft maxims taught
That separate rights are lost in mutual love.

10 March ✶ Women ✶ Alice Walker

Born 1944

Alice Walker is yet another writer whose difficult early years spurred her on towards greatness. As a child, she suffered an accident which left her blind in one eye. But rather than resent her brother, who had shot her with an airgun during a game, she credited him with helping her become a writer as her long recovery forced her to stay at home and recuperate with books by her side. She is best known for her novel *The Color Purple* and for her activism. In her writing Walker coined the term and theory of 'womanism', which specifically refers to feminists of colour whose ideology is grounded in the history and culture of Black women.

They were women then
My mama's generation
Husky of voice—stout of
Step
With fists as well as
Hands
How they battered down
Doors
And ironed
Starched white
Shirts
How they led
Armies
Headragged generals
Across mined
Fields
Booby-trapped
Ditches
To discover books
Desks

A place for us
How they knew what
we
Must know
Without knowing a page
Of it
Themselves.

11 March ✶ What Kind of Times Are These ✶ Adrienne Rich

16 May 1929 – 27 March 2012

Adrienne Rich was born in Baltimore and was surrounded by books in her formative years, growing up in a house with a large library as the daughter of intellectuals. But what was notable about the books she read was that they were almost exclusively by men. In her own career Rich aimed to redress the sexism endemic in literature by becoming a vocal advocate for hardline feminism, especially after becoming a mother – an experience which she said 'radicalized' her. She was also a noted pacifist and a fighter for social justice more broadly – themes explored in her essays and her poetry – which used everyday speech to help convey her meanings to a wide readership. She gained a reputation for refusing many of the prizes bestowed on her, and she notably insisted on sharing her National Book Award with fellow nominees Audre Lorde and Alice Walker, in the name of women everywhere.

There's a place between two stands of trees where the grass
    grows uphill
and the old revolutionary road breaks off into shadows
near a meeting-house abandoned by the persecuted
who disappeared into those shadows.

I've walked there picking mushrooms at the edge of dread, but
    don't be fooled
this isn't a Russian poem, this is not somewhere else but here,
our country moving closer to its own truth and dread,
its own ways of making people disappear.

I won't tell you where the place is, the dark mesh of the woods
meeting the unmarked strip of light—
ghost-ridden crossroads, leafmold paradise:
I know already who wants to buy it, sell it, make it disappear.

And I won't tell you where it is, so why do I tell you
anything? Because you still listen, because in times like these
to have you listen at all, it's necessary
to talk about trees.

12 March ✶ Spring Has Come Back Again ✶ Rainer Maria Rilke, translated by C. F. MacIntyre

4 December 1875 – 29 December 1926

Rainer Maria Rilke is considered to be one of the greatest German-language poets of the early twentieth century. His childhood in Prague was cast under the shadow of his sister's death and he had to endure a number of gruelling years in military school. After studying literature at university, Rilke went on a cultural pilgrimage to Russia, which he claimed was his spiritual fatherland. It was here that he began to view poetry as a transcendent, almost religious, force. It was arguably this awakening that encouraged him to move away from juvenile romantic verse towards writing such wonderful poems as this celebration of spring. Outside of poetry, Rilke also worked as an assistant to the sculptor Auguste Rodin in France, where he was known to be a regular at an artist commune set up by painter Henri Matisse in an old abandoned convent.

Spring has come back again. The earth
is like a child who has memorized
poems, oh, many! . . . now it seems worth
the effort, for she wins the prize.

Her teacher was strict. We loved the white
hair of the old man's beard.
When we ask what the green and the blue are, right
off she knows every word.

Lucky earth, with your holiday,
and all the children coming to play!
We try to catch you. The gayest will do it.

Teacher trained her until she knew it,
and all that's printed in roots and long
unruly stems she sings in song.

13 March ✶ A Brilliant Day ✶
Charles Tennyson Turner

4 July 1808 – 25 April 1879

All siblings have rivalries, but spare a thought for Charles Tennyson Turner, who saw his younger brother Alfred become one of the defining names of Victorian poetry, while his own poetry went largely unread. Which isn't to say he wasn't skilled in his own right; Charles is known to have written a number of sonnets that were much admired by his brother and by Samuel Taylor Coleridge, but he lacked the mastery of a variety of forms that saw Alfred become a national icon. The older Tennyson eventually took on his great-uncle's surname, Turner, in order to inherit his large estate – and perhaps to avoid constant comparison with his brother.

O keen pellucid air! nothing can lurk
Or disavow itself on this bright day;
The small rain-plashes shine from far away,
The tiny emmet glitters at his work;
The bee looks blithe and gay, and as she plies
Her task, and moves and sidles round the cup
Of this spring flower, to drink its honey up,
Her glassy wings, like oars that dip and rise,
Gleam momently. Pure-bosom'd, clear of fog,
The long lake glistens, while the glorious beam
Bespangles the wet joints and floating leaves
Of water-plants, whose every point receives
His light; and jellies of the spawning frog,
Unmark'd before, like piles of jewels seem!

14 March ✶ A Child's Laughter ✶ Algernon Charles Swinburne

5 April 1837 – 10 April 1909

As far as London flatshares go, there can hardly have been any more creative and eccentric than that of the poets Algernon Swinburne, George Meredith and Dante Rossetti. Their house was full of strange habits, eccentric paraphernalia and exotic animals, including peacocks, wombats and kangaroos. Meredith eventually left – apparently because Swinburne would slide down the banisters naked to breakfast, and one day threw an egg at him in an argument. Swinburne also courted scandal and controversy with his rather risqué writing. But his later verse centred more on nature and childhood. Swinburne's unhealthy, hedonistic lifestyle (he was part of the so-called Decadent movement, after all) eventually caught up with him and he became a frail old man who had to be taken care of by his literary agent, with whom he lived for thirty years.

All the bells of heaven may ring,
All the birds of heaven may sing,
All the wells on earth may spring,
All the winds on earth may bring
   All sweet sounds together;
Sweeter far than all things heard,
Hand of harper, tone of bird,
Sound of woods at sundawn stirred,
Welling water's winsome word,
   Wind in warm wan weather,

One thing yet there is, that none
Hearing ere its chime be done
Knows not well the sweetest one
Heard of man beneath the sun,
    Hoped in heaven hereafter;
Soft and strong and loud and light,
Very sound of very light
Heard from morning's rosiest height,
When the soul of all delight
    Fills a child's clear laughter.

Golden bells of welcome rolled
Never forth such notes, nor told
Hours so blithe in tones so bold,
As the radiant mouth of gold
    Here that rings forth heaven.
If the golden-crested wren
Were a nightingale—why, then,
Something seen and heard of men
Might be half as sweet as when
    Laughs a child of seven.

15 March ✶ The Sweet o' the Year ✶ George Meredith

12 February 1828 – 18 May 1909

Swinburne's one-time flatmate, George Meredith, was a major Victorian poet-novelist in the vein of Thomas Hardy, and a pioneer of a more psychological storytelling which paid particular attention to characters' inner lives and motivations. After his wife left him for the artist Henry Wallis, he shared a house with Dante Rossetti and Swinburne (but as we saw above, he did not adjust to this unorthodox way of life and left). Meredith was popular in his lifetime but unlike his contemporaries Tennyson, Hardy and Robert Browning, he is rarely read today – with one exception – 'The Lark Ascending'. Often voted the nation's favourite piece of classical music, it is famed as a piece of work by the composer Ralph Vaughan Williams, but it was inspired by the poem of the same name by Meredith. This poem below, about nature reawakening after a long winter, provides another example of the musicality inherent in Meredith's writing.

Now the frog, all lean and weak,
Yawning from his famished sleep,
Water in the ditch doth seek,
Fast as he can stretch and leap:
Marshy king-cups burning near
Tell him 'tis the sweet o' the year.
Now the ant works up his mound
In the mouldered piny soil,
And above the busy ground
Takes the joy of earnest toil:
Dropping pine-cones, dry and sere,
Warn him 'tis the sweet o' the year.
Now the chrysalis on the wall
Cracks, and out the creature springs,

Raptures in his body small,
Wonders on his dusty wings:
Bells and cups, all shining clear,
Show him 'tis the sweet o' the year.
Now the brown bee, wild and wise,
Hums abroad, and roves and roams,
Storing in his wealthy thighs
Treasure for the golden combs:
Dewy buds and blossoms dear
Whisper 'tis the sweet o' the year.
Now the merry maids so fair
Weave the wreaths and choose the queen,
Blooming in the open air,
Like fresh flowers upon the green;
Spring, in every thought sincere,
Thrills them with the sweet o' the year.
Now the lads, all quick and gay,
Whistle to the browsing herds,
Or in the twilight pastures grey
Learn the use of whispered words:
First a blush, and then a tear,
And then a smile, i' the sweet o' the year.
Now the May-fly and the fish
Play again from noon to night;
Every breeze begets a wish,
Every motion means delight:
Heaven high over heath and mere
Crowns with blue the sweet o' the year.
Now all Nature is alive,
Bird and beetle, man and mole;
Bee-like goes the human hive,
Lark-like sings the soaring soul:
Hearty faith and honest cheer
Welcome in the sweet o' the year.

16 March ✶ The Woodspurge ✶
Dante Gabriel Rossetti

12 May 1828 – 9 April 1882

Dante Gabriel Rossetti was a co-founder of the (originally secret) Pre-Raphaelite Brotherhood along with the painters William Holman Hunt and John Millais. A highly influential visual arts movement, the PRB broadly rejected the practices of the Renaissance of Neo-Classicism in favour of a more medieval aesthetic with emphasis on nature, religious iconography, rich colours and a dark and brooding tone. Born in London to an Anglo-Italian artistic family, he lived up to his name (chosen in tribute to the great Florentine writer Dante Alighieri) by pursuing poetry – like his sister Christina (see 22 July) – alongside his painting. Known as a deeply romantic soul, he once buried a book of his poems in the grave of his young wife – the Pre-Raphaelite muse Elizabeth Siddall. The romance of this anecdote is somewhat undermined by the fact that Rossetti came to regret his gesture and later had the coffin exhumed!

The wind flapp'd loose, the wind was still,
Shaken out dead from tree and hill:
I had walk'd on at the wind's will,—
I sat now, for the wind was still.

Between my knees my forehead was,—
My lips, drawn in, said not Alas!
My hair was over in the grass,
My naked ears heard the day pass.

My eyes, wide open, had the run
Of some ten weeds to fix upon;
Among those few, out of the sun,
The woodspurge flower'd, three cups in one.

From perfect grief there need not be
Wisdom or even memory:
One thing then learnt remains to me,—
The woodspurge has a cup of three.

17 March ✶ Magdalen Walks ✶ Oscar Wilde

16 October 1854 – 30 November 1900

There is arguably nobody in the history of English literature who did quite as much to elevate wit into an art form as Oscar Wilde. Every one of his countless quips, aphorisms and retorts – from for example, his play *The Importance of Being Earnest:* 'I never travel without my diary. One should always have something sensational to read in the train' – is perfectly executed, and uses irony or parody to reveal something meaningful about human nature. But Wilde was much more than a writer of clever one-liners. He was an extremely accomplished poet, playwright, novelist (of the excellent *The Picture of Dorian Gray*), aesthete and the writer of perhaps the most heartbreaking collection of fairy tales, *The Happy Prince*. Yet all his talent, acclaim and celebrity status couldn't protect him from being the victim of an absurd prosecution which saw him imprisoned for a number of private homosexual affairs. Wilde never truly recovered from this ordeal and he died in Paris at the age of forty-six. He doubtless would have been amused to hear that his tomb at the Père Lachaise cemetery is now surrounded by glass to protect the stone, which had begun to erode due to the sheer number of devotees who came to kiss it.

The little white clouds are racing over the sky,
  And the fields are strewn with the gold of the flower of March,
  The daffodil breaks under foot, and the tasselled larch
Sways and swings as the thrush goes hurrying by.

A delicate odour is borne on the wings of the morning breeze,
  The odour of leaves, and of grass, and of newly upturned earth,
  The birds are singing for joy of the Spring's glad birth,
Hopping from branch to branch on the rocking trees.

And all the woods are alive with the murmur and sound of Spring,
  And the rose-bud breaks into pink on the climbing briar,
  And the crocus-bed is a quivering moon of fire
Girdled round with the belt of an amethyst ring.

And the plane to the pine-tree is whispering some tale of love
  Till it rustles with laughter and tosses its mantle of green,
  And the gloom of the wych-elm's hollow is lit with the iris sheen
Of the burnished rainbow throat and the silver breast of a dove.

See! the lark starts up from his bed in the meadow there,
  Breaking the gossamer threads and the nets of dew,
  And flashing adown the river, a flame of blue!
The kingfisher flies like an arrow, and wounds the air.

18 March ✶ Four-Leaf Clover ✶ Ella Higginson

c. 28 January 1862 – 27 December 1940

The American Pacific Northwest is perhaps not a region that immediately brings to mind any famous literary styles or traditions in the way that New England or the South does, but there have been some terrific poets working in the area. One such is Ella Higginson, who was born in Kansas but grew up in Oregon. Later in life she settled in the town of Bellingham in neighbouring Washington, where she was named the state's poet laureate in 1931. Aside from her own writing, Higginson's work saw her implement changes in her own small community – opening the town's first library – and the state more widely as the campaign manager for Frances C. Axtell: the first female senator voted into the Washington State House Representatives. Anyone interested in going on a summer holiday to Alaska can also look up Higginson's traveller's guide.

I know a place where the sun is like gold,
  And the cherry blooms burst with snow,
And down underneath is the loveliest nook,
  Where the four-leaf clovers grow.

One leaf is for hope, and one is for faith,
  And one is for love, you know,
And God put another in for luck—
  If you search, you will find where they grow.

But you must have hope, and you must have faith,
  You must love and be strong—and so—
If you work, if you wait, you will find the place
  Where the four-leaf clovers grow.

19 March ✶ The Larch Grove ✶ Hartley Coleridge

19 September 1796 – 6 January 1849

The oldest son of Samuel Taylor Coleridge, Hartley Coleridge was raised not by his father – who had chronic money troubles preventing him from looking after his children – but by his uncle, the poet Robert Southey at his Lake District home, Greta Hall. Although he was encouraged by his family, and by neighbour William Wordsworth, Hartley was never able to establish himself as a prominent poet. His father rather uncharitably suggested the reason why, saying of his son that he 'is a poet, spite of the forehead, "villainously low", which his mother smuggled into his face'. He was expelled from Oxford for his drinking, and like his father struggled to keep afloat financially. That said, he was a writer of well-received author biographies, many beautiful sonnets and this wonderfully unassuming, bitter-sweet poem about the often-overlooked larch trees.

Line above line the nursling larches planted,
  Still as they climb with interspace more wide,
Let in and out the sunny beams that slanted,
  And shot and crankled down the mountain's side.

The larches grew, and darker grew the shade;
  And sweeter aye the fragrance of the Spring;
Pink pencils all the spiky boughs arrayed,
  And small green needles called the birds to sing.

They grew apace as fast as they could grow,
  As fain the tawny fell to deck and cover,
They haply thought to soothe the pensive woe,
  Or hide the joy of stealthy tripping lover.

Ah, larches! that shall never be your lot;
  Nought shall you have to do with amorous weepers,
Nor shall ye prop the roof of cosy cot,
  But rumble out your days as railway sleepers.

20 March ✶ Spring, the Sweet Spring ✶ Thomas Nashe

November 1567 – c. 1601

Thomas Nashe was a kind of early freelance writer with a tendency for getting into trouble. He published satirical pamphlets and circulated irreverent poetry which did nothing to ingratiate him with the strict Elizabethan censors. Nevertheless, his contribution to literature in just thirty-four years of life is impressive. His prose work is credited with being an important stepping stone to the invention of the modern novel, and he is thought by many to have collaborated with Shakespeare on *Henry VI, Part 1*. His other major collaboration with the playwright Ben Jonson on a lost play, *The Isle of Dogs*, was a rather less felicitous one, given that both authors ended up in jail for its scandalous content. After narrowly escaping execution, Nashe lived in the relative safety and tranquillity of Yarmouth for what remained of his short life.

Spring, the sweet spring, is the year's pleasant king,
Then blooms each thing, then maids dance in a ring,
Cold doth not sting, the pretty birds do sing:
    Cuckoo, jug-jug, pu-we, to-witta-woo!

The palm and may make country houses gay,
Lambs frisk and play, the shepherds pipe all day,
And we hear aye birds tune this merry lay:
    Cuckoo, jug-jug, pu-we, to-witta-woo!

The fields breathe sweet, the daisies kiss our feet,
Young lovers meet, old wives a-sunning sit,
In every street these tunes our ears do greet:
    Cuckoo, jug-jug, pu-we, to witta-woo!
        Spring, the sweet spring!

21 March ✶ Spring Song ✶ Edith Nesbit

15 August 1858 – 4 May 1924

It's strange to think now, but before Edith Nesbit, there wasn't a precedent for children's stories filled with adventure and magic, but set in a relatable real world. Both C. S. Lewis and J. K. Rowling have credited her books – most notably *Five Children and It* – as being huge influences on their own work. But before her immense success as an author of some forty children's titles, Nesbit was an acclaimed poet. And despite suffering from difficult personal circumstances, the worlds of her stories were always blissfully happy and escapist, and never betrayed her own sorrows. Nesbit was known as a charismatic figure, and a legendary hostess of parties attended by the likes of George Bernard Shaw and H. G. Wells. Her political life was also very active and saw her co-found the Fabian Society – a socialist organization that operates to this day.

All winter through I sat alone,
Doors barred and windows shuttered fast,
And listened to the wind's faint moan,
And ghostly mutterings of the past;
And in the pauses of the rain,
'Mid whispers of dead sorrow and sin,
Love tapped upon the window pane:
I had no heart to let him in.

But now, with spring, my doors stand wide;
My windows let delight creep through;
I hear the skylark sing outside;
I see the crocus, golden new.
The pigeons on my window-sill,
Winging and wooing, flirt and flout,—
Now Love must enter if he will,
I have no heart to keep him out.

22 March ✶ Spring Magic ✶ Cicely Mary Barker

28 June 1895 – 16 February 1973

Cicely Mary Barker's childhood was initially defined by the challenges of living with epilepsy, and being home-schooled as a result. But her fortunes improved in her teens when she enrolled in evening classes at her local school of art, and became, aged sixteen, the youngest life member of the Croydon Art Society. At first she sold her art on postcards and greetings cards, but the success of J. M. Barrie's *Peter Pan* in the early part of the twentieth century meant that fairies (her preferred subject) suddenly became very popular. Soon enough, her series of Flower Fairies books became a success. This poem is taken from her first book, *Flower Fairies of the Spring,* published in 1923.

The World is very old;
  But year by year
It groweth new again
  When buds appear.

The World is very old,
  And sometimes sad;
But when the daisies come
  The World is glad.

The World is very old;
  But every Spring
It groweth young again,
  And fairies sing.

23 March ✶ Trees ✶ Joyce Kilmer

6 December 1886 – 30 July 1918

The American poet Joyce Kilmer is not as well known in the UK as some of his war poet counterparts like Wilfred Owen and Siegfried Sassoon, but his legacy lives on in many street names and even a section of forest in his native US. Not only is he beloved for his poetry, which celebrated the natural world, but he was also commended for his selfless bravery after he gave his life in combat, even when, as a father, he wasn't required to enlist.

I think that I shall never see
A poem lovely as a tree.

A tree whose hungry mouth is prest
Against the earth's sweet flowing breast;

A tree that looks at God all day,
And lifts her leafy arms to pray;

A tree that may in Summer wear
A nest of robins in her hair;

Upon whose bosom snow has lain;
Who intimately lives with rain.

Poems are made by fools like me,
But only God can make a tree.

24 March ✶ He Wishes for the Cloths of Heaven ✶ W. B. Yeats

13 June 1865 – 28 January 1939

Ireland may not have an official national poet, but W. B. Yeats would undoubtedly be in contention for the title if it were ever given. He was the first Irishman, in 1923, to receive a Nobel Prize, and much of his career was devoted to forging a new path for Irish literature. Although he spent much of his childhood in London, he kept his Irish heritage close at heart and immersed himself in the country's rich tradition of myths and legends. His interest in spiritualism eventually saw him become a member of Golden Dawn, a society dedicated to ritual magic. Outside of poetry he was a co-founder of Dublin's Abbey Theatre, enjoyed a successful career as a playwright, and even served a period as a senator in the newly formed Irish Free State.

Had I the heavens' embroidered cloths,
Enwrought with golden and silver light,
The blue and the dim and the dark cloths
Of night and light and the half-light,
I would spread the cloths under your feet:
But I, being poor, have only my dreams;
I have spread my dreams under your feet;
Tread softly because you tread on my dreams.

25 March ✶ Pine Tree in Spring ✶ Chinua Achebe

16 November 1930 – 21 March 2013

The Nigerian writer Chinua Achebe was very clearly influenced by W. B. Yeats and named his most famous novel *Things Falls Apart* after a line from a Yeats poem, 'The Second Coming'. Achebe is in his own right one of the most widely read authors of the twentieth century. Christened Albert Chinualumogu by his Christian convert parents, he became involved in the anti-colonial movements in the post-war years, and altered his name. As he pithily explained, like Queen Victoria he 'lost his Albert'. Nelson Mandela ranked among his biggest fans, and once wrote: 'There was a writer named Chinua Achebe . . . in whose company the prison walls fell down.'

Pine tree
flag bearer
of green memory
across the breach of a desolate hour

Loyal tree
that stood guard
alone in austere emeraldry
over Nature's recumbent standard

Pine tree
lost now in the shade
of traitors decked out flamboyantly
marching back unabashed to the colors they betrayed

Fine tree
erect and trustworthy
what school can teach me
your silent, stubborn fidelity?

26 March ✶ I Wandered Lonely as a Cloud ✶ William Wordsworth

7 April 1770 – 23 April 1850

As one of the fathers of English Romanticism along with Samuel Taylor Coleridge, William Wordsworth was perennially concerned with the relationship between man and nature, and with writing poetry that could reach and speak to common people. Indeed, his friendship with Coleridge might be seen as one of the most important and fruitful collaborations in English literary history. Together they wrote *Lyrical Ballads* – which became a blueprint for early Romanticism that set about elevating everyday events and observations by using accessible language. Initially a revolutionary spirit who greatly supported the upheavals against tyranny that he observed while travelling in Europe, Wordsworth's liberalism significantly shifted towards conservatism in his later years. For this he was much ridiculed by the newer generations of Romantics who saw him as a sell-out; Byron, in one of his less creative moments, called him 'Turdsworth', while Shelley wrote a poem expressing his disappointment in his role model. He became Poet Laureate in 1843 and his popularity would go unchallenged until the arrival of the modernists, who thought him overly sentimental. But you can't dispute the simple genius of this poem – perhaps the most famous English lyric about spring, and certainly the most famous poem about daffodils.

I wandered lonely as a cloud
That floats on high o'er vales and hills,
When all at once I saw a crowd,
A host, of golden daffodils;
Beside the lake, beneath the trees,
Fluttering and dancing in the breeze

Continuous as the stars that shine
And twinkle on the milky way,
They stretched in never-ending line
Along the margin of a bay:
Ten thousand saw I at a glance,
Tossing their heads in sprightly dance.

The waves beside them danced; but they
Out-did the sparkling waves in glee:
A poet could not but be gay,
In such a jocund company:
I gazed—and gazed—but little thought
What wealth the show to me had brought:

For oft, when on my couch I lie
In vacant or in pensive mood,
They flash upon that inward eye
Which is the bliss of solitude;
And then my heart with pleasure fills,
And dances with the daffodils.

27 March ✶ Love You More ✶ James Carter

Born 1959

James Carter took a circuitous route to becoming a poet, having worked as a school cook, an unemployment counsellor and a rhythm guitarist in a band. He started to write while training to become a primary school teacher and has never looked back. Today he is an acclaimed children's poet who performs at schools and festivals up and down the UK. He lives in Oxfordshire with his wife, two children and three ukuleles, all of which are named Erik (the ukuleles, not his wife and children!).

Do I love you
to the moon and back?
No I love you
more than that

I love you to the desert sands
the mountains, stars
the planets and

I love you to the deepest sea
and deeper still
through history

Before beyond I love you then
I love you now
I'll love you when

The sun's gone out
the moon's gone home
and all the stars are fully grown

When I no longer say these words
I'll give them to the wind, the birds
so that they will still be heard

I love you

28 March ✶ The Gold Bangles ✶ Mona Arshi

Born 1970

Mona Arshi worked as a human rights lawyer at the advocacy group Liberty, where she was involved in a number of high-profile legal trials, including the Stephen Lawrence case, before turning her talents to poetry. Her debut collection *Small Hands,* which features this poem, won the Forward Prize for best first collection in 2015. She has gone on to win many more prizes, and be a judge of the Forward herself. This piece begins a run of poems devoted to the grandmothers whose wisdom helped guide these writers in their formative years.

In my bedroom dresser, in a little red box
sit two gold bangles.
They are pure yellow gold
and the pair are a set, though I believe
they once belonged to part of a bigger set
some time ago.
They were given to my grandmother
and passed down to my mother
upon her marriage.
They are very simple, wide bands and
wear and age have pitted the surface
and begun to affect
the integrity of their modest design.
I imagine they were the kind of thing
that could be melted down
and refashioned into more ornate jewellery
or sold by weight quite easily
depending on the circumstances.
I believe many girls at the time
in those Punjabi villages
would have been presented with similar items

by their parents before they departed
on their long journeys.
My mother wore them on her journey to England.
When I hold them in my hands
I like to think not of that long period
when she owned them
but the time before that,
her waiting for Papaji
by the gate (like so many other gates)
her wrists,
still unadorned and naked.

29 March ✶ My Grandmother's Love Letters ✶ Hart Crane

21 July 1899 – 27 April 1932

Born in the final months of the nineteenth century, Hart Crane found himself caught between Romantic and Victorian influences, and the emergence of the modernist movement. As such, his work features both more ornate language and an experimental spirit that still seems contemporary today, as seen in this free verse poem that explores the difficulties of keeping loved ones alive through memory. In this case, Crane is trying to bridge the gap to his deceased grandmother, who nurtured his passion for literature while his cold and domineering parents tried to deter his creative dreams.

There are no stars tonight
But those of memory.
Yet how much room for memory there is
In the loose girdle of soft rain.

There is even room enough
For the letters of my mother's mother,
Elizabeth,
That have been pressed so long
Into a corner of the roof
That they are brown and soft,
And liable to melt as snow.

Over the greatness of such space
Steps must be gentle.
It is all hung by an invisible white hair.
It trembles as birch limbs webbing the air.

And I ask myself:

'Are your fingers long enough to play
Old keys that are but echoes:
Is the silence strong enough
To carry back the music to its source
And back to you again
As though to her?'

Yet I would lead my grandmother by the hand
Through much of what she would not understand;
And so I stumble. And the rain continues on the roof
With such a sound of gently pitying laughter.

30 March ✶ A Portable Paradise ✶ Roger Robinson

Born 1982

A self-proclaimed 'British resident with a Trini sensibility', Roger Robinson spent most of his early years in Trinidad with his parents before moving back to the UK to live with his grandmother – about whom this poem was written. His poetry is all about breaking barriers and inviting people to unite in unexpected ways through shared experience; as he so brilliantly put it, 'Poems are empathy machines.' He won the T. S. Eliot Prize in 2019 for his fourth collection, *A Portable Paradise.*

And if I speak of Paradise,
then I'm speaking of my grandmother
who told me to carry it always
on my person, concealed, so
no one else would know but me.
That way they can't steal it, she'd say.
And if life puts you under pressure,
trace its ridges in your pocket,
smell its piney scent on your handkerchief,
hum its anthem under your breath.
And if your stresses are sustained and daily,
get yourself to an empty room – be it hotel,
hostel or hovel – find a lamp
and empty your paradise onto a desk:
your white sands, green hills and fresh fish.
Shine the lamp on it like the fresh hope
of morning, and keep staring at it till you sleep.

31 March ✶ Kissing in Vietnamese ✶ Ocean Vuong

Born 1988

Ocean Vuong is an award-winning Vietnamese-American poet, essayist and novelist – impressive achievements for someone his age, but made even more remarkable by the fact that he was the first literate member of his family. Born in Saigon, he was evacuated as a baby with his young mother to a refugee camp in the Philippines before moving on to the US, where he grew up in Connecticut with his mother, aunt and grandmother. As a child he would often work with his mother at a nail salon, which he says gave him a writer's instinct for observing people. After obtaining a degree in English at Brooklyn College, he entered his debut book of poetry into a competition, in the hope of receiving some feedback – but he got more than he bargained for. The book, *Night Sky with Exit Wounds*, was picked up, published and garlanded with literary prizes.

My grandmother kisses
as if bombs are bursting in the backyard,
where mint and jasmine lace their perfumes
through the kitchen window,
as if somewhere, a body is falling apart
and flames are making their way back
through the intricacies of a young boy's thigh,
as if to walk out the door, your torso
would dance from exit wounds.
When my grandmother kisses, there would be
no flashy smooching, no western music
of pursed lips, she kisses as if to breathe
you inside her, nose pressed to cheek
so that your scent is relearned
and your sweat pearls into drops of gold
inside her lungs, as if while she holds you
death also, is clutching your wrist.
My grandmother kisses as if history
never ended, as if somewhere
a body is still
falling apart.

April

1 April ✶ April 1 ✶ 'Tainant'

As we saw with our earlier run of 'Anon.' poets, there are many great poems circulating that cannot be attributed to any one writer. This witty little rhyme for April Fool's Day, about a rainy start to April, is believed to have been written for a Welsh newspaper in 1917 by a local West Glamorgan resident who submitted it under his pen name, 'Tainant'.

Fed up with winter's chilly blast,
April meant hopes of Spring at last;
But it, with joyous smirk so cool,
Made one and all an 'April fool',
For, while the sun shone brightly and nice,
The sky rain'd April showers – of ice.

2 April ✶ The Spider and the Fly ✶
Mary Botham Howitt

12 March 1799 – 30 January 1888

Parables and morality tales tend to be associated with short fiction, but Mary Botham Howitt begins a run of poems here that provide a strong cautionary lesson in just a matter of lines. A friend and translator of the Danish fairy-tale writer Hans Christian Andersen, Howitt is also known for her own poetic fables – especially this one. Unlike many poets, she enjoyed a happy and collaborative marriage to a fellow writer, William Howitt, and was a voice of change as a member of an anti-slavery movement.

Will you walk into my parlour?' said the Spider to the Fly,
''Tis the prettiest little parlour that ever you did spy;
The way into my parlour is up a winding stair,
And I have many curious things to shew when you are there.'
'Oh no, no,' said the little Fly, 'to ask me is in vain,
For who goes up your winding stair can ne'er come down again.'

'I'm sure you must be weary, dear, with soaring up so high;
Will you rest upon my little bed?' said the Spider to the Fly.
'There are pretty curtains drawn around; the sheets are fine and thin,
And if you like to rest awhile, I'll snugly tuck you in!'
'Oh no, no,' said the little Fly, 'for I've often heard it said,
They never, never wake again, who sleep upon your bed!'

Said the cunning Spider to the Fly, 'Dear friend what can I do,
To prove the warm affection I've always felt for you?
I have within my pantry, good store of all that's nice;
I'm sure you're very welcome – will you please to take a slice?'
'Oh no, no,' said the little Fly, 'kind sir, that cannot be,
I've heard what's in your pantry, and I do not wish to see!'

'Sweet creature!' said the Spider, 'you're witty and you're wise,
How handsome are your gauzy wings, how brilliant are your eyes!
I've a little looking-glass upon my parlour shelf,
If you'll step in one moment, dear, you shall behold yourself.'
'I thank you, gentle sir,' she said, 'for what you're pleased to say,
And bidding you good morning now, I'll call another day.'

The Spider turned him round about, and went into his den,
For well he knew the silly Fly would soon come back again:
So he wove a subtle web, in a little corner sly,
And set his table ready, to dine upon the Fly.
Then he came out to his door again, and merrily did sing,
'Come hither, hither, pretty Fly, with the pearl and silver wing;
Your robes are green and purple – there's a crest upon your head;
Your eyes are like the diamond bright, but mine are dull as lead!'

Alas, alas! how very soon this silly little Fly,
Hearing his wily, flattering words, came slowly flitting by;
With buzzing wings she hung aloft, then near and nearer drew,
Thinking only of her brilliant eyes, and green and purple hue –
Thinking only of her crested head – poor foolish thing! At last,
Up jumped the cunning Spider, and fiercely held her fast.
He dragged her up his winding stair, into his dismal den,
Within his little parlour – but she ne'er came out again!

And now dear little children, who may this story read,
To idle, silly flattering words, I pray you ne'er give heed:
Unto an evil counsellor, close heart and ear and eye,
And take a lesson from this tale, of the Spider and the Fly.

3 April ✶ The Story of Little Suck-a-Thumb ✶ Heinrich Hoffmann

13 June 1809 – 20 September 1894

The nineteenth-century German author Heinrich Hoffmann was a practising psychiatric doctor. But when he wasn't treating patients, he was busy writing macabre cautionary stories for children. His collection *Der Struwwelpeter* is almost as popular in Germany as the Brothers Grimm's fairy tales, and features five humorous (but undeniably dark) illustrated stories about naughty children getting their comeuppance. That book was initially written for his young son as a Christmas present, but it went on to influence other wickedly funny and twisted children's writers such as Maurice Sendak and Roald Dahl. The poem below, with its reference to the 'scissorman', is thought to have inspired the Tim Burton film *Edward Scissorhands*.

One day, Mamma said, 'Conrad dear,
I must go out and leave you here.
But mind now, Conrad, what I say,
Don't suck your thumb while I'm away.
The great tall tailor always comes
To little boys that suck their thumbs.
And ere they dream what he's about
He takes his great sharp scissors
And cuts their thumbs clean off, – and then
You know, they never grow again.'

Mamma had scarcely turn'd her back,
The thumb was in, alack! alack!

The door flew open, in he ran,
The great, long, red-legged scissorman.
Oh! children, see! the tailor's come
And caught our little Suck-a-Thumb.

Snip! Snap! Snip! the scissors go;
And Conrad cries out – Oh! Oh! Oh!
Snip! Snap! Snip! They go so fast;
That both his thumbs are off at last.
Mamma comes home; there Conrad stands,
And looks quite sad, and shows his hands; –
'Ah!' said Mamma, 'I knew he'd come
To naughty little Suck-a-Thumb.'

4 April ✶ Henry King ✶ Hilaire Belloc

27 July 1870 – 16 July 1953

Although Hilaire Belloc authored many well-regarded historical and political texts, he is best known for his bitingly satirical collection called *Cautionary Tales* (which includes this poem) that saw him compared to fellow humorists Edward Lear (see 16 February) and Lewis Carroll (see tomorrow). His poems are some of the most deliriously entertaining of the early twentieth century and were famously admired by Pink Floyd's Syd Barrett – who created music inspired by Belloc's work.

The Chief Defect of Henry King
Was chewing little bits of String.
At last he swallowed some which tied
Itself in ugly Knots inside.
Physicians of the Utmost Fame
Were called at once; but when they came
They answered, as they took their Fees,
'There is no Cure for this Disease.
Henry will very soon be dead.'
His parents stood about his Bed
Lamenting his Untimely Death,
When Henry, with his Latest Breath,
Cried – 'Oh, my Friends, be warned by me,
That Breakfast, Dinner, Lunch, and Tea
Are all the Human Frame requires . . .'
With that, the Wretched Child expires.

5 April ✶ Jabberwocky ✶ Lewis Carroll

27 January 1832 – 14 January 1898

Born Charles Lutwidge Dodgson, Lewis Carroll adopted his pen name after partaking in some linguistic shenanigans which saw him translate his first names into Latin (*Carolus Lodovicus*) and then anglicize the result. This tendency to play games with words defined his career as a pioneering author and poet in the emerging nonsense tradition – until then children's books were often dry and prone to moralizing. As the third of eleven children, Carroll developed a knack for engaging with young ones from early on in his life. While teaching Maths at Christ Church, Oxford, he was known to entertain the dean's children – one of whom was called Alice. She would be immortalized in Carroll's *Alice in Wonderland* books, which fused fun, accessible verse with complicated mathematical theories, social allegories, and what today we might call psychedelic imagery. The poem below is one of his most beloved, and it's recommended that you read it aloud to get the most out of the weird and wonderful words he invented here.

'Twas brillig, and the slithy toves
    Did gyre and gimble in the wabe:
All mimsy were the borogoves,
    And the mome raths outgrabe..

'Beware the Jabberwock, my son!
    The jaws that bite, the claws that catch!
Beware the Jubjub bird, and shun
    The frumious Bandersnatch!'

He took his vorpal sword in hand;
    Long time the manxome foe he sought—
So rested he by the Tumtum tree
    And stood awhile in thought.

And, as in uffish thought he stood,
    The Jabberwock, with eyes of flame,
Came whiffling through the tulgey wood,
    And burbled as it came!

One, two! One, two! And through and through
    The vorpal blade went snicker-snack!
He left it dead, and with its head
    He went galumphing back.

'And hast thou slain the Jabberwock?
    Come to my arms, my beamish boy!
O frabjous day! Callooh! Callay!'
    He chortled in his joy.

'Twas brillig, and the slithy toves
    Did gyre and gimble in the wabe:
All mimsy were the borogoves,
    And the mome raths outgrabe.

6 April ✶ Feeling Icky ✶ Michaela Morgan

As the author of over 150 books, it's a mystery how the poet Michaela Morgan finds the time to do anything else! But alongside her writing she has also worked as a teacher and as a writer-in-residence at several prisons. Like her influences – Lewis Carroll, A. A. Milne and Edward Lear – her poems are spontaneous, whimsical and fantastically inventive. In this spring-time piece she is affectionately subverting Carroll's 'Jabberwocky'. There's little doubt that he would've been flattered as a fellow parodist who pastiched past writers such as Isaac Watts (see 19 October).

'Twas Springy and the seedy flowers
Did blow and blossom all around.
All wafty were the shrubberies
And floral dust drifts to the ground.

Beware the pollen count, dear one.
The spores that spread, the dust that flies!
Beware the blossom, and the sun
And buy more tissues, MEGA size.

He took the nasal spray in hand:
He sniffed hard once, he sniffed hard twice –
His nose was clean, his head was clear,
It really was . . . quite nice.

But as in some relief he stood
The blossom flew, the POLLEN came
And drifted through the tulgey wood
He snivelled as it came.

One two, one two! Achoo! Achoo!
The mega tissue failed its job
With eyes of flame, and nose the same
Our hero sobbed a sob.

Can I defeat the allergy
With sprays and potions, pills and such?
I buy it all, I try it all –
And does it help? Not much.

I would prefer a Jabberwock
or a Bandersnatch – or two
But it is the dust that hunts ME out
and lays me low. Boo hoo.

Beware the pollen count, dear one.
The hives that itch, the eyes that run . . .
Beware the flowers, shrubs and such –
Avoid the breeze and shun the sun.

'Tis Springtime – time to stay inside.
Oh slam the door, close curtains too.
The dreaded season's coming near
No tulgey woods for such as you.
So snufflesniff and sneezesneeze SNEEZE
Just rest your head – and snore.

7 April ✶ Reading ✶ Jacqueline Woodson

Born 1963

Jacqueline Woodson turned a childhood ability to tell fibs into a career telling award-winning stories for readers of all ages. Inspired by the likes of Maya Angelou and Langston Hughes, she endeavours to redress the lack of diversity in children's fiction by writing books which centre around Black characters. This poem, about the joys of books, also contains the spirit of inclusivity in the way that it argues that there is no 'right' or 'wrong' way to read; all that matters is the personal enjoyment you derive from it.

I am not my sister.
Words from the books curl around each other
make little sense
until
I read them again
and again, the story
settling into memory. *Too slow*
the teacher says.
Read faster.
Too babyish, the teacher says.
Read older.
But I don't want to read faster or older or
any way else that might
make the story disappear too quickly
from where it's settling
inside my brain,
slowly becoming
a part of me.
A story I will remember
long after I've read it for the second,
third, tenth,
hundredth time.

8 April ✶ The Burning of the Books ✶ Bertolt Brecht, translated by Tom Kuhn

10 February 1898 – 14 August 1956

Jacqueline Woodson's poem shows the way in which a good book can become a private part of you – no wonder then that the oppressive Nazi regime felt threatened by the power of books which stood opposed to their abhorrent ideologies. And so on 8 April 1933, the German Student Union issued a decree which ignited a retrograde policy of burning titles deemed to be of 'Un-German Spirit'. In this poem, the playwright Bertolt Brecht – who had fled the country when the Nazis came to power – retorts that to have one's book burned is a badge of honour for having spoken out against the oppressive regime. Indeed, his profoundly political dramas such as *Life of Galileo* and *The Resistible Rise of Arturo Ui* are some of the most famous anti-fascist texts ever written. Like Harold Pinter (see 10 February), his name has also been transformed into an adjective: 'Brechtian', referring to a kind of theatre that knowingly draws attention to its own artifice.

When the regime ordered that books with harmful knowledge
Should be publicly burnt, and all around
Oxen were forced to drag cartloads of books
To the pyre, one banished poet
One of the best, discovered, studying the list of the burnt
To his horror, that his books
Had been forgotten. He hurried to his desk
On wings of rage, and wrote a letter to the powers that be.
Burn me! he wrote, his pen flying, burn me!
Don't do this to me! Don't pass me over! Have I not always told
The truth in my books? And now
I am treated by you as a liar! I order you:
Burn me!

9 April ✶ Buffalo Dusk ✶ Carl Sandburg

6 January 1878 – 22 July 1967

As his biographer once noted, Carl Sandburg was the kind of poet whose critics would say of his work that it could have been written by a six-year-old child. But of course to write with such ostensible simplicity and clarity demands a mastery of the form – and six-year-olds don't tend to win the Pulitzer Prize! As a disciple of Walt Whitman, Sandburg rejected many of the practices of his generation in favour of the older American poetic traditions that valued nature and universality. An accomplished author, poet, historian and songwriter, Sandburg resists easy definition. As his friend Fanny Butcher once evocatively put it: 'Trying to write briefly about Carl Sandburg, is like trying to picture the Grand Canyon in one black and white snapshot.'

The buffaloes are gone.
And those who saw the buffaloes are gone.
Those who saw the buffaloes by thousands and how they pawed
 the prairie sod into dust with their hoofs, their great heads
 down pawing on in a great pageant of dusk,
Those who saw the buffaloes are gone.
And the buffaloes are gone.

10 April ✶ The Flower-fed Buffaloes ✶ Nicholas Vachel Lindsay

10 November 1879 – 5 December 1931

We may think of performance or spoken-word poetry as a relatively new form, but Nicholas Vachel Lindsay was already touring America giving dramatic readings well over a hundred years ago. Like Sandburg he was inspired by older notions of American literary idealism, and like Sandburg he hailed from Illinois and wrote frequently about his native Midwest. As a performance poet, Lindsay emphasized rhythm and rhetorical flourish in his work.

The flower-fed buffaloes of the spring
In the days of long ago,
Ranged where the locomotives sing
And the prairie flowers lie low:—
The tossing, blooming, perfumed grass
Is swept away by the wheat,
Wheels and wheels and wheels spin by
In the spring that still is sweet.
But the flower-fed buffaloes of the spring
Left us, long ago.
They gore no more, they bellow no more,
They trundle around the hills no more:—
With the Blackfeet, lying low,
With the Pawnees, lying low,
Lying low.

11 April ✶ An Adieu ✶ Florence Earle Coates

1 July 1850 – 6 April 1927

As the granddaughter of the abolitionist Thomas Earle and a descendant of the passengers on the *Mayflower* (the boat carrying the first English settlers to America), Florence Earle Coates has an undoubtedly impressive lineage. Her success as a poet would only confer more prestige on the family name. She was something of a late starter – she only began to be published in her forties – but soon found fans in literary heavyweights such as Thomas Hardy, W. B. Yeats and Matthew Arnold, who would stay with her when touring the US.

Sorrow, quit me for a while!
  Wintry days are over;
Hope again, with April smile,
  Violets sows and clover.

Pleasure follows in her path,
  Love itself flies after,
And the brook a music hath
  Sweet as childhood's laughter.

Not a bird upon the bough
  Can repress its rapture,
Not a bud that blossoms now
  But doth beauty capture.

Sorrow, thou art Winter's mate,
  Spring cannot regret thee;
Yet, ah, yet—my friend of late—
  I shall not forget thee!

12 April ✶ Anthem ✶ Leonard Cohen

21 September 1934 – 7 November 2016

A poet who happened to sing, a philosopher who happened to play guitar – Leonard Cohen may be regarded primarily as a musician, but the term underplays his extraordinary talents as a writer. Today, the achingly cool Canadian is best known as the man behind hits such as 'Hallelujah', 'Suzanne' and 'Famous Blue Raincoat', but he only turned to music at the age of thirty-three, having started out as a poet and novelist. His lyrics, some of which were originally poems, range from heartbreaking observations on death and lost love, to romantic paeans to his (many) muses, to spiritual meditations on God (he was Jewish, but also embraced Buddhism and Christianity) and hope, as seen in the lines from this song 'Anthem': 'There is a crack in everything. / That's how the light gets in.' His fusion of the divine and profane may bring to mind the Metaphysical poets Donne and Marvell, but Cohen is perhaps most readily aligned with the Spanish surrealist poet Federico García Lorca, who also blurred the boundaries between folk music and poetry, while for U2 singer Bono, he was 'our Shelley . . . our Byron'.

The birds they sang
at the break of day
Start again,
I heard them say,
Don't dwell on what
has passed away
or what is yet to be.

The wars they will
be fought again
The holy dove
be caught again
bought and sold
and bought again;
the dove is never free.

Ring the bells that still can ring.
Forget your perfect offering.
There is a crack in everything.
That's how the light gets in.

We asked for signs
the signs were sent:
the birth betrayed,
the marriage spent;
the widowhood
of every government –
signs for all to see.

Can't run no more
with that lawless crowd
while the killers in high places
say their prayers out loud.
But they've summoned up
a thundercloud
They're going to hear from me.

Ring the bells that still can ring
Forget your perfect offering.
There is a crack in everything.
That's how the light gets in.

You can add up the parts
but you won't have the sum
You can strike up the march,
there is no drum.
Every heart
to love will come
but like a refugee.

Ring the bells that still can ring
Forget your perfect offering.
There is a crack in everything.
That's how the light gets in.

13 April ✶ *from* Boots of Spanish Leather ✶ Bob Dylan

Born 1941

When Bob Dylan was controversially awarded the Nobel Prize for Literature in 2016 'for having created new poetic expressions within the great American song tradition', Leonard Cohen (with a typically wonderful turn of phrase) said that it was like 'pinning a medal on Everest' for being the highest mountain. For sixty years Dylan – who was born to a Jewish family in Minnesota as Robert Zimmerman (and whose stage name is a tribute to Dylan Thomas) – has written songs of literary stature on love and war, childhood and ageing, idealism and cynicism, God and the Devil, and everything else in between. Inspired by the folk singer and memoirist Woody Guthrie and Beat generation poets such as Allen Ginsberg, Dylan brought folk sounds and stories into the mainstream during the 1960s. And with his Nobel Prize – the first given to a songwriter – he was once again helping reshape the broadening of genres by showing that sung lyrics were no less highbrow literature than written verse.

Oh, I'm sailin' away my own true love
I'm sailin' away in the morning
Is there something I can send you from across the sea
From the place that I'll be landing?

No, there's nothin' you can send me, my own true love
There's nothin' I wish to be ownin'
Just carry yourself back to me unspoiled
From across that lonesome ocean [...]

Well, if you, my love, must think that-a-way
I'm sure your mind is roamin'
I'm sure your heart is not with me
But with the country to where you're goin'

So take heed, take heed of the western wind
Take heed of the stormy weather
And yes, there's something you can send back to me
Spanish boots of Spanish leather

14 April ✶ Lincoln Is Dead ✶ George Moses Horton

c. 1798 – 1883

On this day in 1865 President Abraham Lincoln was shot by the radical anti-abolitionist John Wilkes Booth at Ford's Theatre. The poet George Moses Horton, who was a slave for sixty-eight years, wrote this poem in tribute to Lincoln, the great emancipator who brought an end to a century of slavery in the United States. Horton's own remarkable story saw him overcome unimaginable oppression to become the first enslaved American to have a book published with *The Hope of Liberty* in 1829. Before that, Horton honed his craft as a writer by selling his love poems to students at the nearby University of North Carolina. His talents were eventually discovered by a woman who was linked to the university, who helped him get a poem published in her hometown Massachusetts newspaper, this time writing on the injustices of slavery.

He is gone, the strong base of the nation,
   The dove to his covet has fled;
Ye heroes lament his privation,
   For Lincoln is dead.

He is gone down, the sun of the Union,
   Like Phoebus, that sets in the west;
The planet of peace and communion,
   Forever has gone to his rest.

He is gone down from a world of commotion,
   No equal succeeds in his stead;
His wonders extend with the ocean,
   Whose waves murmur, Lincoln is dead.

He is gone and can ne'er be forgotten,
   Whose great deeds eternal shall bloom;
When gold, pearls and diamonds are rotten,
   His deeds will break forth from the tomb.

He is gone out of glory to glory,
   A smile with the tear may be shed,
O, then let us tell the sweet story,
   Triumphantly, Lincoln is dead.

15 April ✶ *from* Spring Song ✶ Federico García Lorca, translated by Martin Sorrell

5 June 1898 – 18/19 August 1936

Like Lincoln, the Spanish poet and dramatist Federico García Lorca was assassinated for his unwavering commitment to a progressive, egalitarian world. Along with the painter Salvador Dalí and the filmmaker Luis Buñuel, Lorca was an instrumental figure in the Spanish surrealist avant-garde movement. He found huge success with his 1928 collection of poems *Gypsy Ballads* and for his great rural tragedies *Blood Wedding*, *Yerma* and *House of Bernarda Alba*. Though he spent time in America – where he wrote his influential collection *Poet in New York* – Lorca returned to Spain as the country was succumbing to the fascist ideology of Francisco Franco. Never yielding his leftist stance, Lorca was secretly and tragically executed by the future dictator's soldiers near the start of the Spanish Civil War in August 1936.

28 March 1919
(Granada)

Happy children emerge
from school
sending tender songs
into mid April air.
Such joy for the deep
silence of the alleyway!
A silence smashed to pieces
by bright new silver laughter.

16 April ✶ April ✶ Edwin Arnold

10 June 1832 – 24 March 1904

Edwin Arnold was born in Gravesend in Kent but spent much of his life in India, where he worked as a schoolmaster. During this period he became immersed in Eastern religion, philosophy and literature, translating the poetic Hindu scripture known as the *Bhagavad Gītā* in 1885, and writing his own epic poem about the life and wisdom of the Buddha called *The Light of Asia* in 1879. He eventually pursued journalism rather than poetry on his return to Britain, becoming the editor of the *Daily Telegraph.*

Blossom of the almond-trees,
April's gift to April's bees,
Birthday ornament of spring,
Flora's fairest daughterling! –
Coming when no flow'rets dare
Trust the cruel outer air;
When the royal king-cup bold
Will not don his coat of gold;
And the sturdy blackthorn spray
Keeps its silver for the May; –
Coming when no flow'rets would,
Save thy lowly sisterhood
Early violets, blue and white,
Dying for their love of light.
Almond blossom, sent to teach us
That the spring-days soon will reach us,
Lest, with longing over-tried,
We die as the violets died.
Blossom, clouding all the tree
With thy crimson 'broidery,
Long before a leaf of green
On the bravest bough is seen;
Ah! when wintry winds are swinging
All thy red bells into ringing,
With a bee in every bell,
Almond bloom, we greet thee well!

17 April ✶ Wet Evening in April ✶ Patrick Kavanagh

21 October 1904 – 30 November 1967

Another poet with a farming background like Robert Burns and Seamus Heaney (whom he influenced), Patrick Kavanagh managed to forge an illustrious writing career despite his lack of education. He left school at twelve, but he discovered and taught himself poetry in his teens before breaking out on to the Irish literary scene in the late 1920s. His most famous poems focus on Irish themes and observations and many are devoted to exalting the beauty of the rural landscapes of his childhood.

The birds sang in the wet trees
And as I listened to them it was a hundred years from now
And I was dead and someone else was listening to them.
But I was glad I had recorded for him
   The melancholy.

18 April ✶ Proverbial Logic ✶ Debjani Chatterjee

Born 1952

The Indian-born British poet and children's writer Debjani Chatterjee lived in more places by the time she was twenty than many people visit in a lifetime, having grown up in India, Japan, Bangladesh, Hong Kong and Egypt, before moving to England in 1972. The author of more than sixty books, in addition to her writing, Chatterjee works as a counsellor. She was awarded an MBE in 2008 for services to literature.

Where there are pandas
there's bamboo, but the converse
is sadly not true.

19 April ✶ April Rise ✶ Laurie Lee

26 June 1914 – 13 May 1997

Laurie Lee was a prodigiously successful poet and a prolific chronicler of his own early life as the author of no less than three autobiographies about his first thirty or so years. *Cider with Rosie* is his famous account of growing up in rural Gloucestershire in the years following the First World War; *As I Walked Out One Midsummer Morning* tells of his remarkable pilgrimage to London on foot through the English countryside; and *A Moment of War* presents his recollections of his experiences of fighting for the Republicans in the Spanish Civil War. In later life he worked as a documentary maker and as the excellently titled Curator of Eccentricities at the Festival of Britain exhibition in 1951, for which he was awarded an MBE. His final words, which he called to his wife – 'I've got a secret' – may go down as the greatest, and most frustrating, in history.

If ever I saw blessing in the air
   I see it now in this still early day
Where lemon-green the vaporous morning drips
   Wet sunlight on the powder of my eye.

Blown bubble-film of blue, the sky wraps round
   Weeds of warm light whose every root and rod
Splutters with soapy green, and all the world
   Sweats with the bead of summer in its bud.

If ever I heard blessing it is there
   Where birds in trees that shoals and shadows are
Splash with their hidden wings and drops of sound
   Break on my ears their crests of throbbing air.

Pure in the haze the emerald sun dilates,
   The lips of sparrows milk the mossy stones,
While white as water by the lake a girl
   Swims her green hand among the gathered swans.

Now, as the almond burns its smoking wick,
   Dropping small flames to light the candled grass;
Now, as my low blood scales its second chance,
   If ever world were blessed, now it is.

20 April ✶ The Catch ✶ Simon Armitage

Born 1963

Simon Armitage is the current Poet Laureate, having taken over the now ten-year post from Carol Ann Duffy in May 2019. Growing up in West Yorkshire, Armitage took inspiration from the fact that Ted Hughes had managed to become a world-renowned poet, having come from a similarly remote nearby valley. After some years working as a probation officer in Greater Manchester, Armitage became a full-time writer and part-time lecturer. His poems can be found on school syllabuses up and down the country as their accessible language, relatable subjects and punkish irreverence all combine to beguile even the most reluctant teen readers.

Forget
the long, smouldering
afternoon. It is

this moment
when the ball scoots
off the edge

of the bat; upwards,
backwards, falling
seemingly

beyond him
yet he reaches
and picks it

out
of its loop
like

an apple
from a branch,
the first of the season.

21 April ✶ Sonnet 7 ✶ John Milton

9 December 1608 – 8 November 1674

Other than Shakespeare (fear not, he's coming up soon!), there is perhaps no writer who can lay a better claim to the title of the greatest English poet than John Milton. And if you need any convincing (T. S. Eliot is one who certainly did), it's worth bearing in mind that his undisputed masterpiece – the twelve-book Biblical epic *Paradise Lost* – was dictated in full, in blank verse, after he went blind in midlife. Milton's career coincided with the most turbulent period in English history (well, until recently . . .) and he wrote polemically against Charles I and in favour of Oliver Cromwell and the anti-monarchists during the Civil War. After the latter's protectorate rule ended, Milton found himself a political enemy of the restored monarchy, and was promptly imprisoned until his family paid his fines. To this day Milton is still cited as one of the great champions of a free, uncensored press.

How soon hath Time, the subtle thief of youth,
    Stol'n on his wing my three-and-twentieth year!
    My hasting days fly on with full career,
    But my late spring no bud or blossom shew'th.
Perhaps my semblance might deceive the truth
    That I to manhood am arriv'd so near;
    And inward ripeness doth much less appear,
    That some more timely-happy spirits endu'th.
Yet be it less or more, or soon or slow,
    It shall be still in strictest measure ev'n
    To that same lot, however mean or high,
Toward which Time leads me, and the will of Heav'n:
    All is, if I have grace to use it so
    As ever in my great Task-Master's eye.

22 April ✶ Sonnet 292 ✶ Francesco Petrarch, translated by Thomas Wentworth Higginson

20 July 1304 – 18/19 July 1374

There is a case to be made that the great Italian poet Francesco Petrarch was to Shakespeare and his contemporaries what Shakespeare is to all writers since. Such was the influence of this man born in Arezzo in the early fourteenth century on the future of English literature, that Tudor writers developed the Petrarchan Sonnet (fourteen lines split into stanzas of eight and six lines) in tribute to the Renaissance pioneer. A keen traveller, humanist and scholar, Petrarch is known as 'the first modern man', and his poems about love, longing and loss – many of which were devoted to his muse Laura (a possibly fictional precursor to Dante's Beatrice and Shakespeare's so-called Dark Lady) – still resonate and inspire today.

Those eyes, 'neath which my passionate rapture rose,
The arms, hands, feet, the beauty that erewhile
Could my own soul from its own self beguile,
And in a separate world of dreams enclose,
The hair's bright tresses, full of golden glows,
And the soft lightning of the angelic smile
That changed this earth to some celestial isle, –
Are now but dust, poor dust, that nothing knows.
And yet I live! Myself I grieve and scorn,
Left dark without the light I loved in vain,
Adrift in tempest on a bark forlorn;
Dead is the source of all my amorous strain,
Dry is the channel of my thoughts outworn,
And my sad harp can sound but notes of pain.

23 April ✶ Sonnet 18 ✶ William Shakespeare

c. 23 April 1564 – 23 April 1616

Brevity may be the soul of wit, but it's not particularly helpful when it comes to trying to summarize the single most important English writer in history. Where to begin and where to end? Well, handily enough, we can do both on 23 April, which is thought to be the day on which he was born and then died fifty-two years later. Not only is it a curious fact, but it perfectly captures Shakespeare's keen sense of equilibrium: in his plays (which could equally entertain the uneducated as they could beguile the scholars), his life (which was defined both by his humble roots in Warwickshire and his success and fame in London where he co-owned the Globe theatre) and in his politics (which were marked by an even-handed understanding). A writer of infinite variety, he was a master of poetry as well as theatre. This sonnet, perhaps the most quoted in the English language, is thought to have been written for a 'fair youth', who though anonymous, continues to live on forever in these lines, just as Shakespeare promises in the final couplet.

Shall I compare thee to a summer's day?
Thou art more lovely and more temperate:
Rough winds do shake the darling buds of May,
And summer's lease hath all too short a date;
Sometime too hot the eye of heaven shines,
And often is his gold complexion dimm'd;
And every fair from fair sometime declines,
By chance or nature's changing course untrimm'd;
But thy eternal summer shall not fade,
Nor lose possession of that fair thou ow'st;
Nor shall death brag thou wander'st in his shade,
When in eternal lines to time thou grow'st:
  So long as men can breathe or eyes can see,
  So long lives this, and this gives life to thee.

24 April ✶ On Quoting Shakespeare ✶ Bernard Levin

9 August 1928 – 7 August 2004

Bernard Levin was a leading journalist for *The Times* and *Sunday Times* for over thirty years who became a household name after appearing on the BBC's satirical programme *That Was The Week That Was*. He was known for his great erudition and for his incisive comic touch that saw him skewer politicians both in his columns and on TV. In this article extract (though sometimes it's called a poem) he mocks the idea that Shakespeare's writing is impenetrable by listing many of the near-countless everyday words and phrases that were coined by Shakespeare and remain central to our means of expression to this day.

If you cannot understand my argument, and declare 'It's Greek to me', you are quoting Shakespeare; if you claim to be more sinned against than sinning, you are quoting Shakespeare; if you recall your salad days, you are quoting Shakespeare; if you act more in sorrow than in anger, if your wish is father to the thought, if your lost property has vanished into thin air, you are quoting Shakespeare; if you have ever refused to budge an inch or suffered from green-eyed jealousy, if you have played fast and loose, if you have been tongue-tied, a tower of strength, hoodwinked or in a pickle, if you have knitted your brows, made a virtue of necessity, insisted on fair play, slept not one wink, stood on ceremony, danced attendance (on your lord and master), laughed yourself into stitches, had short shrift, cold comfort or too much of a good thing, if you have seen better days or lived in a fool's paradise – why, be that as it may, the more fool you, for it is a foregone conclusion that you are (as good luck would have it) quoting Shakespeare; if you think it is early days and clear out bag and baggage, if you think it is high time and that that is the long and short of it, if you believe that the game is up and that truth will out even if it involves your own flesh and blood, if you lie low till the crack of doom because you suspect foul play, if you have your teeth set on edge (at one fell swoop) without rhyme or reason, then – to give the devil his due – if the truth were known (for surely you have a tongue in your head) you are quoting Shakespeare; even if you bid me good riddance and send me packing, if you wish I were dead as a door-nail, if you think I am an eyesore, a laughing stock, the devil incarnate, a stony-hearted villain, bloody-minded or a blinking idiot, then – by Jove! O Lord! Tut, tut! for goodness' sake! what the dickens! but me no buts – it is all one to me, for you are quoting Shakespeare.

25 April ✶ Death, Be Not Proud ✶ John Donne

22 January 1572 – 31 March 1631

John Donne was one of the principal figures in what Samuel Johnson later called the 'metaphysical' group of English poets, whose writing was full of inventive metaphors, far-fetched imagery, philosophical debates and ambiguous messages. Donne's particular interest in the paradoxes of human thought and behaviour may have been informed by the underlying contradictions in his own life. On the one hand, he was a devoted cleric, on the other, he had earlier engaged in a clandestine romance with an MP's daughter. Much of his early life was also defined by secrecy as the child of Roman Catholics in an era in which the religion was still banned in England. He was eventually allowed (and in fact encouraged by King James) to become a preacher and his sermons and devotional works are hugely admired as works of prose. Still, he is best known as an exceptional love poet, as well as a writer on weightier themes such as God and death, as seen in the sonnet below.

Death, be not proud, though some have called thee
Mighty and dreadful, for thou art not so;
For those whom thou think'st thou dost overthrow
Die not, poor Death, nor yet canst thou kill me.
From rest and sleep, which but thy pictures be,
Much pleasure; then from thee much more must flow,
And soonest our best men with thee do go,
Rest of their bones, and soul's delivery.
Thou art slave to fate, chance, kings, and desperate men,
And dost with poison, war, and sickness dwell,
And poppy or charms can make us sleep as well
And better than thy stroke; why swell'st thou then?
One short sleep past, we wake eternally
And death shall be no more; Death, thou shalt die.

26 April ✶ Cradle Song ✶ Thomas Dekker

c. 1572 – 25 August 1632

Even though we don't know much about the life of pamphleteer and playwright Thomas Dekker, we do know that he was a prolific writer – at least forty-two plays can be traced back to him – and he supported himself through his writing, though not always successfully, twice being imprisoned for debt. He also helped arrange the welcoming of James I to London in 1604 and organized four Lord Mayor's pageants. This poem is from his play *Patient Grissel*. It may sound remarkably familiar to fans of the Beatles as a version of the poem was adapted into a beautifully tender song by Paul McCartney for the album *Abbey Road*.

Golden slumbers kiss your eyes,
Smiles awake you when you rise;
Sleep, pretty wantons, do not cry,
And I will sing a lullaby:
Rock them, rock them, lullaby.

Care is heavy, therefore sleep you;
You are care, and care must keep you.
Sleep, pretty wantons, do not cry,
And I will sing a lullaby:
Rock them, rock them, lullaby.

27 April ✶ Say not the Struggle Nought Availeth ✶ Arthur Hugh Clough

1 January 1819 – 13 November 1861

Arthur Hugh Clough was a Victorian poet whose work had a major influence on modernists such as T. S. Eliot in the way that it experimented with language and literary conventions. He worked as an unpaid assistant to the nurse and social reformer Florence Nightingale (who happened to be his wife's cousin). But perhaps his most significant presence at a moment in history came after his death. In 1941, with Britain facing potential defeat in the Second World War, Winston Churchill chose this rousing poem by Clough to quote to the nation in an attempt to galvanize their sense of perseverance and give hope that their struggle would not be in vain.

Say not the struggle nought availeth,
  The labour and the wounds are vain,
The enemy faints not, nor faileth,
  And as things have been they remain.

If hopes were dupes, fears may be liars;
  It may be, in yon smoke concealed,
Your comrades chase e'en now the fliers,
  And, but for you, possess the field.

For while the tired waves, vainly breaking
  Seem here no painful inch to gain,
Far back through creeks and inlets making,
  Comes silent, flooding in, the main.

And not by eastern windows only,
  When daylight comes, comes in the light,
In front the sun climbs slow, how slowly,
  But westward, look, the land is bright.

28 April ✶ Invictus ✶ W. E. Henley

23 August 1849 – 11 July 1903

Continuing with a run of poems about the indomitable human spirit in times of suffering and conflict is this rousing piece by the Victorian W. E. Henley, which kept Nelson Mandela company during his Apartheid-era incarceration on Robben Island. Henley himself endured an extremely difficult childhood – he lost a leg to TB aged twelve, and his father died not long after – which is why so much of his poetry focuses on finding those fathomless reserves of inner-strength and courage in moments of great adversity. Indeed, the word 'Invictus' means 'unconquered' in Latin, and it has been adopted as the name of the sport event founded by Prince Harry for injured soldiers. Henley himself may not be a household name, but most people will be very familiar with the character based on the poet: the pegleg pirate Long John Silver from *Treasure Island*, which was written by Henley's friend Robert Louis Stevenson.

Out of the night that covers me,
    Black as the pit from pole to pole,
I thank whatever gods may be
    For my unconquerable soul.

In the fell clutch of circumstance
    I have not winced nor cried aloud.
Under the bludgeonings of chance
    My head is bloody, but unbowed.

Beyond this place of wrath and tears
    Looms but the Horror of the shade,
And yet the menace of the years
    Finds and shall find me unafraid.

It matters not how strait the gate,
    How charged with punishments the scroll,
I am the master of my fate,
    I am the captain of my soul.

29 April ✶ *from* The Cure of Troy ✶ Seamus Heaney

13 April 1939 – 30 August 2013

Unarguably the greatest Irish poet since W. B. Yeats, Seamus Heaney won the Nobel Prize, like his predecessor, in 1995. Born in County Derry to a family of farmers, he, like fellow Irishman Patrick Kavanagh before him, saw his calling in poetic matters of the soul, rather than soil. But he never forgot his home, and his work often reveals a longing for the landscapes of his past, and a sense of regret at his lack of agricultural vocation – this despite having taught at Harvard University and given readings to crowds of fans. As such, his poetry often focuses on his farming roots, his family and his Catholic background. Despite being almost synonymous with Ireland, Heaney is beloved by readers across the world and can rank President Joe Biden among his fans after the latter recited the lines from Heaney's 'The Cure at Troy' (below) – 'The longed-for tidal wave / Of justice can rise up / And hope and history rhyme' – on receiving the Democratic nomination in 2020. The poem continues our run of pieces about the resilience born of conflict and hardship.

Human beings suffer.
They torture one another.
They get hurt and get hard.
No poem or play or song
Can fully right a wrong
Inflicted and endured.

History says, Don't hope
On this side of the grave,
But then, once in a lifetime
The longed-for tidal wave
Of justice can rise up
And hope and history rhyme.

So hope for a great sea-change
On the far side of revenge.
Believe that a farther shore
Is reachable from here.
Believe in miracles.
And cures and healing wells.

Call miracle self-healing,
The utter self-revealing
Double-take of feeling.
If there's fire on the mountain
And lightning and storm
And a god speaks from the sky

That means someone is hearing
The outcry and the birth-cry
Of new life at its term.
It means once in a lifetime
That justice can rise up
And hope and history rhyme.

30 April ✶ Blood and Lead ✶ James Fenton

Born 1949

James Fenton has enjoyed a sterling career as a war correspondent, literary critic, professor of poetry at Oxford, and award-winning poet. His journalistic background has seen him take a more investigative approach to writing poetry that is more about the discovery than coming at a poem with set, didactic ideas. As he articulately once explained: 'The writing of a poem is like a child throwing stones into a mineshaft. You compose first, then you listen for the reverberation.' Although Fenton is known for his fondness for humour and the music hall tradition, he has also written more sombre pieces such as this one about the Vietnam War, which ended on this date in 1975.

Listen to what they did.
Don't listen to what they said.
What was written in blood
Has been set up in lead.

Lead tears the heart.
Lead tears the brain.
What was written in blood
Has been set up again.

The heart is a drum.
The drum has a snare.
The snare is in the blood.
The blood is in the air.

Listen to what they did.
Listen to what's to come.
Listen to the blood.
Listen to the drum.

May

1 May ✶ The Language of Birds ✶
Samuel Taylor Coleridge

21 October 1772 – 25 July 1834

So far in this anthology we have already met two of Samuel Taylor Coleridge's children (see 7 January and 19 March) and heard about his friendship with the poet Robert Southey and how he spearheaded the Romantic movement with his longtime collaborator William Wordsworth. As for the man himself, Coleridge was born in Devon to a vicar as one of fourteen children. It was assumed that he would follow in his father's footsteps but he dropped out of his studies. The church's loss was ultimately literature's gain, as Coleridge went on to become one of the most influential poets of the last 250 years. His legacy was to create a style of poetry that was more natural or conversational, using the language of the people and drawing on personal and observed experiences. This poem, alternately (and touchingly) titled as 'Answer to a Child's Question', is a perfect illustration of how Coleridge saw poetry as an inclusive form of human communication which could, and should, speak to people of all ages.

Do you ask what the birds say? The Sparrow, the Dove,
The Linnet and Thrush say, 'I love and I love!'
In the winter they're silent – the wind is so strong;
What it says, I don't know, but it sings a loud song.
But green leaves, and blossoms, and sunny warm weather,
And singing, and loving – all come back together.
But the Lark is so brimful of gladness and love,
The green fields below him, the blue sky above,
That he sings, and he sings; and for ever sings he –
'I love my Love, and my Love loves me!'

2 May ✶ The Windhover ✶ Gerard Manley Hopkins

28 July 1844 – 8 June 1889

Some writers see the fruits of their labour receive recognition in their lifetime, but many died years before readers caught up with their trailblazing brilliance. Gerard Manley Hopkins belongs to the latter category as someone whose work was mostly not published until thirty years after his death. His pioneering, experimental style was seen as out of step with what was in vogue at the time. But even in his personal life he was unconventional; raised by Protestants, he converted to Catholicism, despite the pain this initially cost his parents. Religious overtones pervade his work, as do birds such as the windhover in this poem.

I caught this morning morning's minion, king-
  dom of daylight's dauphin, dapple-dawn-drawn Falcon, in his riding
  Of the rolling level underneath him steady air, and striding
High there, how he rung upon the rein of a wimpling wing
In his ecstasy! then off, off forth on swing,
  As a skate's heel sweeps smooth on a bow-bend: the hurl and gliding
  Rebuffed the big wind. My heart in hiding
Stirred for a bird, – the achieve of, the mastery of the thing!

Brute beauty and valour and act, oh, air, pride, plume, here
  Buckle! AND the fire that breaks from thee then, a billion
Times told lovelier, more dangerous, O my chevalier!

 No wonder of it: shéer plód makes plough down sillion
Shine, and blue-bleak embers, ah my dear,
  Fall, gall themselves, and gash gold-vermilion.

3 May ✶ Plovers ✶ Padraic Colum

8 December 1881 – 11 January 1972

Born in County Longford, Ireland, Padraic Colum was the son of a workhouse master and the oldest of eight siblings. He started work at the age of seventeen as a clerk for the Irish Railway Clearing House, but while living in Dublin, he began to pursue his real passion of writing. It was here that he became part of the Celtic Revival Movement and, along with friends such as W. B. Yeats, John Synge and Lady Gregory, founded the iconic Abbey Theatre. Colum wrote poetry and prose, but he had a particularly keen interest in folklore. A close friend of James Joyce, in the 1930s he moved to France, where he had the perhaps unenviable task of helping the former type up his notoriously difficult book *Finnegans Wake*, before moving permanently to the USA, where he taught at Columbia University. This poem about the plover bird continues our avian run.

The Plovers fly and cry around,
Unguided, nestless, without bourn,
Wandering and impetuous,
Turning and flying to return.

These wild birds seen on Ireland's ground
I name upon Hawaiian beaches –
Estrayents, they, of all lands' ends,
They have the oceans for their reaches

My thoughts are like the Plovers' flight,
Unguided, nestless, without bourn,
Wandering and impetuous,
Turning and flying to return.

4 May ✶ Plovers ✶ Paul Muldoon

Born 1951

Another short plover poem comes to us courtesy of another Irishman: the poet and professor Paul Muldoon. A highly regarded writer, Muldoon is noted for his attention to paradox and wordplay, and for what the writer Ruth Padel called 'his sheer delight in the power of words'. In addition to his poetry, Muldoon has worked as the poetry critic for the *New Yorker* magazine and has written for TV, radio and even opera. Today he teaches at Princeton University.

The plovers come down hard, then clear again,
for they are the embodiment of rain.

5 May ✶ Bird ✶ Gareth Owen

Nobody was more surprised than Gareth Owen when he became a writer. The Lancashire-born poet left school at sixteen to go to sea, but eventually ended up as a teacher who began writing poems to entertain his students. His first collection, *Salford Road,* won high praise, and Patric Dickinson said it was 'original, beautiful, serious, funny, real and imaginative. Nothing quite like it has been done before.'

Something fluttered about my heart
Like a bird caught in a snare
I blame the girl on the fourteen bus
It was she who put it there.

6 May ✶ Bustopher Jones: The Cat about Town ✶ T. S. Eliot

26 September 1888 – 4 January 1965

T. S. Eliot is synonymous with both modernist poetry – his masterpieces *The Waste Land* and 'The Love Song of J. Alfred Prufrock' are seminal texts within the movement – and the London literary scene in the interwar period. An American expat living and working largely in Britain, Eliot became the era's foremost arbiter of culture as the literary advisor of Faber and Faber publishers and as a hugely influential and revered critic. Although much of his poetry dealt with urban desolation, decay and despair, he also wrote more cheerily for children, notably in *Old Possum's Book of Practical Cats,* from which this poem is taken.

Bustopher Jones is *not* skin and bones –
In fact, he's remarkably fat.
He doesn't haunt pubs – he has eight or nine clubs,
For he's the St. James's Street Cat!
He's the Cat we all greet as he walks down the street
In his coat of fastidious black:
No commonplace mousers have such well-cut trousers
Or such an impeccable back.
In the whole of St. James's the smartest of names is
The name of this Brummell of Cats;
And we're all of us proud to be nodded or bowed to
By Bustopher Jones in white spats!

His visits are occasional to the *Senior Educational*
And it is against the rules
For any one Cat to belong both to that
And the *Joint Superior Schools*.
For a similar reason, when game is in season
He is found, not at *Fox's*, but *Blimp's*;
But he's frequently seen at the gay *Stage and Screen*
Which is famous for winkles and shrimps.
In the season of venison he gives his ben'son
To the *Pothunter's* succulent bones;
And just before noon's not a moment too soon
To drop in for a drink at the Drones.
When he's seen in a hurry there's probably curry
At the *Siamese* – or at the *Glutton*;
If he looks full of gloom then he's lunched at the *Tomb*
On cabbage, rice pudding and mutton.

So, much in this way, passes Bustopher's day –
At one club or another he's found.
It can be no surprise that under our eyes
He has grown unmistakably round.
He's a twenty-five pounder, or I am a bounder,
And he's putting on weight every day:
But he's so well preserved because he's observed
All his life a routine, so he'd say.
Or, to put it in rhyme: 'I shall last out my time'
Is the word of this stoutest of Cats.
It must and it shall be Spring in Pall Mall
While Bustopher Jones wears white spats!

7 May ✶ How to Get On in Society ✶ John Betjeman

28 August 1906 – 19 May 1984

T. S. Eliot may have had an immeasurable influence on countless poets, but on none perhaps quite as directly as John Betjeman, whom he taught at Highgate School. Though his name may be of German origin, Betjeman might be seen as the archetypal English intellectual eccentric; a gifted mind who drank too much, flunked out of Oxford and still landed on his feet due to his irrepressible talents (and some university contacts in high places). After an early career in journalism and broadcasting, he became a hugely successful writer of wide appeal, often skewering the upper middle class of which he was a part. By his side throughout all his achievements – the crowning one being named Poet Laureate in 1972 – were his two best friends, Archie and Jumbo: a teddy bear and stuffed elephant who were allegedly still in his arms when he died aged seventy-eight.

Phone for the fish-knives, Norman
   As Cook is a little unnerved;
You kiddies have crumpled the serviettes
   And I must have things daintily served.

Are the requisites all in the toilet?
   The frills round the cutlets can wait
Till the girl has replenished the cruets
   And switched on the logs in the grate.

It's ever so close in the lounge, dear,
   But the vestibule's comfy for tea
And Howard is out riding on horseback
   So do come and take some with me.

Now here is a fork for your pastries
   And do use the couch for your feet;
I know what I wanted to ask you—
   Is trifle sufficient for sweet?

Milk and then just as it comes dear?
   I'm afraid the preserve's full of stones;
Beg pardon, I'm soiling the doileys
   With afternoon tea-cakes and scones.

8 May ✶ Soliloquy of a Maiden Aunt ✶ Dollie Radford

3 December 1858 – 7 February 1920

It's hard not to feel a little sorry for Dollie Radford (born Caroline Maitland), a poet who occupied the same literary circles as her day's leading minds and writers – Eleanor Marx, W. B. Yeats, William Morris, D. H. Lawrence, H. G. Wells and George Bernard Shaw – without ever receiving any recognition herself. In fact, Yeats went so far as to belittle her efforts as 'trifling'. It's true that she did mainly write romances (which were not considered highbrow), but she imbued them all with a subversive streak and messages of female autonomy. Indeed, the name of this poem, 'Maiden Aunt', is a term for what we'd today call an independent woman.

The ladies bow, and partners set,
And turn around and pirouette
  And trip the Lancers.

But no one seeks my ample chair,
Or asks me with persuasive air
  To join the dancers.

They greet me, as I sit alone
Upon my solitary throne,
  And pass politely.

Yet mine could keep the measured beat,
As surely as the youngest feet,
  And tread as lightly.

No other maiden had my skill
In our old homestead on the hill –
  That merry May-time

When Allan closed the flagging ball,
And danced with me before them all,
  Until the day-time.

Again I laugh, and step alone,
And curtsey low as on my own
  His strong hand closes.

But Allan now seeks staid delight,
His son there, brought my niece to-night
  These early roses.

Time orders well, we have our Spring,
Our songs, and may-flower gathering,
  Our love and laughter.

And children chatter all the while,
And leap the brook and climb the stile
  And follow after.

And yet – the step of Allan's son,
Is not as light as was the one
  That went before it.

And that old lace, I think, falls down
Less softly on Priscella's gown
  Than when I wore it.

9 May ✶ Ends Meet ✶ Frances Bellerby

29 August 1899 – 30 July 1975

Frances Bellerby (née Parker) was a writer of poetry, short stories, novels and essays, often autobiographical. Born to a working-class curate in Bristol, she settled with her husband in Cornwall; they shared socialist beliefs and were both involved in a voluntary welfare organization based around the idea of shared income. While her prose was sometimes political, her poetry was characterized by a deep regard for the landscape around her, and Cornish poet Charles Causley (see 22 January) praised her for its 'ambience and essence of place'.

My grandmother came down the steps into the garden.
She shone in the gauzy air.
She said: 'There's an old woman at the gate –
See what she wants, my dear.'

My grandmother's eyes were blue like the damsels
Darting and swerving above the stream,
Or like the kingfisher arrow shot into darkness
Through the archway's dripping gleam.

My grandmother's hair was silver as sunlight.
The sun had been poured right over her, I saw,
And ran down her dress and spread a pool for her shadow
To float in. And she would live for evermore.

There was nobody at the gate when I got there.
Not even a shadow hauling along the road,
Nor my yellow snail delicate under the ivy,
Nor my sheltering cold-stone toad.

But the sunflowers aloft were calm. They'd seen no one.
They were sucking light, for ever and a day.
So I busied myself with going away unheeded
And with having nothing to say.

No comment, nothing to tell, or to think,
Whilst the day followed the homing sun.
There was no old woman at my grandmother's gate.

And there isn't at mine.

10 May ✶ Childhood ✶ Frances Cornford

30 March 1886 – 19 August 1960

You can imagine the chaos that would have followed Frances Cornford (born Frances Crofts Darwin) throughout her life, given that both her father (a botanist) and her husband (a classics and philosophy professor at Cambridge) were called – you guessed it – Francis! Eventually the confusion became so much that Frances was referred to in her family by her initials only: FCD, then FCC. Although she never became as famous as her grandfather, Charles Darwin, Cornford was well-known in her lifetime, and her poems were very popular.

I used to think that grown-up people chose
To have stiff backs and wrinkles round their nose,
And veins like small fat snakes on either hand,
On purpose to be grand.
Till through the banisters I watched one day
My great-aunt Etty's friend who was going away,
And how her onyx beads had come unstrung.
I saw her grope to find them as they rolled;
And then I knew that she was helplessly old,
As I was helplessly young.

11 May ✶ Warning ✶ Jenny Joseph

7 May 1932 – 8 January 2018

Jenny Joseph wrote many poems in her career, predominantly on everyday matters and the human condition. But her life's work has largely been defined by the extraordinary success of this one particular poem written in 1961, which, like Cornford's poem above, grapples with ageing (albeit in a lighter tone). A 1996 BBC poll saw it named the country's best loved post-war poem, and lines from it could be found on everything from greetings cards to tea-towels. Joseph's other wide-ranging work unfortunately never received the same recognition, and she inevitably became frustrated that everyone seemed interested in only that poem. That said, it is a truly great one!

When I am an old woman I shall wear purple
With a red hat which doesn't go, and doesn't suit me.
And I shall spend my pension on brandy and summer gloves
And satin sandals, and say we've no money for butter.
I shall sit down on the pavement when I'm tired
And gobble up samples in shops and press alarm bells
And run my stick along the public railings
And make up for the sobriety of my youth.
I shall go out in my slippers in the rain
And pick flowers in other people's gardens
And learn to spit.

You can wear terrible shirts and grow more fat
And eat three pounds of sausages at a go
Or only bread and pickle for a week
And hoard pens and pencils and beermats and things in boxes.

But now we must have clothes that keep us dry
And pay our rent and not swear in the street
And set a good example for the children.
We must have friends to dinner and read the papers.

But maybe I ought to practise a little now?
So people who know me are not too shocked and surprised
When suddenly I am old, and start to wear purple.

12 May ✶ Jenny Kiss'd Me ✶ Leigh Hunt

19 October 1784 – 28 August 1859

You might never have heard of Leigh Hunt, but without him, you almost certainly would never have heard of the likes of John Keats and Percy Shelley. Although he wrote his own vividly atmospheric poetry, Hunt was far more influential as a critic, essayist and as the proprietor of a political and cultural journal called *The Examiner*, in which he published and tirelessly promoted the new generation of Romantic writers. It was in these pages that Hunt also campaigned for parliamentary reform and the abolition of slavery, and launched a satirical attack on the Prince Regent which landed him in (a rather luxurious) prison, where he wrote his masterpiece, *The Story of Rimini*, and met with poets such as Byron. Outside of jail, he was a resident of Hampstead (then still a village outside London), along with Keats – and it is here that he introduced the latter to Shelley. In later life he would also help launch the careers of Victorian writers Robert Browning, Alfred Tennyson and Charles Dickens.

Jenny kiss'd me when we met,
Jumping from the chair she sat in;
Time, you thief, who love to get
Sweets into your list, put that in!
Say I'm weary, say I'm sad,
Say that health and wealth have miss'd me,
Say I'm growing old, but add,
Jenny kiss'd me.

13 May ✶ Invisible Kisses ✶ Lemn Sissay

Born 1967

Another poem about kisses comes to us from one of the most admired poets working in England today. The son of an Ethiopian immigrant, Lemn Sissay was heartbreakingly separated from his mother at a young age when a social worker gave him up for adoption when the former had only intended for him to be temporarily put in foster care while she studied. He was sent to a very religious white family in Lancashire who anglicized his name to Norman Mark Greenwood, before sending him back to care aged twelve. But despite leaving school at fifteen, Sissay was already self-publishing poetry – which had been a solace through his childhood – at eighteen, and since then he has enjoyed success after success, most notably being awarded an MBE and named the official poet of the London 2012 Olympics. Outside of poetry, he has worked in broadcasting and has done much to expose the many problems blighting the care system. He is also the Chancellor of Manchester University.

If there was ever one
Whom when you were sleeping
Would wipe your tears
When in dreams you were weeping;
Who would offer you time
When others demand;
Whose love lay more infinite
Than grains of sand.

If there was ever one
To whom you could cry;
Who would gather each tear
And blow it dry;
Who would offer help
On the mountains of time;
Who would stop to let each sunset
Soothe the jaded mind.

If there was ever one
To whom when you run
Will push back the clouds
So you are bathed in sun;
Who would open arms
If you would fall;
Who would show you everything
If you lost it all.

If there was ever one
Who when you achieve
Was there before the dream
And even then believed;
Who would clear the air
When it's full of loss;
Who would count love
Before the cost.

If there was ever one
Who when you are cold
Will summon warm air
For your hands to hold;
Who would make peace
In pouring pain,
Make laughter fall
In falling rain.

If there was ever one
Who can offer you this and more;
Who in keyless rooms
Can open doors;
Who in open doors
Can see open fields
And in open fields
See harvests yield.

Then see only my face
In reflection of these tides
Through the clear water
Beyond the river side.
All I can send is love
In all that this is
A poem and a necklace
Of invisible kisses.

14 May ✶ Mmenson ✶ Kamau Brathwaite

11 May 1930 – 4 February 2020

Kamau Brathwaite was known as a giant of Caribbean culture for the way in which he established a local poetic vernacular in his writing, and for co-founding the Caribbean Arts Movement. For him, regional words, idioms and rhythms were not secondary to the kind of English the queen speaks but part of a distinct Caribbean intra-national tongue. His work was perhaps partly influenced by T. S. Eliot, whom he admired. For Adrienne Rich, Brathwaite was 'one of the most compelling of late twentieth-century poets' in his own right.

Summon now the kings of the forest,
horn of the elephant,
mournful call of the elephant;

summon the emirs, kings of the desert,
horses caparisoned, beaten gold bent,
archers and criers, porcupine arrows, bows bent;

recount now the gains and the losses:
Agades, Sokoto, El Hassan dead in his tent,
the silks and the brasses, the slow weary tent

of our journeys down slopes, dry river courses;
land of the lion, land of the leopard, elephant
country; tall grasses, thick prickly herbs.
                                        Blow elephant

trumpet; summon the horses,
dead horses, our losses: the bent
slow bow of the Congo, the watering Niger . . .

15 May ✶ If I Woz a Tap-Natch Poet ✶ Linton Kwesi Johnson

Born 1952

Linton Kwesi Johnson, the so-called 'father of dub poetry', was born in Jamaica and moved to London aged eleven. In his teens he joined the Black Panther Movement, and that burning sense of injustice informed his work as a protest poet who had a responsibility, he believed, to fight against oppression with his words. As he put it, 'Writing was a political act and poetry was a cultural weapon.' His work is indeed marked by a vibrant urgency, and like Brathwaite's poetry, it lends itself naturally to performances in which the musical cadences of the language resonate more clearly. Johnson's recorded recitations (accompanied by dub music) are still hugely popular, and his canonical status was secured in 2002 when he became just the second living, and first Black, poet to be published in the Penguin Classics series.

If I woz a tap-natch poet

like Chris Okigbo
Derek Walcott
ar T. S. Eliot

I woodah write a poem
soh dyam deep
dat it bittah-sweet
like a precious
memari
whe mek yu weep
whe mek yu feel incomplete

like wen yu lovah leave
an dow defeat yu kanseed
still yu beg an yu plead
till yu win a repreve
an yu raedy fi rack steady
but di muzik done aready

still
inna di meantime
wid mi riddim
wid mi rime
wid mi ruff base line
wid mi own sense a time

goon poet haffi step in line
caw Bootahlazy mite a gat couple touzan
but Mandela fi him
touzans a touzans a touzans a touzans

if I woz a tap-natch poet
like Kamau Brathwaite
Martin Carter
Jayne Cortez ar Amiri Baraka

I woodah write a poem
soh rude
an rootsy
an subversive
dat it mek di goon poet
tun white wid envy

like a candhumble/voodoo/kumina chant
a ole time ar a slave song
dat get ban
but fram granny
rite
down
to
gran
pickney
each an evry wan
can recite dat-der wan

still
inna meantime
mi gat mi riddim
mi gat mi rime
mi gat mi ruff base line
mi gat mi own sense a time

goon poet haffi step in line
caw Bootahlazy mite a gat couple touzan
but Mandela fi him
touzans a touzans a touzans a touzans

if I woz a tap-natch poet
like Tchikaya U'tamsi
Nicholas Guillen
ar Lorna Goodison

I woodah write a poem
soh beautiful dat it simple
like a plain girl
wid good brains
an nice ways
wid a sexy dispozishan
an plenty compahshan
wid a sweet smile
an a suttle style

still
mi naw goh bow an scrape
an gwaan like a ape
peddlin noh puerile parchment af ethnicity
wid ongle a vaig fleetin hint af hawtenticity
like a black Lance Percival in reverse
ar even worse
a babblin bafoon whe looze im tongue

no sah
nat atall
wid mi riddim
wid mi rime
wid mi ruff base line
wid mi own sense a time

goon poet bettah step in line
caw Bootahlazy mite a gat a couple touzan
but Mandela fi him
touzans a touzans a touzans a touzans

16 May ✶ Roads ✶ Kei Miller

Born 1978

Another Jamaican writer who has become an emerging figure in the British poetry scene over the last decade is poet and novelist Kei Miller. Despite dropping out of his undergraduate studies at the University of the West Indies, Miller came to Britain to complete an MA and then PhD in writing, before launching his career in earnest with his first poetry book in 2006. As seen in this poem, he too blurs the lines between music and writing, and his work often contains biblical references, as well as allusions to mythology and mysticism. His 2014 collection *The Cartographer Tries to Map a Way to Zion* won the prestigious Forward Prize, and was cited by *Wolf Hall* author Hilary Mantel as one of her favourite books of that year.

The secret roads and slaving roads,
the dirging roads, marooning roads.
    Our people sing:
    Alligator dah walk on road
    Yes, alligator dah walk on road

The cow roads and cobbled roads,
the estate roads and blackbush roads.
    Our people sing:
    Go dung a Manuel Road
    Fi go bruck rock stone

The marl roads and bauxite roads
the causeway roads and Chinese roads.
    Our people sing:
    Right tru right tru de rocky road
    Hear Charlie Marley call you

The press-along, the soon-be-done,
The not-an-easy, the mighty-long –
so many roads we trod upon
and every mile, another song.

17 May ✶ The Passionate Shepherd to His Love ✶ Christopher Marlowe

26 February 1564 – 30 May 1593

Christopher Marlowe is best known for what he wrote – notably the wickedly dark, provocative and entertaining play *Doctor Faustus* – and for what he didn't write – namely Shakespeare's entire body of work. Although it's patently nonsense, rumours have circulated for hundreds of years that Marlowe may have faked his own death – he was frequently courting trouble for his perceived atheism and blasphemy (two very serious crimes in Elizabethan England) – and then continued to write under the name of William Shakespeare. The story largely stems from the sense of continuity between the two poets, with Shakespeare taking up the dramatic blank verse that was Marlowe's signature. But his life was certainly dramatic enough in its own right anyway without us having to look into absurd conspiracies; after graduating from Cambridge he was employed as a spy for the Queen before being killed, aged twenty-nine, in a bar brawl in a dockside pub following a possible dispute over the tab. It's quite hard to reconcile the drinker with the writer of these calm and sensitive pastoral lines.

Come live with me and be my love,
And we will all the pleasures prove,
That Valleys, groves, hills, and fields,
Woods, or steepy mountain yields.

And we will sit upon the Rocks,
Seeing the Shepherds feed their flocks,
By shallow Rivers to whose falls
Melodious birds sing Madrigals.

And I will make thee beds of Roses
And a thousand fragrant posies,
A cap of flowers, and a kirtle
Embroidered all with leaves of Myrtle;

A gown made of the finest wool
Which from our pretty Lambs we pull;
Fair lined slippers for the cold,
With buckles of the purest gold;

A belt of straw and Ivy buds,
With Coral clasps and Amber studs:
And if these pleasures may thee move,
Come live with me, and be my love.

The Shepherds' Swains shall dance and sing
For thy delight each May-morning:
If these delights thy mind may move,
Then live with me, and be my love.

18 May ✶ The Nymph's Reply to the Shepherd ✶ Sir Walter Raleigh

c. 1552 – 29 October 1618

Was there a more compelling figure in Elizabethan England than Sir Walter Raleigh (sometimes spelled Ralegh)? The poet, soldier, spy, statesman, aristocrat, royal advisor, explorer, treasure-hunter and rebel was a famously charismatic man – a trace of whose charm is apparent in his distant descendant Hugh Grant – Raleigh curried favour with the Queen (to whom much of his poetry was devoted), who in turn granted him many commissions, including the establishment of an American colony in Virginia. Their relationship soured when the bitterly jealous Elizabeth discovered that Raleigh had married in secret – a transgression for which he was imprisoned. Undeterred by his loss of influence and titles, Raleigh eventually returned to the upper echelons of the court with a series of triumphs, ranging from finding gold in Venezuela, raiding the Spanish at Cadiz, and quashing a coup by the Earl of Essex. Elizabeth's successor, James I, however, was not quite as taken by this silver-tongued maverick, whom he first jailed and later executed for attacking the Spanish against the king's orders. Like Marlowe, he too wrote incongruously bucolic poems, and indeed in this one Raleigh's Nymph is giving her response to Marlowe's Shepherd above.

If all the world and love were young,
And truth in every shepherd's tongue,
These pretty pleasures might me move
To live with thee and be thy love.

Time drives the flocks from field to fold
When rivers rage and rocks grow cold,
And Philomel becometh dumb;
The rest complains of cares to come.

The flowers do fade, and wanton fields
To wayward winter reckoning yields;
A honey tongue, a heart of gall,
Is fancy's spring, but sorrow's fall.

Thy gowns, thy shoes, thy beds of roses,
Thy cap, thy kirtle, and thy posies
Soon break, soon wither, soon forgotten –
In folly ripe, in reason rotten.

Thy belt of straw and ivy buds,
Thy coral clasps and amber studs,
All these in me no means can move
To come to thee and be thy love.

But could youth last and love still breed,
Had joys no date nor age no need,
Then these delights my mind might move
To live with thee and be thy love.

19 May ✶ The Rhodora ✶ Ralph Waldo Emerson

25 May 1803 – 27 April 1882

Ralph Waldo Emerson was a poet, essayist, philosopher, minister, abolitionist and one of the pioneers of 'American Transcendentalism'. It may be a bit of a mouthful but, broadly speaking, it's a movement which treasured real-life experiences over scientific truths. It could perhaps be best distilled in just two words: 'Trust thyself' – Emerson's famous motto which exhorted people to rely on their own perceptions and not received notions. As a poet, as well as a thinker, he was greatly influenced by the likes of Wordsworth and Coleridge, whom he met while visiting England, and he was generally fascinated by British imperialism – although he was also a keen advocate of the individuality of Asian and Middle Eastern culture, which he promoted back in the United States.

In May, when sea-winds pierced our solitudes,
I found the fresh Rhodora in the woods,
Spreading its leafless blooms in a damp nook,
To please the desert and the sluggish brook.
The purple petals fallen in the pool
Made the black water with their beauty gay;
Here might the red-bird come his plumes to cool,
And court the flower that cheapens his array.
Rhodora! if the sages ask thee why
This charm is wasted on the earth and sky,
Tell them, dear, that, if eyes were made for seeing,
Then beauty is its own excuse for Being;
Why thou wert there, O rival of the rose!
I never thought to ask; I never knew;
But in my simple ignorance suppose
The self-same power that brought me there, brought you.

20 May ✶ The Unexplorer ✶ Edna St Vincent Millay

22 February 1892 – 19 October 1950

Edna St Vincent Millay was a Pulitzer Prize-winning writer and was once called 'the greatest woman poet since Sappho' (see 21 November). But, like so many other fantastic female writers of her time, her work was overshadowed by her male counterparts. Perhaps she was punished for her boldness in writing openly on the modern female experience and on her love for both men and women (which, needless to say, was a huge taboo in the early twentieth century). That said, her actual formal style was far more traditional (she wrote Petrarchan sonnets) than that favoured by the modernists of her era. But there was nothing conservative about her personality. A famously wild spirit, she was known to regale all who met her with her effervescence, and she had a reputation for being a rousing live reader. A natural performer, she had initially intended to pursue a career as a concert pianist and there is a definite musicality found in her verse.

There was a road ran past our house
Too lovely to explore.
I asked my mother once—she said
That if you followed where it led
It brought you to the milk-man's door.
(That's why I have not traveled more.)

21 May ✶ I may, I might, I must ✶ Marianne Moore

15 November 1887 – 5 February 1972

A peer and friend of William Carlos Williams and 'H.D.' (Hilda Doolittle), Marianne Moore devoted her writing to experimenting with and subverting literary traditions. She was particularly noted for her ability to find poetry in seemingly trivial things, with Williams commenting of her technique that 'in looking at some apparently small object, one feels the swirl of great events'. Moore didn't only occupy the same circles as many of the twentieth-century greats, but 'The Greatest' himself – Muhammad Ali – who in typically self-assured fashion insisted that they write together, claiming that 'I am a poet too'. It would take a very courageous person to disagree with him . . .

If you will tell me why the fen
appears impassable, I then
will tell you why I think that I
can get across it if I try.

22 May ✶ The Spring ✶ Thomas Carew

1594/5 – 22 March 1640

Thomas Carew was a leading light of 'Cavalier' poetry (referring to a group of royalist supporters of Charles I in the run-up to the Civil War), which was a style of verse that was indebted to the likes of Ben Jonson and John Donne, but overall lighter in tone. Born to a prominent family in Kent, Carew studied law at Cambridge with the intention of following in his father's footsteps, but he then opted to pursue favour at the royal court instead. Like Byron and Swinburne after him, he cultivated a reputation as a debauched pleasure-seeker, and here, in one of his love poems, we see him asking his beloved not to remain cold to him when all of nature is warming up with spring.

Now that the winter's gone, the earth hath lost
Her snow-white robes, and now no more the frost
Candies the grass, or casts an icy cream
Upon the silver lake or crystal stream;
But the warm sun thaws the benumbed earth,
And makes it tender; gives a sacred birth
To the dead swallow; wakes in hollow tree
The drowsy cuckoo, and the humble-bee.
Now do a choir of chirping minstrels bring
In triumph to the world the youthful Spring.
The valleys, hills, and woods in rich array
Welcome the coming of the long'd-for May.
Now all things smile, only my love doth lour;
Nor hath the scalding noonday sun the power
To melt that marble ice, which still doth hold
Her heart congeal'd, and makes her pity cold.
The ox, which lately did for shelter fly
Into the stall, doth now securely lie
In open fields; and love no more is made

By the fireside, but in the cooler shade
Amyntas now doth with his Chloris sleep
Under a sycamore, and all things keep
Time with the season; only she doth carry
June in her eyes, in her heart January.

23 May ✶ Let No One Steal Your Dreams ✶ Paul Cookson

Born 1961

A poet who has given readings of over sixty books in a staggering 3,000 schools, Paul Cookson is one of the country's most beloved children's writers. This wonderfully inspiring poem (for kids and adult dreamers alike) has already been incorporated to quite a few school mottos and mission statements. In his other role as the official poet-in-residence at the National Football Museum, he has united beautiful language with the beautiful game. Cookson has been known to perform with a ukulele – perhaps a showdown with James Carter (see 27 March) is in order soon!

Let no one steal your dreams
Let no one tear apart
The burning of ambition
That fires the drive inside your heart

Let no one steal your dreams
Let no one tell you that you can't
Let no one hold you back
Let no one tell you that you won't

Set your sights and keep them fixed
Set your sights on high
Let no one steal your dreams
Your only limit is the sky

Let no one steal your dreams
Follow your heart
Follow your soul
For only when you follow them
Will you feel truly whole

Set your sights and keep them fixed
Set your sights on high
Let no one steal your dreams
Your only limit is the sky

24 May ✶ If Once You Have Slept on an Island ✶ Rachel Field

19 September 1894 – 15 March 1942

Rachel Field was a National Book Award-winning author, playwright and children's writer. She was born in New York, but spent many summers in Maine, where several of her books are set and where she was inspired by the islands off the coast – as seen in this poem. Her biggest claim to fame, however, is perhaps translating Franz Schubert's 'Ave Maria' into English for use in Disney's *Fantasia*.

If once you have slept on an island
  You'll never be quite the same;
You may look as you looked the day before
  And go by the same old name,

You may bustle about in street and shop;
  You may sit at home and sew,
But you'll see blue water and wheeling gulls
  Wherever your feet may go.

You may chat with the neighbours of this and that
  And close to your fire keep,
But you'll hear ship whistle and lighthouse bell
  And tides beat through your sleep.

Oh, you won't know why, and you can't say how
  Such change upon you came,
But once you have slept on an island,
  You'll never be quite the same!

25 May ✶ Phases of the Moon ✶ Elinor Wylie

7 September 1885 – 16 December 1928

Elinor Wylie is another unjustly neglected female poet and novelist. Born into a prominent New Jersey family, she was trained for a life as a high society wife as decreed by her father, a US solicitor general. But of course she rebelled, and pursued a more fulfilling literary life in which she railed against the limiting and stereotyped expectations society placed on women. Although she was admired in her day, she almost faded into obscurity until she was rediscovered by feminist critics of the 1970s and 1980s.

Once upon a time I heard
That the flying moon was a Phoenix bird;
Thus she sails through windy skies,
Thus in the willow's arms she lies;
Turn to the East or turn to the West
In many trees she makes her nest.
When she's but a pearly thread
Look among birch leaves overhead;
When she dies in yellow smoke
Look in a thunder-smitten oak;
But in May when the moon is full
Bright as water and white as wool,
Look for her where she loves to be
Asleep in a high magnolia tree.

26 May ✶ Love's Philosophy ✶ Percy Bysshe Shelley

4 August 1792 – 8 July 1822

Percy Bysshe Shelley is part of the triumvirate of late Romantics, along with his friends Lord Byron and John Keats. Like the latter, he emphasized natural imagery and drew heavily from classical texts and mythology, but he was perhaps the most explicitly political of the three, using his poetry to champion the people, the indomitable human spirit, and to warn elitist oppressors of their inevitable demise. For a man who was so concerned about the struggles of the common man, Shelley hailed perhaps surprisingly from a very aristocratic lineage, inheriting money and a parliamentary seat from his family. He went to Eton and then Oxford, from which he got expelled after less than a year for writing a polemical pamphlet called 'The Necessity of Atheism'. In the years that followed he was almost as prolific in his romantic life as his work, eloping not once but twice! His second wife, Mary, was the daughter of the social philosopher William Godwin and the women's rights advocate Mary Wollstonecraft, and the author of the Gothic masterpiece *Frankenstein*. That story emerged from a particularly fruitful trip to Lake Geneva with Lord Byron, but Percy Shelley's European gallivanting would ultimately end in tragedy. Sailing a boat called the *Don Juan* (after Byron's epic poem) off the coast of Italy, Shelley was caught in a storm and drowned. His legacy lives on, however, in every political speech that pits 'the many' against 'the few' – a dichotomy established in his electrifying poem, 'The Masque of Anarchy'.

The fountains mingle with the river
  And the rivers with the ocean,
The winds of heaven mix for ever
  With a sweet emotion;
Nothing in the world is single;
  All things by a law divine
In one spirit meet and mingle.
  Why not I with thine?—

See the mountains kiss high heaven
  And the waves clasp one another;
No sister-flower would be forgiven
  If it disdained its brother;
And the sunlight clasps the earth
  And the moonbeams kiss the sea:
What is all this sweet work worth
  If thou kiss not me?

27 May ✶ A Riddle on the Letter H ✶ Catherine Maria Fanshawe

6 July 1765 – 17 April 1834

Catherine Maria Fanshawe is another female poet who should be better known. The daughter of a courtier of George III, she grew up in Surrey but spent much of her life on the warmer shores of Italy. She was praised in her day by Walter Scott, and is best known for this witty brainteaser of a poem (to give yourself a challenge you should avoid looking up at the title above).

’Twas in heaven pronounced, and ’twas mutter’d in hell,
And echo caught faintly the sound as it fell;
On the confines of earth ’twas permitted to rest,
And the depths of the ocean its presence confess’d;
’Twill be found in the sphere when ’tis riven asunder,
Be seen in the lightning and heard in the thunder.
’Twas allotted to man with his earliest breath,
Attends him at birth, and awaits him in death,
Presides o’er his happiness, honour, and health,
Is the prop of his house, and the end of his wealth.
In the heaps of the miser ’tis hoarded with care,
But is sure to be lost on his prodigal heir.
It begins every hope, every wish it must bound,
With the husbandman toils, and with monarchs is crown’d.
Without it the soldier, the seaman may roam,
But woe to the wretch who expels it from home!
In the whispers of conscience its voice will be found,
Nor e’en in the whirlwind of passion is drown’d.
’Twill not soften the heart; but though deaf be the ear,
It will make it acutely and instantly hear.
Yet in shade let it rest, like a delicate flower,
Ah! breathe on it softly – it dies in an hour.

28 May ✶ Vanity ✶ Brian Patten

Born 1946

Brian Patten began his professional career in his mid-teens reporting for a local newspaper in Liverpool about the up-and-coming poets Roger McGough and Adrian Henri. A few years later he would be collaborating with them as a fab three, working on the 1967 book *The Mersey Sound*, which is now considered a modern classic. His funny poems – such as the pithy and witty one below – and humorous performances have made him a favourite among both children and adults. He's come a long, long way from the time he spent in Paris, before his first collection was published, scraping a living by writing poems in chalk on the pavements.

When I broke the mirror I bought a new one.
I didn't like what I saw,
So I took it back to the shop and asked for one
Like the one I'd bought some years before.

29 May ✶ Berserk ✶ Shams-ud-din Muhammad Hafiz

c. 1315 – 1390

Widely known by his pen name Hafiz, the fourteenth-century Persian lyric poet Shams-ud-din Muhammad Hafiz is one of the key figures in Iranian literary history, and a much-read writer the world over. Many of his poems passed into use as sayings and proverbs for everyday life – and he even had the rare distinction of being quoted by Arthur Conan Doyle's fictional detective Sherlock Holmes. Hafiz had many other fans in high places, from Queen Victoria, who reportedly consulted his verse for guidance, to Ralph Waldo Emerson, who called him 'a poet for poets', and Johann Wolfgang von Goethe, who claimed 'he had no peers'. Hafiz mainly wrote ghazals, short sensual poems about love, loss and ways to lead a good life.

Once
In a while
God cuts loose His purse strings,
Gives a big wink to my orchestra.

Hafiz
Does not require
Any more prompting than that
To let
Every instrument inside
Go
Berserk.

30 May ✶ Twinkle, Twinkle, Little Star ✶ Jane Taylor

23 September 1783 – 13 April 1824

Almost everybody in the English-speaking world knows this next poem – the most famous nursery rhyme of all time – but it's safe to assume that almost nobody knows who it is by, and not because it's another 'Anon.' entry. 'Twinkle, Twinkle, Little Star' (originally published as just 'The Star') is attributed to Jane Taylor, a writer and engraver, who collaborated with her sister Ann on this text and others, among some of the first ever children's poems. Her work is thought to have inspired the likes of Robert Browning, and Lewis Carroll included a parody of this nursery rhyme, 'Twinkle, Twinkle, Little Bat', in *Alice's Adventures in Wonderland*.

Twinkle, twinkle, little star,
How I wonder what you are!
Up above the world so high,
Like a diamond in the sky.

When the blazing sun is gone,
When he nothing shines upon,
Then you show your little light,
Twinkle, twinkle, all the night.

Then the traveller in the dark
Thanks you for your tiny spark,
How could he see where to go,
If you did not twinkle so?

In the dark blue sky you keep,
Often through my curtains peep
For you never shut your eye,
Till the sun is in the sky.

As your bright and tiny spark
Lights the traveller in the dark,
Though I know not what you are,
Twinkle, twinkle, little star.

31 May ✶ Mary Had a Little Lamb ✶ Sarah Josepha Hale

24 October 1788 – 30 April 1879

Sarah Josepha Hale received an education inaccessible to other eighteenth-century girls, and was fortunate to marry a husband who also encouraged her scholarly work. This turned out to be a critical asset when she was widowed and needed the full benefit of her education in order to fend for her five children by writing children's poetry. During her tenure as the editor for *Godey's Lady's Book*, a post she held until she was ninety years old, she became highly influential on matters relating to the raising and education of young people, and advocating the virtues of education for girls and the rights to property of women. Perhaps her most seismic legacy (aside from the following ubiquitous nursery rhyme) stems from a letter she wrote to Abraham Lincoln persuading him to institute the nation-wide observance of Thanksgiving, which had previously only been recognized in the Northeast.

Mary had a little lamb,
Its fleece was white as snow;
And everywhere that Mary went
The lamb was sure to go.

It followed her to school one day,
Which was against the rule;
It made the children laugh and play
To see a lamb at school.

And so the teacher turned it out,
But still it lingered near,
And waited patiently about
Till Mary did appear.

Why does the lamb love Mary so?
The eager children cry;
Why, Mary loves the lamb, you know,
The teacher did reply.

June

1 June ✶ The Best Thing in the World ✶ Elizabeth Barrett Browning

6 March 1806 – 29 June 1861

Elizabeth Barrett Browning was one of those all too rare female poets from the nineteenth century who received recognition in her own lifetime. In fact, such was her standing that when William Wordsworth died in 1850, she was widely touted to be the next Poet Laureate. She did at least hold the title of 'Poet Laureate of Hope End', which was bestowed on her by her father, who owned the Hertfordshire estate, and who encouraged her early poetic endeavours. He was, however, less open-minded about her private life and forbade her to marry, so she and Robert Browning had to do so in secret. Initially publishing anonymously, Barrett Browning eventually became synonymous with masterful sonnets and poetry which questioned the role of women in Victorian society. Her influence on later female poets is perhaps best illustrated by the fact that Emily Dickinson had a portrait of Barrett Browning – whom she affectionately referred to as 'that foreign woman' – hanging in her Amherst bedroom.

What's the best thing in the world?
June-rose, by May-dew impearled;
Sweet south-wind, that means no rain;
Truth, not cruel to a friend;
Pleasure, not in haste to end;
Beauty, not self-decked and curled
Till its pride is over-plain;
Light, that never makes you wink;
Memory, that gives no pain;
Love, when *so,* you're loved again.
What's the best thing in the world?
    —Something out of it, I think.

2 June ✶ *from* The Pied Piper of Hamelin ✶ Robert Browning

7 May 1812 – 12 December 1889

Many parents, when they hear that their child wants to devote their life to the infamously unstable profession of poet, try to steer them on to more sensible things. Not so with Robert Browning, who never entertained the idea of being anything other than a poet, and whose mother and father offered nothing but enthusiastic support. This was perhaps in part down to the fact that his father was pushed into the banking industry when he had wanted to follow more scholarly pursuits. With such encouragement fuelling his early years, Browning was able to rise from obscurity to become one of the most important poets of Victorian England. He is best known for his macabre, eerie and dramatic monologue poems, such as 'My Last Duchess' and 'Porphyria's Lover', but this one, an adaptation of the Pied Piper legend, is a rather more humorous, if still dark, effort – and his only foray into children's literature. Browning was, as we've already seen, the husband of Elizabeth Barrett, and he did not remarry even though she died almost thirty years before him.

Into the street the Piper stept,
  Smiling first a little smile,
As if he knew what magic slept
  In his quiet pipe the while;
Then, like a musical adept,
To blow the pipe his lips he wrinkled,
And green and blue his sharp eyes twinkled,
Like a candle-flame where salt is sprinkled;
And ere three shrill notes the pipe uttered,
You heard as if an army muttered;
And the muttering grew to a grumbling;
And the grumbling grew to a mighty rumbling;
And out of the houses the rats came tumbling.

Great rats, small rats, lean rats, brawny rats,
Brown rats, black rats, grey rats, tawny rats,
Grave old plodders, gay young friskers,
   Fathers, mothers, uncles, cousins,
Cocking tails and pricking whiskers,
   Families by tens and dozens,
Brothers, sisters, husbands, wives –
Followed the Piper for their lives.
From street to street he piped advancing,
And step for step they followed dancing,
Until they came to the river Weser
Wherein all plunged and perished
– Save one who, stout as Julius Caesar,
Swam across and lived to carry
(As he the manuscript he cherished)
To Rat-land home his commentary,
Which was, At the first shrill notes of the pipe,
I heard a sound as of scraping tripe,
And putting apples, wondrous ripe,
Into a cider-press's gripe:
And a moving away of pickle-tub-boards,
And a leaving ajar of conserve-cupboards,
And a drawing the corks of train-oil-flasks,
And a breaking the hoops of butter-casks;
And it seemed as if a voice
(Sweeter than by harp or by psaltery
Is breathed) called out, Oh rats, rejoice!
The world is grown to one vast drysaltery!
'So munch on, crunch on, take your nuncheon,
'Breakfast, supper, dinner, luncheon!'
And just as one bulky sugar-puncheon,
Ready staved, like a great sun shone
Glorious scarce an inch before me,
Just as methought it said, 'Come, bore me!'
– I found the Weser rolling o'er me.

3 June ✶ A Short Story of Falling ✶ Alice Oswald

Born 1966

Alice Oswald is a Devon-based, highly skilled poet who worked as a gardener before becoming an award-winning writer. She studied classics at university, and has written works inspired by classical texts such as Homer's *Iliad*. In 2019 she became the first woman to hold the prestigious post of Oxford Professor of Poetry – after forty-five men! Of her poetic interests she said: 'I'm mostly interested in life and vitality, but you can only see that by seeing its opposite. I love erosion: I like the way that the death of one thing is the beginning of something else.'

It is the story of the falling rain
to turn into a leaf and fall again

it is the secret of a summer shower
to steal the light and hide it in a flower

and every flower a tiny tributary
that from the ground flows green and momentary

is one of water's wishes and this tale
hangs in a seed-head smaller than my thumbnail

if only I a passerby could pass
as clear as water through a plume of grass

to find the sunlight hidden at the tip
turning to seed a kind of lifting rain drip

then I might know like water how to balance
the weight of hope against the light of patience

water which is so raw so earthy-strong
and lurks in cast-iron tanks and leaks along

drawn under gravity towards my tongue
to cool and fill the pipe-work of this song

which is the story of the falling rain
that rises to the light and falls again

4 June ✶ Landscape with the Fall of Icarus ✶ William Carlos Williams

17 September 1883 – 4 March 1963

Beginning a little run of poems about the Greek legend of Icarus – the boy who tried to fly using wax wings that melted as he soared too close to the sun – is this piece by the excellently named William Carlos Williams. He was closely associated with the Imagist sub-genre of modernist poetry which, as the name suggests, placed an emphasis on imagery and linguistic clarity. His poems provide snapshot (and often droll or ironic) observations of everyday subjects, and are characterized by their spare use of language, with single words sometimes occupying entire lines. In the medical world like John Keats, Williams called that Romantic poet his 'God', and he was also deeply influenced by Ezra Pound, of whom he said: 'Before meeting Pound is like B.C. and A.D.'

According to Brueghel
when Icarus fell
it was spring

a farmer was ploughing
his field
the whole pageantry

of the year was
awake tingling
near

the edge of the sea
concerned
with itself

sweating in the sun
that melted
the wings' wax

unsignificantly
off the coast
there was

a splash quite unnoticed
this was
Icarus drowning

5 June ✶ Mrs Icarus ✶ Carol Ann Duffy

Born 1955

Continuing with our run of Icarus poems is this very funny little poem by Carol Ann Duffy – a poet of many firsts. Before she was given the post in 2009, there had never been a Scottish, gay or female Poet Laureate. Her work is defined by a sharp, satirical sense of humour – often at the expense of gender inequalities – and alternatively by accessible, hugely relatable evocations of inner worlds, and feelings of grief, nostalgia and hubris. Her poems are ever-present on school syllabuses, and speak to those who don't naturally turn to poetry. This poem comes from her renowned collection *The World's Wife*, which takes an imaginative and ironic look at the women behind history's and mythology's most famous men.

I'm not the first or the last
to stand on a hillock,
watching the man she married
prove to the world
he's a total, utter, absolute, Grade A pillock.

6 June ✶ Icarus ✶ Kae Tempest

Born 1985

One of the most popular spoken word performers working today, Kae Tempest has received much recognition in the worlds of poetry and music, having won the prestigious Ted Hughes prize and been nominated for Best Female Solo Artist at the BRITs. The youngest of five, Tempest studied music at the Brit School, as well as politics and English at Goldsmiths, before becoming a professional poet – opening for leading performance poets such as John Cooper Clarke. Today, Tempest plays sell-out shows and festivals such as Glastonbury, blurring the lines between spoken word and rap. Their work is famed for its compassionate and inclusive tone, and for its timely takes on contemporary politics. This poem concludes our trilogy of pieces inspired by the Icarus myth.

Soaring the skies that had always been beyond his reach,
he felt like a champion
his feet kicked the clouds
his arms were bound in the feathers of his father's labour
Which a little while later would be ashes, vapour,
Cumbersome limbs furnished with powerful things
he heard the wind speak every time he felt his wings beat.
His father flew before him and so the course was set.
He said 'Don't fly by the waves 'cos your wings'll get wet
but don't fly so high that the sun melts the wax'.
He said 'Stay on my path, son. Follow my tracks'.
Well, Icarus enamoured by the feeling of flight
he just had to fly higher, get closer to the light
The sun was hot against him but he carried on ascending
He felt strength in him increasing like the heat that was so
tempting
beneath him was the world he left behind in search of better things
but to achieve that freedom, he sacrificed everything.

I told him
Icarus, come down from the sky you're flying too high
Icarus, heed your father's word, this ain't your territory
No one even noticed as he splashed and hit the sea bed
I wonder what he saw before he fell and if he needed my help.
Would he have asked for it? Probably he wouldn't,
probably he thought he was invincible, he weren't
in principle he burnt he smouldered in those myths
so that we who never flew before can learn from what he did.

See, given the gift of flight
it was too easy to ignore the warnings of his father.
How could he be truly responsible?
When really all he wants to do is soar above his station and become
the sun's equal,
but the sun can have no equal.
Poor Icarus, that flicker in his eye
that distant picture in the sky about to catch the light he saw
Foolish young pride, silly man cub
How can you learn to fly if you ain't even learnt to stand up?
If he'd listened to his father well then he never would've drowned,
but the happiness he felt is one he never would have found.
Gifts are dangerous when they are given and not earned,
and the lesson merely heard is never a lesson learned,
But by the time his father turned, the wax had completely burned,
feathers scattered on the waves, and they just rolled on
unconcerned
But for that small moment before he fell into the sea
Icarus the headstrong had been completely free!

Icarus, come down from the sky you're flying too high
Icarus, heed your father's word this ain't your territory
No one even noticed as he splashed and hit the sea bed
I wonder what he saw before he fell and if he needed my help.
Would he have asked for it? Probably he wouldn't
probably he thought he was invincible, he weren't
in principle he burnt he smouldered in those myths
So that we who never flew before can learn from what he did.

7 June ✶ Bashō in Ireland ✶ Billy Collins

Born 1941

Billy Collins has been called 'the most popular poet in America'. His popularity stems from his conversational, personable approach to poetry and public performances (from TED Talks to readings). But that's not to say that his poems are 'easy' – below the witty, accessible surface lie depths of meaning and emotion. His own poetry, he's said, comes from a place of being 'willing to stop anywhere' and notice the 'amazing set of distractions' found in daily life. This poem is a tribute to the Japanese writer Bashō (whom we'll meet shortly) – another writer who extracted the miraculous from the everyday.

I am like the Japanese poet
who longed to be in Kyoto
even though he was already in Kyoto.

I am not exactly like him
because I am not Japanese
and I have no idea what Kyoto is like.

But once, while walking around
the Irish town of Ballyvaughan
I caught myself longing to be in Ballyvaughan.

The sensation of being homesick
for a place that is not my home
while being right in the middle of it

was particularly strong
when I passed the hotel bar
then the fluorescent depth of a launderette,

also when I stood at the crossroads
with the road signs pointing 3 directions
and the enormous buses making the turn.

it might have had something to do
with the nearby limestone hills
and the rain collecting in my collar,

but then again I have longed
to be with a number of people
while the two of us were sitting in a room

on an ordinary evening
without a limestone hill in sight,
thousands of miles from Kyoto

and the simple wonders of Ballyvaughan,
which reminds me
of another Japanese poet

who wrote how much he enjoyed
not being able to see
his favorite mountain because of all the fog.

8 June ✶ Misty Rain ✶ Matsuo Bashō

1644 – 28 November 1694

The seventeenth-century Japanese writer Bashō (born Matuso Kinsaku) is known as the master of the haiku: a poem typically composed (pre-translation) of lines of five, seven, and five syllables. The craft lies in the fact that they say so much in very few words, often drawing our attention to a fleeting moment of wonder in nature. His pen name, Bashō, comes from the Japanese name for a banana tree that he was gifted while working as a teacher in Edo (modern day Tokyo), and under which he was known to write and meditate. He was deeply interested in Tao and Zen Buddhist philosophy – which is rooted in finding satisfaction in solitude and life's simple, unassuming pleasures – which may explain why his poems can have such a soothing effect on its readers.

Misty rain,
Mount Fuji is unseen for the day:
Enchanting!

9 June ✶ Dragonfly Catcher ✶ Fukuda Chiyo-Ni

1703 – 2 October 1775

The power of the seemingly simplistic haiku form is perhaps best exemplified in this heartbreaking poem by Fukuda Chiyo-Ni, written on losing her son. After studying under Bashō, she became the first woman to be recognized as an accomplished haiku writer and went on to become one of the leading names associated with pioneering the form in pre-modern Japanese literature. Sadly, her personal life was fraught with tragedy, and Fukuda turned to religion after her husband, son and parents all died. She eventually became a Buddhist nun.

> Dragonfly catcher,
> Where today
> have you gone?

10 June ✶ Mosquito at my Ear ✶ Kobayashi Issa, translated by Robert Hass

15 June 1763 – 5 January 1828

Another of the foremost haiku writers is Issa, whose pen name means 'cup of tea' – a fitting name for a practitioner of a form defined by a humble elegance and which elevates everyday objects to the status of literature. After being sent by his agrarian family to study haiku in Edo, Issa became one of the most prolific poets of his age, writing an incredible 20,000 haikus. His preferred subject matter was insects, with this funny poem about a mosquito just one of over 150 he wrote about the bothersome little creature. Like Fukuda Chiyo-Ni above, Issa found solace from the sorrows of his life in poetry, and some of his work does accordingly lean towards the more melancholic aspects of human life.

> Mosquito at my ear—
> does he think
>   I'm deaf?

11 June ✶ A Thousand Martyrs ✶ Aphra Behn

1640 – 16 April 1689

We know very little for certain about the life of extraordinarily influential dramatist and poet Aphra Behn, but what we do know is quite remarkable for a seventeenth-century woman. She travelled to the West Indies, where she befriended a prince, and spent months in Suriname, where she subsequently wrote one of the first English novels, the devastating *Oroonoko*. Like Marlowe and Raleigh, she also worked as a spy for the crown and was allegedly imprisoned for debt when Charles II failed to provide payment for a mission in Belgium. Finally (caught your breath yet?), she escaped prison and became a prolific playwright. Her work is hallmarked with audacity and a light satirical touch, and it is no surprise that she became notorious in London society. She was deplored by many, of course – for her nonconformity to womanly conduct – but also admired by her peers, and by feminists in the twentieth century such as Virginia Woolf and Germaine Greer.

A thousand martyrs I have made,
  All sacrificed to my desire;
A thousand beauties have betrayed,
  That languish in resistless fire.
The untamed heart to hand I brought,
And fixed the wild and wandering thought.

I never vowed nor sighed in vain
  But both, though false, were well received.
The fair are pleased to give us pain,
  And what they wish is soon believed.
And though I talked of wounds and smart,
Love's pleasures only touched my heart.

Alone the glory and the spoil
  I always laughing bore away;
The triumphs, without pain or toil,
  Without the hell, the heav'n of joy.
And while I thus at random rove
Despise the fools that whine for love.

12 June ✶ A Modest Love ✶ Sir Edward Dyer

October 1543 – May 1607

Was there a poet in Elizabethan England who hasn't at some time been suspected of being Shakespeare? Or who wasn't moonlighting as a spy? Edward Dyer, like Marlowe and Raleigh, is one of many such candidates for the former (despite dying six years before Shakespeare's last play was written), but certainly sent out on various missions by the crown. None were more exciting than an ill-fated quest on behalf of Elizabeth I, which ended in arrest in Prague, to find the philosopher's stone, which as Harry Potter fans well know, is a legendary substance which was thought to be able to turn metals into gold. A sense of mystery also extended to his poems, in that many of them are difficult to identify because they were just signed with initials or published anonymously.

The lowest trees have tops, the ant her gall,
The fly her spleen, the little sparks their heat;
The slender hairs cast shadows, though but small,
And bees have stings, although they be not great;
Seas have their source, and so have shallow springs;
And love is love, in beggars as in kings.

Where rivers smoothest run, deep are the fords;
The dial stirs, yet none perceives it move;
The firmest faith is in the fewest words;
The turtles cannot sing, and yet they love:
True hearts have eyes and ears, no tongues to speak;
They hear and see, and sigh, and then they break.

13 June ✶ To My Dear and Loving Husband ✶ Anne Bradstreet

20 March 1612 – 16 September 1672

Anne Bradstreet was, in a sense, the first poet of modern America – or at least the first English settler to have her work published in the North American colonies. A highly educated, aristocratic woman who was used to the finer things in life, she was understandably somewhat piqued by her husband's decision to join the puritan colonies in the relative wilderness of the Americas. Still, she can't have stayed mad at him for too long, given that she wrote this touching poem, still often read at weddings, about the extent of her love for him. In writing directly to him with an autobiographical candour, Bradstreet could be seen to be subverting the era's conventions. It was the New World, after all . . .

If ever two were one, then surely we.
If ever man were loved by wife, then thee.
If ever wife was happy in a man,
Compare with me, ye women, if you can.
I prize thy love more than whole mines of gold,
Or all the riches that the East doth hold.
My love is such that rivers cannot quench,
Nor ought but love from thee give recompense.
Thy love is such I can no way repay;
The heavens reward thee manifold, I pray.
Then while we live, in love let's so persever,
That when we live no more, we may live ever.

14 June ✶ Becoming Anne Bradstreet ✶ Eavan Boland

24 September 1944 – 27 April 2020

As a literary, and quite literal, pioneer, Anne Bradstreet unsurprisingly inspired many other writers, not least the Irish poet Eavan Boland, who wrote this poem about the feeling of being transported by the former's book. Born in Dublin to a diplomat and a painter, Boland spent her early years similarly crossing the Atlantic, growing up between London and New York. She returned to Ireland to study, and set about reclaiming the subjectivity of women in Irish literature in response to writers who had traditionally treated them as mere objects of their verse.

It happens again
As soon as I take down her book and open it.

I turn the page.
My skies rise higher and hang younger stars.

The ship's rail freezes.
Mare Hibernicum leads to Anne Bradstreet's coast.

A blackbird leaves her pine trees
And lands in my spruce trees.

I open my door on a Dublin street.
Her child/her words are staring up at me:

In better dress to trim thee was my mind,
But nought save home-spun cloth, i' th' house I find.

We say *home truths*
Because her words can be at home anywhere—

At the source, at the end and whenever
The book lies open and I am again

An Irish poet watching an English woman
Become an American poet.

15 June ✶ Why so Pale and Wan, Fond Lover? ✶ Sir John Suckling

February 1609 – 1641

In this poem, extracted from one of John Suckling's plays, a man jokingly comments on a friend's attempts to woo a woman. This kind of light and witty subject is typical of Cavalier poets – courtiers who supported King Charles I during the English Civil War – who frequently wrote about sensual pleasures. Suckling himself was a notorious gambler – said to have devised the popular game of cribbage – and something of a libertine. He helped the king by rallying troops to support him in his war against the Scots, but his efforts were ultimately ridiculed for the soldiers' poor performance and daft costumes. Suckling died in France, where he had exiled himself after plotting to help the Earl of Strafford, whom the king had condemned to death, escape from the Tower of London.

Why so pale and wan, fond lover?
    Prithee why so pale?
Will, when looking well can't move her,
    Looking ill prevail?
    Prithee why so pale?

Why so dull and mute, young sinner?
    Prithee why so mute?
Will, when speaking well can't win her,
    Saying nothing do't?
    Prithee why so mute?

Quit, quit for shame, this will not move,
    This cannot take her;
If of herself she will not love,
    Nothing can make her;
    The devil take her.

16 June ✶ *from* Beowulf ✶ Anon., translated by Gerard Benson

A rare example of Anglo-Saxon Old English, *Beowulf* is often seen as the fountainhead of English literature. The revered epic poem, set in pagan Scandinavia, follows a prince on his way to Denmark as he battles various enemies, such as the monster Grendel and his mother (see tomorrow), and a treasure-hoarding dragon. Probably rooted in oral tradition, it was written sometime between the seventh and eleventh centuries, and it survives in a single medieval manuscript in the British Library. This was copied by two different scribes: the first two-thirds are copied down with evident care and interest, modifying the spelling for consistency. This first scribe, however, breaks off mid-sentence, and his job is taken over by a far less assiduous colleague who, it seems, simply copied straight from the source (along with all the mistakes). These are the opening lines in a modern English translation.

Now from the marshlands under the mist-mountains
Came Grendel prowling; branded with God's ire.
This murderous monster was minded to entrap
Some hapless human in that high hall.
On he came under the clouds, until clearly
He could see the great golden feasting place,
Glimmering wine-hall of men. Not his first
Raid was this on the homeplace of Hrothgar.
Never before though and never afterward
Did he encounter hardier defenders of a hall.

17 June ✶ Beowulf ✶ A. F. Harrold

Born 1975

Following on from that extract from *Beowulf* is this parody in haiku form by the children's author and poet A. F. Harrold. The poem opens with a playful spin on the famously debated meaning of the original opening word of '*Hwaet*' – thought to mean 'Lo!', or 'Listen!', or in this case, 'Oi!'. Harrold writes and performs for adults and children, and can be found performing everywhere from schools to bars to Glastonbury Festival, where he once served as the poet-in-residence.

Oi! He kills Grendel,
and its mother. Seasons pass.
The dragon eats him.

18 June ✶ The Sweetness of Dogs ✶ Mary Oliver

10 September 1935 – 17 January 2019

Until her death in 2019, Mary Oliver was one of the most prolific (publishing a new collection almost every year from 1963), revered, and commercially successful poets working in America. She was the kind of poet who straddled literary acclaim (including a Pulitzer Prize) and mainstream appeal, appearing in the *New Yorker* as well as Oprah's *O* magazine. Her immense popularity is rooted in her ability to capture unassuming yet beautiful moments in the natural world, and the gentle, almost therapeutic emotional guidance offered to readers in her verse. This poem comes from a popular collection devoted to dogs.

What do you say, Percy? I am thinking
of sitting out on the sand to watch
the moon rise. It's full tonight.
So we go

and the moon rises, so beautiful it
makes me shudder, makes me think about
time and space, makes me take
measure of myself: one iota
pondering heaven. Thus we sit, myself

thinking how grateful I am for the moon's
perfect beauty and also, oh! how rich
it is to love the world. Percy, meanwhile,
leans against me and gazes up into
my face. As though I were just as wonderful
as the perfect moon.

19 June ✶ Now ✶ Audre Lorde

18 February 1934 – 17 November 1992

Audre Lorde once famously described herself as 'black, lesbian, mother, warrior, poet', which gives a succinct account of her personal identity and the issues addressed in her work. Born in New York to Caribbean immigrants, Lorde struggled with communication in her early years, but at the age of twelve she discovered that she could articulate her thoughts and feelings in verse; she said she was 'thinking in poetry'. Outside of her poetry, and her immense contribution to academic discourse, Lorde was a famed orator and grassroots activist not just in the US but also abroad, notably spending time in Berlin in the 1980s to help develop a burgeoning Afro-German movement.

Woman power
is
Black power
is
Human power
is
always feeling
my heart beats
as my eyes open
as my hands move
as my mouth speaks

I am
are you

Ready.

20 June ✶ Not Waving but Drowning ✶ Stevie Smith

20 September 1902 – 7 March 1971

The novelist and poet Stevie Smith was born in Hull, but she spent all but her first three years in North London. She struggled with mental health issues throughout her life, and was candid about her struggles in her writing – not least in this very famous poem, which sheds light on how depression is often fatally hard to notice or discuss. It serves as a perfect example of Smith's distinctive style, through which she broached serious and moving subjects in a light, deceptively simple vernacular. She was greatly admired by Sylvia Plath (see 20 February) who described herself as 'a desperate Smith addict'.

Nobody heard him, the dead man,
But still he lay moaning:
I was much further out than you thought
And not waving but drowning.

Poor chap, he always loved larking
And now he's dead
It must have been too cold for him his heart gave way,
They said.

Oh, no no no, it was too cold always
(Still the dead one lay moaning)
I was much too far out all my life
And not waving but drowning.

21 June ✶ Dark Sonnet ✶ Neil Gaiman

Born 1960

Neil Gaiman has accrued a cult following as the author of several predominantly fantasy novels, screenplays and comics, such as the hugely popular *Sandman* series. Screen adaptations of his work include the hits *Stardust* and the animated *Coraline*, and the series *American Gods* and *Good Omens*, which he originally wrote with Terry Pratchett. A self-described 'feral child who was raised in libraries', his writing process is rather more civilized, with each of his first drafts committed to paper with a fountain pen. His first book was, rather improbably, a biography of the 1980s pop group Duran Duran. This is one of a handful of poems that he's published – and there's not a single mystical being in sight!

I don't think that I've been in love as such,
Although I liked a few folk pretty well.
Love must be vaster than my smiles or touch,
For brave men died and empires rose and fell
For love: girls followed boys to foreign lands
And men have followed women into Hell.

In plays and poems someone understands
There's something makes us more than blood and bone
And more than biological demands . . .
For me, love's like the wind unseen, unknown.
I see the trees are bending where it's been,
I know that it leaves wreckage where it's blown.
I really don't know what 'I love you' means.
I think it means 'Don't leave me here alone.'

22 June ✶ People Equal ✶ James Berry

28 September 1924 – 20 June 2017

On this day in 1948, a ship called the *Empire Windrush* arrived in England carrying Caribbean migrants who were promised British citizenship. Thousands of West Indians would embark on this 'exodus', including the poet James Berry, who described the *Windrush* as a 'godsend' at the time; although on arriving, they had to endure much prejudice and inequality. Having studied the likes of Wordsworth in his childhood, Berry moved away from the English traditions, and wrote poetry that captured his own voice as a Jamaican.

Some people shoot up tall.
Some hardly leave the ground at all.
Yet – people equal. Equal.

One voice is a sweet mango.
Another is a non-sugar tomato.
Yet – people equal. Equal.

Some people rush to the front.
Others hang back, feeling they can't.
Yet – people equal. Equal.

Hammer some people, you meet a wall.
Blow hard on others, they fall.
Yet – people equal. Equal.

One person will aim at a star.
For another, a hilltop is too far.
Yet – people equal. Equal.

Some people get on with their show.
Others never get on the go.
Yet – people equal. Equal.

23 June ✶ Exclamation ✶ Octavio Paz

31 March 1914 – 19 April 1998

Octavio Paz was a world-renowned poet and essayist who won the Nobel Prize for Literature in 1990. A Mexican national icon, he had attained such a standing through his writing and his political activism that his death was announced by the President in 1998. The son of an assistant to the revolutionary leader Emiliano Zapata, Paz embraced left-wing politics throughout his career. As a poet, he attended an anti-fascist writers' congress in Spain; as a diplomat, he resigned his post as Ambassador to India after the government quashed a student protest in Mexico City. Paz believed poetry to be 'the secret religion of the modern age'. This short poem is a great example of his rootedness in Mexican heritage, for the hummingbird carries a symbolic significance in the country, where the Aztecs believed it was immortal.

Still
    Not on the branch
In the air
        Not in the air
In the instant
            The hummingbird

24 June ✶ Proverbs and Canticles ✶ Antonio Machado

26 July 1875 – 22 February 1939

A major (or should that be *mejor?*) Spanish poet, Antonio Machado grew up in Madrid, where his father was a professor. But after the latter's sudden death, Machado and his brother tried to bring money into the family through the rather unreliable professions of writing and acting. They both eventually travelled to Paris, where Antonio met Oscar Wilde, and where they worked as translators at a publishing house. From that point on, Antonio alternated between living in Spain and France, teaching and studying French and philosophy for an advanced degree. His poems, such as this one, are known for their engagement with existential questions and for commenting on the solitary life of the poet.

I

The mode of dialogue, my friends,
is first to question:
then . . . attend.

II

I have seen in my solitude
very clear things
that are not true.

III

The poet does not pursue
the fundamental I
but the essential you.

IV

Let us give time to time:
that the vessel overflow
first you must let the water brim.

V

In writing verses, seek
to give them a double light: one
to read square by, one oblique.

VI

Let it not signify
whether they pass from hand to hand:
from gold men make a currency.

VII

This, to ponder:
a heart that's solitary
is a heart no longer.

25 June ✶ The Shortest and Sweetest of Songs ✶ George MacDonald

10 December 1824 – 18 September 1905

The prolific Scottish children's writer George MacDonald was born in Aberdeenshire to a prominent literary and religious family. MacDonald studied moral philosophy and science, but he believed that art and imagination can bring us closer to God. The author of fantasy books and fairy tales such as 'The Light Princess', his legacy is perhaps less tied to his own work than to his mentorship of Lewis Carroll and his support for such books as J. M. Barrie's *Peter Pan* and L. Frank Baum's *The Wonderful Wizard of Oz*. The following, as the title suggests, is one of the shortest poems in the world – though it is still double the length of Gavin Ewart's (see 14 February)!

Come
Home.

26 June ✶ *from* what they did yesterday afternoon ✶ Warsan Shire

Born 1988

The poet and activist Warsan Shire holds the estimable title of being the youngest person invited to join the Royal Society of Literature in 2019. The daughter of Somali migrants, her work focuses on ideas of identity, stereotypes, diaspora and integration, and giving a voice to the otherwise voiceless. As she says of her own work: 'Character-driven poetry is important for me – it's being able to tell the stories of those people, especially refugees and immigrants, that otherwise wouldn't be told, or they'll be told really inaccurately.' She received much attention and acclaim when her poetry was featured throughout Beyoncé's critical smash album *Lemonade*.

later that night
i held an atlas in my lap
ran my fingers across the whole world
and whispered
where does it hurt?

it answered
everywhere
everywhere
everywhere.

27 June ✶ The New Colossus ✶
Emma Lazarus

22 July 1849 – 19 November 1887

'The New Colossus' is one of the most quoted poems in American history. When the poet and activist Emma Lazarus was asked to write a poem to fundraise for a pedestal for the Statue of Liberty, she saw it as an opportunity to draw attention to the plight of immigrants coming to the US for a new life – perhaps inspired by the Jewish refugees fleeing persecution in Russia, for whom she had been advocating. Though fellow poet James Russell Lowell praised her sonnet, stating that it 'gives its subject a raison d'être', it wasn't until after her death that her pro-immigration panegyric was engraved on a bronze plaque and mounted on the pedestal of the statue. The sonnet provides the perfect blueprint for how a nation should welcome potential new citizens to this day.

Not like the brazen giant of Greek fame,
With conquering limbs astride from land to land;
Here at our sea-washed, sunset gates shall stand
A mighty woman with a torch, whose flame
Is the imprisoned lightning, and her name
Mother of Exiles. From her beacon-hand
Glows world-wide welcome; her mild eyes command
The air-bridged harbor that twin cities frame.
'Keep, ancient lands, your storied pomp!' cries she
With silent lips. 'Give me your tired, your poor,
Your huddled masses yearning to breathe free,
The wretched refuse of your teeming shore.
Send these, the homeless, tempest-tost to me,
I lift my lamp beside the golden door!'

28 June ✶ Seeker ✶ Rachel Rooney

Born 1962

Rachel Rooney is an award-winning children's author who worked as a primary and special education teacher before re-embracing poetry writing. Her poems and stories include puzzles, riddles, and original perspectives on everyday things. She once said that we should 'start the day and end the day with a poem' – an excellent rule to live by!

Eyes as wide as continents brim with the water between.
Seeks a different future. Looks back on what has been.

Mouth seeks another language. Shapes a different air.
Unfamiliar classroom words. The other, whispered prayer.

Heart seeks home. One it left and one it took along.
Echoes in the distance. Skips to a playground song.

29 June ✶ A Feather from an Angel ✶ Brian Moses

Born 1950

Brian Moses is the author of over 200 children's books, which more than justifies his decision to give up his dreams of rock stardom to become a writer. But he hasn't completely abandoned his musical roots, as he often includes percussion in readings at schools, libraries and festivals.

Anton's box of treasures held
a silver key and a glassy stone,
a figurine made of polished bone
and a feather from an angel.

The figurine was from Borneo,
the stone from France or Italy,
the silver key was a mystery
but the feather came from an angel.

We might have believed him if he'd said
the feather fell from a bleached white crow
but he always replied, 'It's an angel's, I know,
a feather from an angel.'

We might have believed him if he'd said,
'An albatross let the feather fall,'
But he had no doubt, no doubt at all,
his feather came from an angel.

'I thought I'd dreamt him one night,' he'd say,
'But in the morning I knew he'd been there;
he left a feather on my bedside chair,
a feather from an angel.'

And it seems that all my life I've looked
for that sort of belief that nothing could shift,
something simple yet precious as Anton's gift,
a feather from an angel.

30 June ✶ *from* Ecclesiastes

The King James Bible remains one of the bestselling books of all time. It was put together by forty-seven scholars, who were commissioned by the king in 1604 to create a text that would be more accessible to the reading public. It was finally published in 1611. This poetic extract comes from the Book of Ecclesiastes in the Old Testament. It was adapted into a famous song called 'Turn! Turn! Turn!' by the folk singer Pete Seeger in the late 1950s.

To every thing there is a season,
and a time to every purpose under the heaven.
A time to be born, and a time to die;
a time to plant,
and a time to pluck up that which is planted;
A time to kill, and a time to heal;
a time to break down, and a time to build up;
A time to weep, and a time to laugh;
a time to mourn, and a time to dance.
A time to cast away stones,
and a time to gather stones together;
a time to embrace, and a time to refrain from embracing.
A time to seek, and a time to lose;
a time to keep, and a time to cast away.
A time to rend, and a time to sow;
a time to keep silence, and a time to speak;
A time to love, and a time to hate;
a time of war, and a time of peace.

July

1 July ✶ Chilling Out Beside the Thames ✶ John Agard

Born 1949

John Agard's first writing influence was not poetry but punditry, in the form of the radio cricket commentators whose narration he would try to emulate as a boy. Born in British Guiana, now Guyana, he moved to England in 1977 with his wife the poet Grace Nichols (see 1 October), and his work fuses Caribbean and English history, myths and vernacular. As this poem illustrates, Agard's lively writing comments on British culture as both an insider and as an ironic outside observer. Speaking of the humour that typifies his work, Agard said that it 'breaks down boundaries, it topples our self-importance, it connects people, and because it engages and entertains, it ultimately enlightens'.

Summer come, mi chill-out beside the Thames.
Spend a little time with weeping willow.
Check if dem Trafalgar pigeon still salute
old one-eyed one-armed Lord Horatio.

Mi treat mi gaze to Gothic cathedral
Yet mi cyant forget how spider spiral
Is ladder aspiring to eternal truth . . .
Trickster Nansi spinning from Shakespeare sky.

Sudden so, mi decide to play tourist.
Tower of London high-up on mi list.
Who show up but Anne Boleyn with no head on
And headless Raleigh gazing towards Devon.

Jesus lawd, history shadow so bloody.
A-time fo summer break with strawberry.

2 July ✶ About Friends ✶ Brian Jones

10 December 1938 – 25 June 2009

First things first. The poet Brian Jones is not to be confused with the late Rolling Stone. He was, however, cool in his own way, notably shirking literary celebrity status, and eventually retreating to France. Not one for the spotlight, Jones wrote meaningfully about solitude and loneliness, speaking for those without a voice. Such was the sense of personal experience in his writing that readers often mistook his poems for autobiography – sending condolences following a poem about a father's death, even though his own father was still very much alive. Jones's work also had a political bent, and was especially damning of the Margaret Thatcher-led government in the 1980s. His poetry collections were all published between 1966 and 1990, after which he disappeared from the literary world, and from critical recognition. This quietly affecting poem about how friendships become more distant and formal over the years, is a perfect example of why Jones should be rediscovered.

The good thing about friends
is not having to finish sentences.

I sat a whole summer afternoon with my friend
  once
on a river bank, bashing heels on the baked mud
and watching the small chunks slide into the
  water
and listening to them – plop plop plop.
He said, 'I like the twigs when they . . .
  you know . . .
like that.' I said, 'There's that branch . . .'
We both said, 'Mmmm.' The river flowed and
  flowed
and there were lots of butterflies, that afternoon.

I first thought there was a sad thing about
friends
when we met twenty years later.
We both talked hundreds of sentences,
taking care to finish all we said,
and explain it all very carefully,
as if we'd been discovered in places
we should not be, and were somehow ashamed.

I understood then what the river meant by
flowing

3 July ✶ Poem 85 ✶ Catullus, translated by Sir Richard Francis Burton

c. 84 – c. 54 BC

Catullus (Gaius Valerius Catullus) was one of the great Roman lyric poets, whose writing influenced the better-known Ovid, Horace and Virgil. A quite literal example of that cliché of being a 'poet's poet', Catullus did in fact largely address his poems to fellow literary figures. But aside from being interesting in their own right, literary texts from his era also provide remarkable insight into life (and all the scandal) from his era – which broadly coincided with that of Julius Caesar. Only one manuscript has survived, with 116 poems – some passionate, some funny, some just plain crude – that, rather unconventionally for the time, focus on personal matters over heroic characters. This is one of his shortest, but it manages to distil the essence of the human condition in just two lines.

I hate and I love. Why do I do this, perhaps you ask.
I do not know, but I feel it happening and I am tortured.

4 July ✶ Friends ✶ Elizabeth Jennings

18 July 1926 – 26 October 2001

The celebrated poet Elizabeth Jennings grew up, studied and spent her whole life in Oxford, where she was known to encourage student poets. If not spotted in town, she could usually be found on a bus to Stratford-upon-Avon, where she went to watch every Shakespeare play being staged. Jennings's poetry is noted for its traditionalism, and its emphasis on form and directness over emotion and abstraction. Of poetry she once said: 'Only one thing must be cast out, and that is the vague. Only true clarity reaches to the heights and the depths of human, and more than human, understanding.'

I fear it's very wrong of me
And yet I must admit,
When someone offers friendship
I want the *whole* of it.
I don't want everybody else
To share my friends with me.
At least, I want *one* special one,
Who indisputedly,

Likes me much more than all the rest,
Who's always on my side,
Who never cares what others say,
Who lets me come and hide
Within his shadow; in his house –
It doesn't matter where –
Who lets me simply be myself,
Who's always, *always* there.

5 July ✶ Dear Key Workers ✶ Laura Mucha

Born 1982

On this day in 1948, the National Health Service was founded in the UK, providing free healthcare to all citizens. This wonderful poem was written in tribute to the thousands of doctors, nurses, administrators and various other key workers, whose tireless efforts helped save countless lives during the Coronavirus pandemic. It was created by the children's poet and author Laura Mucha – a former lawyer, who works with organizations such as UNICEF to improve the lives of young people – in collaboration with eighty young children.

You sprint, lift and listen
to heartbeats, worries,
and the puff
                    and gasp
of ventilators.
You inject painkillers
                    and courage.

You teach history,
          hockey
                    and hope.
You grow
          imaginations,
                    confidence,
          brains.
You believe in us,
          you care.

You soak, scrub
          and sweep
                    away our fears.

You put out fires
and warm our spirits.
You bring letters,
lifelines,
and love.

You pick, pack, stack,
prepare.
You keep shelves
and bellies full.
You nourish us.
You share.

You govern, guide, inform,
protect,
search, rescue, build,
arrest.
You comfort.
You mend.

You keep our streets clean,
and our minds tidy.
No matter what, you're there.

Thank you.

6 July ✶ The Time of Roses ✶ Thomas Hood

23 May 1799 – 3 May 1845

The early Victorian poet and magazine editor Thomas Hood first broke into the literary world by writing light and witty magazine articles while convalescing with relatives in Dundee. He went on to do caricatures and humorous verse, but also poems that captured the lives of the poor. One such piece, 'The Song of the Shirt', shed light on the exploitation of seamstresses, and was printed anonymously in the famous satirical magazine *Punch*, before going viral. Well, the nineteenth-century version of going viral, which entailed the words being printed just about everywhere – including on handkerchiefs! This poem, however, sees Hood eschew his usual satirical tone for a touching account of a flowering romance.

It was not in the winter
  Our loving lot was cast!
It was the time of roses,
  We plucked them as we passed;

That churlish season never frowned
  On early lovers yet!
Oh, no—the world was newly crowned
  With flowers, when first we met.

'Twas twilight, and I bade you go,
  But still you held me fast;
It was the time of roses,—
  We plucked them as we pass'd!

What else could peer thy glowing cheek,
  That tears began to stud?
And when I asked the like of Love
  You snatched a damask bud,—

And oped it to the dainty core
   Still glowing to the last:
It was the time of roses,
   We plucked them as we passed!

7 July ✶ One Perfect Rose ✶ Dorothy Parker

22 August 1893 – 7 June 1967

Anyone who says that Americans don't have a dry, ironic sense of humour like the British has clearly not read any Dorothy Parker. The critic, poet, author and screenwriter (of the often-adapted 1937 classic film *A Star is Born*) turned cynicism and witticisms into an art in both her literary writing and her articles for all of the major New York publications. But as is sadly often the case with those who make us laugh the most, Parker struggled with depression throughout her life, and was often heard to be dismissive of her own immense talents. Her most notable influence however, was the similarly sharp Edna St Vincent Millay, of whom Parker once said: 'I was following in [her] exquisite footsteps, unhappily in my own horrible sneakers.' Despite being best known for her humour, Parker was also engaged with serious political issues of her day, and she left most of her estate to Martin Luther King, Jr. when she died to help further promote the Civil Rights Movement. Still, she didn't leave the world without offering a few final quips, advocating that her epitaph should read either 'Excuse my dust' or 'If you can read this, you're standing too close'. No doubt Spike Milligan (see 19 January) would have approved!

A single flow'r he sent me, since we met.
   All tenderly his messenger he chose;
Deep-hearted, pure, with scented dew still wet—
   One perfect rose.

I knew the language of the floweret;
   'My fragile leaves,' it said, 'his heart enclose.'
Love long has taken for his amulet
   One perfect rose.

Why is it no one ever sent me yet
   One perfect limousine, do you suppose?
Ah no, it's always just my luck to get
   One perfect rose.

8 July ✶ Wild Strawberries ✶ Helen Dunmore

12 December 1952 – 5 June 2017

The novelist, children's author and poet Helen Dunmore was born in Yorkshire into a very large family, and spent much of her childhood learning poems by heart. Her own work touched on subjects as diverse as war, food and nature. The simplicity of her language can at first conceal the depths of her critically acclaimed work; her collection *Into the Wave*, published shortly before her death, was given a posthumous Book of the Year prize at the 2017 Costa Book Awards.

What I get I bring home to you:
a dark handful, sweet-edged,
dissolving in one mouthful.

I bother to bring them for you
though they're so quickly over,
pulpless, sliding to juice

a grainy rub on the tongue
and the taste's gone. If you remember
we were in the woods at wild strawberry time

and I was making a basket of dockleaves
to hold what you'd picked,
but the cold leaves unplaited themselves

and slid apart, and again unplaited themselves
until I gave up and ate wild strawberries
out of your hands for sweetness.

I lipped at your palm –
the little salt edge there,
the tang of money you'd handled.

As we stayed in the wood, hidden,
we heard the sound system below us
calling the winners at Chepstow,
faint as the breeze turned.

The sun came out on us, the shade blotches
went hazel: we heard names
bubble like stock-doves over the woods

as jockeys in stained silks gentled
those sweat-dark, shuddering horses
down to the walk.

9 July ✶ Song of the Traveller at Evening ✶ Johann Wolfgang von Goethe, translated by Henry Wadsworth Longfellow

28 August 1749 – 22 March 1832

Johann Wolfgang von Goethe (pronounced *Guh-teh*) is one of the towering figures of German literature and European culture more broadly. A poet, novelist, playwright, critic, director, philosopher and even scientist, he enjoyed a long and hugely influential career which (along with the likes of philosopher Immanuel Kant) helped shape the late Enlightenment and early Romantic eras, in the way he promoted ideas of the self, reason and social progress – all of which would be central to post-revolutionary France and America. A man of means, Goethe had the freedom to devote his life to thinking and writing. To call him prolific would be an understatement; his collected works run to an amazing 143 volumes. He is best known for his epic poetic play *Faust*: an adaptation of the medieval German legend of a frustrated academic who gives his soul to the Devil in exchange for a life of unlimited knowledge and satisfaction. This is a far more tranquil poem about a weary traveller finding some much-needed rest.

O'er all the hill-tops
Is quiet now,
In all the tree-tops
Hearest thou
Hardly a breath;
The birds are asleep in the trees:
Wait; soon like these
Thou too shalt rest.

10 July ✶ Eldorado ✶ Edgar Allan Poe

19 January 1809 – 7 October 1849

The nineteenth-century poet and author Edgar Allan Poe has become a byword for dark, atmospheric, Gothic writing. Indeed, his eerie short stories and poems play on human fears and follies, and are credited with starting a trend for modern detective and mystery fiction, as well as popularizing horror as a literary genre. A university dropout, and later discharged from the military, Poe found much more success as a writer of poems such as 'The Raven', taking the rich, Romantic imagery of the likes of Keats and Coleridge, and marrying it with morbid stories of supernatural spirits, decay and death. This poem sees him in rich macabre form, as he tells the tale of a man searching for the mythical land of Eldorado, only to find Death instead.

Gaily bedight,
  A gallant knight,
In sunshine and in shadow,
  Had journeyed long,
  Singing a song,
In search of Eldorado.

  But he grew old—
  This knight so bold—
And o'er his heart a shadow—
  Fell as he found
  No spot of ground
That looked like Eldorado.

And, as his strength
Failed him at length,
He met a pilgrim shadow—
'Shadow,' said he,
'Where can it be—
This land of Eldorado?'

'Over the Mountains
Of the Moon,
Down the Valley of the Shadow,
Ride, boldly ride,'
The shade replied,—
'If you seek for Eldorado!'

11 July ✶ What If This Road ✶ Sheenagh Pugh

Born 1950

Sheenagh Pugh has lived all over Britain, having been born in Birmingham before studying in Bristol and living in Wales, and now Shetland in Scotland. The country's landscapes have been a staple of her work, which has garnered much praise over the years. But she has hit back at snobbish critics who have called her work – which is notable for its direct style – 'populist' and 'too accessible', saying that she hopes both assessments are true.

What if this road, that has held no surprises
these many years, decided not to go
home after all; what if it could turn
left or right with no more ado
than a kite-tail? What if its tarry skin
were like a long, supple bolt of cloth,
that is shaken and rolled out, and takes
a new shape from the contours beneath?
And if it chose to lay itself down
in a new way, around a blind corner,
across hills you must climb without knowing
what's on the other side, who would not hanker
to be going, at all risks? Who wants to know
a story's end, or where a road will go?

12 July ✶ Lean Out of the Window ✶ James Joyce

2 February 1882 – 13 January 1941

The pioneering Irish modernist writer James Joyce may be best known for his experimental 'stream of consciousness' novels, which place us inside his protagonists' racing mind, but his first ever published book was in fact a collection of love poems in 1907 called *Chamber Music*, from which this piece is taken. Despite being praised by his contemporaries T. S. Eliot and Ezra Pound for his proficiency in verse, Joyce did not return to the form until 1932. By that point, he had already published two novels (the semi-autobiographical novel *A Portrait of the Artist as a Young Man* and *Ulysses*, which, after Homer's epic poem the *Odyssey*, takes place over one day in Dublin), and begun work on *Finnegans Wake*, a dense, complex, impenetrable night's dream. This poem, however, should be a little easier to follow than his prose . . .

Lean out of the window,
  Goldenhair,
I heard you singing
  A merry air.

My book is closed;
  I read no more,
Watching the fire dance
  On the floor.

I have left my book,
  I have left my room,
For I heard you singing
  Through the gloom,

Singing and singing
  A merry air,
Lean out of the window,
  Goldenhair.

13 July ✶ Daddy Fell into the Pond ✶ Alfred Noyes

16 September 1880 – 25 June 1958

The writer Alfred Noyes was, in many ways, born about a hundred years too late. Working in the early modernist era, he was far more influenced by earlier, canonical poets such as William Wordsworth, and had no interest in his contemporaries' penchant for literary innovation; in fact, he is said to have especially reviled James Joyce. But despite being out of step with the time, Noyes was one of those rare few poets who managed to translate literary prestige into financial security. His most famous work, the balladic narrative poem 'The Highwayman', ranked near the top of a BBC poll of the nation's favourite poems.

Everyone grumbled. The sky was grey.
We had nothing to do and nothing to say.
We were nearing the end of a dismal day.
And there seemed to be nothing beyond,
  Then
Daddy fell into the pond!

And everyone's face grew merry and bright,
And Timothy danced for sheer delight.
'Give me the camera, quick, oh quick!
He's crawling out of the duckweed.' Click!

Then the gardener suddenly slapped his knee,
And doubled up, shaking silently,
And the ducks all quacked as if they were daft,
And it sounded as if the old drake laughed.
Oh, there wasn't a thing that didn't respond
  When
Daddy fell into the pond!

14 July ✶ Be Like the Bird ✶ Victor Hugo

26 February 1802 – 22 May 1885

14 July is celebrated as the national holiday Bastille Day in France, commemorating the storming of the Paris prison by revolutionary forces in 1789. Who better to mark this day then than perhaps the most famous French writer of them all, Victor Hugo. The author of the epic *Les Misérables* and the *Hunchback of Notre Dame* (both of which you may not have read, but will almost certainly have seen in film or musical form), as well as of many celebrated collections of Romantic poetry, Hugo was a giant of French literature. But he is almost as famous for his politics as a fiercely devoted republican; this despite growing up with royalist sympathies under his mother's influence. His work championed the poor and destitute of Paris, and beguiled the country. In short, he was a national treasure, and as such he was given a state funeral attended by some two million mourners. Today you'd be hard pressed to find any city in France that doesn't have a street bearing his name.

Be like the bird, who
Pausing in his flight
On a limb too slight
Feels it bend beneath him
Yet sings,
Knowing he has wings.

15 July ✶ The Albatross ✶ Charles Baudelaire, translated by George Dillon

9 April 1821 – 31 August 1867

Charles Baudelaire, like Victor Hugo, is one of the great French writers of the nineteenth century, although his fame never quite reached the heights of the former. In fact, the word 'notorious' might be more apt, given that he was a known libertine who burned through his inheritance and wrote about matters that were considered more than a little scandalous in his day. His masterpiece, a collection called *Les Fleurs du Mal* ('The Flowers of Evil') that contains this poem, was in fact the subject of a successful prosecution for causing offence. Aside from its more offensive poems, the book was conceived as a response to the industrialization of Paris, and his poetry was also devoted to finding beauty in the everyday. Although he died relatively young, his legacy lived on, in musical adaptations of his poems by composers such as Claude Debussy; in other literary works such as in T. S Eliot's *The Waste Land,* where it is quoted; and even in the film *The Usual Suspects*, in which a line from one of his stories is instrumental to the plot.

Sometimes, to entertain themselves, the men of the crew
Lure upon deck an unlucky albatross, one of those vast
Birds of the sea that follow unwearied the voyage through,
Flying in slow and elegant circles above the mast.

No sooner have they disentangled him from their nets
Than this aerial colossus, shorn of his pride,
Goes hobbling pitiably across the planks and lets
His great wings hang like heavy, useless oars at his side.

How droll is the poor floundering creature, how limp and weak –
He, but a moment past so lordly, flying in state!
They tease him: One of them tries to stick a pipe in his beak;
Another mimics with laughter his odd lurching gait.

The Poet is like that wild inheritor of the cloud,
A rider of storms, above the range of arrows and slings;
Exiled on earth, at bay amid the jeering crowd,
He cannot walk for his unmanageable wings.

16 July ✶ Envy ✶ Mary Lamb

3 December 1764 – 20 May 1847

With a name that cannot help but bring to mind a certain nursery rhyme, the writer Mary Lamb was, rather fittingly, a celebrated author of children's stories and poetry. Along with her brother, the better-established poet and essayist Charles Lamb, she co-wrote the popular collection *Tales from Shakespeare*, in which they adapted the Bard's plays into more accessible stories for younger readers. The two siblings were also well known for their friendship with the early Romantics including Wordsworth, Coleridge and Blake, who provided illustrations for their book. Lamb sadly suffered from poor mental health (leading to episodes of violence), and was known to be such a serious person that her brother claimed she never told a joke before the age of fifty. While humour was clearly not her forte, poems such as this one about overcoming gnawing feelings of envy and discovering one's own self-worth, reveal her ability to reassure and console.

This rose-tree is not made to bear
The violet blue, nor lily fair,
  Nor the sweet mignionet:
And if this tree were discontent,
Or wished to change its natural bent,
  It all in vain would fret.

And should it fret, you would suppose
It ne'er had seen its own red rose,
  Nor after gentle shower
Had ever smelled its rose's scent,
Or it could ne'er be discontent
  With its own pretty flower.

Like such a blind and senseless tree
As I've imagined this to be,
  All envious persons are:
With care and culture all may find
Some pretty flower in their own mind,
  Some talent that is rare.

17 July ✶ The Book of My Enemy Has Been Remaindered ✶ Clive James

7 October 1939 – 24 November 2019

While Mary Lamb takes a rather affecting and earnest look at our human inclination towards envy, the beloved broadcaster, journalist, memoirist, author and poet Clive James offers a typically cynical take on the joy derived from the failure of others. Born in Sydney, James spent most of his adult life in the UK, where he became a familiar figure and leading cultural voice. His work ranged from the very highbrow – translating Dante – to the more popular – writing TV reviews for the *Observer* and hosting his own TV programmes, including several on the more bizarre Japanese game shows. The last decade of his life was blighted by increasingly poor health, but he approached his illness with the same candour and humour that defined his entire career, writing a weekly column for the *Guardian* called 'Reports of my Death . . .'

The book of my enemy has been remaindered
And I am pleased.
In vast quantities it has been remaindered.
Like a van-load of counterfeit that has been seized
And sits in piles in a police warehouse,
My enemy's much-prized effort sits in piles
In the kind of bookshop where remaindering occurs.
Great, square stacks of rejected books and, between them, aisles
One passes down reflecting on life's vanities,
Pausing to remember all those thoughtful reviews
Lavished to no avail upon one's enemy's book –
For behold, here is that book
Among these ranks and banks of duds,
These ponderous and seemingly irreducible cairns
Of complete stiffs.

The book of my enemy has been remaindered
And I rejoice.
It has gone with bowed head like a defeated legion
Beneath the yoke.
What avail him now his awards and prizes,
The praise expended upon his meticulous technique,
His individual new voice?
Knocked into the middle of next week
His brainchild now consorts with the bad buys,
The sinkers, clinkers, dogs and dregs,
The Edsels of the world of movable type,
The bummers that no amount of hype could shift,
The unbudgeable turkeys.

Yea, his slim volume with its understated wrapper
Bathes in the glare of the brightly jacketed *Hitler's War Machine,*
His unmistakably individual new voice
Shares the same scrapyard with a forlorn skyscraper
Of *The Kung-Fu Cookbook,*
His honesty, proclaimed by himself and believed in by others,
His renowned abhorrence of all posturing and pretence,
Is there with *Pertwee's Promenades and Pierrots –*
One Hundred Years of Seaside Entertainment,
And (oh, this above all) his sensibility,
His sensibility and its hair-like filaments,
His delicate, quivering sensibility is now as one
With *Barbara Windsor's Book of Boobs,*
A volume graced by the descriptive rubric
'My boobs will give everyone hours of fun'.

Soon now a book of mine could be remaindered also,
Though not to the monumental extent
In which the chastisement of remaindering has been meted out
To the book of my enemy,
Since in the case of my own book it will be due
To a miscalculated print run, a marketing error –
Nothing to do with merit.
But just supposing that such an event should hold
Some slight element of sadness, it will be offset
By the memory of this sweet moment.
Chill the champagne and polish the crystal goblets!
The book of my enemy has been remaindered
And I am glad.

18 July ✶ The Curse ✶ J. M. Synge

16 April 1871 – 24 March 1909

The Irish playwright and poet J. M Synge gives us another funny, albeit rather violent, poem about taking pleasure from an enemy's suffering. The prefix refers to his drama *The Playboy of the Western World*, which managed to unite both Protestants and Catholics in their revulsion at its profanity and bloodthirstiness – which shouldn't come as a shock, to judge by this poem. A contemporary of W. B. Yeats, Synge met his fellow Irishman and poet in Paris, where he had gone to study. And it was the former who encouraged him to return to his Irish roots, imploring him to 'give up Paris . . . Go to the Aran Islands. Live there as if you were one of the people themselves; express a life that has never found expression.' And that's precisely what Synge did, capturing the essence of rustic, Irish folk life in his literature and photography. Today he is considered one of the most important chroniclers of Irish folklore and heritage.

To a sister of an enemy of the author's
who disapproved of 'The Playboy'

Lord, confound this surly sister,
Blight her brow with blotch and blister,
Cramp her larynx, lung, and liver,
In her guts a galling give her.
Let her live to earn her dinners
In Mountjoy with seedy sinners:
Lord, this judgment quickly bring,
And I'm your servant, J. M. Synge.

19 July ✶ A Singing Lesson ✶ Jean Ingelow

17 March 1820 – 20 July 1897

Born to an English banker father and a Scottish mother, Jean Ingelow seemed destined to become only a minor Victorian writer – producing mainly religious, romantic and children's verses – until the success of her 1863 collection *Poems*, which was printed in over twenty editions. It was a huge hit in both England and in America. Such was her reputation across the pond, that when Lord Tennyson (a friend of hers) died, her US-based fans wrote to Queen Victoria imploring her to appoint Ingelow as the next Poet Laureate. An American newspaper article once described her as 'shy, delicate, and reserved', with 'a true English aversion to being looked at, and a still greater horror of being written about'. And so, respecting her wishes, we'll leave this intro here.

A nightingale made a mistake—
  She sang a few notes out of tune—
Her heart was ready to break,
  And she hid from the moon.
She wrung her claws, poor thing,
  But was far too proud to weep;
She tuck'd her head under her wing,
  And pretended to be asleep.

A lark, arm-in-arm with a thrush,
  Came sauntering up to the place;
The nightingale felt herself blush,
  Though feathers hid her face.
She knew they had heard her song,
  She felt them snicker and sneer;
She thought that this life was too long,
  And wished she could skip a year.

‘Oh, nightingale,’ cooed a dove,
  ‘Oh, nightingale, what’s the use?
You, a bird of beauty and love,
  Why behave like a goose?
Don’t skulk away from our sight
  Like a common, contemptible fowl;
You bird of joy and delight,
  Why behave like an owl?

‘Only think of all you have done—
  Only think of all you can do;
A false note is really fun
  From such a bird as you!
Lift up your proud little crest;
  Open your musical beak;
Other birds have to do their best,
  But you need only speak.’

The nightingale shyly took
  Her head from under her wing,
And, giving the dove a look,
  Straightway began to sing.
There was never a bird could pass—
  The night was divinely calm—
And the people stood on the grass
  To hear that wonderful psalm.

The nightingale did not care—
  She only sang to the skies;
Her song ascended there,
  And there she fixed her eyes.
The people who listened below
  She knew but little about—
And this tale has a moral, I know,
  If you’ll try to find it out.

20 July ✶ 'Call for the Robin-Redbreast' ✶ John Webster

c. 1580 – c. 1632

John Webster was an Elizabethan/Jacobean playwright famed for his gripping, and often bloody tragedies, such as *The White Devil* and *The Duchess of Malfi*, which are still popular with audiences today. A younger contemporary of Shakespeare, he collaborated with some of the other great dramatists of the day, such as Thomas Dekker and Thomas Middleton. The son of a coach-maker, he was involved in the family business, and also received legal training (which comes up in his plays), perhaps leaving him little time to write more than his fairly modest output. Fans of the film *Shakespeare in Love* may remember Webster as the strange and brooding teen – a joke at the expense of his tendency to write dark, death-filled plays. This poem, sung by a mad character in *The White Devil*, is similarly bleak, and is known as a 'dirge', meaning a lament for the dead, as opposed to the modern usage which relates to something slow or dull.

Call for the robin-redbreast and the wren,
Since o'er shady groves they hover
And with leaves and flow'rs do cover
The friendless bodies of unburied men.
Call unto his funeral dole
The ant, the field-mouse, and the mole,
To rear him hillocks that shall keep him warm
And, when gay tombs are robb'd, sustain no harm;
But keep the wolf far thence, that's foe to men,
For with his nails he'll dig them up again.

21 July ✶ *from* Satyricon ✶ Petronius, translated by A. S. Kline

c. 27 AD – 66 AD

Gaius Petronius Arbiter is the author of *Satyricon*, a prose and verse text that contained thirty short poems (including this one) and two long within it. As the title gives away, it is a largely satirical piece that mocks an array of rather vulgar characters (one of which is thought to have inspired Gatsby in F. Scott Fitzgerald's novel). But it also serves as a valuable account of the lives of common people in the Roman Empire in the first century AD. Petronius himself is thought to have been a wealthy nobleman and an idle hedonist who provoked the ire of the Stoic philosophers who were against his profligate pleasure seeking. Despite his reputation, he did manage to get into Emperor Nero's court, but their relationship fractured when popular opinion turned against Petronius's decadent behaviour. Things went from bad to worse for him, and his end came when he was wrongly convicted of a plot to assassinate the emperor. This little poem, about the corruption endemic in the legal system reveals his famously biting wit.

What use are laws, where only money rules
and the plaintiff without it can never win?
Even those with a Cynic's purse, these days,
have been known to betray truth for money.
So a lawsuit's no more than a public auction,
with the noble jurors approving the purchase.

22 July ✶ Song ✶ Christina Rossetti

5 December 1830 – 29 December 1894

Despite being the sister of one of the Pre-Raphaelite Brotherhood's founders, Dante Gabriel Rossetti, and despite embracing many of the central themes explored by this group – namely, love, death, religion and aesthetics – the Victorian poet Christina Rossetti was not included in their group. It was, after all, a *brother*hood. Still, this didn't stop her from becoming one of the most successful poets of her day. She was an incredibly prolific writer, experimenting throughout her life with many forms of verse and drawing inspiration from the religious tradition as well as folk tales and romantic themes. Her poetry is often infused with a sense of compassion and reassurance, which we can still rely on for guidance to this day. This wise and moving poem, for instance, is often read at funerals.

When I am dead, my dearest,
　Sing no sad songs for me;
Plant thou no roses at my head,
　Nor shady cypress tree:
Be the green grass above me
　With showers and dewdrops wet;
And if thou wilt, remember,
　And if thou wilt, forget.

I shall not see the shadows,
　I shall not feel the rain;
I shall not hear the nightingale
　Sing on, as if in pain;
And dreaming through the twilight
　That doth not rise nor set,
Haply I may remember,
　And haply may forget.

23 July ✶ The Ivy Green ✶ Charles Dickens

7 February 1812 – 9 June 1870

The foremost Victorian novelist of such esteemed titles as *Great Expectations*, *David Copperfield* and *Oliver Twist*, Charles Dickens was also a handy poet. His name is another that has been turned into an adjective, in this case 'Dickensian', referring usually to urban hardship, dastardly male or sentimentalized female characters. His work was rich in timely allusions and often skewered the elite classes and those in positions of power – from factory owners to schoolmasters – and was rather more affectionate towards the poor and downtrodden. Perhaps this is unsurprising given his own, well, Dickensian, upbringing; his father was put in a debtors' prison, and he had to go to work in a warehouse. But despite being a very popular author and a celebrity – his novels, each published in serial form, were like the box sets of their day – he was always under some kind of financial pressure to produce more work, mainly owing to the fact that he had ten children!

Oh, a dainty plant is the Ivy green,
That creepeth o'er ruins old!
Of right choice food are his meals, I ween,
In his cell so lone and cold.
The wall must be crumbled, the stone decayed,
To pleasure his dainty whim:
And the mouldering dust that years have made
Is a merry meal for him.
Creeping where no life is seen,
A rare old plant is the Ivy green.

Fast he stealeth on, though he wears no wings,
And a staunch old heart has he.
How closely he twineth, how tight he clings,
To his friend the huge Oak Tree!
And slily he traileth along the ground,
And his leaves he gently waves,
As he joyously hugs and crawleth round
The rich mould of dead men's graves.
Creeping where grim death has been,
A rare old plant is the Ivy green.

Whole ages have fled and their works decayed,
And nations have scattered been;
But the stout old Ivy shall never fade,
From its hale and hearty green.
The brave old plant, in its lonely days,
Shall fatten upon the past:
For the stateliest building man can raise,
Is the Ivy's food at last.
Creeping on, where time has been,
A rare old plant is the Ivy green.

24 July ✶ Ithaka ✶ C. P. Cavafy, translated by Edmund Keeley

29 April 1863 – 29 April 1933

The twentieth-century Greek poet C. P. Cavafy was born in Egypt, and spent most of his early years moving between England and Greece. Although he had such distinguished fans as W. H. Auden and E. M. Forster, Cavafy was little known in his lifetime, owing to the fact he made no attempt to get his poems published. Instead, he mainly circulated his work amongst friends and in the occasional pamphlet. He was brought to wider attention after a collection of his poems was finally published in 1961 and was rediscovered again in 2001, when Leonard Cohen released a song, 'Alexandra Leaving', based on one of his poems. Today he is seen as an important figure in twentieth-century LGBTQIA+ poetry.

As you set out for Ithaka
hope your road is a long one,
full of adventure, full of discovery.
Laistrygonians, Cyclops,
angry Poseidon—don't be afraid of them:
you'll never find things like that on your way
as long as you keep your thoughts raised high,
as long as a rare excitement
stirs your spirit and your body.
Laistrygonians, Cyclops,
wild Poseidon—you won't encounter them
unless you bring them along inside your soul,
unless your soul sets them up in front of you.

Hope your road is a long one.
May there be many summer mornings when,
with what pleasure, what joy,
you enter harbors you're seeing for the first time;
may you stop at Phoenician trading stations
to buy fine things,
mother of pearl and coral, amber and ebony,
sensual perfume of every kind—
as many sensual perfumes as you can;
and may you visit many Egyptian cities
to learn and go on learning from their scholars.

Keep Ithaka always in your mind.
Arriving there is what you're destined for.
But don't hurry the journey at all.
Better if it lasts for years,
so you're old by the time you reach the island,
wealthy with all you've gained on the way,
not expecting Ithaka to make you rich.

Ithaka gave you the marvelous journey.
Without her you wouldn't have set out.
She has nothing left to give you now.

And if you find her poor, Ithaka won't have fooled you.
Wise as you will have become, so full of experience,
you'll have understood by then what these Ithakas mean.

25 July ✶ *from* Song of the Open Road ✶ Walt Whitman

31 May 1819 – 26 March 1892

The history of American literature only extends a few hundred years, but there is a strong case to be made that what Shakespeare is to England, or Goethe is to Germany, Walt Whitman is to the US. In fact, on the first publication of his book *Leaves of Grass*, one critic declared, 'An American bard at last!' – although that review was a little biased, given that it was written by Whitman himself. Eventually, though, he would receive praise from others – and a lot of it. The Transcendentalist poet Emerson said of Whitman's first collection that it was the most extraordinary piece of wit and wisdom that America has yet contributed, while years after his death the modernist Ezra Pound said that he was 'America's poet'. Whitman himself is often seen as a bridge between those two literary movements, combining natural observations and the self with formal experimentation; indeed, he is often called 'the father of free verse'. He is also talked about as being a democratic poet – who spoke to and listened to the people (especially soldiers during the Civil War) and captured them and the national spirit in his beautiful verse, as seen in this poem.

Afoot and light-hearted, I take to the open road,
Healthy, free, the world before me,
The long brown path before me leading wherever I choose.

Henceforth I ask not good-fortune, I myself am good fortune,
Henceforth I whimper no more, postpone no more, need nothing,
Done with indoor complaints, libraries, querulous criticisms,
Strong and content, I travel the open road.

The earth, that is sufficient,
I do not want the constellations any nearer,
I know they are very well where they are,
I know they suffice for those who belong to them.

(Still here I carry my old delicious burdens,
I carry them, men and women, I carry them with me wherever I go,
I swear it is impossible for me to get rid of them,
I am fill'd with them, and I will fill them in return.)

26 July ✶ Song of the Open Road ✶ Ogden Nash

19 August 1902 – 19 May 1971

A sure sign of greatness is being pastiched, and so, further cementing Whitman's status as an American icon, is this little comic tribute to his poem 'Song of the Open Road' by Ogden Nash. The descendant of the very serious General Francis Nash – the man after whom the city of Nashville, Tennessee is named – Ogden was known for not taking anything, least of all himself, too seriously. Instead he was famed for his sharp, whimsical sense of humour and his playful use of rhyme and language, often making up words as he went along. A Harvard dropout, he worked at the same advertising firm as the novelist F. Scott Fitzgerald, before going on to work at the *New Yorker* magazine. Like Spike Milligan, he was a master of quips, such as 'In chaos sublunary / What remains constant but buffoonery?'

I think that I shall never see
A billboard lovely as a tree.
Indeed, unless the billboards fall
I'll never see a tree at all.

27 July ✶ Ego Tripping (there may be a reason why) ✶ Nikki Giovanni

Born 1943

One of the best-known contemporary American writers, Nikki Giovanni is the author of dozens of books of award-winning verse, essays, memoirs, anthologies and children's poetry. Born in Knoxville, Tennessee, Giovanni rose to prominence as part of the Black Arts and Civil Rights movements on moving to New York in the late 1960s, writing widely distributed, polemical poems that aimed to illuminate social awareness. While her later work softened slightly in tone, it still remained deeply entrenched in racial and gender politics, although deliberately designed to be accessible to readers of all ages. Throughout an illustrious career that has seen her work as a TV producer and interviewer, and found a publishing cooperative, Nik-Tom Ltd – which gave a platform to the likes of Gwendolyn Brooks (see 14 January) – Giovanni has devoted herself to teaching, and has been a professor at Virginia Tech University since 1987. Of her work she has said: 'My dream was not to publish or to even be a writer: my dream was to discover something no one else had thought of. I guess that's why I'm a poet. We put things together in ways no one else does.'

I was born in the congo
I walked to the fertile crescent and built
   the sphinx
I designed a pyramid so tough that a star
   that only glows every one hundred years falls
   into the center giving divine perfect light
I am bad

I sat on the throne
   drinking nectar with allah
I got hot and sent an ice age to europe
   to cool my thirst
My oldest daughter is nefertiti
   the tears from my birth pains
   created the nile
I am a beautiful woman

I gazed on the forest and burned
   out the sahara desert
   with a packet of goat's meat
   and a change of clothes
I crossed it in two hours
I am a gazelle so swift
   so swift you can't catch me

   For a birthday present when he was three
I gave my son hannibal an elephant
   He gave me rome for mother's day
My strength flows ever on

My son noah built new/ark and
I stood proudly at the helm
   as we sailed on a soft summer day
I turned myself into myself and was
   jesus
   men intone my loving name
   All praises All praises
I am the one who would save

I sowed diamonds in my back yard
My bowels deliver uranium
  the filings from my fingernails are
  semi-precious jewels
  On a trip north
I caught a cold and blew

My nose giving oil to the arab world
I am so hip even my errors are correct
I sailed west to reach east and had to round off
  the earth as I went
  The hair from my head thinned and gold was laid
  across three continents

I am so perfect so divine so ethereal so surreal
I cannot be comprehended
  except by my permission

I mean . . . I . . . can fly
  like a bird in the sky . . .

28 July ✶ The Sail ✶ Mikhail Lermontov

15 October 1814 – 27 July 1841

A leading Romantic poet and novelist, Mikhail Lermontov is seen as one of the key figures in nineteenth-century Russian literature and a major influence on later existential and psychological novelists in his country and beyond. The son of an army captain, he was brought up by his grandmother before being sent to boarding school, where he immersed himself in poetry, and developed a keen sense of caustic humour. He shot to stardom in his late twenties when he wrote a widely circulated elegy in tribute to his hero, Pushkin, who had died in a duel (see 26 February). 'The Death of a Poet' was a thinly veiled attack on the ruling classes, whom Lermontov blamed for Pushkin's death. The result of such invective saw him exiled to the mountains for a period. He would again be exiled for duelling with the French ambassador. Lermontov wasn't so lucky in his next duel, against an old friend who had had enough of being teased by his comrade. And so Lermontov died aged just twenty-six, albeit fittingly, just like his idol Pushkin.

Amid the blue haze of the ocean
A sail is passing, white and frail.
What do you seek in a far country?
What have you left at home, lone sail?

The billows play, the breezes whistle,
And rhythmically creaks the mast.
Alas, you seek no happy future,
Nor do you flee a happy past.

Below the mirrored azure brightens,
Above the golden rays increase –
But you, wild rover, pray for tempests
As if in tempests there was peace!

29 July ✶ Past, Present, Future ✶ Emily Brontë

30 July 1818 – 19 December 1848

We have already met some writer siblings – the Rossettis, the Tennysons – but none have perhaps been quite so collectively influential as the three Brontë sisters, who we'll be meeting over the next three days. Let's begin with Emily, the second youngest of the four surviving siblings, who is undoubtedly best known for her 1847 novel *Wuthering Heights*, which divided critics at the time of its publication, with one reviewer stating, 'The incidents are too coarse and disagreeable to be attractive.' Little did he know that it would go on to become a favourite of generations of readers, and even inspire a hit pop song by Kate Bush. Together with her sisters Anne and Charlotte, Emily published a volume of poetry called *Poems by Currer, Ellis and Acton Bell* – these being the androgynous first names they adopted to stand a chance of getting published. Like her sisters, Emily was employed as a teacher and governess, and while little is known about her life and character, we have these revealing words that her sister Charlotte wrote after she died of tuberculosis: 'She had no worldly wisdom; her powers were unadapted to the practical business of life. An interpreter ought always to have stood between her and the world.' Here is a poem by 'Ellis Bell'.

Tell me, tell me, smiling child,
What the past is like to thee?
'An Autumn evening soft and mild
With a wind that sighs mournfully.'

Tell me, what is the present hour?
'A green and flowery spray
Where a young bird sits gathering its power
To mount and fly away.'

And what is the future, happy one?
'A sea beneath a cloudless sun;
A mighty, glorious, dazzling sea
Stretching into infinity.'

30 July ✶ Home ✶ Anne Brontë

17 January 1820 – 28 May 1849

The youngest, and perhaps most overlooked, member of the Brontë family, Anne grew up at the Haworth parsonage where, like her sisters, she was encouraged by her father to study in order to be able to become a governess and support herself, as there were few marriage prospects for a poor clergyman's daughter in Yorkshire. She found her work as a governess lonely, but it did inspire her novels *Agnes Gray* and *The Tenant of Wildfell Hall.* Unfortunately for her, her sister Charlotte's novel *Jane Eyre* about the same subject was a commercial success and undoubtedly overshadowed Anne's work. Anne sadly died shortly after her sister Emily of the same disease, aged twenty-nine.

How brightly glistening in the sun
  The woodland ivy plays!
While yonder beeches from their barks
  Reflect his silver rays.

That sun surveys a lovely scene
  From softly smiling skies;
And wildly through unnumbered trees
  The wind of winter sighs:

Now loud, it thunders o'er my head,
  And now in distance dies
But give me back my barren hills
  Where colder breezes rise;

Where scarce the scattered, stunted trees
  Can yield an answered swell,
But where a wilderness of health
  Returns the sound as well.

For yonder garden, fair and wide,
   With groves of evergreen,
Long winding walks, and borders trim,
   And velvet lawns between;

Restore to me that little spot,
   With grey walls compassed round,
Where knotted grass neglected lies,
   And weeds usurp the ground

Though all around this mansion high
   Invites the foot to roam,
And though its halls are fair within –
   Oh, give me back my HOME!

31 July ✶ Speak of the North ✶ Charlotte Brontë

21 April 1816 – 31 March 1855

The eldest of the Brontë sisters, Charlotte survived all her siblings, making it to the comparatively grand old age of thirty-eight. Despite not being particularly fond of children, Charlotte, like her sisters, worked as a governess. Although she had a reputation for being shy and unassuming, Brontë took the bold step of writing to the Poet Laureate, Robert Southey, when she was twenty to show him her poems. His reply? The poems were good, but women shouldn't write! Charlotte of course wisely did not listen to him, and went on to write many more poems and a number of novels, including *Jane Eyre*. After *Jane Eyre* was published, and made her a literary star, she never completed another poem.

Speak of the North! A lonely moor
Silent and dark and trackless swells,
The waves of some wild streamlet pour
Hurriedly through its ferny dells.

Profoundly still the twilight air,
Lifeless the landscape; so we deem
Till like a phantom gliding near
A stag bends down to drink the stream.

And far away a mountain zone,
A cold, white waste of snow-drifts lies,
And one star, large and soft and lone,
Silently lights the unclouded skies.

August

1 August ✶ Let Us Go, Then, Exploring ✶ Virginia Woolf

25 January 1882 – 28 March 1941

Virginia Woolf is one of the most revered writers of the early twentieth century. An era-defining novelist of psychologically penetrating works such as *Mrs Dalloway*, her aim in much of her work was to authentically capture 'an ordinary mind on an ordinary day'. But there is nothing ordinary about her exquisite, often daring writing, which broached such themes as gender fluidity, womanhood, and mental health that would have been considered highly sensitive at the time. Woolf was never one to follow patriarchal conventions; in 1929 she published the foundational feminist essay *A Room of One's Own*, which compelled women to follow their own paths, and not let men dictate their lives. As part of the so-called 'Bloomsbury Set' – a group of London intellectuals, writers, artists and critics – Woolf helped shape the cultural discourse of the day. A version of this poem first appeared in her novel *Orlando*, and was then published in a similar anthology to this one, edited by Vita Sackville-West and Harold Nicolson.

Let us go, then, exploring
This summer morning,
When all are adoring
The plum blossom and the bee.
And humming and hawing
Let us ask of the starling
What he may think
On the brink
Of the dustbin whence he picks
Among the sticks
Combings of scullion's hair.
What's life, we ask;
Life, Life, Life! cries the bird
As if he had heard.

2 August ✶ The Sands of Dee ✶ Charles Kingsley

12 June 1819 – 23 January 1875

For August, we are going to have a nine-day run of poems about rivers, seas and oceans. We'll be going in chronological order, so kicking us off is the Victorian poet, novelist and priest Charles Kingsley. A one-time chaplain to Queen Victoria and private tutor to the Prince of Wales, he was also a professor of modern history at Cambridge and a friend of Charles Darwin. Despite his religious background, he was in fact open to the theory of evolution proposed by Darwin, as seen even in his famous children's novel, *The Water Babies*. This folk-story poem takes us to calmer climes on the bank of the River Dee.

'O Mary, go and call the cattle home,
And call the cattle home,
And call the cattle home
Across the sands of Dee.'
The western wind was wild and dank with foam,
And all alone went she.

The western tide crept up along the sand,
And o'er and o'er the sand,
And round and round the sand,
As far as eye could see.
The rolling mist came down and hid the land:
And never home came she.

'Oh! is it weed, or fish, or floating hair,
A tress of golden hair,
A drownèd maiden's hair
Above the nets at sea?
Was never salmon yet that shone so fair
Among the stakes of Dee.'

They rowed her in across the rolling foam,
The cruel crawling foam,
The cruel hungry foam,
To her grave beside the sea:
But still the boatmen hear her call the cattle home
Across the sands of Dee.

3 August ✶ The Maldive Shark ✶ Herman Melville

1 August 1819 – 28 September 1891

Call him Herman. The author of *Moby-Dick*, considered by some to be 'the great American novel', was also a proficient poet of well-crafted and complex verse, and is seen as a key figure alongside Walt Whitman and Emily Dickinson in the nineteenth-century poetic revival in the US. After working as a teacher for a period, he became a seaman – a profession which would come to define his literature. Not only did he observe creatures such as the evocatively described shark in this poem, and whales such as Moby-Dick, but it also took him across the globe and imbued him with new cultural ideas and criticisms of western imperialism. His early writing was met with success, but his later novels were commercial failures, so he turned to poetry. He died in relative obscurity, before his reputation was revived by the likes of D. H. Lawrence.

About the Shark, phlegmatical one,
Pale sot of the Maldive sea,
The sleek little pilot-fish, azure and slim,
How alert in attendance be.
From his saw-pit of mouth, from his charnel of maw
They have nothing of harm to dread,
But liquidly glide on his ghastly flank
Or before his Gorgonian head;
Or lurk in the port of serrated teeth
In white triple tiers of glittering gates,
And there find a haven when peril's abroad,
An asylum in jaws of the Fates!
They are friends; and friendly they guide him to prey,
Yet never partake of the treat—
Eyes and brains to the dotard lethargic and dull,
Pale ravener of horrible meat.

4 August ✶ Sea Shell ✶ Amy Lowell

9 February 1874 – 12 May 1925

Pulitzer Prize-winning writer Amy Lowell did not seem destined for a career in poetry, but as she put it, 'God made me a business woman, and I made myself a poet.' Her first poem was printed when she was thirty-six, but Lowell more than made up for lost time after that, publishing over 650 poems in about twelve years. Despite being a great admirer of Keats, and even writing a biography on him, Lowell became associated with the Imagist movement, which, as we've already seen with William Carlos Williams (see 4 June), railed against ornate Romanticism with its promotion of clear language and imagery. She was a great supporter of the likes of Ezra Pound and 'H.D.' (whom we'll meet shortly), and edited collections of their work. Lowell herself was another in a long list of female poets who was largely forgotten until the 1970s and the emergence of feminist literary theory.

Sea Shell, Sea Shell,
   Sing me a song, O Please!
A song of ships, and sailor men,
   And parrots, and tropical trees,

Of islands lost in the Spanish Main
Which no man ever may find again,
Of fishes and corals under the waves,
And seahorses stabled in great green caves.

Sea Shell, Sea Shell,
Sing of the things you know so well.

5 August ✶ Above the Dock ✶ T. E. Hulme

16 September 1883 – 28 September 1917

T. E. Hulme was one of the leading members of the Imagist movement. In fact, he was possibly even more instrumental in its development than Ezra Pound, who laid claim to many of Hulme's ideas. Perhaps bringing a zeal for experimentation from his science studies at UCL, Hulme set about modernizing what he perceived to be a stagnant literary landscape, by creating poetry that bypassed the intellect and left an instant impression on its readers. Sadly, Hulme was killed in action in the First World War, leaving behind only a small body of work. Still, the little that he did write proved to be hugely influential on a generation of Imagist poets.

Above the quiet dock in mid night,
Tangled in the tall mast's corded height,
Hangs the moon. What seemed so far away
Is but a child's balloon, forgotten after play.

6 August ✶ Oread ✶ 'H.D.'

10 September 1886 – 27 September 1961

Another important Imagist poet is Hilda Doolittle, often known just as 'H.D.'. Those initials today are more likely to bring to mind a high definition screen, but fittingly, her poetry was marked by strong, crisp and clear imagery, and appeared in the first Imagist anthology, which was compiled by Ezra Pound (with whom she had a relationship); and she was also associated with the likes of William Carlos Williams, Marianne Moore and Richard Aldington, whom she married. In her later years she underwent therapy with Sigmund Freud, in the hope of better understanding her trauma of losing a brother in the First World War. She, like Amy Lowell, was reclaimed by the 1970s feminist movement, and thankfully preserved from anonymity. This is one of her most famous poems, which reveals her interest in Ancient Greek stories; the word *oread* means mountain nymph in Greek.

Whirl up, sea—
whirl your pointed pines,
splash your great pines
on our rocks,
hurl your green over us,
cover us with your pools of fir.

7 August ✶ Sea Fever ✶ John Masefield

1 June 1878 – 12 May 1967

John Masefield was the Poet Laureate for almost forty years, and yet today he is not as well-known as some of his contemporaries. That said, he does hold the honour of being the last poet to have his ashes interred in Poets' Corner in Westminster Abbey. Much of his writing focuses on maritime scenes and stories, unsurprisingly given that, like Herman Melville, he spent many of his early years as a merchant seaman. Eventually, after quite literally jumping ship at port in New York, he returned to London to pursue his childhood dream of being a writer. As he put it himself, 'I was going to be a writer, come what might.' And that's what he did, enjoying a prolific career that saw him write novels, plays, children's books and histories, as well as countless poems, with this one perhaps his most famous.

I must go down to the seas again, to the lonely sea and the sky,
And all I ask is a tall ship and a star to steer her by;
And the wheel's kick and the wind's song and the white sail's
shaking,
And a grey mist on the sea's face, and a grey dawn breaking.

I must go down to the seas again, for the call of the running tide
Is a wild call and a clear call that may not be denied;
And all I ask is a windy day with the white clouds flying,
And the flung spray and the blown spume, and the sea-gulls crying.

I must go down to the seas again, to the vagrant gypsy life,
To the gull's way and the whale's way where the wind's like a
whetted knife;
And all I ask is a merry yarn from a laughing fellow-rover,
And quiet sleep and a sweet dream when the long trick's over.

8 August ✶ Lobster ✶ Ted Hughes

17 August 1930 – 28 October 1998

The Poet Laureate between 1984 and 1998, Ted Hughes is undoubtedly more readily associated with the period of his life in the 1950s and early 1960s, when he met and married fellow writer Sylvia Plath, when they were both students at Cambridge University. The marriage was notoriously unhappy, indeed tragic. Ted Hughes is best known for his evocative writing on nature and animals, or even both, as in this light-hearted poem, but his body of work includes not only poetry, but beloved children books such as *The Iron Man*, several volumes of translations of writers from Ovid to Lorca, and an edited anthology of Shakespeare. At his funeral, Seamus Heaney gave a powerful tribute to Hughes's talent and wide-ranging influence, saying: 'No death in my lifetime has hurt poets more.'

This is the Lobster's song:
'Has anybody seen a
Heavy duty Knight
Dancing through the fight
Like a ballerina?
I was a thrilling sight!
Alas, not for long!

'It was the stupid sea,
The fumbling, mumbling sea,
The sea took me apart
And lost my clever wits
And lost my happy heart
And then jammed all the bits
Back together wrong.
Now I'm just a fright.
I don't know what to do.
I'm feeling pretty blue.'

9 August ✶ From the Wave ✶ Thom Gunn

29 August 1929 – 25 April 2004

Thom Gunn published his first book of poems while he was still a student at Cambridge. What followed was a long career that saw him publish over thirty books. In the 1970s he moved to the US, following his long-term partner to San Francisco, where he also taught. His writing was eclectic in its forms and references, from iambic pentameter to free verse, from Dante to Allen Ginsberg. In the 1990s he was seen as one of the key voices chronicling the tragedy of the AIDS pandemic, and his later work reflects more on grief and mortality. This poem, however, is a beautiful observation about how surfers become one with the sea.

It mounts at sea, a concave wall
  Down-ribbed with shine,
And pushes forward, building tall
  Its steep incline.

Then from their hiding rise to sight
  Black shapes on boards
Bearing before the fringe of white
  It mottles towards.

Their pale feet curl, they poise their weight
  With a learn'd skill.
It is the wave they imitate
  Keeps them so still.

The marbling bodies have become
  Half wave, half men,
Grafted it seems by feet of foam
  Some seconds, then,

Late as they can, they slice the face
    In timed procession:
Balance is triumph in this place,
    Triumph possession.

The mindless heave of which they rode
    A fluid shelf
Breaks as they leave it, falls and, slowed,
    Loses itself.

Clear, the sheathed bodies slick as seals
    Loosen and tingle;
And by the board the bare foot feels
    The suck of shingle.

They paddle in the shallows still;
    Two splash each other;
Then all swim out to wait until
    The right waves gather.

10 August ✶ Siren Song ✶ Margaret Atwood

Born 1939

One of the best-known contemporary writers, and Canada's major literary export, Margaret Atwood is known worldwide for her fiction, essays and poetry, as well as for her environmental activism. Her dystopian 1985 novel *The Handmaid's Tale* has been adapted into a film, opera and, recently, a major TV series. Atwood rejects the label of 'science fiction' for her novel, preferring the term 'speculative fiction', which she feels emphasizes the plausibility of the worlds she describes. As a poet, Atwood urges the reader to take ownership rather than trying to look for the author in the poem.

This is the one song everyone
would like to learn: the song
that is irresistible:

the song that forces men
to leap overboard in squadrons
even though they see the beached skulls

the song nobody knows
because anyone who has heard it
is dead, and the others can't remember.

Shall I tell you the secret
and if I do, will you get me
out of this bird suit?

I don't enjoy it here
squatting on this island
looking picturesque and mythical

with these two feathery maniacs,
I don't enjoy singing
this trio, fatal and valuable.

I will tell the secret to you,
to you, only to you.
Come closer. This song

is a cry for help: Help me!
Only you, only you can,
you are unique

at last. Alas
it is a boring song
but it works every time.

11 August ✶ Leisure ✶ W. H. Davies

3 July 1871 – 26 September 1940

The Welsh writer W. H. Davies spent part of his life as a homeless drifter. Born in Newport, Davies was raised by his grandparents after the death of his father. At twenty-two, Davies used his inheritance to travel across the Atlantic, where he train-hopped across the US and Canada, supporting himself by begging. Returning to Britain and settling in London, Davies wrote poetry about urban life and the natural world. He was championed by many of the great writers of his day, including George Bernard Shaw, who wrote the preface to his memoir, *The Autobiography of a Super-Tramp.*

What is this life if, full of care,
We have no time to stand and stare?

No time to stand beneath the boughs
And stare as long as sheep or cows:

No time to see, when woods we pass,
Where squirrels hide their nuts in grass:

No time to see, in broad daylight,
Streams full of stars, like skies at night:

No time to turn at Beauty's glance,
And watch her feet, how they can dance:

No time to wait till her mouth can
Enrich that smile her eyes began?

A poor life this if, full of care,
We have no time to stand and stare.

12 August ✶ The Tyger ✶ William Blake

28 November 1757 – 12 August 1827

One of the great British poets and painters, William Blake was a Renaissance man in the Romantic era. A radical thinker, he prized originality and freedom above other forms of success. Occasionally, his singularity led others to believe that he was simply a madman; a reputation which probably wasn't helped by the fact that Blake claimed to have had visions of God and angels throughout his life; unsurprisingly, he spoke often about the supremacy of the imagination over rationality. This, possibly his best-known poem, is from his self-illustrated collection *Songs of Innocence and Experience*, in which he explores the inevitable human transition from childlike purity to adult pain and sorrow. 'The Tyger' belongs to the latter state, in contrast with the innocent 'Lamb' it mentions towards the end.

Tyger, Tyger, burning bright,
In the forests of the night;
What immortal hand or eye
Could frame thy fearful symmetry?

In what distant deeps or skies
Burnt the fire of thine eyes?
On what wings dare he aspire?
What the hand, dare seize the fire?

And what shoulder, & what art,
Could twist the sinews of thy heart?
And when thy heart began to beat,
What dread hand? & what dread feet?

What the hammer? what the chain,
In what furnace was thy brain?
What the anvil? what dread grasp,
Dare its deadly terrors clasp?

When the stars threw down their spears
And water'd heaven with their tears:
Did he smile his work to see?
Did he who made the Lamb make thee?

Tyger, Tyger, burning bright,
In the forests of the night:
What immortal hand or eye,
Dare frame thy fearful symmetry?

13 August ✶ To the Virgins, to Make Much of Time ✶ Robert Herrick

August 1591 – October 1674

Robert Herrick was a Cavalier poet who remained devoted to King Charles I until the latter's execution in January 1649. But his support for the Crown would cost him his job as a country vicar, and he spent the years after the Civil War relying on friends and relatives for financial help. It was during this unstable period that Herrick turned to poetry, writing over a thousand poems for a collection called *Hesperides*. The Restoration of the monarchy in 1660 saw Herrick return to his parsonage in Devon, where he lived until the very impressive age (especially at that time) of eighty-three. It's somewhat ironic, then, that he is best known for this *carpe diem* poem which implores the reader to make the most of a fleeting life.

Gather ye rosebuds while ye may,
  Old Time is still a-flying:
And this same flower that smiles to-day
  To-morrow will be dying.

The glorious lamp of heaven, the sun,
  The higher he's a-getting,
The sooner will his race be run,
  And nearer he's to setting.

That age is best which is the first,
  When youth and blood are warmer;
But being spent, the worse, and worst
  Times still succeed the former.

Then be not coy, but use your time,
  And while ye may, go marry:
For having lost but once your prime,
  You may for ever tarry.

14 August ✶ The Mower to the Glow-Worms ✶ Andrew Marvell

31 March 1621 – 16 August 1678

We move on from a *carpe diem* poem to Andrew Marvell, a poet who certainly wasted no time in getting ahead in life, leaving his childhood town of Hull to attend Cambridge University from the age of twelve. Unlike Herrick and the other Cavaliers, Marvell was a republican, but he managed to negotiate the fraught and bifurcated politics of the era by showing respect to both sides in his writing; in his poem *A Horatian Ode*, he both expresses sadness at the death of Charles I and admiration for Oliver Cromwell. As such, when the monarchy was restored, Marvell managed to escape any royal retribution, and he was even able to convince Charles II not to execute his old colleague and friend John Milton for his revolutionary writing. The Restoration period also saw Marvell become an MP for Hull, and he wrote many sardonic pieces at the expense of corrupt politicians. Catholics were another subject of his satire, and it was rumoured for centuries that he was poisoned to death by Jesuits who felt ridiculed by his verses. Recent research suggests that he was indeed poisoned, but by some dubious treatment for his malaria.

Ye living lamps, by whose dear light
The nightingale does sit so late,
And studying all the summer night,
Her matchless songs does meditate;

Ye country comets, that portend
No war nor prince's funeral,
Shining unto no higher end
Than to presage the grass's fall;

Ye glow-worms, whose officious flame
To wand'ring mowers shows the way,
That in the night have lost their aim,
And after foolish fires do stray;

Your courteous lights in vain you waste,
Since Juliana here is come,
For she my mind hath so displac'd
That I shall never find my home.

15 August ✶ Let My Country Awake ✶ Rabindranath Tagore

7 May 1861 – 7 August 1941

Today is Indian Independence Day, and so we turn to the 'Bard of Bengal', Rabindranath Tagore. A writer across many genres, a philosopher and painter, Tagore was the first Indian – and the first non-European – to win the Nobel Prize for Literature, in 1913. Tagore was homeschooled until the age of seventeen, when he was sent to England to finish his studies, which he never did. Instead, he returned to India to manage his family's estates, which sparked a new interest in social reforms. Tagore was respected both in India – he was a good friend of Mahatma Gandhi – and in Europe, where he met Einstein to discuss religion and truth, and was given a knighthood by George V, which he renounced in protest against British policies and the Jallianwala Bagh massacre in 1919.

Where the mind is without fear and the head is held high;
Where knowledge is free;
Where the world has not been broken up into fragments by
  narrow domestic walls;
Where words come out from the depth of truth;
Where tireless striving stretches its arms towards perfection;
Where the clear stream of reason has not lost its way into the
  dreary desert sand of dead habit;
Where the mind is led forward by thee into ever-widening
  thought and action –
Into that heaven of freedom, my Father, let my country awake.

16 August ✶ Village Song ✶ Sarojini Naidu

13 February 1879 – 2 March 1949

The poet and activist Sarojini Naidu was called the 'Nightingale of India' by Mahatma Gandhi, in tribute to the melodious delicacy of her verse. But she was also known as a tireless campaigner for Indian independence and for women's rights. Having studied in London and Cambridge, she wrote most of her poetry in a succinct English on themes that were close to her politics, as well as romances, tragedies and children's texts. As an influential figure in the nationalist fight against British rule, Naidu met and collaborated with the likes of Gandhi and Tagore, and took part in civil disobedience protests that led to her imprisonment. In the years following independence, Naidu became the first woman ever to hold the position of governor in the Commonwealth Dominion of India, taking the post for the province of Uttar Pradesh.

Honey, child, honey, child, whither are you going?
Would you cast your jewels all to the breezes blowing?
Would you leave the mother who on golden grain has fed you?
Would you grieve the lover who is riding forth to wed you?

Mother mine, to the wild forest I am going,
Where upon the champa boughs the champ buds are blowing;
To the köil-haunted river-isles where lotus lilies glisten,
The voices of the fairy-folk are calling me listen!

Honey, child, honey, child, the world is full of pleasure,
Of bridal-songs and cradle-songs and sandal-scented leisure.
Your bridal robes are in the loom, silver and saffron glowing,
Your bridal cakes are on the hearth: O whither are you going?

The bridal-songs and cradle-songs have cadences of sorrow,
The laughter of the sun to-day, the wind of death to-morrow.
Far sweeter sound the forest-notes where forest-streams are falling;
O mother mine, I cannot stay, the fairy-folk are calling.

17 August ✶ The Lion ✶ W. J. Turner

13 October 1889 – 18 November 1946

In case you were wondering whether the great British painter and fan of ships J. M. W. Turner also dabbled in poetry, you should note the arrangement of the initials in the name of this Australian-born poet, biographer and journalist. W. J. Turner arrived in England at the age of eighteen to pursue a career in writing, and soon found himself a satellite of the Bloomsbury Group (see 1 August). He was friends with the war poet Siegfried Sassoon, and also with the great Irish poet W. B. Yeats, who was a big admirer, and with whom he collaborated on BBC poetry programmes. Outside of poetry, he also wrote music criticism for the *New Statesman*, and today his name is perhaps more readily associated with the biographies he wrote of Mozart and Beethoven.

Strange spirit with inky hair,
Tail tufted stiff in rage,
I saw with sudden stare
Leap on the printed page.

The stillness of its roar
For midnight deserts torn
Clove silence to the core
Like the blare of a great horn

I saw the sudden sky;
Cities in crumbling sand;
The stars fall wheeling by;
The lion roaring stand:

The stars fall wheeling by,
Their silent, silver strain,
Cold on his glittering eye,
Cold on his craven mane

The full-orbed moon shone down,
The silence was so loud,
From jaws wide-open thrown
His voice hung like a cloud.

Earth shrank to blackest air;
That spirit stiff in rage
Into some midnight lair
Leapt from the printed page

18 August ✶ Two Guns in the Sky for Daniel Harris ✶ Raymond Antrobus

Born 1986

On 18 August 2016, a young father and deaf man called Daniel Harris was tragically shot and killed by police in America while trying to communicate using sign language. This poem, by the Jamaican-British poet Raymond Antrobus, who is also deaf, provides a moving tribute to the victim, and a devastating account of what transpired. Antrobus's poetry has seen him become the first poet to win the Rathbone Folio Prize, as well as the Ted Hughes prize. This was an especially poignant award to receive, given that Hughes once clumsily described the faces of deaf children as 'alert and simple / Like faces of little animals' in a poem. In response, Antrobus took Hughes's poem and struck it out in black pen, before writing his own poem with the lines: 'Ted is alert and simple. / Ted lacked a subtle wavering aura of sound / and responses to Sound.'

When Daniel Harris stepped out of his car
the policeman was waiting. Gun raised.

I use the past tense though this is irrelevant
in Daniel's language, which is sign.

Sign has no future or past; it is a present language.
You are never more present than when a gun

is pointed at you. What language says this
if not sign? But the police officer saw hands

waving in the air, fired and Daniel dropped
his hands, his chest bleeding out onto concrete

metres from his home. I am in Breukelen Coffee House
in New York, reading this news on my phone,

when a black policewoman walks in, two guns
on her hips, my friend next to me reading

the comments section: *Black Lives Matter*.
Now what could we sign or say out loud

when the last word I learned in ASL was *alive?*
Alive — both thumbs pointing at your lower abdominal,

index fingers pointing up like two guns in the sky.

19 August ✶ An Ordinary Day ✶ Norman MacCaig

14 November 1910 – 23 January 1996

The Scottish poet Norman MacCaig is not very well known today, perhaps due to the fact that his reputation was tarnished by his refusal as a committed pacifist to fight in the Second World War. Though he was born and based in Edinburgh throughout most of his life, he often cloistered himself away in the remoteness of the Highlands. His lively and often funny poetry drew many admirers, not least his contemporaries Ted Hughes and Seamus Heaney. If you live in or have visited Scotland, you may well have inadvertently held a piece of MacCaig's poetry in your hands, as a verse from his poem 'Moorings' can be found on a Scottish ten-pound note.

I took my mind a walk
Or my mind took me a walk –
Whichever was the truth of it.

The light glittered on the water
Or the water glittered in the light.
Cormorants stood on a tidal rock

With their wings spread out,
Stopping no traffic. Various ducks
Shilly-shallied here and there

On the shilly-shallying water.
An occasional gull yelped. Small flowers
Were doing their level best

To bring to their kerbs bees like
Ariel charabancs. Long weeds in the clear
Water did Eastern dances, unregarded

By shoals of darning needles. A cow
Started a moo but thought
Better of it . . . And my feet took me home

And my mind observed to me,
Or I to it, how ordinary
Extraordinary things are or

How extraordinary ordinary
Things are, like the nature of the mind
And the process of observing.

20 August ✶ The Cataract of Lodore ✶
Robert Southey

12 August 1774 – 21 March 1843

Robert Southey, as we have seen, was the brother-in-law, friend, neighbour and literary collaborator of Samuel Taylor Coleridge, as well as the Poet Laureate who told a young Charlotte Brontë that women shouldn't be writers. That particular instance of closed-mindedness is illustrative of the conservatism that defined his later years – but like Wordsworth, Southey was, in his younger days, a fierce liberal who wrote in support of the French Revolution. And although he was an early advocate of social reform such as workers' rights and universal education, his entry into the establishment caused him to turn away from the radical ideals of his youth. As such, he was targeted by the new generation of Romantics such as Shelley and Byron who criticized his hypocrisy – with Southey retorting that Byron was a 'Satanic' poet. His status today is considerably less than that of his contemporaries, although he did give us the word 'zombie'.

'How does the water
Come down at Lodore?'
My little boy asked me
Thus, once on a time;
And moreover he tasked me
To tell him in rhyme.
Anon, at the word,
There first came one daughter,
And then came another,
To second and third
The request of their brother,
And to hear how the water
Comes down at Lodore,
With its rush and its roar,

As many a time
They had seen it before.
So I told them in rhyme,
For of rhymes I had store;
And 'twas in my vocation
For their recreation
That so I should sing;
Because I was Laureate
To them and the King.

From its sources which well
In the tarn on the fell;
From its fountains
In the mountains,
Its rills and its gills;
Through moss and through brake,
It runs and it creeps
For a while, till it sleeps
In its own little lake.
And thence at departing,
Awakening and starting,
It runs through the reeds,
And away it proceeds,
Through meadow and glade,
In sun and in shade,
And through the wood-shelter,
Among crags in its flurry,
Helter-skelter,
Hurry-skurry.
Here it comes sparkling,
And there it lies darkling;
Now smoking and frothing
Its tumult and wrath in,
Till, in this rapid race
On which it is bent,
It reaches the place
Of its steep descent.

The cataract strong
Then plunges along,
Striking and raging
As if a war raging
Its caverns and rocks among;
Rising and leaping,
Sinking and creeping,
Swelling and sweeping,
Showering and springing,
Flying and flinging,
Writhing and ringing,
Eddying and whisking,
Spouting and frisking,
Turning and twisting,
Around and around
With endless rebound:
Smiting and fighting,
A sight to delight in;
Confounding, astounding,
Dizzying and deafening the ear with its sound.

Collecting, projecting,
Receding and speeding,
And shocking and rocking,
And darting and parting,
And threading and spreading,
And whizzing and hissing,
And dripping and skipping,
And hitting and splitting,
And shining and twining,
And rattling and battling,
And shaking and quaking,
And pouring and roaring,
And waving and raving,
And tossing and crossing,
And flowing and going,

And running and stunning,
And foaming and roaming,
And dinning and spinning,
And dropping and hopping,
And working and jerking,
And guggling and struggling,
And heaving and cleaving,
And moaning and groaning;

And glittering and frittering,
And gathering and feathering,
And whitening and brightening,
And quivering and shivering,
And hurrying and skurrying,
And thundering and floundering;

Dividing and gliding and sliding,
And falling and brawling and sprawling,
And driving and riving and striving,
And sprinkling and twinkling and wrinkling,
And sounding and bounding and rounding,
And bubbling and troubling and doubling,
And grumbling and rumbling and tumbling,
And clattering and battering and shattering;

Retreating and beating and meeting and sheeting,
Delaying and straying and playing and spraying,
Advancing and prancing and glancing and dancing,
Recoiling, turmoiling and toiling and boiling,
And gleaming and streaming and steaming and beaming,
And rushing and flushing and brushing and gushing,
And flapping and rapping and clapping and slapping,
And curling and whirling and purling and twirling,
And thumping and plumping and bumping and jumping,
And dashing and flashing and splashing and clashing;
And so never ending, but always descending,
Sounds and motions for ever and ever are blending
All at once and all o'er, with a mighty uproar, –
And this way the water comes down at Lodore.

21 August ✶ The Laird o' Cockpen ✶ Carolina Oliphant

16 August 1766 – 26 October 1845

It's one thing that female writers were historically overshadowed by their male counterparts, but it's another that they rarely received the credit for their work. That was the case with the Scottish poet Carolina Oliphant, Lady Nairne, who wrote anonymously or under initialled pseudonyms such as B.B., only to find her hugely popular songs attributed to Robert Burns – who didn't really need the extra recognition! And yet, even then, she didn't reveal her identity, knowing it would bring her husband and standing as a noblewoman into disrepute.

The laird o' Cockpen, he's proud an' he's great,
His mind is ta'en up wi' the things o' the State;
He wanted a wife, his braw house to keep,
But favour wi' wooin' was fashious to seek.

Down by the dyke-side a lady did dwell,
At his table head he thocht she'd look well,
M'Leish's ae dochter o' Clavers-ha' Lea,
A penniless lass wi' a lang pedigree.

His wig was weel pouther'd and as gude as new,
His waistcoat was white, his coat it was blue;
He put on a ring, a sword, and cock'd hat,
And wha could refuse the laird wi' a' that?

He took the grey mare, and rade cannily,
And rapp'd at the yett o' Clavers-ha' Lea;
'Gae tell Mistress Jean to come speedily ben, –
She's wanted to speak to the laird o' Cockpen.'

Mistress Jean she was makin' the elderflower wine;
'An' what brings the laird at sic a like time?'
She put aff her apron, and on her silk goun,
Her mutch wi' red ribbons, and gaed awa' doun.

An' when she cam' ben, he bowed fu' low,
An' what was his errand he soon let her know;
Amazed was the laird when the lady said 'Na',
And wi' a laigh curtsie she turned awa'.

Dumfounder'd was he, nae sigh did he gie,
He mounted his mare – he rade cannily;
An' aften he thought, as he gaed through the glen,
She's daft to refuse the laird o' Cockpen.

22 August ✶ Watermelons ✶ Charles Simic

Born 1938

Charles Simic was born in Yugoslavia, or modern-day Serbia, just before the outbreak of the Second World War, and spent most of his early childhood fleeing the bombs that ravaged his home – or, as he put it with a typically humorous touch, 'My travel agents were Hitler and Stalin.' He spent a year in Paris, where he learned the poetry of Baudelaire and Rimbaud by heart, and moved to the US with his family when he was sixteen, where he started to learn English. His first poetry in that language was published by the age of just twenty. By the 1970s, he had cultivated a reputation as being an original and innovative poet in the Imagist vein – with this short, amusing poem serving as an apt example.

Green Buddhas
On the fruit stand.
We eat the smile
And spit out the teeth.

23 August ✶ The Unseen Life of Trees ✶ Chrissie Gittins

Chrissie Gittins is an award-winning poet who writes for both children and adults. She is often to be found touring, performing at festivals from West Cork to London, and in schools as far afield as Wester Ross. Gittins has also served as a writer-in-residence at the Refugee Council and at Belmarsh Prison, and her brilliant nature poetry has seen her appear on the BBC's *Countryfile* programme.

When the fraying skeins of silver birch
sway in the wind they think of
lulling water in the floating harbour,

the dried out plants on a deck,
the bespoke barge door cut to close
on a trapezium.

A sparse beech globe of yellow
holds an afternoon with two young friends,
who will walk through their vivid lives

beyond the end of mine.
A ball of mistletoe hangs
way up in spindle branches balancing

a trowel, a ginger cake,
and a framed copy of Jessop's 1802
'Design for Improving the Harbour of Bristol'.

Umber banks of oak climb the hillside
dragging children by the hand.
'There will be time,' they whisper,

canopy to canopy.
'There will be time, before
all our leaves stretch out across the frosted ground.'

24 August ✶ *from* To Penhurst ✶ Ben Jonson

c. 11 June 1572 – c. 6 August 1637

Ben Jonson's standing as a playwright was perhaps second only to his friend Shakespeare. But while he eventually became a leading figure of the literary establishment and a favourite of King James I – receiving the patronage of the court, for which he produced extravagantly staged, musical plays known as masques – his early career was defined by infamy and scandal. In 1597 he was imprisoned by decree of Elizabeth I for writing an allegedly slanderous satire at her expense. Shortly after release, Jonson again found himself in prison for killing one of his actors in a duel. Although he never courted quite so much controversy again, his plays and epigrams (short, pithy poems) were famed for their ruthless satirical streak. But he was an accomplished poet, who was able to discard his mocking tone for one of equanimity, as in this poem dedicated to the warm hospitality of the Sidney family, and the bountiful, natural splendour of their home.

Then hath thy orchard fruit, thy garden flowers,
    Fresh as the air, and new as are the hours.
The early cherry, with the later plum,
    Fig, grape, and quince, each in his time doth come;
The blushing apricot and woolly peach
    Hang on thy walls, that every child may reach.
And though thy walls be of the country stone,
    They're reared with no man's ruin, no man's groan;
There's none that dwell about them wish them down;
    But all come in, the farmer and the clown,
And no one empty-handed, to salute
    Thy lord and lady, though they have no suit.

25 August ✶ Church Going ✶ Philip Larkin

9 August 1922 – 2 December 1985

Philip Larkin was called the greatest English poet of the post-war era by *The Times*, and yet despite his fame, he spent almost his entire career working as a librarian at the University of Hull. A notorious grouch, Larkin's poetry is shot through with a sense of sadness and disappointment, and he observed of his own work that 'deprivation' was for him 'what daffodils were for Wordsworth'. But his work could scarcely be described as dour, as it is often marked by an ironic detachment and inspired turns of phrase. Despite being something of a recluse who eschewed attention – he turned down the invitation to become Poet Laureate – he was considered the main figure in the literary movement known, rather unhelpfully, as 'The Movement', which aimed to re-establish the importance of traditional English forms and expression in the face of American modernism.

Once I am sure there's nothing going on
I step inside, letting the door thud shut.
Another church: matting, seats, and stone,
And little books; sprawlings of flowers, cut
For Sunday, brownish now; some brass and stuff
Up at the holy end; the small neat organ;
And a tense, musty, unignorable silence,
Brewed God knows how long. Hatless, I take off
My cycle-clips in awkward reverence,

Move forward, run my hand around the font.
From where I stand, the roof looks almost new –
Cleaned or restored? Someone would know: I don't.
Mounting the lectern, I peruse a few
Hectoring large-scale verses, and pronounce
'Here endeth' much more loudly than I'd meant.

The echoes snigger briefly. Back at the door
I sign the book, donate an Irish sixpence,
Reflect the place was not worth stopping for.

Yet stop I did: in fact I often do,
And always end much at a loss like this,
Wondering what to look for; wondering, too,
When churches fall completely out of use
What we shall turn them into, if we shall keep
A few cathedrals chronically on show,
Their parchment, plate and pyx in locked cases,
And let the rest rent-free to rain and sheep.
Shall we avoid them as unlucky places?

Or, after dark, will dubious women come
To make their children touch a particular stone;
Pick simples for a cancer; or on some
Advised night see walking a dead one?
Power of some sort or other will go on
In games, in riddles, seemingly at random;
But superstition, like belief, must die,
And what remains when disbelief has gone?
Grass, weedy pavement, brambles, buttress, sky,

A shape less recognisable each week,
A purpose more obscure. I wonder who
Will be the last, the very last, to seek
This place for what it was; one of the crew
That tap and jot and know what rood-lofts were?
Some ruin-bibber, randy for antique,
Or Christmas-addict, counting on a whiff
Of gown-and-bands and organ-pipes and myrrh?
Or will he be my representative,

Bored, uninformed, knowing the ghostly silt
Dispersed, yet tending to this cross of ground
Through suburb scrub because it held unspilt
So long and equably what since is found
Only in separation – marriage, and birth,
And death, and thoughts of these – for which was built
This special shell? For, though I've no idea
What this accoutred frowsty barn is worth,
It pleases me to stand in silence here;

A serious house on serious earth it is,
In whose blent air all our compulsions meet,
Are recognised, and robed as destinies.
And that much never can be obsolete,
Since someone will forever be surprising
A hunger in himself to be more serious,
And gravitating with it to this ground,
Which, he once heard, was proper to grow wise on,
If only that so many dead lie round.

26 August ✶ The Fly ✶ Miroslav Holub, translated by George Theiner

13 September 1923 – 14 July 1998

For the Czech writer Miroslav Holub, poetry was something of a secondary pursuit, the main object of his focus being his work as an immunologist; indeed, he even turned down a two-year stipend that would have allowed him to switch his attention to his writing. Still, Holub never saw biology and literature as strictly polarized disciplines, and his work occasionally contains images or metaphors derived from the world of science. Which isn't to say that his writing is overly complex – in fact his poems were written in such an accessible way that they might appeal to people who usually steer clear of poetry.

She sat on a willow-trunk
watching
part of the battle of Crécy,
the shouts,
the gasps,
the groans,
the trampling and the tumbling.

During the fourteenth charge
of the French cavalry
she mated
with a brown-eyed male fly
from Vadincourt.

She rubbed her legs together
as she sat on a disembowelled horse
meditating
on the immortality of flies.

With relief she alighted
on the blue tongue
of the Duke of Clervaux.

When silence settled
and only the whisper of decay
softly circled the bodies

and only
a few arms and legs
still twitched jerkily under the trees,

she began to lay her eggs
on the single eye
of Johann Uhr,
the Royal Armourer.

And thus it was
that she was eaten by a swift
fleeing
from the fires of Estrées.

27 August ✶ Sonnet: To the Poppy ✶ Anna Seward

12 December 1742 – 25 March 1809

Anna Seward is a lesser known but widely admired early Romantic poet. She was born to a clergyman who, unusually for a father at that time, was a considerable advocate of female education. By the age of three, Seward is said to have been able to recite Milton by heart, and by seven she was already considered a promising writer. She grew up and lived her whole life in the Bishop's Palace in Lichfield, where her father was a canon of the Cathedral, and it was here that she befriended the botanist and poet Erasmus Darwin (grandfather of Charles), who supported her work. Later called 'the Swan of Lichfield', most of her poems were edited and published posthumously by Walter Scott.

While summer roses all their glory yield
  To crown the votary of love and joy,
  Misfortune's victim hails, with many a sigh,
  Thee, scarlet Poppy of the pathless field,
Gaudy, yet wild and lone; no leaf to shield
  Thy flaccid vest that, as the gale blows high,
  Flaps, and alternate folds around thy head.
  So stands in the long grass a love-crazed maid,
Smiling aghast; while stream to every wind
  Her garish ribbons, smeared with dust and rain;
  But brain-sick visions cheat her tortured mind,
And bring false peace. Thus, lulling grief and pain,
  Kind dreams oblivious from thy juice proceed,
  Thou flimsy, showy, melancholy weed.

28 August ✶ Invitation to Love ✶ Paul Dunbar

27 June 1872 – 9 February 1906

Born to freed slaves from Kentucky, Paul Laurence Dunbar was one of the first Black American poets to achieve international success. Motivated to write from a very young age, Dunbar had to overcome many challenges due to his financial limitations and discrimination. For instance, he was the only Black American in his high school in Dayton, Ohio, where he met Orville Wright – of airplane-inventing Wright Brothers fame – with whom he edited a local paper. They remained close friends, and Wright provided the monetary backing for Dunbar to publish his first collection of poems, *Oak and Ivy*, in 1893 – while he was still working as an elevator operator. From that point on, Dunbar lived off his writing, and didn't stop until his early death at the age of thirty-three. Writing in both standard English and in dialect styles, he was lauded for the technical expertise that underpins his work, which offered a personal insight into the Black American experience in the late nineteenth century. The poet Nikki Giovanni (see 27 July) said of Dunbar: 'There is no poet, black or nonblack, who measures his achievement . . . Even today. He wanted to be a writer and he wrote.'

Come when the nights are bright with stars
Or come when the moon is mellow;
Come when the sun his golden bars
Drops on the hay-field yellow.
Come in the twilight soft and gray,
Come in the night or come in the day,
Come, O love, whene'er you may,
And you are welcome, welcome.

You are sweet, O Love, dear Love,
You are soft as the nesting dove.
Come to my heart and bring it to rest
As the bird flies home to its welcome nest.

Come when my heart is full of grief
Or when my heart is merry;
Come with the falling of the leaf
Or with the redd'ning cherry.
Come when the year's first blossom blows,
Come when the summer gleams and glows,
Come with the winter's drifting snows,
And you are welcome, welcome.

29 August ✶ Harlem ✶ Langston Hughes

1 February 1901 – 22 May 1967

The writer and civil rights campaigner Langston Hughes is best known as one of the pioneering figures of the Harlem Renaissance – a New York-based cultural movement that embraced Black American artistic traditions and heritage across music, literature, dance, fashion, theatre and visual art in the 1920s and 1930s. He was also one of the first to fuse jazz music and poetry, creating a new kind of verse that was often improvised, and always imbued with a sense of musicality. Although he is predominantly thought of as a New Yorker, Hughes grew up in the Midwest, and was mainly raised by his grandmother, who introduced him to the ideas of Black identity and pride that he would go on to transmit to generations of Americans.

What happens to a dream deferred?

Does it dry up
like a raisin in the sun?
Or fester like a sore—
And then run?
Does it stink like rotten meat?
Or crust and sugar over—
like a syrupy sweet?

Maybe it just sags
like a heavy load.

Or does it explode?

30 August ✶ Lord Ullin's Daughter ✶ Thomas Campbell

27 July 1777 – 15 June 1844

Time works in mysterious ways. In his own lifetime, the Scottish poet Thomas Campbell was for a period even more well regarded than his fellow Romantics Wordsworth and Coleridge. (Well, at least by Byron, who, as we've seen, was not too fond of Wordsworth.) Today he is considered, at best, a minor poet, his status perhaps diminished by the strong imperialist overtone of his most significant works, which celebrate colonial expansion. There is a statue of him outside the University of Glasgow (at least for now), and he is remembered as one of the instigators of a plan to found the university that is now UCL – the first university in England to welcome students of any religion or social background, and the first to welcome women. This poem from 1809 was a particular favourite of the painter J. M. W. Turner, who produced twenty illustrations based on the text.

A Chieftain to the Highlands bound,
  Cries, 'Boatman, do not tarry!
And I'll give thee a silver pound
  To row us o'er the ferry.'

'Now who be ye, would cross Lochgyle,
  This dark and stormy water?'
'O, I'm the chief of Ulva's isle,
  And this Lord Ullin's daughter.

'And fast before her father's men
  Three days we've fled together,
For should he find us in the glen,
  My blood would stain the heather.

'His horsemen hard behind us ride;
  Should they our steps discover,
Then who will cheer my bonny bride
  When they have slain her lover?'

Outspoke the hardy Highland wight:
  'I'll go, my chief – I'm ready:
It is not for your silver bright,
  But for your winsome lady.

'And by my word! the bonny bird
  In danger shall not tarry:
So though the waves are raging white,
  I'll row you o'er the ferry.'

By this the storm grew loud apace,
  The water-wraith was shrieking;
And in the scowl of heaven each face
  Grew dark as they were speaking.

But still, as wilder blew the wind,
  And as the night grew drearer,
Adown the glen rode armed men-
  Their trampling sounded nearer.

'O haste thee, haste!' the lady cries,
  'Though tempests round us gather;
I'll meet the raging of the skies,
  But not an angry father.'

The boat has left a stormy land,
  A stormy sea before her, –
When, oh! too strong for human hand
  The tempest gather'd o'er her.

And still they row'd amidst the roar
  Of waters fast prevailing:
Lord Ullin reach'd that fatal shore,
  His wrath was chang'd to wailing.

For sore dismay'd, through storm and shade,
  His child he did discover:
One lovely hand she stretch'd for aid,
  And one was round her lover.

'Come back! Come back!' he cried in grief,
  'Across this stormy water:
And I'll forgive your Highland chief,
  My daughter! – oh, my daughter!'

'Twas vain: the loud waves lash'd the shore,
  Return or aid preventing;
The waters wild went o'er his child,
  And he was left lamenting.

31 August ✶ What's the Railroad to Me? ✶ Henry David Thoreau

12 July 1817 – 6 May 1862

It is a cliché to say that a writer or thinker was ahead of their time, but it's a sentiment that truly does apply to Henry David Thoreau, whose interest in environmentalism and advocacy of civil disobedience would become instrumental to ecological and civil rights movements of the mid-twentieth century. Like Ralph Waldo Emerson – with whom he lived, and whose children he tutored for a period – Thoreau was a Transcendentalist writer who believed in individual, sensory and spiritual experiences, and rejected institutions, famously saying: 'That government is best which governs least.' He took his philosophy of self-reliance to something of an extreme when he retreated from the world to live in a woodland cabin for two years, writing about it in his memoir *Walden* – now seen as a touchstone text for anyone eager to live simply and immerse themselves in nature. His poetry, you will not be surprised to learn and see below, is filled with rich and vivid observations and celebrations of natural beauty.

What's the railroad to me?
I never go to see
Where it ends.
It fills a few hollows,
And makes banks for the swallows,
It sets the sand a-blowing,
And the blackberries a-growing.

September

1 September ✶ It's Not What I'm Used To ✶ Jan Dean

Born 1950

For children and parents, early September will invariably be filled with the excitement, and occasional dread, associated with the start of the school year. This poem by Jan Dean playfully, but touchingly, captures the trepidation felt by a child moving to a new school. Dean herself knows at first hand children's experiences at school, since she has regularly visited them to give readings and run workshops. As a prolific writer whose work has been featured in over a hundred anthologies, her main aim has been, she says, to create poetry 'which doesn't leave children out'.

I don't want to go to Juniors . . .

The chairs are too big
I like my chair small, so I fit
Exactly
And my knees go
Just so
Under the table.

And that's another thing –
The tables are too big.
I like my table to be
Right
For me
So my workbook opens
Properly.
And my pencil lies in the space at the top
The way my thin cat stretches into a long line
On the hearth at home.

Pencils – there's another thing.
Another problem.
Up in Juniors they use pens and ink.
I shall really have to think

About ink.

2 September ✶ Science Block Toilets ✶ Steven Camden

Born 1979

Steven Camden is an award-winning performance poet and writer also known as Polarbear. He is the author of three young adult novels and a play, but is probably best known for his debut poetry collection *Everything All At Once* (where this poem appears), which chronicles a week-in-the-life of teenagers at a secondary school. The musicality of his writing, which is influenced by hip hop rhythms, becomes even more apparent when it is read aloud, by the author himself, at schools, at festivals, on the radio – or by you.

The drip of the tap like
the tick of a clock
as I sit on the top of the seat gripping the lock
It's break-time and I'm hiding
not from anyone
really
I just wanted some time without anyone near me
to breathe
in the midst of the chaos and noise
hyena girls and megaphone boys
police captain mannequin teachers
a gaggle of mad daggering laminate features
leeches attach on to top of the pack creatures
between bells they speak spells to keep sweet the divas
a legion of chair feet screeches
and I feel the bones in my ears crack
the CD skips
between these lips, my tongue whispers
You won't ever get these years back.
So I'm here
to sit
while the crowds are outside
in my graffitied bubble

I pause and unwind.
And I read lines, scribbled and scratched into patterns
declarations of feelings
bad stuff that's happened

Sophie loves Toby 4 eva

NO, COS SOPHIE KISSED JONAH
ON THE COACH DOWN TO DEVON

No I never Why you lying?

No she's not. I saw you. Slapper. Stop crying.

I HATE MATHS!

me too!

CARA G IS A BITCH

No SHE'S NOT
YOU ARE
FOR SCRIBBLING THIS

The voices ring out
ricochet off the walls
and I'm trapped
in a casket of angry catcalls
my hand falls from the lock. I reach for my bag. The door
starts to creak. I smell bleach and I gag
and the voices are screeching
the volume has risen
my toilet seat haven morphed into a prison

Then the bell goes
and no ring ever sounded so sweet
I pull open the door as I get to my feet
quick check in the mirror
Face is fine. All clear.
The tap drips approval and
the one voice I hear
is a small one
from a cubicle deep down
inside me
saying,
Next time you want peace
just go to the library.

3 September ✶ Busted ✶ Kwame Alexander

Born 1968

Kwame Alexander is a bestselling author of thirty-five books of poetry and children's fiction. He only really began to pursue poetry seriously when he realized that it could impress a girl he liked. As he charmingly tells it, 'I decided I wanted to be a poet when I wrote a poem for a girl I liked in college. Later, she married me. Yay for poetry!' After studying under Nikki Giovanni (see 27 July) at Virginia Tech University, Alexander has gone on to enjoy a prize-laden career. This includes a Newbery Medal for his young adult verse novel *The Crossover*, which was turned into a series on Disney +. This fun poem about a distracted pupil will resonate with all of us who have ever been caught not paying attention at an important moment, be it in a classroom or a meeting room.

Nicholas, I've warned you
about not paying attention
in my class.
This is your final warning.
Next time, it's down to the office.
Now, can anyone answer
the question correctly?

I can, I can, Ms. Hardwick, says Winnifred,
the teacher's pet (and a pain in the *class*).
What is the correct phrase, Winnifred?
Nip in the bud, not butt, Ms Hardwick, she answers, then adds,
Sorta like when you prune a flower
in the budding stage, to keep it from growing.
Then she rolls her eyes. In your direction.

Precisely. It is a metaphor
for dealing with a problem
when it is still small
and before it grows
into something LARGER, Ms. Hardwick says,
looking dead at you.

Ironically, Nicholas, by not paying attention,
you have stumbled upon another literary device
called a malapropism. Do you know what that means?
And of course you do, but before
you can tell her Winnifred raises
her hand and starts spelling it:
M-A-L-A-P-R-O-P-I-S-M, from
the French term mal à propos, *meaning*
when a person, or in this case, a boy,
uses a word that sounds like another
just to be funny.

Excellent, Winnifred, and since
You're such a comedian, Nicholas, Ms. Hardwick howls,
how about you finish reading
The Adventures of Huckleberry Finn
and find
an example of malapropism
in the text
to present
in class next week.

ARRGGGHH!

4 September ✶ Homework ✶ Allen Ginsberg

3 June 1926 – 5 April 1997

If you were to go to a liberal protest rally in America at any time between the 1950s and the 1970s, chances are you would bump into Allen Ginsberg. A legendary cult figure in the hippie, counterculture era – in fact, he's thought to have come up with the term 'flower power' – he was a fervent campaigner against the Vietnam War, for free speech, and civil rights throughout his life. Along with writers William S. Burroughs and Jack Kerouac, among others, Ginsberg helped spark the Beat Generation – a literary movement that challenged established political, social and economic norms and values, and championed the spiritual awakening of the individual, much as the Transcendentalists had done a century earlier. Hugely popular with young, rebellious souls and creative, bohemian types, Ginsberg also frequently courted the wrath of the authorities, who censored and tried to ban some of his more controversial poems. The poem below, one of his later poems, is not quite as inflammatory, but it does reveal Ginsberg's disdain at the pollution and corruption that blights the world.

Homage Kenneth Koch

If I were doing my Laundry I'd wash my dirty Iran
I'd throw in my United States, and pour on the Ivory Soap, scrub up
  Africa,
   put all the birds and elephants back in the jungle,
I'd wash the Amazon river and clean the oily Carib & Gulf of Mexico,
Rub that smog off the North Pole, wipe up all the pipelines in
  Alaska,
Rub a dub dub for Rocky Flats and Los Alamos, Flush that sparkly
  Cesium
   out of Love Canal
Rinse down the Acid Rain over the Parthenon & Sphinx, Drain

Sludge out
of the Mediterranean basin & make it azure again,
Put some blueing back into the sky over the Rhine, bleach the little Clouds
so snow return white as snow,
Cleanse the Hudson Thames & Neckar, Drain the Suds out of Lake Erie
Then I'd throw big Asia in one giant Load & wash out the blood & Agent Orange,
Dump the whole mess of Russia and China in the wringer, squeeze out the tattletail
Gray of U.S. Central American police state,
& put the planet in the drier & let it sit 20 minutes or an Aeon till it came out clean.

5 September ✶ Autumn ✶ Alexander Posey

3 August 1873 – 27 May 1908

Alexander Posey grew up in what is now Oklahoma, in a Muscogee Creek family. Although Muscogee was his first language, his father encouraged him to go to the local university where he began to write poetry, in English. Most of his poems, like this one below, were about the raw beauty in nature. In 1901 he founded the *Eufaula Indian Journal*, the first Native American daily newspaper, and using a fictional persona, he wrote and published *The Fus Fixico Letters*. These satirical letters, written in his Muscogee Creek dialect, remain an important record of Native American politics and culture at a crucial moment in history for the Creek Nation.

In the dreamy silence
Of the afternoon, a
Cloth of gold is woven
Over wood and prairie;
And the jaybird, newly
Fallen from the heaven,
Scatters cordial greetings,
And the air is filled with
Scarlet leaves, that, dropping,
Rise again, as ever,
With a useless sigh for
Rest—and it is Autumn.

6 September ✶ Autumn Song ✶ Paul Verlaine, translated by Arthur Symons

30 March 1844 – 8 January 1896

The so-called 'prince of poets', Paul Verlaine, was one of the great French poets of the late nineteenth century, following in the footsteps of his literary heroes Victor Hugo and Charles Baudelaire. He was one of the pioneers of the Symbolist movement – which placed an emphasis on metaphor-rich, often surreal writing, at the expense of realism. Despite being married, Verlaine became besotted with the teenage poetry sensation Arthur Rimbaud, and left his family to pursue a whirlwind romance. But as is so often the case when two poets get together, their relationship was stormy and volatile, and it eventually turned violent when Verlaine shot his lover in the wrist. The assault saw Verlaine imprisoned for two years, where, unlike his friend Oscar Wilde, he enjoyed a fruitful writing period.

When a sighing begins
In the violins
Of the autumn-song,
My heart is drowned
In the slow sound
Languorous and long

Pale as with pain,
Breath fails me when
The hours toll deep.
My thoughts recover
The days that are over,
And I weep.

And I go
Where the winds know,
Broken and brief,
To and fro,
As the winds blow
A dead leaf.

7 September ✶ *from* Le Bateau Ivre ✶ Arthur Rimbaud, translated by Norman Cameron

20 October 1854 – 10 November 1891

At nine years old Arthur Rimbaud was writing polemical essays, by fifteen he was a prize-winning poet, and by twenty-one he had retired, having created a body of work that would see him remembered as one of the titans of nineteenth-century French poetry. The son of an army captain and a strict mother, Rimbaud ran away from home several times before definitively leaving to live in Paris with the poet Paul Verlaine, to whom he had sent a particularly persuasive bit of fan mail and some poems. As we have already seen, the two had a difficult relationship, which was defined by partying, poverty, and finally, a pistol. Despite the wrist injury – a grave one for a writer! – Rimbaud continued to write for a couple more years. This extract is taken from his famous 100-line poem, 'Le Bateau Ivre' ('The Drunken Boat'), which presents a dream-like story about a boat that voyages downstream, alone.

I know how the sky splits in lightning, and what moves
Currents and surf and water-spouts; the evening light
I know; I've seen dawn risen like a flock of doves.
Sometimes I've seen what man's believed he had in sight.

I've seen the low sun stained with an uncanny dread,
Illuminating with its long and violet rays,
Like actors in an ancient drama, waves that spread
Their shudders all throughout their overlapping maze.

8 September ✶ Eiffel Tower ✶
Guillaume Apollinaire

6 August 1880 – 9 November 1918

Arthur Rimbaud's work was a precursor to surrealism, a term coined by the poet and art critic Guillaume Apollinaire. Born in Rome to a Polish aristocrat mother, Apollinaire eventually moved to Paris where he became part of a social milieu that served as a Who's Who of Europe's greatest minds and artists – from Picasso and Marc Chagall to Gertrude Stein, Andre Breton and Jean Cocteau. Despite his estimable reputation in the art world, Apollinaire also cultivated an image as an *enfant terrible*, which led him to become one of the prime suspects when the Mona Lisa was stolen from the Louvre in 1911. This poem comes from *Calligrammes* – his pioneering book of 'concrete poetry', where the visual image relates to the meaning of each poem's words.

S
A
LUT
M
O N
D E
DONT
JE SUIS
LA LAN
GUE É
LOQUEN
TE QUESA
B O U C H E
O PARIS
TIRE ET TIRERA
TOU JOURS
AUX A L
LEM ANDS

Translation: Hello, world, where I am the eloquent tongue, which Paris will forever stick out at the Germans.

9 September ✶ Fishes' Nightsong ✶ Christian Morgenstern

6 May 1871 – 31 March 1914

While Apollinaire was busy writing poems in the form of the Eiffel Tower (among many other shapes), the German poet and humorist Christian Morgenstern took things much further in his visual poem about fishes which features no words at all! Instead we have an assortment of dashes and shapes that look a little like several smiley emoticons aligned on top of each other. What could it possibly mean? Are these characters showing us fish swimming amidst waves? Are they bubbles? Or some kind of mysterious code? Over 110 years later and we're still none the wiser, which is of course the timeless brilliance of this poem. Morgenstern himself was more than just an impish nonsense writer and comic poet; he also worked as a journalist, translator and philosophical essayist.

10 September ✶ Little Fish ✶ D. H. Lawrence

11 September 1885 – 2 March 1930

The son of a Nottingham coal miner, Lawrence knew he didn't want to go down the same route as his father, and worked as a clerk and teacher before pursuing writing. Today he is regarded as one of the major writers of the early twentieth century, who wrote insightfully and without idealization about relationships and the modern, industrialized world. But in his own lifetime Lawrence's career was overshadowed by the scandals provoked by his explicit novels – in particular *Lady Chatterley's Lover*, which was banned from publication in full between 1928 and 1960, when it was the subject of an obscenity trial. His reputation, outside of his admirers such as Virginia Woolf and E. M. Forster, who called him the 'greatest imaginative novelist of our generation', was still damaged when he died in France in 1930, after years of travelling the world.

The tiny fish enjoy themselves
in the sea.
Quick little splinters of life,
their little lives are fun to them
in the sea.

11 September ✶ Thirteen Ways of Looking at a Blackbird ✶ Wallace Stevens

2 October 1879 – 2 August 1955

The words 'lawyer', 'businessman' and 'poet' are not too often seen together, but Wallace Stevens was in fact all three throughout his career. Even when his poetry began to receive significant acclaim in his forties, he remained a vice president at an insurance company. His first collection, *Harmonium*, in which this poem appears, was published in 1923 and is still considered an iconic text, rich in symbolism, abstract thought and innovation. Although largely bracketed together with the modernists, and as someone who occupied the same circles as the likes of E. E. Cummings, William Carlos Williams and Marianne Moore, Stevens is also often called a neo-Romantic who was greatly influenced by European poetry from the previous century. Stevens wrote well into his seventies, winning both the National Book Award and the Pulitzer Prize in the final years of his life. In an obituary, William Carlos Williams compared his talent to that of Milton and Dante.

I

Among twenty snowy mountains,
The only moving thing
Was the eye of the blackbird.

II

I was of three minds,
Like a tree
In which there are three blackbirds.

III

The blackbird whirled in the autumn winds.
It was a small part of the pantomime.

IV

A man and a woman
Are one.
A man and a woman and a blackbird
Are one.

V

I do not know which to prefer,
The beauty of inflections
Or the beauty of innuendoes,
The blackbird whistling
Or just after.

VI

Icicles filled the long window
With barbaric glass.
The shadow of the blackbird
Crossed it, to and fro.
The mood
Traced in the shadow
An indecipherable cause.

VII

O thin men of Haddam,
Why do you imagine golden birds?
Do you not see how the blackbird
Walks around the feet
Of the women about you?

VIII

I know noble accents
And lucid, inescapable rhythms;
But I know, too,
That the blackbird is involved
In what I know.

IX

When the blackbird flew out of sight,
It marked the edge
Of one of many circles.

X

At the sight of blackbirds
Flying in a green light,
Even the bawds of euphony
Would cry out sharply.

XI

He rode over Connecticut
In a glass coach.
Once, a fear pierced him,
In that he mistook
The shadow of his equipage
For blackbirds.

XII

The river is moving.
The blackbird must be flying.

XIII

It was evening all afternoon.
It was snowing
And it was going to snow.
The blackbird sat
In the cedar-limbs.

12 September ✶ They Knew What They Wanted ✶ John Ashbery

28 July 1927 – 3 September 2017

John Ashbery was a hugely influential American writer whose poetry often took on the form of a verbal collage. As he explained, his poems were like 'a snapshot of whatever is going on in my head at the time'. The result of such an approach was a poetic style that was wholly original, rich with allusions and dense in its imagery, but at times, well, a little hard to follow. Even W. H. Auden admitted that when he gave the Yale Younger Poets Prize to Ashbery in 1956, he didn't have a clue what his manuscript, titled *Some Trees*, was about! The rest of us then stand little chance at really getting to the bottom of what some of Ashbery's poetry 'means', but there is great pleasure to be derived from reading a poem that opens itself up to subjective interpretation in such a way. The obscurity of his verse certainly didn't harm his critical or commercial reception, as he published over twenty volumes of poetry and won dozens more prizes. He was also a celebrated translator of French poets (including Rimbaud), a lecturer and an art critic, who knew Andy Warhol. This poem, which boasts a number of playful, curious juxtapositions of images about modern America, can perhaps best be seen as a kind of literary pop art.

They all kissed the bride.
They all laughed.
They came from beyond space.
They came by night.

They came to a city.
They came to blow up America.
They came to rob Las Vegas.
They dare not love.

They died with their boots on.
They shoot horses, don't they?
They go boom.
They got me covered.

They flew alone.
They gave him a gun.
They just had to get married.
They live. They loved life.

They live by night.
They drive by night.
They knew Mr. Knight.
They were expendable.

They met in Argentina.
They met in Bombay.
They met in the dark.
They might be giants.

They made me a fugitive.
They made me a criminal.
They only kill their masters.
They shall have music.

They were sisters.
They still call me Bruce.
They won't believe me.
They won't forget.

13 September ✶ JOMO ✶ Michael Leunig

Born 1945

Some poets have drawn little illustrations to accompany their poems. But Michael Leunig often does things the other way round, writing poems to give added texture to his work as a cartoonist. His work, which is often political, satirical, and occasionally controversial, appears in books and in numerous newspapers in his native Australia. Some of his regular characters, such as Mr Curly, seen below, promote a gentle, easy-going life, but many of Leunig's other pieces have been more direct in their criticism of conflict and consumerism. This poem, about JOMO (Joy Of Missing Out), is an uplifting play on the widely used acronym FOMO (Fear Of Missing Out).

JOMO (Joy Of Missing Out.)

Oh the joy of missing out.
When the world begins to shout
And rush towards that shining thing;
The latest bit of mental bling –
Trying to have it, see it, do it,
You simply know you won't go through it;
The anxious clamouring and need
This restless hungry thing to feed.

Instead, you feel the loveliness;
The pleasure of your emptiness.
You spurn the treasure on the shelf
In favour of your peaceful self;
Without regret, without a doubt.
Oh the joy of missing out.

Leunig

14 September ✶ The Cod ✶ Lord Alfred Douglas

22 October 1870 – 20 March 1945

Mention of Lord Alfred Douglas is usually followed by mention of Oscar Wilde. The two embarked on a relationship in the early 1890s that would, as we've already seen, lead to a trial and the imprisonment of Wilde. Douglas would also find himself in prison some thirty years later when he was jailed for six months for his criminal libel of then cabinet minister Winston Churchill. As for his writing, Douglas can only be considered as something of a minor poet, but he did receive praise for his sonnets and light verse, this example being perhaps the most playful.

There's something very strange and odd
About the habits of the Cod.

For when you're swimming in the sea,
He sometimes bites you on the knee.

And though his bites are not past healing,
It is a most unpleasant feeling.

And when you're diving down below,
He often nips you on the toe.

And though he doesn't hurt you much,
He has a disagreeable touch.

There's one thing to be said for him, –
It is a treat to see him swim.

But though he swims in graceful curves,
He rather gets upon your nerves.

15 September ✶ Autumn ✶ John Clare

13 July 1793 – 20 May 1864

Born to an agricultural family, John Clare became a farmhand while he was still a child, receiving only a primary school education. Having saved up money to buy a book of poems, Clare immersed himself in poetry and began writing his own. Eventually he was picked up by a publisher, in the hope that given his background as a 'peasant poet' who wrote in dialect, he could become a nineteenth-century and English Robert Burns. Despite receiving critical acclaim, however, his success made him feel out of place both in London's literary circles and among his rural neighbours. This contributed to Clare reaching a breaking point, and he spent the last decades of his life in an asylum where he was prone to lapses of delusion in which he believed he was Byron or Shakespeare. His posthumous life as a poet does have a happier ending, though, as he was rediscovered in the twentieth century and held up as one of the great nature poets, who had a finely tuned eye and ear for the beauties – both the majestic and the subtle – found in the English countryside.

The thistledown's flying, though the winds are all still,
On the green grass now lying, now mounting the hill,
The spring from the fountain now boils like a pot;
Through stones past the counting it bubbles red-hot.

The ground parched and cracked is like overbaked bread,
The greensward all wracked is, bents dried up and dead.
The fallow fields glitter like water indeed,
And gossamers twitter, flung from weed unto weed.

Hill-tops like hot iron glitter bright in the sun,
And the rivers we're eying burn to gold as they run;
Burning hot is the ground, liquid gold is the air;
Whoever looks round sees Eternity there.

16 September ✶ And the Days Are Not Full Enough ✶ Ezra Pound

30 October 1885 – 1 November 1972

A literary giant of the early twentieth century, the poet and academic Ezra Pound is seen as the father of the modernist movement. Born in rural Idaho and raised in Pennsylvania, Pound lived in England between 1908 and 1920. It was here that he picked up where T. E. Hulme had left off, developing the Imagist movement that would be adopted by the likes of 'H.D.' and William Carlos Williams. Admired for his own poetry – especially his incomplete, experimental epic *The Cantos*, published in parts over decades – Pound was as well known for his work as an editor and champion of modernist writers, such as James Joyce and T. S. Eliot. In the 1920s Pound left London for Paris, before moving to Italy, where he strengthened his admiration for Mussolini and the Fascist party. He stayed in Italy after the Second World War broke out, broadcasting radio commentaries which were viewed as treasonous by the US. After the war, he was incarcerated in the US until 1958, when he returned to Italy. While his politics remain a stain on his reputation, the extent of Pound's impact on modern literature cannot be overstated.

And the days are not full enough
And the nights are not full enough
And life slips by like a field mouse
                    Not shaking the grass.

17 September ✶ *from* The Burning of the Leaves ✶ Laurence Binyon

10 August 1869 – 10 March 1943

The art historian and poet Laurence Binyon was the son of a Lancaster clergyman, the second of nine children. Aside from his own poetry, he wrote acclaimed books on painting and a much-admired translation of Dante's *Divine Comedy*, which preserved the original, complicated rhyme scheme. The traumas of the First World War led him to write some of his greatest poems, including 'For the Fallen', which is often recited at Remembrance Day services. Twenty years later, Binyon would find himself returning to war poetry, with this poem capturing the devastation of the London Blitz.

Now is the time for the burning of the leaves.
They go to the fire; the nostril pricks with smoke
Wandering slowly into a weeping mist.
Brittle and blotched, ragged and rotten sheaves!
A flame seizes the smouldering ruin and bites
On stubborn stalks that crackle as they resist.

The last hollyhock's fallen tower is dust;
All the spices of June are a bitter reek,
All the extravagant riches spent and mean.
All burns! The reddest rose is a ghost;
Sparks whirl up, to expire in the mist: the wild
Fingers of fire are making corruption clean.

Now is the time for stripping the spirit bare,
Time for the burning of days ended and done,
Idle solace of things that have gone before:
Rootless hope and fruitless desire are there;
Let them go to the fire, with never a look behind.
The world that was ours is a world that is ours no more.

They will come again, the leaf and the flower, to arise
From squalor of rottenness into the old splendour,
And magical scents to a wondering memory bring;
The same glory, to shine upon different eyes.
Earth cares for her own ruins, naught for ours.
Nothing is certain, only the certain spring.

18 September ✶ Everything is Going to Be All Right ✶ Derek Mahon

23 November 1941 – 1 October 2020

The Irish poet Derek Mahon won a scholarship to study French at Trinity College Dublin, where he wrote poems and met future poets Michael Longley and Eavan Boland. While teaching at a school in Belfast in the late 1960s, Mahon published his first poetry collection, and he continued to write prolifically for the next fifty years. Often compared to W. H. Auden, Gerard Manley Hopkins and Louis MacNeice, Mahon wrote with a certain formality in an age of free verse, on Ireland, art and nature. He found the latter to be an inexhaustible source of replenishment and optimism – as seen in this poem.

How should I not be glad to contemplate
the clouds clearing beyond the dormer window
and a high tide reflected on the ceiling?
There will be dying, there will be dying,
but there is no need to go into that.
The poems flow from the hand unbidden
and the hidden source is the watchful heart;
The sun rises in spite of everything
and the far cities are beautiful and bright.
I lie here in a riot of sunlight
watching the day break and the clouds flying.
Everything is going to be all right.

19 September ✶ Rhapsody ✶ William Stanley Braithwaite

6 December 1878 – 8 June 1962

William Stanley Braithwaite was born into an affluent family, but when his father died, Braithwaite had to leave school and find work. Luckily for him, he was employed at a publisher in Boston, Massachusetts, which instilled in him a love of both reading and writing poetry. He published his first book at the age of twenty-six, and swiftly became a leading literary figure through his work as a critic, editor and anthologist of an annual collection of 'magazine verse', in which he sourced the best, and often unheralded, poems in print circulation. Although the anthologies made little money, they did help shape the landscape of American poetry, not least in the way they promoted the poets of the Harlem Renaissance in the 1920s. Somehow he found the time to father seven children, including his daughters Fiona Lydia Rossetti and Katherine Keats, named after his literary heroes.

I am glad daylong for the gift of song,
  For time and change and sorrow;
For the sunset wings and the world-end things
  Which hang on the edge of to-morrow.
I am glad for my heart whose gates apart
  Are the entrance-place of wonders,
Where dreams come in from the rush and din
  Like sheep from the rains and thunders.

20 September ✶ The Guest House ✶ Rumi, translated by Coleman Barks

30 September 1207 – 17 December 1273

The thirteenth-century poet Jalaluddin Rumi (popularly known simply as Rumi) is undoubtedly the most revered Persian and Muslim poet in history, whose enduring resonance and universality has seen him become one of the bestselling poets in the US today. A proponent of Sufism – a branch of Islam rooted in mysticism – Rumi's poetry is filled with guidance on how to live a spiritual, meditative, loving and fulfilling life to the extent that his six-volume poem of 27,000 lines called *Masnavi* has been dubbed 'the Quran in Persian'. Such was his impact that a religious order devoted to his teaching was established after his death and continued for many centuries. That said, the real appeal of Rumi is his ability to impart wisdom and shed light on human experiences beyond the specifics of Islam. As the renowned Rumi translator Shahram Shiva brilliantly explained: 'He does not offend anyone, and he includes everyone . . . [his poems] can be heard in churches, synagogues, Zen monasteries, as well as in the downtown New York art/performance/music scene.' This poem, for instance, can certainly be read as a reminder that even life's hardships should be embraced because they can, unbeknownst to us, lead us into new pleasures.

This being human is a guest house.
Every morning a new arrival.

A joy, a depression, a meanness,
some momentary awareness comes
as an unexpected visitor.

Welcome and entertain them all!
Even if they're a crowd of sorrows,
who violently sweep your house

empty of its furniture,
still, treat each guest honorably.
He may be clearing you out
for some new delight.

The dark thought, the shame, the malice,
meet them at the door laughing,
and invite them in.

Be grateful for whoever comes,
because each has been sent
as a guide from beyond.

21 September ✶ On the Departure of the Nightingale ✶ Charlotte Smith

4 May 1749 – 28 October 1806

Charlotte Turner Smith was an early Romantic poet, novelist and translator who managed to cultivate a fruitful writing career alongside a very trying life. After her father gambled his fortune away, Charlotte was married, aged fifteen, to Benjamin Smith, the son of a merchant and plantation owner, though this turned out to be a marriage of extreme inconvenience, as Smith also ended up in all kinds of financial problems that landed him and his wife in debtors' prison. But it was here that Charlotte Smith wrote and published her first collection of sonnets, receiving enough income to pay their way out of prison. Charlotte would continue to use writing as a means of providing for her family (of nine children) after leaving her husband. Her work is seen as instrumental in revitalizing the sonnet form, and was admired by the likes of Wordsworth and Coleridge.

Sweet poet of the woods, a long adieu!
  Farewell soft minstrel of the early year!
Ah! 'twill be long ere thou shalt sing anew,
  And pour thy music on the night's dull ear.
Whether on spring thy wandering flights await,
  Or whether silent in our groves you dwell,
The pensive muse shall own thee for her mate,
  And still protect the song she loves so well.
With cautious step the love-lorn youth shall glide
  Through the lone brake that shades thy mossy nest;
And shepherd girls from eyes profane shall hide
  The gentle bird who sings of pity best:
For still thy voice shall soft affections move,
  And still be dear to sorrow and to love!

22 September ✶ Chrysanthemum ✶ Robin Hyde

19 January 1906 – 23 August 1939

The New Zealand writer Iris Guiver Wilkinson, better known by her pseudonym Robin Hyde, had a short, but eventful life. At eighteen she suffered a knee injury, which slowed her down physically, but not professionally. A year later she became a journalist and by the end of the decade she was a columnist for a number of publications. Despite being commissioned to write for the society pages, Hyde managed to deliver some hard-hitting journalism on poverty alongside 'who wore what'-style pieces. Later she set sail to England, only to wind up caught in the Sino-Japanese War en route. Unfazed, she headed to the front line to write about the events unfolding in China before being caught by the authorities and sent to England, where she spent her final years working for pacifist groups in the run-up to the Second World War.

See that dishevelled head,
Its bronze curls all undone?
I am that one,
The stubborn slattern of your garden bed;
No sweetness for you here, but bittersweet
Admission that my hour must needs be fleet;
A frosty tang of wit, an autumn face,
Perchance the memory of some sharper grace,
That shone beneath the imperial yellow tiles
Nor needed stoop for princely sulks or smiles;
Tatterdemalion courage here, a ghost
To captain some obscure, defeated host . . .
Many the springtime maidens, crisp as snow . . .
Yet hapless sir, we know
Your fate . . . to lose me most

23 September ✶ There Was a Little Girl ✶ Henry Wadsworth Longfellow

27 February 1807 – 24 March 1882

Like Florence Earle Coates and Robert Lowell, Henry Wadsworth Longfellow was a descendant of the first group of English settlers who came to America on the *Mayflower*. That Longfellow would reach the very top of his profession was no surprise, given that he was already publishing poems in the local Massachusetts paper at the age of thirteen, and was offered a professorship by the age of eighteen. Eventually he became a professor at Harvard, where he taught the main Romance languages – which he'd mastered while travelling around Europe – as well as studying Dutch, Danish, Swedish, German, Finnish and Icelandic. Longfellow is first and foremost regarded as a seminal American poet, and a versatile one too – as capable of writing stirring epics as amusing verses for children such as this one.

There was a little girl,
        Who had a little curl,
Right in the middle of her forehead.
        When she was good,
        She was very good indeed,
But when she was bad she was horrid.

24 September ✶ The Art of Biography ✶ Edmund Clerihew Bentley

10 July 1875 – 30 March 1956

We all know the feeling of sitting bored and distracted at the back of a classroom, passing the time by doodling or exchanging notes with a friend. But it's safe to say that none of us created a whole new poetic form that would still be used over a century later. That's exactly what the future poet, humorist, detective novelist and *Telegraph* journalist Edmund Clerihew Bentley did during a particularly dull chemistry lesson at St Paul's School. Named after its creator, the clerihew is an amusing four-line poem that usually names a famous subject in the first line and tries to offer some biographical detail about them using innovative rhymes in the next three, although this one is about biography more generally.

The Art of Biography
Is different from Geography.
Geography is about Maps,
But Biography is about Chaps.

25 September ✶ Celia Celia ✶ Adrian Mitchell

24 October 1932 – 20 December 2008

Another funny four-liner comes to us via Adrian Mitchell – a poet, novelist and dramatist. His career in writing began as a freelance arts critic for a number of national titles. He was the first person to print an interview with the Beatles. As a playwright he wrote *Tyger* about the life of William Blake which was staged at the National Theatre and he adapted *The Lion, the Witch and the Wardrobe* for the Royal Shakespeare Company. Much of his writing was defined by strong, sometimes radical, left-wing views, and he was known to give passionate performances and readings at anti-war rallies – he became a pacifist after a period of national service in the RAF. That said, many of his poems reveal a pure zeal for life itself, and there are many witty pieces to be found amidst his collections for both adults and children.

When I am sad and weary
When I think all hope has gone
When I walk along High Holborn
I think of you with nothing on

26 September ✶ The Dog Who Bit the Ball ✶ Pam Ayres

Born 1947

Continuing our run of light-hearted poems is this piece by Pam Ayres, who has been one of the UK's most beloved poets since she won the TV talent show *Opportunity Knocks* in 1975. Ayres never looked back following that breakthrough moment, publishing many books of bestselling poetry, performing for the Queen, and appearing on countless radio and TV programmes. Her writing is simple, accessible and invariably funny, but it is also thought-provoking and illuminating in the way that it gives a new perspective on everyday observations.

I am the dog who bit the ball,
And ruined the game of goals.
I wasn't to know, that balls don't go,
If you've added a couple of holes.
The kids and dad, they all went mad,
They sent me indoors, they did,
The ball was new, a beautiful blue,
And it cost them several quid.

The shame, the shame, I ruined the game.
And made the family crabby,
I jumped for it, I shook it a bit,
And it went from hard to flabby,
'Bad dog!' they said, 'Go in your bed!'
And in disgrace I go,
I offered a paw, but nobody saw,
Nobody wanted to know.

Here comes the boss, she's ever so cross,
Her face is black as thunder,
I'm in my bed, expression of dread,
My tail ducked down and under,
With hands on hips and scold on lips,
She tells me I'm a *menace*,
I'm finding it tough, this football stuff,
Anyone care for tennis?

The rule, you see, for dogs like me,
Is simple, I'll recite it:
Don't kick a ball for terriers small,
And think that they won't bite it.
I'm not too grand to lick her hand,
I sidle up and risk it . . .
I think I've won . . . look, everyone!
She's gone to get a biscuit!

27 September ✶ Waltzing Matilda ✶ Banjo Paterson

17 February 1864 – 5 February 1941

Andrew Barton Paterson, better known as Banjo Paterson (a pen name he took from his favourite horse), was voted the Greatest Australian of all time in a national newspaper poll conducted in 2013. Growing up in the outback between Sydney and Melbourne, Paterson developed a rich mental storehouse of experiences of living in rustic, rural Australia, which he would then use to create his hugely popular, almost mythological folk stories and ballads about bush life. This song, 'Waltzing Matilda', about a nomadic traveller, for which Paterson wrote the lyrics, has been adopted as Australia's unofficial national anthem, and has been covered by at least 500 different recording artists.

Oh! there once was a swagman camped in the Billabong,
  Under the shade of a Coolabah tree;
And he sang as he looked at his old billy boiling
  'Who'll come a-waltzing Matilda with me.'

Who'll come a-waltzing Matilda, my darling,
  Who'll come a-waltzing Matilda with me?
Waltzing Matilda and leading a water-bag –
  Who'll come a-waltzing Matilda with me?

Down came a jumbuck to drink at the water-hole,
  Up jumped the swagman and grabbed him in glee;
And he sang as he put him away in his tucker-bag,
  'You'll come a-waltzing Matilda with me!'

Down came the Squatter a-riding his thoroughbred;
  Down came Policemen – one, two, and three.
'Whose is the jumbuck you've got in the tucker-bag?
  You'll come a-waltzing Matilda with me.'

But the swagman, he up and he jumped in the water-hole,
  Drowning himself by the Coolabah tree;
And his ghost may be heard as it sings in the Billabong,
  'Who'll come a-waltzing Matilda with me?'

28 September ✶ The Lion and Albert ✶ Marriott Edgar

5 October 1880 – 5 May 1951

George Marriott Edgar, known professionally without his first name, was an actor, comedian, script writer and poet who hailed from an old established theatrical family. Following on in his ancestors' footsteps, or rather heels, Edgar first rose to prominence playing pantomime dames, and toured his act around the globe. In 1929 he had a career-defining meeting with the famous comic actor Stanley Holloway, with whom he went to Hollywood and worked as a monologue writer. One such was this funny narrative poem, which was performed by Holloway with words and music composed by Edgar. Despite his success around the world, Edgar filled his poem with Lancastrian allusions that hark back to his family's roots.

There's a famous seaside place called Blackpool,
That's noted for fresh air and fun,
And Mr and Mrs Ramsbottom
Went there with young Albert, their son.

A grand little lad was young Albert,
All dressed in his best; quite a swell
With a stick with an 'orse's 'ead 'andle
The finest that Woolworth's could sell.

They didn't think much to the Ocean:
The waves, they was fiddlin' and small,
There was no wrecks and nobody drownded,
Fact, nothing to laugh at at all.

So, seeking for further amusement,
They paid and went into the zoo,
Where they'd Lions and Tigers and Camels,
And old ale and sandwiches too.

There were one great big Lion called Wallace;
His nose were all covered with scars —
He lay in a somnolent posture,
With the side of his face on the bars.

Now Albert had heard about Lions,
How they was ferocious and wild —
To see Wallace lying so peaceful,
Well, it didn't seem right to the child.

So straightway the brave little feller,
Not showing a morsel of fear,
Took his stick with its 'orse's 'ead 'andle
And shoved it in Wallace's ear.

You could see that the lion didn't like it,
For giving a kind of a roll,
He pulled Albert inside the cage with 'im,
And swallowed the little lad 'ole.

Then Pa, who had seen the occurrence,
And didn't know what to do next.
Said, 'Mother! Yon lions 'et Albert,'
And Mother said, 'Well, I am vexed!'

Then Mr and Mrs Ramsbottom —
Quite rightly, when all's said and done —
Complained to the Animal Keeper,
That the lion had eaten their son.

The keeper was quite nice about it;
He said, 'What a nasty mishap.
Are you sure that it's your boy he's eaten?'
Pa said,'Am I sure? There's his cap!'

The manager had to be sent for.
He came and he said, 'What's to do?'
Pa said, 'Yon lion's 'et Albert,
And 'im in his Sunday clothes, too.'

Then Mother said, 'Right's right, young feller;
I think it's a shame and a sin,
For a lion to go and eat Albert,
And after we've paid to come in.'

The manager wanted no trouble,
He took out his purse right away,
Saying, 'How much to settle the matter?'
And Pa said, 'What do you usually pay?'

But Mother had turned a bit awkward
When she thought where her Albert had gone.
She said, 'No! someone's got to be summonsed!' —
So that was decided upon.

Then off they went to the P'lice Station,
In front of the Magistrate chap;
They told 'im what happened to Albert,
And proved it by showing his cap.

The Magistrate gave his opinion
That no one was really to blame
And he said that he hoped the Ramsbottoms
Would have further sons to their name.

At that Mother got proper blazing,
'And thank you, sir, kindly,' said she.
'What, waste all our lives raising children
To feed ruddy lions? Not me!'

29 September ✶ *from* Beth Gêlert ✶ William Robert Spencer

9 January 1770 – 22/23 October 1834

William Robert Spencer was, as the name suggests, part of the aristocratic Spencer family to which Winston Churchill and Princess Diana also belonged. A professional wit, Spencer won the admiration and favour of many literary and political figures of his day, including Byron, Walter Scott and the Prince of Wales. He served as an MP for a short period before resigning his seat to take on the rather less exciting-sounding position of Commissioner of Stamps in order to better provide for his family of seven children. As a poet he is best known for his ballad 'Beth Gêlert' (from which this is an extract), a re-telling of a Welsh legend about a faithful dog, wrongly believed to be a killer by his owner.

The spearmen heard the bugle sound,
   And cheerily smil'd the morn;
And many a brach, and many a hound,
   Obey'd Llewelyn's horn.

And still he blew a louder blast,
   And gave a lustier cheer;
'Come, Gêlert, come, wer't never last
   Llewelyn's horn to hear.—

'Oh where does faithful Gêlert roam,
   The flower of all his race;
So true, so brave, a lamb at home,
   A lion in the chase?'

'Twas only at Llewelyn's board
   The faithful Gêlert fed;
He watch'd, he serv'd, he cheer'd his Lord,
   And sentinel'd his bed.

In sooth he was a peerless hound,
  The gift of royal John;
But, now no Gêlert could be found,
  And all the chase rode on.

And now, as o'er the rocks and dells
  The gallant chidings rise,
All Snowdon's craggy chaos yells
  The many-mingled cries!

That day Llewelyn little lov'd
  The chase of hart and hare;
And scant and small the booty proved,
  For Gêlert was not there.

Unpleas'd Llewelyn homeward hied,
  When near the portal-seat,
His truant Gêlert he espied,
  Bounding his lord to greet.

But, when he gain'd his castle-door,
  Aghast the chieftain stood;
The hound all o'er was smear'd with gore,
  His lips, his fangs, ran blood.

Llewelyn gaz'd with fierce surprise;
  Unused such looks to meet,
His favourite check'd his joyful guise,
  And crouch'd, and lick'd his feet.

Onward, in haste, Llewelyn pass'd,
  And on went Gêlert too;
And still, where'er his eyes he cast,
  Fresh blood-gouts shock'd his view.

O'erturn'd his infant's bed he found,
With blood-stain'd covert rent;
And all around the walls and ground
With recent blood besprent.

He call'd his child—no voice replied—
He search'd with terror wild;
Blood, blood he found on every side,
But nowhere found his child.

'Hell-hound! my child's by thee devour'd,'
The frantic father cried;
And to the hilt his vengeful sword
He plung'd in Gêlert's side.

His suppliant looks, as prone he fell,
No pity could impart;
But still his Gêlert's dying yell
Passed heavy o'er his heart.

Arous'd by Gêlert's dying yell,
Some slumb'rer wakened nigh:—
What words the parent's joy could tell
To hear his infant's cry!

Conceal'd beneath a tumbled heap
His hurried search had miss'd,
All glowing from his rosy sleep,
The cherub boy he kiss'd.

Nor scath had he, nor harm, nor dread,
But, the same couch beneath,
Lay a gaunt wolf, all torn and dead,
Tremendous still in death.

Ah, what was then Llewelyn's pain!
   For now the truth was clear;
His gallant hound the wolf had slain
   To save Llewelyn's heir.

Vain, vain was all Llewelyn's woe:
   'Best of thy kind, adieu!
The frantic blow, which laid thee low,
   This heart shall ever rue.'

And now a gallant tomb they raise,
   With costly sculpture deck'd;
And marbles storied with his praise
   Poor Gêlert's bones protect.

There never could the spearman pass,
   Or forester, unmoved;
There, oft the tear-besprinkled grass
   Llewelyn's sorrow proved.

And there he hung his horn and spear,
   And there, as evening fell,
In fancy's ear he oft would hear
   Poor Gêlert's dying yell.

And, till great Snowdon's rocks grow old,
   And cease the storm to brave,
The consecrated spot shall hold
   The name of 'Gêlert's Grave'.

30 September ✶ *from* The Epic of Gilgamesh ✶ Anon.

The Epic of Gilgamesh is widely considered to be the oldest existing extended piece of literature, thought to have originated at some point in the third millennium BC and written on tablets in the second millennium BC. Or, put it another way, it's at least 1,500 years older than Homer's *Iliad* – often cited as one of the earliest literary texts. The Gilgamesh tale is thought to have emerged in Sumerian poems (see Enheduanna on 5 February), before being collated on tablets as a single narrative – fragments of which were unearthed in 1849 in modern-day Iraq by a real-life Indiana Jones, the English archaeologist Austen Henry Layard, who was looking for evidence to corroborate events in the Bible. The story told by these great unknown poets is a mythological account of a deified, but actual historical king, of the state of Uruk in Mesopotamia, on a quest to discover the meaning of life and how to gain immortality after the death of a friend.

At the very first glimmer of brightening dawn,
there rose from the horizon a dark cloud of black,
and bellowing within it was Adad the Storm God.
The gods Shullat and Hanish were going before him,
bearing his throne over mountain and land.

The god Errakal was uprooting the mooring-poles,
Ninurta, passing by, made the weirs overflow.
The Anunnaki gods carried torches of fire,
scorching the country with brilliant flashes.

The stillness of the Storm God passed over the sky,
and all that was bright then turned into darkness.
[He] charged the land like a *bull* [*on the rampage,*]
he smashed [it] in pieces [*like a vessel of clay.*] . . .

Even the gods took fright at the Deluge,
they left and went up to the heaven of Anu,
lying like dogs curled up in the open.
The goddess cried out like a woman in childbirth.

October

1 October ✶ Epilogue ✶ Grace Nichols

Born 1950

October is Black History Month in the UK. It's a period in which we remember and continue to champion the struggle for equality undertaken by leading civil rights figures in the UK and overseas, and celebrate Black arts, culture and heritage. This poem by Grace Nichols starts a week-long run of poems by some of the very best Black British and Black American poets. Grace Nichols is a Caribbean-British writer, born and educated in Guyana, before she moved to the UK in 1977 with her husband, the poet John Agard (see 1 July). Her poetry has been influenced by the oral storytelling traditions of her homeland, and she writes for both children and adults on issues including migration and assimilation, as seen in this short, reflective poem.

I have crossed an ocean
I have lost my tongue
from the root of the old one
a new one has sprung.

2 October ✶ The Benin Bronze ✶ George the Poet

Born 1991

George Mpanga, better known as George the Poet, is one of the leading young British spoken word artists who seamlessly blend music (he was also shortlisted for a BRIT award), literary expression and incisive social commentary. He grew up in North London in a Ugandan family and attended Cambridge University, where he pivoted away from grime and rap towards poetry; he cites a range of eclectic influences, from rapper Tupac Shakur to Maya Angelou. In 2019, he rejected an MBE in protest against Britain's colonial past.

I used to Live on the wall of a palace
Till I was torn off in malice
The figure adorned in the attire of a king
Headed the great African empire of Benin.
Two of his officials are either side of him; he's
Standing and they're kneeling right beside the king.
He's depicted in the centre as bigger () than
Everybody cos he was an emperor figure.

He ruled much of what is now southern Nigeria but his
Power can be gauged by other criteria. For ex-
Ample: the "Oba", as he was called hosted
European subjects who were utterly enthralled by the
Organisation of Benin society –
No inner-rivalry or impropriety.
He controlled trade from the upper echelons right
Back down to the village – thus monopolising se-
curity and favours. The smaller figures in the
Background of the image are European traders. I re-
Member these guys, they were Portuguese, al-
Ways caught disease in the scorching heat but they were
Guided through the King's court with ease to negotiate the

Purchase of pepper, gold and Ivory.
Oba was happy to export these commodities but
As for me, I was never told that I could leave.
The Europeans knew I wasn't for sale. Yet
Every time they visited they kept an open eye for me.
Over the sixteenth and seventeenth centuries the
Kings continued to trade pepper, gold and Ivory.
And other goods exclusive to our soil.
Most commonly: rubber and palm oil.

Since our exports were much distinguished they at-
Tracted business from the Dutch and English whose
Ships gave a direct link to Western markets,
We were the only suppliers – the rest departed
Leaving our king to monopolise trade in the area . . .
Which gave him warier outlook on the Western
Visitors who used some Africans as partners . . .
The rest as prisoners.

Anyway, back to me. Oba and his
officials are in the foreground, as you can see, to con-
Vey their dominance of the relationship; they were
Commonly accommodating trading ships that were
Often laden with brass from European nations be-
Fore all the invasions. The
People of Benin made art with the brass. And
All of the images charted the past.
Every single scene covers
Kings and queen mothers . . .
I was on the
Palace wall of the man that balanced all of the land.

By the late 19th century the Oba suspected Britain's
Only ambition was colonialism, and even
Though he'd envisioned a continuation of this har-
Monious system, he figured "if I sever ties then we

Won't be imprisoned." So in
1896 when he ended their trade agreement
The British decided to invade the region. They re-
Quested a meeting with the trade officials, but ar-
Rived in Benin concealing blades and pistols.
Only two Brits survived; the
Rest were slain as soon as their ships arrived.
And even though it was a well-deserved victory,
It wasn't long before we felt the burn, literally.
The British response was a thousand marines.
All I remember was the sounds of the screams as they
Raided our cities, raped and pillaged the in-
Digenous people of the ancient village. I
Can't erase the image. They circled around as our
Civilisation was burned to the ground.
And what was once the royal decor . . .
Had now become the spoils of war

3 October ✶ Songs for the People ✶
Frances Ellen Watkins Harper

24 September 1825 – 22 February 1911

Frances Ellen Watkins Harper was an abolitionist and suffragist, and one of the first Black American women to have her literary work published. Orphaned at the age of three, she was raised in Baltimore by her uncle, an educator and civil rights campaigner who helped shape Watkins Harper's own activism in later years. As a teenager she worked in a bookshop, where she fell in love with reading and began writing her own poetry. Her first collection came out when she was just twenty years old, and set her on a path to become one of the century's most successful writers, and a leading, stirring voice in the anti-slavery movement. Not only did she further the cause through her writing, but Watkins Harper also helped fleeing slaves travel through the celebrated Underground Railroad, a network of secret routes and safe houses, and refused to give up her seat on a segregated tram some hundred years before Rosa Parks. In 1896 she co-founded the National Association of Colored Women, which still exists to this day.

Let me make the songs for the people,
  Songs for the old and young;
Songs to stir like a battle-cry
  Wherever they are sung.

Not for the clashing of sabres,
  For carnage nor for strife;
But songs to thrill the hearts of men
  With more abundant life.

Let me make the songs for the weary,
  Amid life's fever and fret,
Till hearts shall relax their tension,
  And careworn brows forget.

Let me sing for little children,
  Before their footsteps stray,
Sweet anthems of love and duty,
  To float o'er life's highway.

I would sing for the poor and aged,
  When shadows dim their sight;
Of the bright and restful mansions,
  Where there shall be no night.

Our world, so worn and weary,
  Needs music, pure and strong,
To hush the jangle and discords
  Of sorrow, pain, and wrong.

Music to soothe all its sorrow,
  Till war and crime shall cease;
And the hearts of men grown tender
  Girdle the world with peace.

4 October ✶ 'I've learned to sing a song of hope' ✶ Georgia Douglas Johnson

10 September 1880 – 15 May 1966

Georgia Douglas Johnson was a poet and playwright who picked up the mantle left by Frances Ellen Watkins Harper in becoming the next prominent Black female voice in American literature. Born and raised in Atlanta, she spent most of her adult life in Washington DC, where she became a kind of ambassador for the New York-based Harlem Renaissance. After her husband died, Douglas Johnson turned her house into a salon where the leading Black artists of her day – including Langston Hughes and Alice Dunbar-Nelson – came to discuss, debate and develop their intellectual theories, creative ideas and political opinions. As a writer herself, Douglas Johnson wrote a nationally syndicated newspaper column, twenty-eight plays and some two hundred poems.

I've learned to sing a song of hope,
I've said goodbye to despair,
I caught the note in a thrush's throat,
I sang – and the world was fair!
I've learned to sing a song of joy
It bends the skies to me,
The song of joy is the song of hope
Grown to maturity.

I've learned to laugh away my tears
As through the dark I go,
For love and laughter conquer fears
My heart has come to know.

I've learned a song of happiness
It is a song of love,
For love alone is happiness
And happiness is love.

5 October ✶ Le sporting-club de Monte Carlo (for Lena Horne) ✶ James Baldwin

2 August 1924 – 1 December 1987

The writer and activist James Baldwin was born in New York during the Harlem Renaissance period. He grew up with nine siblings in the custody of a strict stepfather. The young Baldwin would flee for the sanctuary of the library. After a period of living in Greenwich Village with a budding actor called Marlon Brando, Baldwin moved to Paris to escape the stifling racial segregation in the US. Of his move he said: 'I could see that I carried myself, which is my home, with me. You can never escape that. I am the grandson of a slave, and I am a writer. I must deal with both.' Baldwin wrote many essays on identity and race, and became a hugely important figure within the civil rights movement. Beyond his non-fiction works, he is celebrated for his novels such as *Go Tell It on the Mountain*, *Giovanni's Room* and *If Beale Street Could Talk*, and for his poems. This one is dedicated to the American singer and activist Lena Horne.

The lady is a tramp
    a camp
    a lamp

The lady is a sight
    a might
    a light
the lady devastated
an alley or two
reverberated through the valley
which leads to me, and you

the lady is the apple
of God's eye:
He's cool enough about it
but He tends to strut a little
when she passes by

the lady is a wonder
daughter of the thunder
smashing cages
legislating rages
with the voice of ages
singing us through.

6 October ✶ Don't Let Me Be Lonely [Mahalia Jackson is a genius] ✶ Claudia Rankine

Born 1963

Here is another poem dedicated to a legendary Black American musician – in this case the soul singer Mahalia Jackson, which comes to us via the acclaimed American poet and playwright Claudia Rankine. Born in Kingston, Jamaica, she has become one of the most urgent and respected voices in contemporary American literature as the editor of several anthologies, and the writer of two plays and five collections of poetry. Her most famous is the award-winning book-length poem *Citizen: An American Lyric* from 2014. A convention-defying, genre-resisting piece of poetry that offers an insight into Black life in America, it became the first text to be nominated in both poetry and criticism categories by the National Critics Circle Awards. Rankine is also a professor of poetry at Yale University. This poem is a perfect illustration of how Rankine subverts received poetic forms in her writing.

Mahalia Jackson is a genius. Or Mahalia Jackson has genius. The man I am with is trying to make a distinction. I am uncomfortable with his need to make this distinction because his inquiry begins to approach subtle shades of racism, classism, or sexism. It is hard to know which. Mahalia Jackson never finished the eighth grade, or Mahalia's genius is based on the collision of her voice with her spirituality. True spirituality is its own force. I am not sure how to respond to all this. I change the subject instead.

We have just seen George Wein's documentary, *Louis Armstrong at Newport, 1971*. In the auditorium a room full of strangers listened to Mahalia Jackson sing 'Let There Be Peace on Earth' and stood up and gave a standing ovation to a movie screen. Her clarity of vision crosses thirty years to address intimately each of us. It is as if her voice has always been dormant within us, waiting to be awakened, even though 'it had to go through its own lack of answers, through terrifying silence, (and) through the thousand darknesses of murderous speech'.

Perhaps Mahalia, like Paul Celan, has already lived all our lives for us. Perhaps that is the definition of genius. Hegel says, 'Each man hopes and believes he is better than the world which is his, but the man who is better merely expresses this same world better than the others.' Mahalia Jackson sings as if it is the last thing she intends to do. And even though the lyrics of the song are, 'Let there be peace on earth and let it begin with me,' I am hearing, *Let it begin in me.*

7 October ✶ Autobiographia Literaria ✶ Frank O'Hara

27 March 1926 – 25 July 1966

Frank O'Hara might be described as the American Apollinaire. Like the French writer (see 8 September), O'Hara was also as influential in the world of art criticism as he was in literature, with a particular interest in surrealism, and sadly, like Apollinaire, he died at a young age. But O'Hara achieved so much in his forty short years. His expertise in art saw him become a curator of the Museum of Modern Art in New York, and together with John Ashbery, whom he met at Harvard, he was a central figure of the so-called New York School of creatives, who were inspired by avant-garde art movements. This poem is a play on the title of Coleridge's book *Biographia Literaria*, and likewise celebrates the privilege and joy of poetry.

When I was a child
I played by myself in a
corner of the schoolyard
all alone.

I hated dolls and I
hated games, animals were
not friendly and birds
flew away.

If anyone was looking
for me I hid behind a
tree and cried out 'I am
an orphan.'

And here I am, the
center of all beauty!
writing these poems!
Imagine!

8 October ✶ A Good Poem ✶ Roger McGough

Born 1937

Roger McGough is a Liverpool legend who, along with Adrian Henri and Brian Patten (see 28 May), wrote the bestselling anthology *The Mersey Sound* in 1967, which was seen to reinvigorate British poetry with its wit, warmth and accessibility. But in a parallel universe we may have been talking about Roger McGough the rock star, as in the mid-1960s he formed a group with Mike McCartney (yes, the brother of Paul) called The Scaffold, which scored a number one hit in 1968. Though he never did quite rival the Beatles, his illustrious literary career has seen him publish over fifty books of poetry for adults and children.

I like a good poem
one with lots of fighting
in it. Blood, and the
clanging of armour. Poems

against Scotland are good,
and poems that defeat
the French with crossbows.
I don't like poems that

aren't about anything.
Sonnets are wet and
a waste of time.
Also poems that don't

know how to rhyme.
If I was a poem
I'd play football and
get picked for England.

9 October ✶ Boots, Boots, Boots ✶ Leroy F. Jackson

15 July 1881 – 8 April 1958

Leroy F. Jackson was a Canadian-born American professor and researcher at a number of universities during the early twentieth century. His career was interrupted by the outbreak of the First World War, which saw Jackson go over to fight in Europe – but even within a military setting, he eventually found himself teaching again as part of the Army Educational Corps. Following the conflict, he became the director of an experimental progressive school, before taking up a position to help provide education for Native Americans. Outside of his important contributions to scholarship and education, Jackson wrote a number of books of playful children's nursery rhymes. This poem seems to allude to Rudyard Kipling's similarly titled 'Boots', which captures the drudgery of endless marching in the army. But for Jackson's narrator, 'boots' are almost a symbol of excitement and adventure.

Buster's got a popper gun,
A reg'lar one that shoots,
And Teddy's got an engine
With a whistler that toots.
But I've got something finer yet—
A pair of rubber boots.
Oh, it's boots, boots, boots,
A pair of rubber boots!
I could walk from here to China
In a pair of rubber boots.

10 October ✶ Shame Is the Cape I Wear ✶ Inua Ellams

Born 1984

Born in Nigeria but based in London, Inua Ellams is a poet, playwright and graphic artist who has performed all over the world in venues ranging from the Royal Opera House to the Glastonbury Festival. He has written a sell-out play for the National Theatre, as well as scripts for other stage and screen projects. Ellams's work has been lauded for its engagement with themes of 'identity, displacement and destiny' and for the way in which it incorporates elements of Nigerian storytelling. His poetry first appeared in pamphlet form in 2005, and a full collection, *The Actual*, was then published in 2020. Defined by his range, he is best characterized perhaps by a description of him as the 'love child of the rapper Mos Def and John Keats'.

after Maria Mazziotti Gillan

On the first day of holidays, my mother leaves a dark blue
wrapper on her bed, her polished boots in one corner, and
in no time I assemble a superhero costume to defend our
house against the plague of lizards: their spindly children,

tongues flicking, nodding under afternoon heat—they are
a reptilian evil. Every hero needs a nemesis. This cotton
cape casts me as Naija's Superman and they threaten life
in the Lagos metropolis. No matter the property you buy,

how tight-shut the gutters, how climb-proof the walls, also
how sharp their crown of barbwires, lizards come. Father,
who insists a clean well-swept backyard helps, is away and
the long-tailed legions are confidently swarming all about

the place, across air vents, up the garden's wire mesh too
thin to survive their claws. Anyway, I'm hovering by that
mesh, a rubber band stretched between my fingers, cape
flowing and a quiver of toothpick-thick bristles, one curled

against the taut elastic. I catch a lizard's beady steady eyes,
take aim, fire, and watch the bristle break through its back,
first piercing its soft stomach, and my aim just gets better.
An hour, and there are bodies piled. Above, a commotion of

flies, excitable over the stiffening flesh and blood, and I have
watched my shadow lengthen to cover the gray and redhead
corpses, the backyard a silent killing field, and I could almost
feel that flowing cape deflate. Sometimes I think that little

boy in his mother's work boots has followed me my whole life
through. There he is when I'm laughing at a party and find a
crimson drink spilled across the clean carpet or when I look
in a mirror to see what the years have done to me or when

I flick through news channels and catch a wartime president
speak of quick victories, of collateral damage and first-class
weapons, the locals broken behind soldiers and men in tweed
who will fabricate stories of jubilant cheers and fist pumps,

and shame is the cape I wear that day, shame and that little
boy, that shadow, is there his head hanging down as it did
then, his hands shaking.

11 October ✶ Masses ✶ César Vallejo, translated by Robert Bly

16 March 1892 – 15 April 1938

Born in a small village in Peru to parents of mixed Spanish and Quechua heritage, modernist poet César Vallejo was the youngest of eleven children. This meant that his family had limited means, and Vallejo had to work in a sugar plantation in his youth, before moving to Lima, where he studied at university and obtained a degree in Spanish literature. In the capital, Vallejo underwent an intellectual, political and creative awakening; he discovered the works of Marx and Darwin, met the intellectual avant-garde, and published his first poetry collection. In the 1920s Vallejo travelled to Paris and the Soviet Union, and later moved to Spain during the Civil War, where this poem is set, joining the Congress of Antifascist Writers in Madrid (along with Octavio Paz). While he was moderately successful during his lifetime, his wife published many of his works after his death, which gave him a posthumous reputation as a poetic master and innovator in the vein of his older contemporaries Rainer Maria Rilke and James Joyce.

When the battle was over,
And the fighter was dead, a man came toward him
And said to him: 'Do not die; I love you so!'
But the corpse, how sad! went on dying.

And two came near, and repeated it.
'Do not leave us! Courage! Return to life!'
But the corpse, how sad! went on dying.

Twenty arrived, a hundred, a thousand, five hundred thousand,
Shouting: 'So much love, and it can do nothing against death!'
But the corpse, how sad! went on dying.

Millions of persons stood around him,
All with the same request: 'Stay here, brother!'
But the corpse, how sad! Went on dying.

Then all the men on the earth
Stood around him; the corpse looked at them sadly, deeply moved;
He sat up slowly,
Put his arms around the first man; started to walk . . .

12 October ✶ Do Not Go Gentle into that Good Night ✶ Dylan Thomas

27 October 1914 – 9 November 1953

Undoubtedly the most famous Welsh poet, Dylan Thomas wrote all of his poetry in English, was not bilingual, and actively renounced the idea of Welsh nationalism. And yet underlying most of his work is a profound sense of place and heritage. As his first biographer put it, 'No major English poet has ever been as Welsh as Dylan.' Thomas was born in Swansea, and was an unremarkable student, but he did however show a keen literary mind, and wrote the majority of his most famous poems in his adolescence. Moving to London to pursue a writing career, Thomas was quickly discovered by leading names such as T. S. Eliot, and soon enough became a star in his own right. After the Second World War, Thomas began supplementing his earnings through scriptwriting and radio commissions for the BBC – including the acclaimed radio drama *Under Milk Wood*.

Do not go gentle into that good night,
Old age should burn and rave at close of day;
Rage, rage against the dying of the light.

Though wise men at their end know dark is right,
Because their words had forked no lightning they
Do not go gentle into that good night.

Good men, the last wave by, crying how bright
Their frail deeds might have danced in a green bay,
Rage, rage against the dying of the light.

Wild men who caught and sang the sun in flight,
And learn, too late, they grieved it on its way,
Do not go gentle into that good night.

Grave men, near death, who see with blinding sight
Blind eyes could blaze like meteors and be gay,
Rage, rage against the dying of the light.

And you, my father, there on the sad height,
Curse, bless, me now with your fierce tears, I pray.
Do not go gentle into that good night.
Rage, rage against the dying of the light.

13 October ✶ *from* Piers Plowman ✶ William Langland

c. 1332 – c. 1386

Very little is known about the medieval writer William Langland, the mysterious poet generally accepted to have been the writer of the fourteenth-century narrative poem *Piers Plowman,* a text considered one of the most important in the canon of English literature. The story follows a narrator called Will who falls asleep in a valley and wanders through various dream visions, filled with characters from medieval society and allegorical personifications such as Reason, Truth and Glutton. The depth of knowledge about Christian morals suggests that Langland might have been a member of the clergy. The fragmentary and incomplete manuscripts are some of the most impenetrable Middle English texts, but luckily we have modern translations that allow us to enjoy this weird and wonderful tale.

With all the woe in this world his wife and his maid
Brought him to his bed and bundled him in it.
And after all this excess he had a fit of sloth
So that he slept Saturday and Sunday till the sun set.
When he was awake and wiped his eyes,
The first word he spoke was, 'Where is the bowl?'
His spouse scolded him for his sin and wickedness,
And right so Repentance rebuked him at that time.
'As with words as well as with deeds you've done evil in your life,
Shrive yourself and be ashamed, and show it with your mouth.'
'I, Glutton,' he began, 'admit I'm guilty of this:
That I've trespassed with my tongue, I can't tell how often;
Sworn by God's soul and his sides "So God help me!"
Where there was no need for it nine hundred times.
And over-stuffed myself at supper and sometimes at midday,
So that I, Glutton, got rid of it before I'd gone a mile,

And spoiled what might have been saved and dispensed to the hungry;
Over-indulgently on feast days I've drunk and eaten both,
And sometimes sat so long there that I slept and ate at once;
To hear tales in taverns I've taken more drink;
Fed myself before noon on fasting days.'
'This full confession,' said Repentance, 'will gain favour for you.'

14 October ✶ *from* The Summoner's Tale ✶ Geoffrey Chaucer

c. 1340 – 25 October 1400

Geoffrey Chaucer has been called 'the father of English literature' – not only for his authorship of texts of timeless appeal, but also more literally for his use of the English language in his verse, at a time in which literary conventions dictated that texts should be written in French or Latin. Unlike William Langland, we have a lot more biographical information about Chaucer at our disposal. Born in London to an affluent family of winemakers, Chaucer embarked on a life in public service, and was personally acquainted with King Richard II and his predecessor, King Edward III, who, for reasons still unknown, granted Chaucer 'a gallon of wine daily for the rest of his life'. His work often took him travelling abroad, where he encountered work by such literary figures as Petrarch and Boccaccio, from which he would borrow certain plot devices and forms. His masterpiece, *The Canterbury Tales*, was written, unsurprisingly, when he was living in Kent in the 1380s. This collection follows a group of pilgrims from all walks of life who engage in a competition to tell the best story on their journey from London to visit Canterbury Cathedral.

'Lo here my faith, in me shall be no lack.'
  'Then put thine hand adown right by my back,'
Said this man, 'and grope well behind,
Beneath my buttock, there thou shalt find
A thing that I have hid in privity.'
  'Ah,' thought this friar, 'that shall go with me.'
And down his hand he launched to the cleft,
In hope for to find there a gift.
And when this sick man felt this friar
About his tail groping there and here,
Amid his hand he let the friar a fart;

There is no *capel* drawing in a cart, *horse*
That might have let a fart of such a sound.
The friar up start, as doth a wood lion: *fierce*
'Ah, false churl,' quoth he, 'for God's bones,
This hast thou in despite done *for the nonce*: *on purpose*
Thou shalt *abie* this fart, if that I may.' *suffer for*
His *meiny*, which that heard of this affray, *servants*
Came leaping in, and chased out the friar,
And forth he went with a full angry *cheer* *mood*
And fetch'd his fellow, there as lay his store:
He looked as it were a wild boar,
And ground with his teeth, so was he wroth.
A sturdy pace down to the court he go'th,
Where as there *wonn'd* a man of great honour, *dwelt*
To whom that he was always confessor:
This worthy man was lord of that village.
This friar came, as he were in a rage,
Where as this lord sat eating at his board:
Unnethes might the friar speak one word, *hardly*
Till at last he said, 'God you *see*.' *save*

15 October ✶ *from* Telling Tales Prologue (Grime Mix) ✶ Patience Agbabi

Born 1965

If ever we needed proof of the enduring appeal of Chaucer, we should look no further than *Telling Tales*, a book written over 600 years later. Patience Agbabi received an Arts Council grant to produce a poetry collection inspired by *The Canterbury Tales*, and the result offers an incredibly engaging modern-day interpretation of the classic medieval text. The piece, written to be performed, pays special attention to the oral tradition that shaped Chaucer's original, but is written in Agbabi's signature style, which fuses poetry with the rhythms and cadences of rap and hip hop. As she describes her poetic approach, 'The written must be spoken. The chasm between page and stage must be healed.'

see my jaw dropping neat Anglo-Saxon,
I got ink in my veins more than Caxton
and it flows hand to mouth, here's a mouthfeast,
verbal feats from the streets of the South-East
but my April, she blooms every shire's end,
fit or vint, rich or skint, she inspires them
from the grime to the clean-cut iambic,
rime royale, rant or rap, get your slam kick
on this Routemaster bus: get cerebral,
Tabard Inn to Canterbury Cathedral,
poet pilgrims competing for free picks,
Chaucer Tales, track by track, here's the remix
from below-the-belt base to the topnotch;
I won't stop all the clocks with a stopwatch
when the tales overrun, run offensive,
or run clean out of steam, they're authentic
cos we're keeping it real, reminisce this:
Chaucer Tales were an unfinished business.

16 October ✶ I Would Like to be a Dot in a Painting by Miró ✶ Moniza Alvi

Born 1954

Born in Lahore to a Pakistani father and British mother, Moniza Alvi moved with her family to Hertfordshire in England when she was just a few months old. Her poetry, which has won and been shortlisted for numerous awards, reflects on her experiences of being caught between two cultures and races. Her poems are often whimsical and entertaining, and sometimes feature surreal images and symbols. This poem is a personal tribute to the famous Spanish surrealist painter Joan Miró.

Barely distinguishable from other dots,
it's true, but quite uniquely placed.
And from my dark centre

I'd survey the beauty of the linescape
and wonder – would it be worthwhile
to roll myself towards the lemon stripe,

Centrally poised, and push my curves
against its edge, to give myself
a little attention?

But it's fine where I am.
I'll never make out what's going on
around me, and that's the joy of it.

The fact that I'm not a perfect circle
makes me more interesting in this world.
People will stare forever –

Even the most unemotional get excited.
So here I am, on the edge of animation,
a dream, a dance, a fantastic construction,

A child's adventure.
And nothing in this tawny sky
can get too close, or move too far away.

17 October ✶ A Brief History of Modern Art in Poetry ✶ Brian Bilston

Born 1970

Known as the 'Poet Laureate of Twitter', Brian Bilston has amassed a huge online following for his hilarious poems. He takes as his subjects everything from celebrities and pop culture, to current affairs and everyday objects, or in this case, the history of art, and dissects them with economical expression and incisive wit. A man of mystery, whose real identity has been kept under wraps, Bilston (a pseudonym), has been dubbed 'the Banksy of Poetry', a reference to the famously stealthy street artist.

1. Impressionism

Roses sway in softened reds
Violets swim in murky blues.
Sugar sparkles in the light.
Blurring into golden you.

2. Surrealism

Roses are melting
Violets are too.
Ceci n'est pas le sucre.
Keith is a giant crab.

3. Social Realism

Roses are dead.
Violence is rife.
Don't sugar coat
This bitter life.

4. Abstract Expressionism

5. Pop Art

Roses go BLAM!
Violets go POW!
Sugar is COOL!
You are so WOW!

6. Conceptual Art

Roses are red,
Coated in blood:
A deer's severed head
Drips from above.

18 October ✶ Puzzle ✶ Matt Goodfellow

Born 1980

The popular children's poet Matt Goodfellow dreamed of being a rock star before realizing he was handier with a pen and paper than a guitar. After working as a primary school teacher who wrote poetry on the side, Goodfellow eventually gained enough traction to become a full-time poet. He travels up and down the country visiting schools, where he brings poetry alive with readings from his books and organizing creative writing workshops.

we are
all
jigsaw pieces

before
we
are gone

we
must
find
a way

to
fit
together
as

one

19 October ✶ Against Idleness and Mischief ✶ Isaac Watts

17 July 1674 – 25 November 1748

Isaac Watts was a minister, theologian, philosopher, poet, and the author of about 750 hymns, many of which can be heard in churches around the world to this day. The son of a religious non-conformist, Watts grew up on the fringes of society, and had to attend the somewhat misleadingly named Dissenting Academy in the village of Stoke Newington (now part of North London) rather than attend the Anglican-run Oxford and Cambridge. He would spend the rest of his life in the area, working as a tutor and as a pastor of an independent London chapel, where he promoted education over religious tribalism. As an educator, his children's poetry veered towards the didactic – as most poetry for younger readers was in those days – and this poem implores kids to spend their days 'In Books, or Work, or healthful Play', which, books aside, doesn't sound like a whole lot of fun! The poem was famously parodied by Lewis Carroll in his poem beginning 'How doth the little crocodile . . .' in *Alice in Wonderland.*

How doth the little busy Bee
  Improve each shining Hour,
And gather Honey all the day
  From every opening Flower!

How skilfully she builds her Cell!
  How neat she spreads the Wax!
And labours hard to store it well
  With the sweet Food she makes.

In Works of Labour or of Skill
  I would be busy too:
For *Satan* finds some Mischief still
  For idle Hands to do.

In Books, or Work, or healthful Play
  Let my first Years be past,
That I may give for every Day
  Some good Account at last.

20 October ✶ The Flattered Flying Fish ✶ E. V. Rieu

10 February 1887 – 11 May 1972

E. V. Rieu was a celebrated translator and editor, and the man behind the Penguin Classics range, which has helped shape the literary canon since its creation in 1946. His translations of Homer and the four Gospels of the New Testament were particularly lauded, especially for the way in which they avoided literalness in favour of more natural, modern forms of expression that nevertheless preserved the meaning of the original. In his spare time, Rieu also wrote poetry for children, including this fun, nonsensical verse, which is anything but didactic!

Said the Shark to the Flying Fish over the phone:
'Will you join me tonight? I am dining alone.
Let me order a nice little dinner for two!
And come as you are, in your shimmering blue.'

Said the Flying Fish: 'Fancy remembering me,
And the dress that I wore at the Porpoises' Tea!'
'How could I forget?' said the Shark in his guile:
'I expect you at eight!' and rang off with a smile.

She has powdered her nose; she has put on her things;
She is off with one flap of her luminous wings.
O little one, lovely, light hearted and vain,
The Moon will not shine on your beauty again!

21 October ✶ City Jungle ✶ Pie Corbett

Born 1954

Pie Corbett is an educator and children's writer. He has devoted his career to improving literacy across the country and training teachers to inspire their pupils, even advising the Department of Education on their school policies. He is the creator and advocate of what's known as the 'Talk for Writing' approach of learning and teaching, which emphasizes the importance of speaking and listening in the process of learning to read and write; as he put it, 'A ten-year-old being able to spot the subjunctive will not improve children's reading and writing, let alone enrich their lives.' As a writer and editor of poetry collections, he has over 250 titles to his name.

Rain splinters town.
  Lizard cars cruise by;
their radiators grin.

Thin headlights stare –
  shop doorways keep
their mouths shut.

At the roadside
  hunched houses cough.

Newspapers shuffle by,
  hands in their pockets.
The gutter gargles.

A motorbike snarls;
  Dustbins flinch.

Streetlights bare
  their yellow teeth.

The motorway's
   cat-black tongue
lashes across
   the glistening back
of the tarmac night.

22 October ✶ Old Foxy ✶ Sue Hardy-Dawson

Born 1963

Sue Hardy-Dawson is a Yorkshire-born poet, artist and illustrator, who has been widely featured in children's poetry anthologies and has published solo collections filled with lyrical and innovative verse. Hardy-Dawson is dyslexic, and takes a special interest in encouraging reluctant readers and writers. This poem is reminiscent of the calligrams we discovered last month.

The
urban
fox waits for Monday night's
feast, of Sunday's roast chicken bones,
jellied and greased. Lunch in
the lamplight. Fish heads
with leeks, crisp
rinds of
bacon
and pizza
midweek.
Brave bin
buccaneer,
midnight's
dark thief, of
pittas with curry,
smoked ham or
corned beef. So
while the house
dozes and Heel-
Nipper sleeps, Old
Foxy hunts hedges
then craftily creeps
up on packed lunches,
down wild city streets,
for the cold fatty flavours
of half-eaten treats.
Then
with
sliced
mutton
sliver and
sausage for
sweet, slinks
back in the
shadows, to
his grand
country
seat.

23 October ✶ My Cats ✶ Charles Bukowski

16 August 1920 – 9 March 1994

The German-American Charles Bukowski is a writer of cult appeal and status both in the US and Europe, but whose transgressive and sometimes controversial writing has seen him largely overlooked by critics and anthologists. Dubbed the 'laureate of American lowlife' by *Time* magazine, his thousands of poems, short stories and novels reflect the urban, underground scene of his hometown of LA, and focus on regular people worn down by life. His most famous book, *The Post Office*, is an autobiographical novel about his years working in – you guessed it – a post office, and the tedium that came with it. He considered his readership to be, as he charmingly put it, 'the defeated, demented and the damned' – in other words the societal outsiders who may not have seen themselves represented in other types of 'highbrow' literature. This poem is the perfect representation of his crisp, unvarnished style – influenced by the likes of Ernest Hemingway and Li Bai – which blends absurdity, humour and a self-aware melancholy.

I know. I know.
they are limited, have different
needs and
concerns.

but I watch and learn from them.
I like the little they know,
which is so
much.

they complain but never
worry,
they walk with a surprising dignity.
they sleep with a direct simplicity that

humans just can't
understand.

their eyes are more
beautiful than our eyes.
and they can sleep 20 hours
a day
without
hesitation or
remorse.

when I am feeling
low
all I have to do is
watch my cats
and my
courage
returns.

I study these
creatures.

they are my
teachers.

24 October ✶ To Autumn ✶ John Keats

31 October 1795 – 23 February 1821

The boy-wonder of the late Romantic period, John Keats composed his entire literary output in just six years before his tragically early death from tuberculosis at twenty-five. We will never know what other masterpieces he would have gone on to write, but it is hard to imagine that the exquisite odes, sonnets and narrative epics that he left us could be surpassed. Keats initially pursued a career in medicine, working first at an apothecary's and then as an apprentice to a surgeon at Guy's Hospital. But despite the draw of a stable job, Keats – thankfully for us – decided to pursue poetry, and was given a platform to do so by Leigh Hunt and his *Examiner* magazine (see 12 May). In 1818, he moved to Hampstead, where he wrote the majority of his most celebrated poems, and became famously besotted with his neighbour, Fanny Brawne. But Keats's life was blighted by chronic illness, and he travelled to Rome, hoping the climate would aid his recovery. He died there a year later, his grave bearing the epitaph he wrote for himself: 'Here lies one whose name was writ in water' – assuming that he would be quickly forgotten. Instead, his legacy became that of one of the most revered writers in the history of English literature, whose reflections on love, nature, solitude and death would echo through the generations.

Season of mists and mellow fruitfulness,
  Close bosom-friend of the maturing sun;
Conspiring with him how to load and bless
  With fruit the vines that round the thatch-eves run;
To bend with apples the moss'd cottage-trees,
  And fill all fruit with ripeness to the core;
    To swell the gourd, and plump the hazel shells
  With a sweet kernel; to set budding more,
And still more, later flowers for the bees,
Until they think warm days will never cease,
    For summer has o'er-brimm'd their clammy cells.

Who hath not seen thee oft amid thy store?
Sometimes whoever seeks abroad may find
Thee sitting careless on a granary floor,
Thy hair soft-lifted by the winnowing wind;
Or on a half-reap'd furrow sound asleep,
Drows'd with the fume of poppies, while thy hook
Spares the next swath and all its twined flowers:
And sometimes like a gleaner thou dost keep
Steady thy laden head across a brook;
Or by a cyder-press, with patient look,
Thou watchest the last oozings hours by hours.

Where are the songs of spring? Ay, Where are they?
Think not of them, thou hast thy music too,—
While barred clouds bloom the soft-dying day,
And touch the stubble-plains with rosy hue;
Then in a wailful choir the small gnats mourn
Among the river sallows, borne aloft
Or sinking as the light wind lives or dies;
And full-grown lambs loud bleat from hilly bourn;
Hedge-crickets sing; and now with treble soft
The red-breast whistles from a garden-croft;
And gathering swallows twitter in the skies.

25 October ✶ The Charge of the Light Brigade ✶ Alfred, Lord Tennyson

6 August 1809 – 6 October 1892

Alfred, Lord Tennyson was the longest ever serving Poet Laureate, his post spanning forty-two years during the reign of Queen Victoria. The fourth son of twelve children (one of whom, Charles, we've already met: see 13 March), his career did not get off to a good start as his first two collections were critically derided. It would prove to be third time lucky, as in 1842 he published a new double-volume collection that became an instant hit. Some claimed that his later poetry, as Laureate, suffered from the role's demands to write stately, propagandist verse, but this poem about a valiant but disastrous action during the Battle of Balaclava on 25 October 1854, by British soldiers against the Russians in the Crimean War, is one of his most famous efforts. At its best, Tennyson's poetry was rich with bold and evocative imagery, and musical in its expression. And for T. S. Eliot, he was 'the saddest of all English poets', who dealt openly with grief and loss, such as in the magnum opus *In Memoriam,* which gave us the immortal line: ''Tis better to have loved and lost / Than never to have loved at all.'

I

Half a league, half a league,
Half a league onward,
All in the valley of Death
  Rode the six hundred.
'Forward, the Light Brigade!
Charge for the guns!' he said.
Into the valley of Death
  Rode the six hundred.

II

'Forward, the Light Brigade!'
Was there a man dismayed?
Not though the soldier knew
  Someone had blundered.
  Theirs not to make reply,
  Theirs not to reason why,
  Theirs but to do and die.
  Into the valley of Death
  Rode the six hundred.

III

Cannon to right of them,
Cannon to left of them,
Cannon in front of them
  Volleyed and thundered;
Stormed at with shot and shell,
Boldly they rode and well,
Into the jaws of Death,
Into the mouth of hell
  Rode the six hundred.

IV

Flashed all their sabres bare,
Flashed as they turned in air
Sabring the gunners there,
Charging an army, while
  All the world wondered.
Plunged in the battery-smoke
Right through the line they broke;
Cossack and Russian
Reeled from the sabre stroke
  Shattered and sundered.
Then they rode back, but not
  Not the six hundred.

V

Cannon to right of them,
Cannon to left of them,
Cannon behind them
  Volleyed and thundered;
Stormed at with shot and shell,
While horse and hero fell.
They that had fought so well
Came through the jaws of Death,
Back from the mouth of hell,
All that was left of them,
  Left of six hundred.

VI

When can their glory fade?
O the wild charge they made!
  All the world wondered.
Honour the charge they made!
Honour the Light Brigade,
  Noble six hundred!

26 October ✶ Renouncement ✶ Alice Meynell

11 October 1847 – 27 November 1922

One of the writers considered to replace Tennyson as Poet Laureate was Alice Meynell. Born in London and raised in Italy, Meynell endured quite a difficult childhood, marked by chronic illness. During her convalescence she converted to Catholicism. This was a defining moment for Meynell, who began to write religious verse which attracted the attention of the editor Wilfrid Meynell, whom she would go on to marry. As a feminist, she co-founded the Catholic Women's Suffrage Society, and through her poetry and journalism she actively promoted women's rights, pacifism and anti-colonialist arguments.

I must not think of thee; and, tired yet strong,
I shun the thought that lurks in all delight—
  The thought of thee—and in the blue heaven's height,
And in the sweetest passage of a song.
Oh, just beyond the fairest thoughts that throng
  This breast, the thought of thee waits hidden yet bright;
But it must never, never come in sight;
I must stop short of thee the whole day long.
But when sleep comes to close each difficult day,
  When night gives pause to the long watch I keep,
And all my bonds I needs must loose apart,
Must doff my will as raiment laid away,—
  With the first dream that comes with the first sleep
I run, I run, I am gathered to thy heart.

27 October ✶ I Sit and Sew ✶ Alice Dunbar-Nelson

19 July 1875 – 18 September 1935

The first generation of Black Americans to be born free after the Civil War reached maturity to find that their own struggle for equality had barely begun. Alice Dunbar-Nelson developed a complex understanding of ethnicity and gender, drawing on a plethora of influences from mixed-race parents and the Creole communities with which she became involved. From the depths of great collective suffering and fear came great art, and Dunbar-Nelson contributed significantly to the artistic blossoming of the Harlem Renaissance. An assiduous diarist, talented poet, lifelong political activist and erudite modernist thinker, Alice Dunbar-Nelson played an important role in empowering Black women, and her writings offer a unique perspective on racism and the everyday life of Black American women in the late nineteenth and early twentieth century.

I sit and sew—a useless task it seems,
My hands grown tired, my head weighed down with dreams—
The panoply of war, the martial tred of men,
Grim-faced, stern-eyed, gazing beyond the ken
Of lesser souls, whose eyes have not seen Death,
Nor learned to hold their lives but as a breath—
But—I must sit and sew.

I sit and sew—my heart aches with desire—
That pageant terrible, that fiercely pouring fire
On wasted fields, and writhing grotesque things
Once men. My soul in pity flings
Appealing cries, yearning only to go
There in that holocaust of hell, those fields of woe—
But—I must sit and sew.

The little useless seam, the idle patch;
Why dream I here beneath my homely thatch,
When there they lie in sodden mud and rain,
Pitifully calling me, the quick ones and the slain?
You need me, Christ! It is no roseate dream
That beckons me—this pretty futile seam,
It stifles me—God, must I sit and sew?

28 October ✶ Dover Beach ✶ Matthew Arnold

24 December 1822 – 15 April 1888

Matthew Arnold is one of the major poets and critics of the Victorian era, though his standing was largely overshadowed by his contemporaries Alfred Tennyson and Robert Browning even in his own time. His place beside these two literary giants was something of which he was keenly aware, writing to his mother, 'It might be fairly urged that I have less poetical sentiment than Tennyson, and less intellectual vigour and abundance than Browning.' Where he excelled, he assessed, was in fusing the two traits together in line with modern development. And Arnold is indeed today held up as one of the first modern poets, with this famous poem often cited as an example of the clear expression and disillusionment with the world that would define many modernist texts. He is also thought to have been the first to use the term 'philistines' to refer to middle-class anti-intellectuals.

The sea is calm tonight.
The tide is full, the moon lies fair
Upon the straits; on the French coast the light
Gleams and is gone; the cliffs of England stand,
Glimmering and vast, out in the tranquil bay.
Come to the window, sweet is the night-air!
Only, from the long line of spray
Where the sea meets the moon-blanched land,
Listen! you hear the grating roar
Of pebbles which the waves draw back, and fling,
At their return, up the high strand,
Begin, and cease, and then again begin,
With tremulous cadence slow, and bring
The eternal note of sadness in.

Sophocles long ago
Heard it on the Ægean, and it brought
Into his mind the turbid ebb and flow
Of human misery; we
Find also in the sound a thought,
Hearing it by this distant northern sea.

The Sea of Faith
Was once, too, at the full, and round earth's shore
Lay like the folds of a bright girdle furled.
But now I only hear
Its melancholy, long, withdrawing roar,
Retreating, to the breath
Of the night-wind, down the vast edges drear
And naked shingles of the world.

Ah, love, let us be true
To one another! for the world, which seems
To lie before us like a land of dreams,
So various, so beautiful, so new,
Hath really neither joy, nor love, nor light,
Nor certitude, nor peace, nor help for pain;
And we are here as on a darkling plain
Swept with confused alarms of struggle and flight,
Where ignorant armies clash by night.

29 October ✶ The Sea is Calm Tonight ✶ Lawrence Ferlinghetti

24 March 1919 – 22 February 2021

One of the many artists to respond to 'Dover Beach' was the American poet, publisher, painter and anarchist Lawrence Ferlinghetti, whose poem picks up at the same place as Arnold's. Born in New York to Italian and Jewish parents, Ferlinghetti spent time studying and living in Paris in his twenties before moving to San Francisco – the place that would become his home for the next seventy years and where he would become a legendary figure as one of the pioneers of the city's literary renaissance and progressive, far-left politics. As the co-founder of the City Lights bookshop and publisher, he helped launch the careers of the likes of Allen Ginsberg. Although associated with the Beat Generation, Ferlinghetti didn't see his own poetry as belonging to that genre, and indeed his work does seem more indebted to the likes of T. S. Eliot and William Carlos Williams. But his aim was also to wrest poetry away from intellectual and academic traditions, describing his work as 'wide open', and always writing in a way that would be accessible and interesting to readers.

The sea is calm tonight
off Dover Beach
The birds at dusk
cry out syllables
of some deconstructed word
we are yet unable
to decipher
to explain existence
And they lift the last light
with their wings
And fly away with it
over the horizon
Keeping the secret

30 October ✶ Little Orphant Annie ✶ James Whitcomb Riley

7 October 1849 – 22 July 1916

James Whitcomb Riley was an American writer, commonly known as the 'Hoosier poet' because of his use of Indiana dialect, and the 'Children's poet' because of his bestselling collection *Rhymes of Childhood*. Riley was a budding poet while working odd jobs, and he began performing his pieces when he started working for a patent-medicine travelling act as a jingle-writer and performer. He later worked as a journalist for an Indiana newspaper, all the while submitting his poetry to other local publications (initially under a pseudonym). Over time he developed a reputation as a rural poet, and slowly but surely his work began to be noticed outside his home state. By the 1890s, when his book of verses first appeared, Riley had achieved national fame. This, one of his most successful poems, inspired *Annie*, the famous Broadway musical and film.

Little Orphant Annie's come to our house to stay,
An' wash the cups an' saucers up, an' brush the crumbs away,
An' shoo the chickens off the porch, an' dust the hearth, an' sweep,
An' make the fire, an' bake the bread, an' earn her board-an'-keep;
An' all us other childern, when the supper things is done,
We set around the kitchen fire an' has the mostest fun
A-list'nin' to the witch-tales 'at Annie tells about,
An' the Gobble-uns 'at gits you
        Ef you
          Don't
            Watch
              Out!

Onc't they was a little boy wouldn"t say his prayers,—
So when he went to bed at night, away up stairs,
His Mammy heerd him holler, an' his Daddy heerd him bawl,

An' when they turn't the kivvers down, he wasn't there at all!
An' they seeked him in the rafter-room, an' cubby-hole, an' press,
An' seeked him up the chimbly-flue, an' ever'wheres, I guess;
But all they ever found was thist his pants an' roundabout—
An' the Gobble-uns'll git you
Ef you
Don't
Watch
Out!

An' one time a little girl 'ud allus laugh an' grin,
An' make fun of ever'one, an' all her blood an' kin;
An' onc't, when they was 'company', an' ole folks was there,
She mocked 'em an' shocked 'em, an' said she didn't care!
An' thist as she kicked her heels, an' turn't to run an' hide,
They was two great big Black Things a-standin' by her side,
An' they snatched her through the ceilin' 'fore she knowed what she's about!
An' the Gobble-uns'll git you
Ef you
Don't
Watch
Out!

An' little Orphant Annie says when the blaze is blue,
An' the lamp-wick sputters, an' the wind goes woo-oo!
An' you hear the crickets quit, an' the moon is gray,
An' the lightnin'-bugs in dew is all squenched away,—
You better mind yer parents, an' yer teachers fond an' dear,
An' churish them 'at loves you, an' dry the orphant's tear,
An' he'p the pore an' needy ones 'at clusters all about,
Er the Gobble-uns'll git you
Ef you
Don't
Watch
Out!

31 October ✶ It's Halloween ✶ Jack Prelutsky

Born 1940

The first person to be named Children's Poet Laureate in the US, Jack Prelutsky, admitted that he was never interested in poetry in his own childhood, owing to a dangerously dull teacher who sucked all the joy out it. In fact, he only stumbled into poetry by accident, when he sent a collection of illustrations to a publisher which were accompanied by short poems that he wrote off the cuff. The editor was instantly impressed, and from then Prelutsky has gone on to write over seventy bestselling children's books. Unlike a certain Isaac Watts (see 19 October), he believes that kids' poetry is at its best, and most educational, when it can make its readers laugh. Like Roger McGough, Prelutsky could have perhaps in another life been a celebrated musician, having played in the same New York coffee-houses as a pre-fame Bob Dylan. This poem is a joyous, rather than eerie, celebration of Halloween.

It's Halloween! It's Halloween!
The moon is full and bright
And we shall see what can't be seen
On any other night:

Skeletons and ghosts and ghouls,
Grinning goblins fighting duels,
Werewolves rising from their tombs,
Witches on their magic brooms.

In masks and gowns
  we haunt the street
And knock on doors
  for trick or treat.

Tonight we are
  the king and queen,
For oh tonight
  it's Halloween!

November

1 November ✶ All Hallows ✶ Louise Glück

Born 1943

Today is All Hallows' Day – a Christian day of celebration in honour of all of the church's saints. This poem marking the occasion is by the American poet Louise Glück, who won the Nobel Prize for Literature in 2020 for 'her unmistakeable poetic voice that with austere beauty makes individual existence universal'. Many of her works are brief, using everyday language to explore everyday life. Others contain beautiful passages about nature, and draw from classical and Biblical mythology to modern psychoanalysis to help articulate complex emotions. Glück was born in New York City, raised in Long Island, and educated nearby at Sarah Lawrence College and Columbia University. Alongside her now multi-award-winning writing life, she can be found teaching the lucky students of Yale and Stanford.

Even now this landscape is assembling.
The hills darken. The oxen
sleep in their blue yoke,
the fields having been
picked clean, the sheaves
bound evenly and piled at the roadside
among cinquefoil, as the toothed moon rises:

This is the barrenness
of harvest or pestilence.
And the wife leaning out the window
with her hand extended, as in payment,
and the seeds
distinct, gold, calling
Come here
Come here, little one

And the soul creeps out of the tree.

2 November ✶ *from* The Fairie Queene ✶ Edmund Spenser

1552/53 – 13 January 1599

Edmund Spenser was one of the greatest Elizabethan poets. His most famous work, the epic, six-volume poem *The Faerie Queene*, was written as a symbolic tribute to Elizabeth I herself. Born to poor cloth-makers in London, Spenser managed to obtain a scholarship to a good school before going on to study at Cambridge. He eventually found work as a secretary at court, where he met the likes of Philip Sidney and Walter Raleigh, under whom he served in colonial campaigns in Ireland. Hoping to become a courtier himself, Spenser sought to gain the crown's favour through his poetry, and so he wrote *The Faerie Queene*, which, among many other things, served as a pro-Anglican allegory. The book received the royal seal of approval and Spenser was given an annual payment of £50 as reward. This short extract should give a flavour of the metaphorical, fantastical nature of the poem as it follows the Redcrosse Knight (a symbol for virtue, holiness and St George) in his battle with a dragon (representing evil, unsurprisingly).

His blazing eyes, like two bright shining shields,
  Did burne with wrath, and sparkled living fyre;
  As two broad Beacons, set in open fields,
  Send forth their flames farre off to every shyre,
  And warning give, that enemies conspyre,
  With fire and sword the region to invade;
  So flam'd his eyne with rage and rancorous yre:
  But farre within, as in a hollow glade,
Those glaring lampes were set, that made a dreadfull shade.

So dreadfully he towards him did pas,
Forelifting up aloft his speckled brest,
And often bounding on the brused gras,
As for great joyance of his newcome guest.
Eftsoones he gan advance his haughtie crest,
As chauffed Bore his bristles doth upreare;
And shoke his scales to battell readie drest;
That made the *Redcrosse* knight nigh quake for feare,
As bidding bold defiance to his foeman neare.

3 November ✶ *from* The Hoard ✶ J. R. R. Tolkien

3 January 1892 – 2 September 1973

Another poem about a dragon comes to us via J. R. R. Tolkien – perhaps the most famous fantasy writer of them all. The author of *The Hobbit* and *The Lord of the Rings* – still among the bestselling books in the world – was responsible for the rise of fantasy as a literary genre in the mid-twentieth century and its subsequent explosion in popularity. Like Spenser, Tolkien is revered for creating entire worlds with his words, building histories, cultures and fellowships of fantastical creatures, as well as inventing complete languages from scratch. Born in South Africa but raised in the West Midlands, Tolkien showed a remarkable gift for writing from an early age. At Oxford he studied Classics and English – with a bit of German, Nordic and Gothic thrown into the mix. After serving as a soldier in the First World War, he took up a post at the *Oxford English Dictionary,* focusing on Germanic etymology, and later worked as an academic, professor and translator of medieval texts such as *Beowulf* (see 16 June), which Tolkien would count 'among my most valued sources'.

There was an old dragon under grey stone;
his red eyes blinked as he lay alone.
His joy was dead and his youth spent,
he was knobbed and wrinkled, and his limbs bent
in the long years to his gold chained;
in his heart's furnace the fire waned.
To his belly's slime gems stuck thick,
silver and gold he would snuff and lick:
he knew the place of the least ring
beneath the shadow of his black wing.
Of thieves he thought on his hard bed,
and dreamed that on their flesh he fed,
their bones crushed, and their blood drank:

his ears drooped and his breath sank.
Mail-rings rang. He heard them not.
A voice echoed in his deep grot:
a young warrior with a bright sword
called him forth to defend his hoard.
His teeth were knives, and of horn his hide,
but iron tore him, and his flame died.

4 November ✶ The Fairies ✶ William Allingham

19 March 1824 – 18 November 1889

Sticking with fantastical creatures, we move on to this much-loved poem by the Irish writer William Allingham. For much of his adult life Allingham worked in customs offices in Ireland and England, writing his verse, including this one, alongside his more prosaic career. Although he wrote many popular collections – some of which were illustrated by Pre-Raphaelite artists such as Dante Rossetti and John Millais – he is best known for his posthumously published *Diary*, which features revealing (and indiscreet) accounts of his famous artistic friends, including Tennyson and Thomas Carlyle. He was married to the celebrated Victorian painter and illustrator Helen Allingham.

Up the airy mountain,
Down the rushy glen,
We daren't go a-hunting
For fear of little men;
Wee folk, good folk,
Trooping all together;
Green jacket, red cap,
And white owl's feather!

Down along the rocky shore
Some make their home,
They live on crispy pancakes
Of yellow tide-foam;
Some in the reeds
Of the black mountain-lake,
With frogs for their watchdogs,
All night awake.

High on the hill-top
The old King sits;
He is now so old and grey
He's nigh lost his wits.
With a bridge of white mist
Columbkill he crosses,
On his stately journeys
From Slieveleague to Rosses;
Or going up with the music
On cold starry nights,
To sup with the Queen
Of the gay Northern Lights.

They stole little Bridget
For seven years long;
When she came down again
Her friends were all gone.
They took her lightly back,
Between the night and morrow,
They thought that she was fast asleep,
But she was dead with sorrow.
They have kept her ever since
Deep within the lake,
On a bed of fig-leaves,
Watching till she wake.

By the craggy hillside,
Through the mosses bare,
They have planted thorn trees
For my pleasure, here and there.
Is any man so daring
As dig them up in spite,
He shall find their sharpest thorns
In his bed at night.

Up the airy mountain,
Down the rushy glen,
We daren't go a-hunting
For fear of little men;
Wee folk, good folk,
Trooping all together;
Green jacket, red cap,
And white owl's feather!

5 November ✶ Solitude ✶ Alexander Pope

21 May 1688 – 30 May 1744

Alexander Pope is one of the greatest satirists in the history of English literature. His devastating sense of humour, usually masterfully employed to mock members of the establishment or the social concerns of his day, was undoubtedly cultivated in response to the hardships he faced in his youth. Despite being the son of fairly wealthy parents, his Catholic background saw him barred from university and positions of public office as a result of the 1673 Test Acts. From adolescence he developed numerous ailments that afflicted him throughout his life, but this coincided with his emergence as a self-taught poet; this poem was written, incredibly, when he was twelve. In his early adult years, he wrote well-reviewed pastoral pieces, as well as a verse essay on poetry itself, written in the heroic couplet style that would become his trademark. Although he does not have quite as many mentions as Shakespeare, apart from 'Anon.' and the Bible, Pope is the second-most featured writer in the *Oxford Dictionary of Quotations*, and has provided us with many expressions that we still use today, such as when we 'damn with faint praise', warn that 'a little learning is a dangerous thing', or admit that 'to err is human, to forgive, divine'.

Happy the man, whose wish and care
  A few paternal acres bound,
Content to breathe his native air,
          In his own ground.

Whose herds with milk, whose fields with bread,
  Whose flocks supply him with attire,
Whose trees in summer yield him shade,
          In winter fire.

Blest, who can unconcernedly find
  Hours, days, and years slide soft away,
In health of body, peace of mind,
          Quiet by day,

Sound sleep by night; study and ease,
  Together mixed; sweet recreation;
And innocence, which most does please,
          With meditation.

Thus let me live, unseen, unknown;
  Thus unlamented let me die;
Steal from the world, and not a stone
          Tell where I lie.

6 November ✶ *from the* Odyssey ✶ Homer, translated by George Chapman

c. eighth century BC

For about 3,000 years up until about thirty years ago, the name Homer would evoke the father of western literature, rather than the lovably buffoonish father of the Simpson family. Unlike the animated Homer, the Greek poet was a near-peerless genius, whose epics, the *Iliad* and the *Odyssey* – about the mythological Trojan War and the warrior king Odysseus's attempt to return home after the battle, respectively – have influenced almost every great writer and literary movement from the Greek philosophers all the way to the modernists. That said, we really don't know anything concrete about Homer or even when he was alive. There are even those who believe that Homer wasn't a single person at all, but a kind of totemic figure to whom these works have been attributed. This extract from George Chapman's 1614 translation of the *Odyssey* (famously admired by Keats) is a playful passage from Book 9 in which the titular hero tricks the blind, one-eyed monster Cyclops.

'Good guest, again afford my taste thy aid,
And let me know thy name, and quickly now,
That in thy recompense I may bestow
A hospitable gift on thy desert,
And such a one as shall rejoice thy heart.
For to the Cyclops too the gentle earth
Bears gen'rous wine, and Jove augments her birth,
In store of such, with show'rs; but this rich wine
Fell from the river that is mere divine,
Of nectar and ambrosia.' This again
I gave him, and again; nor could the fool abstain,
But drunk as often. When the noble juice
Had wrought upon his spirit, I then gave use
To fairer language, saying: 'Cyclop! now,

As thou demand'st, I'll tell my name; do thou
Make good thy hospitable gift to me.
My name is No-Man; No-Man each degree
Of friends, as well as parents, call my name.'
He answer'd, as his cruel soul became:
'No-Man! I'll eat thee last of all thy friends;
And this is that in which so much amends
I vow'd to thy deservings, thus shall be
My hospitable gift made good to thee.'

7 November ✶ *from* Map of the New World ✶ Derek Walcott

23 January 1930 – 17 March 2017

Derek Walcott was a Nobel Prize-winning poet, playwright and essayist. Born in St Lucia, he felt from an early age that he was destined to become a poet, and published his first piece of verse in a local newspaper at the age of fourteen. By the end of his teens he had self-published two collections of poetry, with his mother covering the printing costs, which he paid her back by selling the volumes to his friends. From these humble beginnings, Walcott went on to become one of the leading Caribbean voices of his generation, his 1992 Nobel Prize citation praising the merging of his 'profound, rhapsodic reverie upon his remote birthplace – its people, its landscape, and its history – with the central, classical tradition of western civilization'. Indeed, while his most famous work, the long poem *Omeros*, is a very loose adaptation of Homer's *Iliad* largely set on his home island, the following poem may serve as a kind of mini prequel to the *Odyssey*.

Archipelagoes

At the end of this sentence, rain will begin.
At the rain's edge, a sail.

Slowly the sail will lose sight of islands;
into a mist will go the belief in harbours
of an entire race.

The ten-years war is finished.
Helen's hair, a grey cloud.
Troy, a white ashpit
by the drizzling sea.

The drizzle tightens like the strings of a harp.
A man with clouded eyes picks up the rain
and plucks the first line of the *Odyssey*.

8 November ✶ *from* Metamorphoses ✶ Ovid, translated by Sir Samuel Garth, John Dryden, et al.

20 March 43 BC – c. 17 AD

One of the most read and revered Latin poets, Ovid (Publius Ovidius Naso) has, along with Virgil, arguably helped shape western culture more than any other Roman writer. Following his dream of becoming a poet instead of a lawyer – the profession for which he'd studied in Rome – Ovid achieved immediate success with his first collection of romantic verse, *Amores*. His most celebrated work, *Metamorphoses*, is a broad fifteen-book epic poem describing countless mythical transformations, some of which have become part of our collective imagination – for instance, Pygmalion's statue who turns into a woman, or the nymph Daphne who becomes a laurel tree. The themes and style of this work have been hugely influential on poets including Dante, Chaucer and Shakespeare, and have inspired artists and sculptors throughout the ages. For reasons that are still unknown (Ovid writes of a *carmen et error*, a 'poem and a mistake') he was exiled by Emperor Augustus to Tomis, on the Black Sea, and was never allowed to return to Rome. Here, in what is now a famous cautionary tale, vain Narcissus falls in love with his own reflection and is transformed into a flower.

There stands a fountain in a darksome wood,
Nor stain'd with falling leaves nor rising mud;
Untroubled by the breath of winds it rests,
Unsully'd by the touch of men or beasts;
High bow'rs of shady trees above it grow,
And rising grass and chearful greens below.
Pleas'd with the form and coolness of the place,
And over-heated by the morning chace,
Narcissus on the grassie verdure lyes:
But whilst within the chrystal fount he tries
To quench his heat, he feels new heats arise.

For as his own bright image he survey'd,
He fell in love with the fantastick shade;
And o'er the fair resemblance hung unmov'd,
Nor knew, fond youth! it was himself he lov'd.
The well-turn'd neck and shoulders he descries,
The spacious forehead, and the sparkling eyes;
The hands that Bacchus might not scorn to show,
And hair that round Apollo's head might flow;
With all the purple youthfulness of face,
That gently blushes in the wat'ry glass.
By his own flames consum'd the lover lyes,
And gives himself the wound by which he dies.
To the cold water oft he joins his lips,
Oft catching at the beauteous shade he dip
His arms, as often from himself he slips
Nor knows he who it is his arms pursue
With eager clasps, but loves he knows not who.

9 November ✶ *from* Translations from Horace ✶ John Dryden

9 August 1631 – 1 May 1700

John Dryden was England's first Poet Laureate. He was able to become a leading poet of the day by keeping himself insulated from the volatile political situation of the Restoration era. His poetry was at first written in favour of Oliver Cromwell – he even worked for the secretary of state of the Protectorate – and then in praise of Charles II as a force of national unity after the return of the monarchy. He continued to support James II, but ultimately found himself out of favour, and out of a job as Laureate, after the arrival of the new King and Queen, William and Mary, to whom he refused to pledge allegiance. Undeterred, he re-invented himself as a translator and, unusually for a poet, his work on Virgil, and later Homer, Ovid and Horace, made him a very wealthy man. This much-quoted extract comes from a poem written in imitation of Horace's Ode 3.29. Dryden is also known as the first person to suggest that a sentence shouldn't end in a preposition – a legacy *of* which to be proud.

Happy the Man, and happy he alone,
  He, who can call to day his own:
  He who, secure within, can say
To morrow do thy worst, for I have liv'd to day.
  Be fair, or foul, or rain, or shine,
The joys I have possest, in spight of fate, are mine.
  Not Heav'n it self upon the past has pow'r;
But what has been, has been, and I have had my hour.

10 November ✶ Ode 3.2 ✶ Horace, translated by A. S. Kline

65 – 8 BC

Perhaps best known for coining the saying *carpe diem* ('seize the day'), Horace (Quintus Horatius Flaccus) was one of the foremost poets, satirists and critics during the reign of Emperor Augustus. The son of a freed slave, he studied in Rome and in Athens, where he embraced the republican ideals and joined Brutus's rebel army against Augustus at the Battle of Philippi. Disillusioned with their defeat, he returned to Rome and began his career as a poet, where his fellow writer Virgil introduced him to Maecenas, Augustus's powerful advisor and protector of the arts. They became lifelong friends, and Maecenas gifted Horace – who famously wrote about pursuing a life marked by simplicity, tranquillity and balance – a villa in the Roman countryside. There, Horace was able to concentrate on writing his Odes and his Epistles, such as *Ars Poetica* (*The Art of Poetry*), which remains an illuminating text for students of poetry and classics to this day.

It's sweet and fitting to die for one's country.
Yet death chases after the soldier who runs,
and it won't spare the cowardly back
or the limbs, of peace-loving young men.

Virtue, that's ignorant of sordid defeat,
shines out with its honour unstained, and never
takes up the axes or puts them down
at the request of a changeable mob.

Virtue, that opens the heavens for those who
did not deserve to die, takes a road denied
to others, and scorns the vulgar crowd
and the bloodied earth, on ascending wings.

And there's a true reward for loyal silence:
I forbid the man who divulged those secret
rites of Ceres, to exist beneath
the same roof as I, or untie with me

the fragile boat: often careless Jupiter
included the innocent with the guilty,
but lame-footed Punishment rarely
forgets the wicked man, despite his start.

11 November ✶ Dulce et Decorum Est ✶ Wilfred Owen

18 March 1893 – 4 November 1918

11 November marks the anniversary of the Armistice that brought an end to the First World War after four years of bloodshed. We pay tribute to the sacrifices made by soldiers in this run of poems by the poets of the Great War. We begin with one of the most celebrated and widely read, Wilfred Owen. Born in Shropshire, Owen fell in love with poetry in his early adolescence, showing a particular interest in Keats and the Romantics. He was wounded on his first posting at the front and sent to convalesce at a hospital in Edinburgh, where he met Siegfried Sassoon, who would encourage him to capture the atrocities of the trenches in his writing, and bring the horrors to life for those reading at home. Between 1917 and his death (one week before the Armistice in November 1918), Owen wrote all of his poems, but only five were published in his lifetime. This one, perhaps his most famous, takes its title from the line 'It's sweet and fitting to die for one's country' in the poem by Horace above, but applies it ironically, damningly calling it 'the old Lie'.

Bent double, like old beggars under sacks,
Knock-kneed, coughing like hags, we cursed through sludge,
Till on the haunting flares we turned our backs
And towards our distant rest began to trudge.
Men marched asleep. Many had lost their boots
But limped on, blood-shod. All went lame; all blind;
Drunk with fatigue; deaf even to the hoots
Of gas-shells dropping softly behind.

Gas! GAS! Quick, boys!—An ecstasy of fumbling
Fitting the clumsy helmets just in time;
But someone still was yelling out and stumbling
And flound'ring like a man in fire or lime.—
Dim through the misty panes and thick green light,
As under a green sea, I saw him drowning.

In all my dreams before my helpless sight,
He plunges at me, guttering, choking, drowning.

If in some smothering dreams, you too could pace
Behind the wagon that we flung him in,
And watch the white eyes writhing in his face,
His hanging face, like a devil's sick of sin;
If you could hear, at every jolt, the blood
Come gargling from the froth-corrupted lungs,
Obscene as cancer, bitter as the cud
Of vile, incurable sores on innocent tongues,—
My friend, you would not tell with such high zest
To children ardent for some desperate glory,
The old Lie: *Dulce et decorum est*
Pro patria mori.

12 November ✶ The Soldier ✶ Rupert Brooke

3 August 1887 – 23 April 1915

Unlike Wilfred Owen, Rupert Brooke was already a well-established poet by the start of the First World War. A friend of Virginia Woolf since his university days, Brooke became associated with the Bloomsbury Group, although some believe that he was more respected for his looks – Yeats called him 'the handsomest young man in England' – than for his literary skills. He began writing almost immediately from the front line, and a few of his poems, such as this one, were published the following year, to much acclaim and recognition. His poetry reveals some of the optimism and feelings of national pride that marked the early days of the war, though they still acknowledge the human toll of battle. By the time a collection of his works was published in May 1915, Brooke had tragically died while stationed with the navy in Greece. He is buried in an olive grove on the Greek island of Skyros – a corner of a foreign field that is forever England, to borrow a line from this poem.

If I should die, think only this of me:
    That there's some corner of a foreign field
That is for ever England. There shall be
    In that rich earth a richer dust concealed;
A dust whom England bore, shaped, made aware,
    Gave, once, her flowers to love, her ways to roam;
A body of England's, breathing English air,
    Washed by the rivers, blest by suns of home.

And think, this heart, all evil shed away,
    A pulse in the eternal mind, no less
        Gives somewhere back the thoughts by England given;
Her sights and sounds; dreams happy as her day;
    And laughter, learnt of friends; and gentleness,
        In hearts at peace, under an English heaven.

13 November ✶ Returning, We Hear the Larks ✶ Isaac Rosenberg

25 November 1890 – 1 April 1918

Isaac Rosenberg was a poet and painter who is now mainly remembered as a war poet. The son of Jewish immigrants from Russia, Rosenberg did not have much of an education, but his artistic talent and originality granted him a place to study at the Slade School of Art, where he began to devote some of his time to writing. His early work, the collections *Night and Day* and *Youth*, were very much influenced by the Romantics. In 1915, after the publication of the latter, he enrolled in the British Army and fought, more out of a sense of desperation than patriotism, commenting that 'Nothing can justify war'. In the three years he spent fighting, his poetry became more mature and distinctive, often drawing inspiration from the Old Testament. His promising career was tragically cut short when he died in the Battle of Arras at the age of twenty-eight.

Sombre the night is:
And, though we have our lives, we know
What sinister threat lurks there.

Dragging these anguished limbs, we only know
This poison-blasted track opens on our camp—
On a little safe sleep.

But hark! Joy—joy—strange joy.
Lo! Heights of night ringing with unseen larks:
Music showering on our upturned listening faces.

Death could drop from the dark
As easily as song—
But song only dropped,

Like a blind man's dreams on the sand
By dangerous tides;
Like a girl's dark hair, for she dreams no ruin lies there,
Or her kisses where a serpent hides.

14 November ✶ The General ✶ Siegfried Sassoon

8 September 1886 – 1 September 1967

Although perhaps slightly eclipsed by his protégé Wilfred Owen, Siegfried Sassoon is regarded as another hugely important war poet. Unlike many of his peers, he survived the conflict. The son of a wealthy merchant family, he enjoyed a fairly comfortable life in the build-up to the war, studying at Cambridge, playing cricket, and writing verse which achieved moderate success. Having enlisted in the army, on a wave of patriotism that swept up a number of idealistic young men, he quickly saw war for all its senseless destruction. His poetry, which had once been influenced by the Romantics, now unflinchingly captured the death and suffering around him in graphic detail – as would Owen's verse after the two men met. After finishing his convalescent leave, he wrote a bold letter to his commanding officer called *Finished with the War: A Soldier's Declaration*, which was read out in Parliament and caused a storm with such lines as 'I believe that this War is being deliberately prolonged by those who have the power to end it'. After the war he continued to write poetry, and also worked as a magazine editor, lecturer, biographer and novelist.

'Good-morning, good-morning!' the General said
When we met him last week on our way to the line.
Now the soldiers he smiled at are most of 'em dead,
And we're cursing his staff for incompetent swine.
'He's a cheery old card,' grunted Harry to Jack
As they slogged up to Arras with rifle and pack.

But he did for them both by his plan of attack.

15 November ✶ My November Guest ✶ Robert Frost

26 March 1874 – 29 January 1963

Like other American literary giants of the twentieth century, such as Ezra Pound and T. S. Eliot, Robert Frost really came to prominence as a poet in England. Although he only spent three years in the outskirts of London before the First World War, it was there that he published his first two collections and met a number of fellow poets, including Edward Thomas, T. E. Hulme and Pound himself, who helped promote his early publications. Many of these poems had been written years earlier in the decade that Frost spent fruitlessly tending a farm in New Hampshire that he had inherited from his grandfather. But though he ultimately failed to cultivate land, he did later succeed in cultivating a reputation as an American legend, who became the only writer to win four Pulitzer Prizes for poetry. It is hard to pin down the literary movement to which Frost belonged. His verse, formal in structure and often nature-orientated, is reminiscent of nineteenth-century traditions, but his use of colloquial language and simple expression aligns him more closely to the modernists. And although he is often remembered as a folksy writer who captured the characters and landscapes of rural life, his best poems are also often tinged with a sense of melancholy and loneliness, as seen in this one.

My sorrow, when she's here with me,
  Thinks these dark days of autumn rain
Are beautiful as days can be;
She loves the bare, the withered tree;
  She walks the sodden pasture lane.

Her pleasure will not let me stay.
    She talks and I am fain to list:
She's glad the birds are gone away,
She's glad her simple worsted grey
    Is silver now with clinging mist.

The desolate, deserted trees,
    The faded earth, the heavy sky,
The beauties she so truly sees,
She thinks I have no eye for these,
    And vexes me for reason why.

Not yesterday I learned to know
    The love of bare November days
Before the coming of the snow,
But it were vain to tell her so,
    And they are better for her praise.

16 November ✶ Snow ✶ Edward Thomas

3 March 1878 – 9 April 1917

Edward Thomas is perhaps not as well-known as his friend Robert Frost, but his reputation is based entirely on three years of verse writing between 1914 and 1917. In his lifetime, Thomas was better known as a biographer and literary critic, and he also helped launch the career of the nomadic poet W. H. Davies (see 11 August). His first poetry collection was released under a pseudonym, and was largely influenced by Frost, with whom he would go on long rambles in the countryside. Amused by Thomas's indecisiveness about which route to follow, Frost wrote what is now undoubtedly his most famous poem, 'The Road Not Taken'. Although intended as a playful bit of poetic teasing, Thomas (and most readers since) read it as a serious meditation on uncertainty, and took it as a final encouragement to enlist in the army. Tragically, the decision cost Thomas his life as he died at the Battle of Arras (like Isaac Rosenberg). Though considered a war poet today, he didn't really attempt to capture the realities of the conflict directly, instead embedding images and references to the war in his poems about the English countryside.

In the gloom of whiteness,
In the great silence of snow,
A child was sighing
And bitterly saying: 'Oh,
They have killed a white bird up there on her nest,
The down is fluttering from her breast.'
And still it fell through that dusky brightness
On the child crying for the bird of the snow.

17 November ✶ In Tenebris ✶ Ford Madox Ford

17 December 1873 – 26 June 1939

Ford Madox Ford was born Ford Hermann Hueffer to a German emigré journalist and the daughter of the Pre-Raphaelite artist Ford Madox Brown. Best known for his novel *The Good Soldier*, Ford was also a major literary trendsetter in his work as the critic, editor and founder of the publications *The English Review* (which promoted the likes of D. H. Lawrence, Ezra Pound and H. G. Wells) and the Paris-based *Transatlantic Review* (which featured works by Joyce, Hemingway and Gertrude Stein). During the First World War, Ford worked as a propagandist along with Hilaire Belloc and G. K. Chesterton, before enlisting voluntarily, aged forty-one – experiences he later fictionalized in his other major work, the four-part series of novels *Parade's End*. After the war, he changed his surname from Hueffer to Ford so as to appear less Germanic (much like a certain family that we know today as the Windsors). The author Anthony Burgess went so far as to label Ford the greatest British novelist of the twentieth century, while Hemingway called him a 'well clothed, up-ended hogshead' – which doesn't sound too much like a compliment!

All within is warm,
  Here without it's very cold,
  Now the year is grown so old
And the dead leaves swarm.

In your heart is light,
  Here without it's very dark,
  When shall I hear the lark?
When see aright?

Oh, for a moment's space!
  Draw the clinging curtains wide
  Whilst I wait and yearn outside
Let the light fall on my face.

18 November ✶ Elegy Written in a Country Churchyard ✶ Thomas Gray

26 December 1716 – 30 July 1771

Thomas Gray was an accomplished eighteenth-century poet, yet he has gone down in history as something of a one-hit wonder. But what a hit it is! His 'Elegy Written in a Country Churchyard' took almost a decade to complete and is a timeless reflection on life and death that is considered to be one of the greatest ever pieces of English verse. The poem takes grand, tragic themes of loss and mortality, and addresses them with a refined poetic poise that quietly confers grace and significance on its humble subjects; beyond being an elegy for the dead, it is also a beautifully moving ode to 'the homely joys' of their unknown lives. While Gray may reveal his own fears of being forgotten in the poem's end, this work has gone on to inspire generations of future poets from Shelley, Tennyson and Thomas Hardy – who used the line 'Far from the madding crowd' as a title for a novel – to T. S. Eliot and G. K. Chesterton, who pastiched it directly (see tomorrow's poem). As a shy, unassuming man who turned down the laureateship due to a lack of belief in his talents, Gray would likely have been bemused by the enduring popularity of this poem. In his own lifetime he was also known as a witty writer of light, humorous verse, including a mock lament about his schoolfriend Horace (son of Prime Minister Robert) Walpole's cat. He is buried in the very churchyard in Buckinghamshire thought to have inspired the 'Elegy'.

The curfew tolls the knell of parting day,
    The lowing herd wind slowly o'er the lea,
The plowman homeward plods his weary way,
    And leaves the world to darkness and to me.

Now fades the glimm'ring landscape on the sight,
    And all the air a solemn stillness holds,
Save where the beetle wheels his droning flight,
    And drowsy tinklings lull the distant folds;

Save that from yonder ivy-mantled tow'r
    The moping owl does to the moon complain
Of such, as wand'ring near her secret bow'r,
    Molest her ancient solitary reign.

Beneath those rugged elms, that yew-tree's shade,
    Where heaves the turf in many a mould'ring heap,
Each in his narrow cell for ever laid,
    The rude forefathers of the hamlet sleep.

The breezy call of incense-breathing Morn,
    The swallow twitt'ring from the straw-built shed,
The cock's shrill clarion, or the echoing horn,
    No more shall rouse them from their lowly bed.

For them no more the blazing hearth shall burn,
    Or busy housewife ply her evening care:
No children run to lisp their sire's return,
    Or climb his knees the envied kiss to share.

Oft did the harvest to their sickle yield,
    Their furrow oft the stubborn glebe has broke;
How jocund did they drive their team afield!
    How bow'd the woods beneath their sturdy stroke!

Let not Ambition mock their useful toil,
    Their homely joys, and destiny obscure;
Nor Grandeur hear with a disdainful smile
    The short and simple annals of the poor.

The boast of heraldry, the pomp of pow'r,
    And all that beauty, all that wealth e'er gave,
Awaits alike th' inevitable hour.
    The paths of glory lead but to the grave.

Nor you, ye proud, impute to these the fault,
    If Mem'ry o'er their tomb no trophies raise,
Where thro' the long-drawn aisle and fretted vault
    The pealing anthem swells the note of praise.

Can storied urn or animated bust
    Back to its mansion call the fleeting breath?
Can Honour's voice provoke the silent dust,
    Or Flatt'ry soothe the dull cold ear of Death?

Perhaps in this neglected spot is laid
    Some heart once pregnant with celestial fire;
Hands, that the rod of empire might have sway'd,
    Or wak'd to ecstasy the living lyre.

But Knowledge to their eyes her ample page
    Rich with the spoils of time did ne'er unroll;
Chill Penury repress'd their noble rage,
    And froze the genial current of the soul.

Full many a gem of purest ray serene,
    The dark unfathom'd caves of ocean bear:
Full many a flow'r is born to blush unseen,
    And waste its sweetness on the desert air.

Some village-Hampden, that with dauntless breast
    The little tyrant of his fields withstood;
Some mute inglorious Milton here may rest,
    Some Cromwell guiltless of his country's blood.

Th' applause of list'ning senates to command,
The threats of pain and ruin to despise,
To scatter plenty o'er a smiling land,
And read their hist'ry in a nation's eyes,

Their lot forbade: nor circumscrib'd alone
Their growing virtues, but their crimes confin'd;
Forbade to wade through slaughter to a throne,
And shut the gates of mercy on mankind,

The struggling pangs of conscious truth to hide,
To quench the blushes of ingenuous shame,
Or heap the shrine of Luxury and Pride
With incense kindled at the Muse's flame.

Far from the madding crowd's ignoble strife,
Their sober wishes never learn'd to stray;
Along the cool sequester'd vale of life
They kept the noiseless tenor of their way.

Yet ev'n these bones from insult to protect,
Some frail memorial still erected nigh,
With uncouth rhymes and shapeless sculpture deck'd,
Implores the passing tribute of a sigh.

Their name, their years, spelt by th' unletter'd muse,
The place of fame and elegy supply:
And many a holy text around she strews,
That teach the rustic moralist to die.

For who to dumb Forgetfulness a prey,
This pleasing anxious being e'er resign'd,
Left the warm precincts of the cheerful day,
Nor cast one longing, ling'ring look behind?

On some fond breast the parting soul relies,
Some pious drops the closing eye requires;
Ev'n from the tomb the voice of Nature cries,
Ev'n in our ashes live their wonted fires.

For thee, who mindful of th' unhonour'd Dead
Dost in these lines their artless tale relate;
If chance, by lonely contemplation led,
Some kindred spirit shall inquire thy fate,

Haply some hoary-headed swain may say,
'Oft have we seen him at the peep of dawn
Brushing with hasty steps the dews away
To meet the sun upon the upland lawn.

'There at the foot of yonder nodding beech
That wreathes its old fantastic roots so high,
His listless length at noontide would he stretch,
And pore upon the brook that babbles by.

'Hard by yon wood, now smiling as in scorn,
Mutt'ring his wayward fancies he would rove,
Now drooping, woeful wan, like one forlorn,
Or craz'd with care, or cross'd in hopeless love.

'One morn I miss'd him on the custom'd hill,
Along the heath and near his fav'rite tree;
Another came; nor yet beside the rill,
Nor up the lawn, nor at the wood was he;

'The next with dirges due in sad array
Slow thro' the church-way path we saw him borne.
Approach and read (for thou canst read) the lay,
Grav'd on the stone beneath yon aged thorn.'

The Epitaph

Here rests his head upon the lap of Earth
A youth to Fortune and to Fame unknown.
Fair Science frown'd not on his humble birth,
And Melancholy mark'd him for her own.

Large was his bounty, and his soul sincere,
Heav'n did a recompense as largely send:
He gave to Mis'ry all he had, a tear,
He gain'd from Heav'n ('twas all he wish'd) a friend.

No farther seek his merits to disclose,
Or draw his frailties from their dread abode,
(There they alike in trembling hope repose)
The bosom of his Father and his God.

19 November ✶ Elegy in a Country Churchyard ✶ G. K. Chesterton

29 May 1874 – 14 June 1936

G. K. Chesterton was one of the most important and widely respected English literary figures of the early twentieth century. A prolific writer of books, poems, essays and articles, Chesterton was admired by his contemporaries and friends, Hilaire Belloc and T. S. Eliot among them, for the consistent excellence of his work. He began his career at a publishing house before becoming a newspaper columnist, a role which he would continue to hold throughout his literary career, and which would inform the tone of his poetry, which Eliot called 'first-rate journalistic balladry'. As a novelist he is best known for his highbrow detective and thriller fiction (including the *Father Brown* series), and as a biographer he is credited with reviving critical interest in Charles Dickens. Referred to once as 'the prince of paradox', Chesterton was famous for being an avid debater, and he could often be found trading witty barbs and opinions with his close friend George Bernard Shaw. This great anti-war and anti-government poem is an ironic take on the previous poem by Thomas Gray.

The men that worked for England
They have their graves at home:
And birds and bees of England
About the cross can roam.

But they that fought for England,
Following a falling star,
Alas, alas for England
They have their graves afar.

And they that rule in England,
In stately conclave met,
Alas, alas for England
They have no graves as yet.

20 November ✶ The Spaces Between ✶
Liz Lochhead

Born 1947

Liz Lochhead was the Makar, or National Poet of Scotland, between 2011 and 2016, but she is perhaps better known as the playwright behind a Scots adaptation of the French dramatist Molière's *Tartuffe* and the marvellously titled *Mary Queen of Scots Got Her Head Chopped Off*. After graduating from the Glasgow School of Art, Lochhead spent a period working as a high school teacher before she won the BBC Scotland Poetry competition and had her first collection published. As a dramatist, her poems also seem to be written with readings or performances in mind; they're noted for their humorous, lively, rhythmic nature, and for the way in which they seek to bring Scots vernacular and the voices of Scots women back to the literary fore. The musicality of her verse has seen her collaborate with a number of singer-songwriters, and she has even sung backing vocals on a track by a Glaswegian hip hop group.

(for Leslie McGuire)

The boy is ten and today it is his birthday.
Behind him on the lawn
his mother and his little sister
unfurl a rainbow crayoned big and bright
on a roll of old wallpaper.
His father, big-eyed, mock-solemn, pantomimes ceremony
as he lights the ten candles on the cake.
Inside her living-room
his grandmother puts her open palm to the window.
Out in the garden, her grandson
reaches up, mirrors her, stretching fingers
and they smile and smile as if they touched
warm flesh not cold glass.

More than forty thousand years ago
men or women splayed their fingers thus
and put their hands to bare rock, they
chewed ochre, red-ochre, gritted charcoal and blew,
blew with projectile effort that really took it out of them,
their living breath. Raw gouts of pigment
spattered the living stencil
that was each's own living hand
and made their mark.
The space of absence
was the clean, stark, picture of their presence
and it pleased them.
We do not know why they did it
and maybe they did not either but
they knew they must.
It was the cold cave wall
and they knew they were up against it.

The birthday boy is juggling.
He has been spending time in the lockdown learning
but though he still can't keep it up for long
his grandmother dumb-shows most extravagant applause.
She toasts them all in tea
from her *Best Granny in the World mug,* winking
and licking her lips ecstatically as they cut the cake,
miming hunger, miming prayer
for her hunger to be sated.
The slim girl dances and her grandmother claps
and claps again, blinking tears.
Another matched high-five at her window.

Neither the blown candles or the blown kisses
will leave any permanent mark
– unless love does? –
on them on this the only afternoon
they will be all alive together on just this day the boy is ten.

21 November ✶ Fragment 16 ✶ Sappho

c. 630 – c. 570 BC

As we have seen many times in this anthology, throughout history female poets of genius have frequently been overlooked or else actively sidelined by male peers and critics. But well over two millennia ago, the Ancient Greeks recognized Sappho as a counterpart to Homer, calling her 'the poetess' (while the latter was 'the poet'). The philosopher Plato even called her 'the tenth muse', a perceived equal to the nine traditional muses of mythology. As with Homer, there is little concrete biographical information available that can shed light on her life. We know she lived on the island of Lesbos in circa 600 BC and was exiled at some point with her family to Sicily, due, it is believed, to political tensions. It's thought that she wrote some 10,000 lines of verse, of which only around 650 have survived, mostly as fragments. As a poet she is well regarded for her natural, vivid expression and use of clear, simple language – a link between the ancients and the modernists! From the nineteenth century onwards she would be claimed by many female poets as a pre-feminist icon, and has been adopted by many LGBTQIA+ readers for her candid writing about her love for women.

Some men say an army of horse and some men say an army
  on foot
and some men say an army of ships is the most beautiful thing
on the black earth. But I say it is
what you love.

Easy to make this understood by all.
For she who overcame everyone
in beauty (Helen)
left her fine husband

behind and went sailing to Troy.

Not for her children nor her dear parents
had she a thought, no –
 ] led her astray

 ] for
 ] lightly
 ] reminded me now of Anaktoria
 who is gone.

22 November ✶ *from the* Aeneid ✶
Virgil, translated by A. S. Kline

c. 70 – 18 BC

Virgil (Publius Vergilius Maro), arguably the greatest of all Roman poets, was born in Mantua in northern Italy, studied in Rome, and spent much of his adult life in Naples. His first poetry collection, *Eclogues*, comprised ten beautiful pastoral poems and was a huge success, allowing him to join Maecenas's circle of intellectuals (along with Horace: see 10 November). His masterpiece, the *Aeneid*, was to the Romans what Homer's *Iliad* and *Odyssey* were to the Greeks. Presented in twelve books, it follows the journey of young Trojan prince Aeneas from the recently destroyed Troy to Latium, where, according to a prophecy, he would build a city and start a lineage destined to rule the world: the Romans. Featuring a narrative technique that we might today call a flashback, the *Aeneid* also goes back to the Trojan War, and it is here, in this extract, that the story originates of how the Greeks managed to invade Troy by hiding themselves in a wooden horse.

'Pull the statue to her house,' they shout,
'and offer prayers to the goddess's divinity.'

We breached the wall, and opened up the defences of the city.
All prepare themselves for the work and they set up wheels
allowing movement under its feet, and stretch hemp ropes
round its neck. That engine of fate mounts our walls
pregnant with armed men. Around it boys, and virgin girls,
sing sacred songs, and delight in touching their hands to the ropes:
Up it glides and rolls threateningly into the midst of the city.

O my country, O Ilium house of the gods, and you,
Trojan walls famous in war! Four times it sticks at the threshold
of the gates, and four times the weapons clash in its belly:
yet we press on regardless, blind with frenzy,
and site the accursed creature on top of our sacred citadel.
Even then Cassandra, who, by the god's decree, is never
to be believed by Trojans, reveals our future fate with her lips.
We unfortunate ones, for whom that day is our last,
clothe the gods' temples, throughout the city, with festive branches.
Meanwhile the heavens turn, and night rushes from the Ocean,
wrapping the earth, and sky, and the Myrmidons' tricks,
in its vast shadow: through the city the Trojans
fall silent: sleep enfolds their weary limbs.

23 November ✶ *from* The Divine Comedy ✶ Dante, translated by Henry Wadsworth Longfellow

1265 – 1321

Undoubtedly the greatest ever Italian poet, Florentine Dante Alighieri was born into an aristocratic family. He began writing poetry at an early age, dedicating his verses to Beatrice, whom he met at the age of nine and who would go on to inspire much of his writing. Involved in Florence's political life, and torn between two rival factions, Dante was sent into exile due to his hostility towards Pope Boniface. He spent this period as something of an outsider, wandering through the courts of northern Italy, and working on – among other things – his most famous work, *The Divine Comedy*. Structured into three large sections, this allegorical masterpiece is a first-person verse narration of the poet's descent into Hell, through Purgatory, and into Heaven. It follows this fictional Dante, who is led on his strange and symbol-laden journey first by the Roman poet Virgil and then by his beloved Beatrice, who represents hope and redemption. The text is regarded as an early piece of Renaissance literature with its classical influences and its revolutionary approach to language, using 'vulgar' Italian and Tuscan dialect instead of Latin – much like Chaucer's use of English. In this extract from a translation by the poet Henry Wadsworth Longfellow (see 23 September), Virgil leads Dante through the gates of Hell, which bear the famous admonition: 'Abandon hope all ye who enter here.'

'Through me the way is to the city dolent;
Through me the way is to eternal dole;
Through me the way among the people lost.

Justice incited my sublime Creator;
Created me divine Omnipotence,
The highest Wisdom and the primal Love.

Before me there were no created things,
Only eterne, and I eternal last.
All hope abandon, ye who enter in!'

These words in sombre colour I beheld
Written upon the summit of a gate;
Whence I: 'Their sense is, Master, hard to me!'

And he to me, as one experienced:
'Here all suspicion needs must be abandoned,
All cowardice must needs be here extinct.'

24 November ✶ And Were You Pleased? ✶ Lord Dunsany

24 July 1878 – 25 October 1957

The Anglo-Irish Lord Dunsany, born Edward John Moreton Drax Plunkett into one of Ireland's oldest aristocratic families, grew up in the country's oldest house, Dunsany Castle. Another of his claims to fame is that he held the unlikely double honour of being the Irish national champion of both pistol-shooting and chess. As a writer he was best known for his fantasy stories and novels – preceding J. R. R. Tolkien, whom he greatly influenced, in establishing the genre. He also wrote several essays and successful plays as well as poems, which though less widely read today, were admired by W. B. Yeats, who curated and edited a collection of Dunsany's poetry.

'And were you pleased?' they asked of Helen in Hell.
'Pleased?' answered she, 'when all Troy's towers fell,
And dead were Priam's sons, and lost his throne?
And such a war was fought as none had known;
And even the gods took part; and all because
Of me alone! Pleased?

I should say I was!'

25 November ✶ On Wenlock Edge ✶
A. E. Housman

26 March 1859 – 30 April 1936

Despite being best known as the author of the acclaimed collection *A Shropshire Lad*, the poet A. E. Housman actually never lived in that county, but in neighbouring Worcestershire. It was here that he grew up as the son of a solicitor, the eldest of seven children. Showing academic prowess from an early age, he received a scholarship to go to Oxford, where, owing either to complacency or unrequited love for his roommate, he flunked his exams. But this was just a blip, and Housman spent the next years studying classics independently, becoming a published scholar and eventually a professor at UCL and Cambridge. As a poet, his legacy rests almost entirely on the aforementioned collection, which has not been out of print since 1896. It comprises evocative short lyrics on themes ranging from youth to death, loss to nostalgia, city to countryside, and Englishness more generally, Ted Hughes describing them as 'to my mind the most perfect expression of something deeply English and a whole mood of English history'.

On Wenlock Edge the wood's in trouble;
    His forest fleece the Wrekin heaves;
The gale, it plies the saplings double,
    And thick on Severn snow the leaves.

'Twould blow like this through holt and hanger
    When Uricon the city stood:
'Tis the old wind in the old anger,
    But then it threshed another wood.

Then, 'twas before my time, the Roman
    At yonder heaving hill would stare:
The blood that warms an English yeoman,
    The thoughts that hurt him, they were there.

There, like the wind through woods in riot,
    Through him the gale of life blew high;
The tree of man was never quiet:
    Then 'twas the Roman, now 'tis I.

The gale, it plies the saplings double,
    It blows so hard, 'twill soon be gone:
To-day the Roman and his trouble
    Are ashes under Uricon.

26 November ✶ Comet ✶ Kate Wakeling

Born 1981

Kate Wakeling grew up in Yorkshire and Birmingham and attended Cambridge University, where she studied music before moving on to SOAS to gain a PhD in Balinese gamelan music. Her first collection of poems for children, *Moon Juice* won the CLIPPA prize in 2017 and was nominated for the Carnegie Medal in 2018. This poem perfectly blends her musicality and performance skills with her literary prowess, and comes with the instruction to read it as quickly as possible.

I'm a spinning, winning, tripping, zipping, super-sonic ice queen:
see my moon zoom, clock my rocket, watch me splutter tricksy space-steam.

I'm the dust bomb, I'm the freeze sneeze, I'm the top galactic jockey
made (they think) of gas and ice and mystery bits of something rocky.

Oh I sting a sherbet orbit, running rings round star or planet;
should I shoot too near the sun, my tail hots up: *ouch – OUCH – please fan it!*

And I'm told I hold the answer to the galaxy's top question:
that my middle's made of history (no surprise I've indigestion)

but for now I sprint and skid and whisk and bolt and belt and bomb it;
I'm that hell-for-leather, lunging, plunging, helter-skelter COMET.

27 November ✶ Contentment ✶ Thomas Burke

29 November 1886 – 22 September 1945

It's something of a fool's errand to try to put together a meaningful account of Thomas Burke's life. Many of the biographical details that emerged about him were riddled with exaggerations and fabrications, most of which stemmed from Burke himself, who tried to amplify his close connections to the working classes. In truth, Burke was born in Clapham (not East London as he claimed) and spent some of his childhood at a house for middle-class boys, whose families had status but little money. He worked for a period as an office assistant before making a name for himself with stories set in poverty-stricken areas of London. This poem argues that a financially poor man can be rich in life-affirming experiences.

What though a man be money-poor?
There's honeysuckle by the door.
  Peacefully perfumed lavender,
  And wilding weed and gossamer.

There's plenty cheese and plenty bread,
And russet ale, and apples red;
  And breezes from the garden bring
  A busy voice that loves to sing

Songs of our happy English clime,
Of Lily, Lavender, and Lime!
  And children in the sunshine shout
  For joy that tedious school is out.

Indeed, with friends, and cheese and bread,
And russet ale, and apples red,
  And honeysuckle by the door—
  How shall a man be counted poor?

28 November ✶ Happiness ✶ Raymond Carver

25 May 1938 – 2 August 1988

Raymond Carver is widely considered to be one of the greatest American short-story writers of the twentieth century. His fiction and poems are almost immediately recognizable for their clear and concise minimalism and for the un-idealized, ordinary working people who inhabit them. A father of two by the age of twenty, Carver spent much of his early life fitting his studies and writing around odd jobs, from bookshop assistant to janitor to tulip picker. His writing drew greatly on the insights he gleaned and people he met while working outside the literary world. As such, he defended his characters when critics described them as being despair-filled. 'The waitress, the bus driver, the mechanic, the hotel keeper,' he said. 'They're good people. People doing the best they could.'

So early it's still almost dark out.
I'm near the window with coffee,
and the usual early morning stuff
that passes for thought.
When I see the boy and his friend
walking up the road
to deliver the newspaper.
They have on caps and sweaters,
and the one boy has a bag over his shoulder.
They are so happy
they aren't saying anything, these boys.
I think if they could, they would take
each other's arm.
It's early in the morning,
and they are doing this thing together.
They come on, slowly.
The sky is taking on light,
though the moon still hangs palely over the water.

Such beauty that for a minute
death and ambition, even love
doesn't enter into this.
Happiness. It comes on
unexpectedly. And goes beyond, really,
any early morning talk about it.

29 November ✶ Chaudhri Sher Mobarik Looks at the Loch ✶ Imtiaz Dharker

Born 1954

Born in Pakistan but raised in Glasgow, Imtiaz Dharker once described herself as a 'Scottish Muslim Calvinist'. Much of her writing focuses on displacement, disparate identities, cultural conflicts and faith – often through the specific lens of women's experiences of these issues. Her poetry finds the unique in the mundane and the beautiful in the ordinary, and is marked by an emphasis on evocative visual imagery. Meanwhile, Duffy herself said, 'If there were to be a World Laureate, then for me the role could only be filled by Imtiaz Dharker.'

Light shakes out the dishrag sky
and scatters the water with sequins. *Look, hen!*
says my father, *Loch Lomond!* as if
it were all his doing, as if he owned it,
laird of Lomond, laird of the language.
He is proud to say hen and even more loch
with an *och* not an *ock,* to speak
proper Glaswegian like a true-born Scot,
and he makes the right sound at the back
of the throat because he can say *khush*
and *khwab* and *khamosh,* because the sounds
for happy and dream are the words that swim
In the water for him, so he says it again
Hen! Look! The loch!

30 November ✶ Sassenachs ✶ Jackie Kay

Born 1961

30 November is Saint Andrew's Day, the Scottish national day. How better to mark it than with a poem by Jackie Kay, who was the Scots Makar from 2016 to 2021? Born to a Nigerian father and Scottish mother in Edinburgh, she was adopted by a Glasgow family as a baby. Kay initially considered pursuing a career in acting before a teacher sent her early poetry efforts to the celebrated Scottish writer Alasdair Gray, who encouraged her to continue on this path. Since her award-winning first semi-autobiographical collection, *The Adoption Papers*, she has written poems, books and plays that reflect on her upbringing, background and identity, and on diverse themes such as slavery, Scottishness and the Bible. This lively and conversational poem playfully broaches the topic of Scottish pride (and traditional aversion to England). 'Sassenach' is an old slang Celtic term referring to English people.

Me and my best pal (well, she was
till a minute ago) are off to London.
First trip on an intercity alone.
When we got on we were the same
kind of excited – jigging on our seats,
staring at everyone. But then,
I remembered I had to be sophisticated.
So when Jenny started shouting,
'Look at that, the land's flat already,'
when we were just outside Glasgow
(Motherwell actually) I'd feel myself flush.
Or even worse, 'Sassenach country!
Wey Hey Hey.' The tartan tammy
sitting proudly on top of her pony;
the tartan scarf swinging like a tail.
The nose pressed to the window,

'England's not so beautiful, is it?'
And we haven't even crossed the border!
And the train's jazzy beat joins her:
Sassenachs Sassenachs here we come.
Sassenachs Sassenachs Rum Tum Tum
Sassenachs Sassenachs How do you do.
Sassenachs Sassenachs WE'LL GET YOU.
Then she loses momentum, so out come
the egg mayonnaise sandwiches and
the big bottle of Bru. 'My ma's done us proud,'
says Jenny, digging in, munching loud.
The whole train is an egg and I'm inside it.
I try and remain calm; Jenny starts it again,
Sassenachs Sassenachs Rum Tum Tum.

Finally we get there: London, Euston;
and the first person on the platform
gets asked – 'Are you a genuine Sassenach?'
I want to die, but instead I say, *'Jenny!'*
He replies in that English way –
'I beg your pardon,' and Jenny screams
'Did you hear that Voice?'
And we both die laughing, clutching
our stomachs at Euston.

December

1 December ✶ Two Seasons ✶ Valerie Bloom

Born 1956

Born in Jamaica to a family of nine children, Valerie Bloom's first taste of literary recognition came when she was just a school child, when one of her poems was published in a national newspaper. Success in youth writing competitions followed, which encouraged Bloom to pursue her talent as a career. She arrived in the UK in the late 1970s to study English with African and Caribbean Studies at the University of Kent, and has lived here ever since. Over the last forty years she has established herself as an important Caribbean poetic voice, who has written about island life and migration for both adults and children, often using Jamaican dialect, as in this poem. Like many other writers in this anthology, Bloom has combined her poetry with a love of music; she has written lyrics for a jazz ensemble, and even worked once as a steel-pan teacher. She is, as this poem reveals, not the biggest fan of the British climate!

We don' have a Springtime like some folk
Who live in dem colder place,
but we have a time when de soft rain come,
an' tease open de seedcase
o' de poincianna and de trumpet tree,
An' whisper to de young cane to wake
when de guangu blossom is pink an' white
powder-puff, prettying up de earth face.
But not Spring like in dem colder place.

We no have no Summer when Springtime done,
no change o' season as such,
but we have a time when de asphalt bubble
in de hot sun, when yuh dare not touch
de tarmac wid yuh barefoot, when de heat is
a dancin' dervish who will wi' grab yuh
an' spin yuh till de sweat is a river flowin' down,
an' yuh too tired fe do anything much.
But we don' have a Summer as such.

We no have no Autumn like Europe,
we don' have de American Fall,
but dere is a time when de flame tree in the Forest
light de woodland like a fireball,
when de blue mahoe leaf dem turn bright bronze,
de almond look like wearing henna,
when de nightfall flicker wid peeni-wallie,
an' grasshopper an' tree frog call
to de moon. But we don' have Autumn or Fall.

We don' have no Winter wid snow an' sleet,
an ice like a carpet pon de grung,
but we have a time when de fee-fee twist
purple an' white up de road bank, an' young
tangerine an' ugli fruit swell an' yellow in
de gentle sun; when de cool breeze finger
draw de sweater round de shoulder,
an de sorrel tas'e tart pon de tongue.
But no ice like a carpet pon de grung.

We don't have de four season dem,
Summer, Winter, Autumn an' Spring,
but de dry season wid the noisy bees
an' de shrill call o' de cling-cling,
an' de sun turnin' de sea into a hot bath,
an' de grass bake so dat it crackle like parchment
under yuh foot; when de beach dem crowded
wid folk cooling off; de season when mango is king.
But no Summer, Winter, Autumn an' Spring.

No, we don't have four different season,
just two, de wet an' de dry,
an' in de rainy season de storm cloud dem
cover over de face o' de sky,
de road an' de river dem lose dem bank,
an' de hurricane dem sometimes come callin'
fe borrow de roof an' fe tear up de tree dem
like paper. But de earth always revive by an' by,
in de two season, de wet an' de dry.

2 December ✶ Snow ✶ Louis MacNeice

12 September 1907 – 3 September 1963

Louis MacNeice was an Irish poet, playwright and novelist who was an inspiration to his fellow younger countrymen Paul Muldoon, Derek Mahon and Seamus Heaney. Born the son of a bishop of the Church of Ireland, MacNeice was sent to boarding school in England, where he lived most of his life. And although he never forgot his Irish heritage, he felt perpetually caught between two identities: an Irishman in England, and an Englishman in Ireland. Although never quite as successful as his lifelong university friend W. H. Auden, MacNeice was well regarded by both critics and readers. Prevented by bad eyesight to sign up to serve in the war in 1939, he joined the BBC, where his work included writing radio plays that starred Dylan Thomas. He wrote poetry on the side, and was published by T. S. Eliot at Faber and Faber. Of poetry he said, marvellously, that it 'must be honest before anything else'.

The room was suddenly rich and the great bay-window was
Spawning snow and pink roses against it
Soundlessly collateral and incompatible:
World is suddener than we fancy it.

World is crazier and more of it than we think,
Incorrigibly plural. I peel and portion
A tangerine and spit the pips and feel
The drunkenness of things being various.

And the fire flames with a bubbling sound for world
Is more spiteful and gay than one supposes—
On the tongue on the eyes on the ears in the palms of one's hands—
There is more than glass between the snow and the huge roses.

3 December ✶ The Herd-Boy ✶
Lu Yu, translated by Arthur Waley

733 – 804

Many poets have their literary niches, writing in individual styles or on particular themes. But none perhaps focused their writing quite as specifically as Lu Yu, who is famed for having written the first in-depth text about tea. *The Classic of Tea* traces the entire story of tea, from its production and harvesting to its brewing, and finally its consumption, as part of China's traditional ceremonies. When he wasn't busy writing about or drinking tea, Lu Yu was a prolific poet of the Song Dynasty, who is thought to have written some 10,000 poems – most of which have survived to this day.

In the southern village the boy who minds the ox
With his naked feet stands on the ox's back.
Through the hole in his coat the river wind blows;
Through his broken hat the mountain rain pours.
On the long dyke he seemed to be far away;
In the narrow lane suddenly we were face to face.

The boy is home and the ox is back in its stall;
And a dark smoke oozes through the thatched roof.

4 December ✶ Make Me a Picture of the Sun ✶ Emily Dickinson

10 December 1830 – 15 May 1886

One of the greatest American poets, Emily Dickinson knew more than most about life and death, spirit and solitude, beauty and sorrow, despite being a reclusive soul who rarely left her home, let alone her hometown of Amherst, Massachusetts. Born to an affluent family, Dickinson enjoyed a comfortable upbringing in which she received an extensive education. Yet from her teens onwards she seemed to live under a cloud of melancholy and anxiety, which, by the time she reached her late twenties, saw her retreat from the world into the security of the home. But in all these years cloistered away, she led a rich literary life, reading widely, composing poetry, and conversing with friends in exquisitely written letters. Dickinson asked her sister Lavinia to burn all her correspondence on her death, but, luckily for us, she made no mention of a treasure trove of notebooks filled with nearly 2,000 poems (only eleven of which had been printed in her lifetime), which were duly passed on to be published. It would take over half a century before critics and readers began to look past Dickinson's personal life and recognize the artistry of her verse. Today she is something of a cult, romantic figure who gave her life to the pursuit of poetic grace, and who has inspired several films and TV series.

Make me a picture of the sun –
So I can hang it in my room –
And make believe I'm getting warm
When others call it 'Day'!

Draw me a Robin – on a stem –
So I am hearing him, I'll dream,
And when the Orchards stop their tune –
Put my pretense – away –

Say if it's really – warm at noon –
Whether it's Buttercups – that 'skim' –
Or Butterflies – that 'bloom'?
Then – skip – the frost – upon the lea –
And skip the Russet – on the tree –
Let's play those – never come!

5 December ✶ A Moment ✶
Mary Elizabeth Coleridge

23 September 1861 – 25 August 1907

The fourth member of the Coleridge family that we've met in this anthology, Mary's place on the family tree is as the great-grand-niece of the great Samuel Taylor. Although she never reached the lofty heights of her forebear, she was known in her lifetime as an accomplished novelist and essayist, and has posthumously been recognized for her poetry – owing to the fact that she published her verse either anonymously or under the pseudonym 'Anodos'. Tutored at home, her lack of classmates was perhaps compensated for by regular visits by illustrious family friends including Robert Browning and Tennyson. The lyricism of her writing has inspired a number of composers, including Benjamin Britten, to adapt her poetry into musical arrangements.

The clouds had made a crimson crown
Above the mountains high.
The stormy sun was going down
In a stormy sky.

Why did you let your eyes so rest on me,
And hold your breath between?
In all the ages this can never be
As if it had not been.

6 December ✶ The Future ✶ Nick Drake

Born 1961

Along with Brian Jones (see 2 July), Nick Drake is another poet who could be easily mistaken for his musical namesake – the hugely popular English folk singer-songwriter of the 1970s. This Nick Drake also deserves recognition as an excellent contemporary poet, who writes with imagination, wit, psychological insight and conscience – especially in his work responding to the global warming crisis. A man of many talents, Drake has also written a book on W. B. Yeats, as well as numerous film scripts, plays, an opera libretto and a series of crime novels.

Dear mortals,
I know you are busy with your colourful lives;
You grow quickly bored
And detest moralizing.
I have no wish to waste the little time that remains
On arguments and heated debates.
I wish I could entertain you
With some magnificent propositions and glorious jokes;
But the best I can do is this:
I haven't happened yet; but I will.
I am the future, but before I appear
Please
Close the scrolls of information,
Let the laptop
Sleep,
Sit still
And shut your eyes.
Listen
Things are going to change –
Don't open your eyes, not yet! –
I'm not trying to frighten you.
Think of me not as a wish or a nightmare
But as a story you have to tell yourselves

Not with an ending
In which everyone lives happily ever after,
Or a B-movie apocalypse,
But maybe starting with the line
'To be continued . . .'
And see what happens next.
Remember this;
I am not written in stone
But in time
So please don't shrug and say
What can we do,
It's too late, etc., etc., etc. . . .

Dear mortals,
You are such strange creatures
With your greed and your kindness,
And your hearts like broken toys.
You carry fear with you everywhere
Like a tiny god
In its box of shadows.
You love shopping and festivals
And good food.
You love to dance
In the enchantment of time
Like angels in a forest of mirrors.
Your lives are held
In the beautiful devices
Familiar in your hands.
And perhaps you lie to yourselves
Because you're afraid of the dark.
So always remember
We are in this together,
Face to face and eye to eye.
I hold you in my hands
As I am held in yours.
We are made for each other.
Now – open your eyes
And tell me what you see.

7 December ✶ Caedmon's Hymn ✶ Caedmon, translated by Paul Muldoon

c. 658 – 680 AD

The fountainhead of all English literature was an illiterate Northumbrian animal caretaker. Or at least that's how the story of Caedmon goes (thought to be the first English poet known by name), according to the eighth-century monk and historian Bede. Writing in his *Ecclesiastical History of the English People*, Bede tells the tale of a lay worker at Whitby Abbey who is said to have been granted the gift of verse by a vision in his sleep. On waking, the previously linguistically limited Caedmon could suddenly and mysteriously recite a beautiful religious song, using words that he previously hadn't known. This hymn is the only recorded piece of poetry supposedly composed by Caedmon.

Now we must praise to the skies the keeper of the
heavenly kingdom,
The might of the measurer, all he has in mind,
The work of the Father of Glory, of all manner
of marvel,

Our eternal Master, the main mover.
It was he who first summoned up, on our behalf,
Heaven as a roof, the holy Maker.

Then this middle-earth, the Watcher over humankind,
Our eternal master, would later assign
The precinct of men, the Lord Almighty.

8 December ✶ The Hippopotamus Song ✶ Michael Flanders

1 March 1922 – 14 April 1975

Michael Flanders was one half of the comedy duo Flanders and Swann, the Lennon and McCartney of light musical revue shows in the later post-war years. Born to a family with a music and theatre background, Flanders seemed destined to become an actor himself until he contracted polio while serving in the Second World War. But after the war he reunited with his old school friend Donald Swann, and together the duo wrote dozens of songs for West End productions. Eventually they gained enough traction in the industry to perform their own shows, which became sell-out hits in Britain and across the Atlantic. Flanders then realized his dream of becoming an actor, appearing in films and shows with the RSC. This song is a classic from the Flanders and Swann double act.

A bold Hippopotamus was standing one day
On the banks of the cool Shalimar,
He gazed at the bottom as it peacefully lay
By the light of the evening star.
Away on a hilltop sat combing her hair
His fair Hippopotamine maid;
The Hippopotamus was no ignoramus
And sang her this sweet serenade:

> Mud, mud, glorious mud,
> Nothing quite like it for cooling the blood!
> So follow me, follow,
> Down to the hollow
> And there let us wallow
> In glorious mud!

The fair Hippopotama he aimed to entice
From her seat on that hilltop above,
As she hadn't got a ma to give her advice,
Came tiptoeing down to her love.
Like thunder the forest re-echoed the sound
Of the song that they sang as they met.
His inamorata adjusted her garter
And lifted her voice in duet:

> Mud, mud, glorious mud,
> Nothing quite like it for cooling the blood!
> So follow me, follow,
> Down to the hollow
> And there let us wallow
> In glorious mud!

Now more Hippopotami began to convene
On the banks of that river so wide.
I wonder now what am I to say of the scene
That ensued by the Shalimar side?
They dived all at once with an ear-splitting splosh
Then rose to the surface again,
A regular army of Hippopotami
All singing this haunting refrain:

> Mud, mud, glorious mud,
> Nothing quite like it for cooling the blood!
> So follow me, follow,
> Down to the hollow
> And there let us wallow
> In glorious mud!

9 December ✶ These Are the Hands ✶
Michael Rosen

Born 1946

Michael Rosen is undoubtedly one of the nation's favourite writers, who has written some 140 books, holding the title of Children's Laureate between 2007 and 2009. Rosen began his career in educational TV at the BBC, but ended up forging a long and garlanded career in print instead. His first book of children's poetry was published in 1974, and over the next five decades he has beguiled, entertained and guided generations of children (and their parents) with his writing. His most famous work is the family adventure picture book *We're Going on a Bear Hunt*, but he has also written books that sensitively broach topics such as grief and loss. Rosen is a popular voice on radio and in newspaper columns, and he was in the thoughts of the whole country when he spent forty-seven days in Intensive Care after contracting Covid-19 in 2020. This poem from 2008 captures his long-standing admiration for the NHS which saved his life.

For the 60th anniversary of the NHS

These are the hands
That touch us first
Feel your head
Find the pulse
And make your bed.

These are the hands
That tap your back
Test the skin
Hold your arm
Wheel the bin
Change the bulb
Fix the drip
Pour the jug
Replace your hip.

These are the hands
That fill the bath
Mop the floor
Flick the switch
Soothe the sore
Burn the swabs
Give us a jab
Throw out sharps
Design the lab.

And these are the hands
That stop the leaks
Empty the pan
Wipe the pipes
Carry the can
Clamp the veins
Make the cast
Log the dose
And touch us last.

10 December ✶ Address to a Child During a Boisterous Winter Evening ✶ Dorothy Wordsworth

25 December 1771 – 25 January 1855

Dorothy Wordsworth was the sister of William Wordsworth. Despite being largely inseparable in adult life, the two spent their adolescent years living with different relatives after the death of their parents. Reunited in their twenties, they lived together at Dove Cottage in the Lake District, even after William had married her friend Mary Hutchinson. Although she wrote some poetry herself, and shared the Romantics' interest in the natural world, Dorothy had no burning desire to pursue literary recognition, writing: 'I should detest the idea of setting myself up as an author . . . give [William] the Pleasure of it.' But her role in inspiring her brother, and in actively helping shape his poetry, should not be understated. Her diaries – published as the *Grasmere Journal* after her death – provide illuminating accounts of daily life spent in the company of William and such fellow Lake District Romantics as Coleridge and Southey.

What way does the wind come? What way does he go?
He rides over the water, and over the snow,
Through wood, and through vale; and o'er rocky height,
Which the goat cannot climb, takes his sounding flight;
He tosses about in every bare tree,
As, if you look up, you plainly may see;
But how he will come, and whither he goes,
There's never a scholar in England knows.

He will suddenly stop in a cunning nook,
And ring a sharp 'larum; but, if you should look,
There's nothing to see but a cushion of snow,
Round as a pillow, and whiter than milk,
And softer than if it were covered with silk.

Sometimes he'll hide in the cave of a rock,
Then whistle as shrill as the buzzard cock;
— Yet seek him, and what shall you find in the place?
Nothing but silence and empty space;
Save, in a corner, a heap of dry leaves,
That he's left, for a bed, to beggars or thieves!

As soon as 'tis daylight tomorrow, with me
You shall go to the orchard, and then you will see
That he has been there, and made a great rout,
And cracked the branches, and strewn them about;
Heaven grant that he spare but that one upright twig
That looked up at the sky so proud and big
All last summer, as well you know,
Studded with apples, a beautiful show!

Hark! over the roof he makes a pause,
And growls as if he would fix his claws
Right in the slates, and with a huge rattle
Drive them down, like men in a battle:
— But let him range round; he does us no harm,
We build up the fire, we're snug and warm;
Untouched by his breath see the candle shines bright,
And burns with a clear and steady light.

Books have we to read, but that half-stifled knell,
Alas! 'tis the sound of the eight o'clock bell.
— Come, now we'll to bed! And when we are there
He may work his own will, and what shall we care?
He may knock at the door — we'll not let him in;
May drive at the windows — we'll laugh at his din;
Let him seek his own home wherever it be;
Here's a cozie warm house for Edward and me.

11 December ✶ On Children ✶ Kahlil Gibran

6 January 1883 – 10 April 1931

The Lebanese-American poet and artist Kahlil Gibran is one of the bestselling poets of all time. Born in a village in Lebanon, Gibran moved to the US with his family when he was twelve, before returning to his homeland to study in Beirut. In the following years he lived in Boston, New York and Paris, where his art brought him to the attention of the sculptor August Rodin who called him 'the William Blake of the twentieth century'. Back in New York, Gibran began publishing poetry collections in Arabic and started to gain a large following amongst immigrants, who were drawn to the simple and direct style of his writing, and to his great understanding of the feelings of solitude and displacement. His first English-language book was published in 1918, and it was followed by his masterpiece, *The Prophet* – a collection of prose poetry parables and fables about the different facets of human existence. It cleverly married Gibran's influences, ranging from Transcendentalism to Symbolism, Classicism to Sufism, the Renaissance to Surrealism. The book is one of the most translated books of all times, and was known to be a favourite (among others) of Elvis Presley's. This, one of the twenty-six poems in *The Prophet,* begins a run of poems designed to inspire.

And a woman who held a babe against her
  bosom said, Speak to us of Children.
And he said:
Your children are not your children.
They are the sons and daughters of Life's
  longing for itself.
They come through you but not from you,
And though they are with you yet they belong
  not to you.

You may give them your love but not your thoughts,
For they have their own thoughts.
You may house their bodies but not their souls,
For their souls dwell in the house of tomorrow, which you cannot visit, not even in your dreams.
You may strive to be like them, but seek not to make them like you.
For life goes not backward nor tarries with yesterday.
You are the bows from which your children as living arrows are sent forth.
The archer sees the mark upon the path of the infinite, and He bends you with His might that His arrows may go swift and far.
Let your bending in the archer's hand be for gladness;
For even as He loves the arrow that flies, so He loves also the bow that is stable.

12 December ✶ Desiderata ✶ Max Ehrmann

26 September 1872 – 9 September 1945

Another inspirational piece comes to us courtesy of Max Ehrmann, who is known almost exclusively for this prose poem filled with perfectly articulated guidance and reassurance. Its sage, almost parental, tone perhaps stems from the fact that it was written by Ehrmann when he was already in his fifties. Before then he had studied philosophy at Harvard, and later worked as a lawyer and in his family manufacturing business. Although some of his poems were published during these years, he retired from his job to focus on his writing when he entered his forties. Ehrmann did not receive much recognition in his lifetime as, though 'Desiderata' was popular, it spent many years circulating without attribution until it was posthumously published by his wife. Since then it has featured on posters and has been quoted in speeches by politicians – and even appears tattooed on the back of Johnny Depp's character Captain Jack Sparrow in *The Pirates of the Caribbean*.

Go placidly amid the noise and haste, and remember what peace there may be in silence. As far as possible without surrender be on good terms with all persons. Speak your truth quietly and clearly; and listen to others, even the dull and the ignorant; they too have their story. Avoid loud and aggressive persons they are vexations to the spirit. If you compare yourself with others, you may become vain and bitter; for always there will be greater and lesser persons than yourself. Enjoy your achievements as well as your plans. Keep interested in your own career, however humble; it is a real possession in the changing fortunes of time. Exercise caution in your business affairs; for the world is full of trickery. But let this not blind you to what virtue there is; many persons strive for high ideals; and everywhere life is full of heroism. Be yourself. Especially, do not feign affection. Neither be cynical about love for in the face of all aridity and disenchantment it is as perennial as the grass. Take kindly the counsel of the years, gracefully surrendering the things of youth. Nurture strength of spirit to shield you in sudden misfortune. But do not distress yourself with dark imaginings. Many fears are born of fatigue and loneliness. Beyond a wholesome discipline, be gentle with yourself. You are a child of the universe,no less than the trees and the stars; you have a right to be here. And whether or not it is clear to you, no doubt the universe is unfolding as it should. Therefore be at peace with God, whatever you conceive Him to be, and whatever your labors and aspirations, in the noisy confusion of life keep peace with your soul. With all its sham, drudgery, and broken dreams, it is still a beautiful world. Be cheerful. Strive to be happy.

13 December ✶ As You Go Through Life ✶ Ella Wheeler Wilcox

5 November 1850 – 30 October 1919

Continuing our run of motivating poems, this is one by Ella Wheeler Wilcox, an American writer famed for her optimistic verse. Born into an intellectual family, Wheeler Wilcox was encouraged to immerse herself in reading, and published her first poem at the age of thirteen. A career of writing immensely popular poetry followed, and given that her bestselling collections had such titles as *Poems of Cheer*, *Poems of Pleasure* and *Poems of Passion*, it seems that she was very aware that her writing served to gladden the heart rather than test the brain. And only the most snobbish critic could scoff at the joy she brought to thousands, including soldiers in the First World War, to whom she would give readings.

Don't look for the flaws as you go through life;
  And even when you find them,
It is wise and kind to be somewhat blind
  And look for the virtue behind them.
For the cloudiest night has a hint of light
  Somewhere in its shadows hiding;
It is better by far to hunt for a star,
  Than the spots on the sun abiding.

The current of life runs ever away
  To the bosom of God's great ocean.
Don't set your force 'gainst the river's course
  And think to alter its motion.
Don't waste a curse on the universe--
  Remember it lived before you.
Don't butt at the storm with your puny form,
  But bend and let it go o'er you.

The world will never adjust itself
  To suit your whims to the letter.
Some things must go wrong your whole life long,
  And the sooner you know it the better.
It is folly to fight with the Infinite,
  And go under at last in the wrestle;
The wiser man shapes into God's plan
  As water shapes into a vessel.

14 December ✶ If ✶ Rudyard Kipling

30 December 1865 – 18 January 1936

Rudyard Kipling was both the first English-language author to be awarded the Nobel Prize for Literature, and, at forty-one, the youngest writer to be bestowed the honour to date. But his standing as one of the literary greats of the late Victorian and early twentieth century has been the subject of continued re-appraisal over the years due to the profoundly dated overtones of his pro-colonial writing. Born in Bombay to artist parents, Kipling's early life was shaped by this imperialist background, and he spent many years travelling around the Commonwealth. It was in India that he began to establish himself as a writer, first as a journalist and then as a short story author, with locally inspired collections such as *The Jungle Book* still hugely popular to this day. He would go on to write volumes of stories, travel journals, letters, science fiction, military profiles and poetry. This much beloved, oft-quoted and frequently parodied inspirational poem was voted the UK's favourite in a BBC poll.

If you can keep your head when all about you
  Are losing theirs and blaming it on you,
If you can trust yourself when all men doubt you,
  But make allowance for their doubting too;
If you can wait and not be tired by waiting,
  Or being lied about, don't deal in lies,
Or being hated, don't give way to hating,
  And yet don't look too good, nor talk too wise:

If you can dream—and not make dreams your master;
  If you can think—and not make thoughts your aim;
If you can meet with Triumph and Disaster
  And treat those two impostors just the same;
If you can bear to hear the truth you've spoken
  Twisted by knaves to make a trap for fools,
Or watch the things you gave your life to, broken,
  And stoop and build 'em up with worn-out tools:

If you can make one heap of all your winnings
  And risk it on one turn of pitch-and-toss,
And lose, and start again at your beginnings
  And never breathe a word about your loss;
If you can force your heart and nerve and sinew
  To serve your turn long after they are gone,
And so hold on when there is nothing in you
  Except the Will which says to them: 'Hold on!'

If you can talk with crowds and keep your virtue,
  Or walk with Kings—nor lose the common touch,
If neither foes nor loving friends can hurt you,
  If all men count with you, but none too much;
If you can fill the unforgiving minute
  With sixty seconds' worth of distance run,
Yours is the Earth and everything that's in it,
  And—which is more—you'll be a Man, my son!

15 December ✶ Written with a Diamond on her Window at Woodstock ✶ Elizabeth I

7 September 1533 – 24 March 1603

It's true that the word 'poet' is probably not the first that would come to mind if asked to describe Queen Elizabeth I. But the monarch who ruled during the golden age of English literature, the era of Shakespeare, Spenser, Sidney, Marlowe, Raleigh, Donne and many others, was also a dab hand at poetry and rhetoric herself. Born to Henry VIII and his wife number two of six, Anne Boleyn, Elizabeth was initially a source of disappointment to the king, who had hoped for a male heir. What he didn't know is that Elizabeth would go on to become arguably the most formidable monarch in English history, who quashed numerous uprisings and oversaw the defeat of the Spanish Armada. Before she took to the throne, Elizabeth had spent a year under house arrest by her sister Queen Mary, a Catholic, who feared her sibling was plotting against her. And so, locked away in a Tower at Woodstock Palace in Oxfordshire, Elizabeth pleaded her innocence in this immortal eleven-word poem, inscribed on a window.

Much suspected by me,
Nothing proved can be,
Quoth Elizabeth prisoner.

16 December ✶ Lochinvar ✶ Sir Walter Scott

15 August 1771 – 21 September 1832

Walter Scott was one of the most popular writers of the Romantic era, whose romance-laden narrative poems and novels saw him become the bestselling author of his day, rivalled only by Lord Byron. Despite having written dozens of books, most of which are defined by complicated historical plots, Scott in fact had a day job in the law, working as a judge, administrator and clerk in the Scottish courts. On top of that, Scott (in an episode befitting one of his stories) was responsible for rediscovering the Crown Jewels of Scotland, which had been hidden away for over a century. Few, if any, writers before or since have managed to marry commercial success with such a lofty literary reputation (on both sides of the Atlantic). Not everyone was such a fan, however. E. M. Forster called his work 'flat', and Mark Twain went so far as to name a sinking boat in his book *Huckleberry Finn* 'The Walter Scott'. Still, his legacy is a towering one – quite literally in Edinburgh and Glasgow, where there are giant monuments in his honour.

O, young Lochinvar is come out of the west,
Through all the wide Border his steed was the best;
And save his good broadsword he weapons had none,
He rode all unarm'd, and he rode all alone.
So faithful in love, and so dauntless in war,
There never was knight like the young Lochinvar.

He staid not for brake, and he stopp'd not for stone,
He swam the Eske river where ford there was none;
But ere he alighted at Netherby gate,
The bride had consented, the gallant came late:
For a laggard in love, and a dastard in war,
Was to wed the fair Ellen of brave Lochinvar.

So boldly he enter'd the Netherby Hall,
Among bride's-men, and kinsmen, and brothers and all:
Then spoke the bride's father, his hand on his sword,
(For the poor craven bridegroom said never a word,)
'O come ye in peace here, or come ye in war,
Or to dance at our bridal, young Lord Lochinvar?'

'I long woo'd your daughter, my suit you denied;—
Love swells like the Solway, but ebbs like its tide—
And now I am come, with this lost love of mine,
To lead but one measure, drink one cup of wine.
There are maidens in Scotland more lovely by far,
That would gladly be bride to the young Lochinvar.'

The bride kiss'd the goblet: the knight took it up,
He quaff'd off the wine, and he threw down the cup.
She look'd down to blush, and she look'd up to sigh,
With a smile on her lips and a tear in her eye.
He took her soft hand, ere her mother could bar,—
'Now tread we a measure!' said young Lochinvar.

So stately his form, and so lovely her face,
That never a hall such a galliard did grace;
While her mother did fret, and her father did fume,
And the bridegroom stood dangling his bonnet and plume;
And the bride-maidens whisper'd, ''Twere better by far
To have match'd our fair cousin with young Lochinvar.'

One touch to her hand, and one word in her ear,
When they reach'd the hall-door, and the charger stood near;
So light to the croupe the fair lady he swung,
So light to the saddle before her he sprung!
'She is won! we are gone, over bank, bush, and scaur;
They'll have fleet steeds that follow,' quoth young Lochinvar.

There was mounting 'mong Graemes of the Netherby clan;
Forsters, Fenwicks, and Musgraves, they rode and they ran:
There was racing and chasing on Cannobie Lee,
But the lost bride of Netherby ne'er did they see.
So daring in love, and so dauntless in war,
Have ye e'er heard of gallant like young Lochinvar?

17 December ✶ On Snow ✶ Jonathan Swift

30 November 1667 – 19 October 1745

Jonathan Swift, along with his friend Alexander Pope (see 5 November), is considered to be the greatest English satirical writer. Born in Dublin, he would spend most of his life moving back and forth between Ireland and England. At the beginning of his career, he worked for an English diplomat who introduced him to the royal court. During these years he began writing his scathing, humorous prose pieces, but their outrageous nature is thought to have offended Queen Anne, who saw to it that Swift would not receive a church position in England as he had hoped. Back in Ireland (this time more or less for good) he started writing pamphlets – some deadpan, some serious, all polemical – and he produced his best-known work, *Gulliver's Travels*, which was published as if a real travelogue by a seaman called Lemuel Gulliver. Although often misleadingly labelled as a children's fantasy book, it is, in fact, a playfully imaginative yet wickedly caustic piece of satire at the expense of human and political folly, corruption and conflict. Swift only really turned to poetry later in life. This is a wonderful wintry poem that also doubles as a riddle (well, providing you don't look at the title!).

A Riddle

From Heaven I fall, though from earth I begin.
No lady alive can show such a skin.
I'm bright as an angel, and light as a feather,
But heavy and dark, when you squeeze me together.
Though candour and truth in my aspect I bear,
Yet many poor creatures I help to insnare.
Though so much of Heaven appears in my make,
The foulest impressions I easily take.
My parent and I produce one another,
The mother the daughter, the daughter the mother.

18 December ✶ The Skater ✶ Vladimir Nabokov

22 April 1899 – 2 July 1977

Vladimir Nabokov was a Russian-American writer best known for his scandalous novel *Lolita*. Its publication transformed him into an international literary star, but Nabokov's journey to get to that point was one filled with incident and turmoil. Born to an aristocratic family in St Petersburg, he had an uneventful childhood before the Bolshevik revolution swept the nation, forcing anti-Soviets to flee the nation. They arrived in Germany where his father, a pro-democracy statesman, was mistakenly assassinated. Based in Berlin, Nabokov began writing a number of Russian-language novels, before the rise of Nazis caused him to flee again, this time with the help of Russian-Jewish emigrés who felt indebted to his father's earlier campaigns against anti-Semitism in their homeland. After a period in France, Nabokov eventually arrived in the US, where he became a university literature lecturer. He switched his attention to writing for an American audience, producing thematically daring and formally experimental novels as well as short stories, memoirs and poetry.

He had a muse as his ice-skating teacher,
Terpischore in winter guise – behold:
his brow is bared, he wears black riding breeches,
upon his chest there burns a medal's gold.

He whirls, and underneath the diamond lightning
of his intelligence-defying skate
breaks off its curve and, star-like, widens
the image of a flower ornate.

And thus, upon the ice compact and silky,
a sunflower is outlined. But wait –
have I myself, by that melodious whistling,
not flashed before you with a poem's skate?

I left behind a single verbal figure,
an instantly unfolding flower, inked.
And yet tomorrow, vertical and silent,
the snow will dust the scribble-scrabbled rink.

19 December ✶ A Winter Night ✶ William Barnes

22 February 1801 – 7 October 1886

William Barnes was born to a farming family in Dorset, England. He worked as a solicitor's clerk before becoming a schoolmaster and then later was ordained. Over his long life he wrote some 800 poems, many of which were written in his native Dorset dialect and were pastoral in theme. His legacy as a writer has been somewhat eclipsed by his fellow Dorset resident, and one-time pupil, Thomas Hardy, although Hardy credited Barnes with being 'the most interesting link between present and past forms of rural life that England possessed'.

It was a chilly winter's night;
And frost was glitt'ring on the ground,
And evening stars were twinkling bright;
And from the gloomy plain around
Came no sound,
But where, within the wood-girt tow'r,
The churchbell slowly struck the hour;

As if that all of human birth
Had risen to the final day,
And soaring from the wornout earth
Were called in hurry and dismay,
Far away;
And I alone of all mankind
Were left in loneliness behind.

20 December ✶ Ode to Winter ✶ Gillian Clarke

Born 1937

Gillian Clarke held the title of National Poet of Wales between 2008 and 2016, in recognition of her long career in which she has written over a hundred poems and has published several collections for both children and adults. She has worked in broadcasting and education, and is the co-founder of Ty Newydd, the National Writing Centre of Wales. Her work is marked by an immediacy that's born of a vivid sense of detail and a lively musicality that stems from her use of rhyme and alliteration. Clarke has written many poems in response to momentous events in the UK and beyond, but she also harks back to history and heritage. Of Welsh poetry she has said: 'Poetry is the national art in Wales. It's an unbroken ancient tradition.'

We hoard light, hunkered in holt and burrow,
in cave, cwtsh, den, earth, hut, lair.
Sun blinks. Trees take down their hair.
Dusk wipes horizons, seeps into the room,
the last flame of geranium in the gloom.

In the shortening day, bring in the late flowers
to crisp in a vase, beech to break into leaf,
a branch of lark. Take winter by the throat.
Feed the common birds, tits and finches,
the spotted woodpecker in his opera coat.

Let's learn to love the icy winter moon,
or moonless dark and winter constellations,
Jupiter's glow, a slow, incoming plane,
neighbourly windows, someone's flickering screen,
a lamp-lit page, drawn curtains.

Let us praise intimacy, talk and books,
music and silence, wind and rain,
the beautiful bones of trees, taste of cold air,
darkening fields, the glittering city,
that winter longing, hiraeth, something like prayer.

Under the stilled heartbeat of trees,
wind-snapped branches, mulch and root,
a million bluebell bulbs lie low
ready to flare in lengthening light,
after the dark, the frozen earth, the snow.

Out there, fox and buzzard, kite and crow
are clearing the ground for the myth.
On the darkest day bring in the tree,
cool and pungent as forest. Turn up the music.
Pour us a glass. Dress the house in pagan finery.

21 December ✶ Where Art Thou, Mother Christmas? ✶ Roald Dahl

13 September 1916 – 23 November 1990

The BFG, Willy Wonka, Mr Fox, Matilda, The Twits – some of the most amusing, bemusing, delightful and dastardly characters ever to appear in children's literature – incredibly all came from one brilliant mind. Roald Dahl is quite rightly recognized as one of the greatest storytellers of the twentieth century; his books have been fuelling and shaping the imaginations of kids all over the world for generations, and have sold a scarcely comprehensible 250 million copies. Dahl relished telling tales and poems filled with wordplay, grotesque caricatures and plenty of dark humour. His greatest asset was perhaps the fact that he never lost the child's perspective, the memories of his own unhappy years spent at the hands of horrid schoolmasters clearly still in mind. His early adulthood, however, was filled with adventures (fittingly, as he was named after Roald Amundsen, the first man to reach the South Pole), working and travelling in Africa before serving as an RAF pilot, and later as an America-based intelligence officer, during the Second World War. It was here in the US that he began writing, and from then on he wrote prolifically, both for children and for adults, for whom he spared no macabre thrills.

(Written for Great Ormond Street Hospital)

Where art thou, Mother Christmas?
I only wish I knew
Why Father should get all the praise
And no one mentions you.

I'll bet you buy the presents
And wrap them large and small
While all the time that rotten swine
Pretends he's done it all.

So Hail To Mother Christmas
Who shoulders all the work!
And down with Father Christmas,
That unmitigated jerk!

22 December ✶ You Do Not Need a Chimney for Santa Claus to Come ✶ Hollie McNish

Born 1983

Hollie McNish is one of the country's leading performance poets, and another, like Kae Tempest – whom she has supported on tour – who blurs the distinctions between poetry and music. She is one of very few poets to record an album at the historic Abbey Road Studios. Before McNish broke on to the poetry scene at open mic events, she graduated from Cambridge with a degree in languages and worked as a roadside diner chef, shop assistant and education officer. Today her events fill venues and rack up millions of views online. This touching Christmas poem was written for the charity Home-Start, which supports families with young children in difficult circumstances.

You do not need a chimney
for Santa Claus to come
You do not need a fireplace
to hand your stocking from

That stuff is just from telly
Do not believe the films
You do not need a great big house
for Santa to come in.

He's got a sleigh, for goodness sake
and loads of elves at hand:
Mrs Claus behind the scenes
computing all the plans;

Flying, glowing reindeer
galloping the Christmas air
Of course he can manage
a few quick flights of stairs –

the top flat of a tower block;
the barge on a canal;
a spare room in a friend's house;
a hostel; a hotel

So snuggle into sleep now
and don't listen to anyone
who says you need a chimney
for Santa Claus to come

23 December ✶ Talking Turkeys ✶
Benjamin Zephaniah

Born 1958

Benjamin Zephaniah is one of Britain's most distinctive contemporary writers, and a leading Dub (Reggae) poet and children's author. Born in the Birmingham suburb of Handsworth – which he called 'the Jamaican capital of Europe' – Zephaniah was already a local legend from the age of fifteen, known for his rousing, socially conscious poetry. Seeking to reach more people, he moved to London in his early twenties, where he published his first collection. Strongly influenced by Rastafarianism – a Jamaican religious movement that began in the 1930s that places emphasis on the power of words and music – and his Jamaican heritage, Zephaniah has written in dialect and with a keen sense of musicality. In fact, he has also enjoyed success as a musician, and he was the first person to record with The Wailers after the death of Bob Marley, for a tribute song for Nelson Mandela. This typically lively and amusing poem is the perfect example of Zephaniah's trademark way of taking on important issues – in this instance it's animal rights — and introducing them to young readers in a way that is fun, but never sugar-coated. A self-described 'anarchist' with strong political convictions, he famously publicly rejected an OBE (Order of the British Empire) in 2003 for its imperial connotations.

Be nice to yu turkeys dis christmas
Cos' turkeys just wanna hav fun
Turkeys are cool, turkeys are wicked
An every turkey has a Mum.
Be nice to yu turkeys dis christmas,
Don't eat it, keep it alive,
It could be yu mate, an not on your plate
Say, Yo! Turkey I'm on your side.

I got lots of friends who are turkeys
An all of dem fear christmas time,
Dey wanna enjoy it, dey say humans destroyed it
An humans are out of dere mind,
Yeah, I got lots of friends who are turkeys
Dey all hav a right to a life,
Not to be caged up an genetically made up
By any farmer an his wife.

Turkeys just wanna play reggae
Turkeys just wanna hip-hop
Can yu imagine a nice young turkey saying,
'I cannot wait for de chop',
Turkeys like getting presents, dey wanna watch
christmas TV,
Turkeys hav brains an turkeys feel pain
In many ways like yu an me.

I once knew a turkey called
Turkey
He said 'Benji explain to me please,
Who put de turkey in christmas
An what happens to christmas trees?',
I said 'I am not too sure turkey
But it's nothing to do wid Christ Mass
Humans get greedy an waste more dan need be
An business men mek loadsa cash'.

Be nice to yu turkey dis christmas
Invite dem indoors fe sum greens
Let dem eat cake an let dem partake
In a plate of organic grown beans,
Be nice to yu turkey dis christmas
An spare dem de cut of de knife,
Join Turkeys United an dey'll be delighted
An yu will mek new friends 'FOR LIFE'.

24 December ✶ A Visit from St Nicholas ✶ Clement Clarke Moore

15 July 1779 – 10 July 1863

Today is Christmas Eve and so we can hardly bypass the poem which begins with some of the most famous lines ever written: ''Twas the night before Christmas . . .' The poem is credited with creating the image of Santa Claus in a sleigh pulled by reindeer – all but Rudolph are first named here. For years nobody knew who was behind the hit poem. It was initially published anonymously in a New York newspaper in 1823, but it was only in 1837 that a poetry editor revealed that his friend Clement Clarke Moore – a highly esteemed scholar in classical languages – was the mysterious author.

'Twas the night before Christmas, when all through the house
Not a creature was stirring, not even a mouse;
The stockings were hung by the chimney with care,
In hopes that St Nicholas soon would be there;
The children were nestled all snug in their beds;
While visions of sugar-plums danced in their heads;
And mamma in her 'kerchief, and I in my cap,
Had just settled our brains for a long winter's nap –
When out on the lawn there arose such a clatter,
I sprang from my bed to see what was the matter.
Away to the window I flew like a flash,
Tore open the shutters and threw up the sash.
The moon on the breast of the new-fallen snow,
Gave a lustre of midday to objects below;
When what to my wondering eyes did appear,
But a miniature sleigh and eight tiny reindeer,
With a little old driver so lively and quick,
I knew in a moment it must be St Nick.
More rapid than eagles his coursers they came,
And he whistled, and shouted, and called them by name:

'Now, Dasher! now, Dancer! now, Prancer and Vixen!
On, Comet! on, Cupid! on, Doner and Blitzen!
To the top of the porch! to the top of the wall!
Now dash away! dash away! dash away all!'
As leaves that before the wild hurricane fly,
When they meet with an obstacle, mount to the sky;
So up to the house-top the coursers they flew
With the sleigh full of toys, and St Nicholas too –
And then, in a twinkling, I heard on the roof
The prancing and pawing of each little hoof.
As I drew in my head, and was turning around,
Down the chimney St Nicholas came with a bound.
He was dressed all in fur, from his head to his foot,
And his clothes were all tarnished with ashes and soot;
A bundle of toys he had flung on his back,
And he looked like a pedlar just opening his pack.
His eyes – how they twinkled! his dimples, how merry!
His cheeks were like roses, his nose like a cherry!
His droll little mouth was drawn up like a bow,
And the beard on his chin was as white as the snow;
The stump of a pipe he held tight in his teeth,
And the smoke, it encircled his head like a wreath;
He had a broad face and a little round belly
That shook, when he laughed, like a bowl full of jelly.
He was chubby and plump, a right jolly old elf,
And I laughed when I saw him, in spite of myself;
A wink of his eye and a twist of his head
Soon gave me to know I had nothing to dread;
He spoke not a word, but went straight to his work,
And filled all the stockings; then turned with a jerk,
And laying his finger aside of his nose,
And giving a nod, up the chimney he rose;
He sprang to his sleigh, to his team gave a whistle,
And away they all flew like the down of a thistle.
But I heard him exclaim, ere he drove out of sight:
'Happy Christmas to all, and to all a good night!'

25 December ✶ The Christmas Rose ✶
Cecil Day-Lewis

27 April 1904 – 22 May 1972

Merry Christmas! This festive poem comes to us courtesy of the former Poet Laureate, Cecil Day-Lewis. In his early years Day-Lewis was a radical Marxist who became a member of the British Communist Party whose verse was influenced by that of his university friend W. H. Auden. But in later years, after a stint working in the Ministry of Information during the Second World War, he became a much more traditional lyric writer, and a symbol of the establishment once he was appointed Laureate. Before, and even after, getting his major breakthrough as a poet, Day-Lewis supplemented his income by moonlighting as a detective novelist called Nicholas Blake, publishing nineteen titles. He was the father (no sleuthing skills needed here) of the actor Daniel Day-Lewis.

What is the flower that blooms each year
In flowerless days,
Making a little blaze
On the bleak earth, giving my heart some cheer?

Harsh the sky and hard the ground
When the Christmas rose is found.
Look! Its white star, low on earth,
Rays a vision of rebirth.

Who is the child that's born each year –
His bedding, straw:
His grace, enough to thaw
My wintering life, and melt a world's despair?

Harsh the sky and hard the earth
When the Christmas child comes forth.
Look! around a stable throne
Beasts and wise men are at one.

What men are we that, year on year,
We Herod-wise
In our cold wits devise
A death of innocents, a rule of fear?

Hushed your earth, full-starred your sky
For a new nativity:
Be born in us, relieve our plight,
Christmas child, you rose of light!

26 December ✶ The Listeners ✶ Walter de la Mare

25 April 1873 – 22 June 1956

Walter de la Mare was a celebrated writer of fiction and poetry for both adults and children, famed for his fantastical imagination and dreamlike imagery. He wrote several collections, such as *Songs of Childhood* – a title that's more than a little reminiscent of Blake, a profound influence on his work – and nonsense verse. Some of his serious poetry was occasionally criticized for its childlike tone. As his contemporary, the novelist and playwright J. B. Priestley put it, de la Mare was 'one of that most lovable order of artists who never lose sight of their childhood, but re-live it continually in their work'. But he is also remembered as a master of supernatural fiction for adults, and is revered for his tales of the uncanny. In his early career, de la Mare had to supplement his writing by working as a clerk for an oil company, but before turning forty he was granted a Civil List pension for his services to writing which allowed him to concentrate fully on his literature. It was not an opportunity he squandered, as he became an internationally respected literary figure.

'Is there anybody there?' said the Traveller,
  Knocking on the moonlit door;
And his horse in the silence champed the grasses
  Of the forest's ferny floor:
And a bird flew up out of the turret,
  Above the Traveller's head:
And he smote upon the door again a second time;
  'Is there anybody there?' he said.
But no one descended to the Traveller;
  No head from the leaf-fringed sill
Leaned over and looked into his grey eyes,
  Where he stood perplexed and still.
But only a host of phantom listeners

That dwelt in the lone house then
Stood listening in the quiet of the moonlight
To that voice from the world of men:
Stood thronging the faint moonbeams on the dark stair,
That goes down to the empty hall,
Hearkening in an air stirred and shaken
By the lonely Traveller's call.
And he felt in his heart their strangeness,
Their stillness answering his cry,
While his horse moved, cropping the dark turf,
'Neath the starred and leafy sky;
For he suddenly smote on the door, even
Louder, and lifted his head:—
'Tell them I came, and no one answered,
That I kept my word,' he said.
Never the least stir made the listeners,
Though every word he spake
Fell echoing through the shadowiness of the still house
From the one man left awake:
Ay, they heard his foot upon the stirrup,
And the sound of iron on stone,
And how the silence surged softly backward,
When the plunging hoofs were gone.

27 December ✶ One Art ✶ Elizabeth Bishop

8 February 1911 – 6 October 1979

The poet Elizabeth Bishop was brought up by her grandparents in Massachusetts and attended Vassar College. It was there that she met the poet Marianne Moore, who became a lifelong friend, and where she began working on her own writing. After completing her studies, she travelled extensively in Europe and Northern Africa, and then settled in Florida, where she composed many of the poems that would form part of her first collection, *North and South*, and the Pulitzer Prize-winning follow-up, *Poems: North & South – A Cold Spring*. A close friend of poet Robert Lowell (whom we'll meet next), their poetic styles could not have been more different; where Lowell was confessional, she was reserved, known for her quiet observation. Bishop later lived in Brazil with the architect Lota de Macedo Soares for fourteen years, before returning to Massachusetts, accepting a teaching position at Harvard. Bishop only published 101 poems.

The art of losing isn't hard to master;
so many things seem filled with the intent
to be lost that their loss is no disaster.

Lose something every day. Accept the fluster
of lost door keys, the hour badly spent.
The art of losing isn't hard to master.

Then practice losing farther, losing faster:
places, and names, and where it was you meant
to travel. None of these will bring disaster.

I lost my mother's watch. And look! my last, or
next-to-last, of three loved houses went.
The art of losing isn't hard to master.

I lost two cities, lovely ones. And, vaster,
some realms I owned, two rivers, a continent.
I miss them, but it wasn't a disaster.

—Even losing you (the joking voice, a gesture
I love) I shan't have lied. It's evident
the art of losing's not too hard to master
though it may look like (*Write* it!) like disaster.

28 December ✶ Epilogue ✶ Robert Lowell

1 March 1917 – 12 September 1977

Robert Lowell is another poet, like Henry Longfellow and Florence Earle Coates, who could trace their lineage back to the first *Mayflower* American settlers. There is even a popular rhyme that stresses his family's grand social position: 'And this is good old Boston, / The home of the bean and the cod, / Where the Lowells talk only to Cabots, / And the Cabots talk only to God.' Much of Lowell's poetry engages with his New England background, his roots and privilege. A Pulitzer Prize and National Book Award winner, Lowell was one of the most venerated US poets of the post-war era, and hailed on the cover of *Time* magazine in 1967 as 'America's Greatest Poet'. His early work was influenced by his Christian beliefs, but his style had drastically changed by the late 1950s, when he published *Life Studies*, his major, career-defining collection. In it, Lowell wrote in free verse and freely about his personal life in a so-called 'confessional' manner, similar in nature to the work of his one-time student Sylvia Plath. This poem, the last in his final collection, is typically inward-looking but seemingly (and ironically) damning of his work being based on personal recollections.

Those blessèd structures, plot and rhyme—
why are they no help to me now
I want to make
something imagined, not recalled?
I hear the noise of my own voice:
The painter's vision is not a lens,
it trembles to caress the light.
But sometimes everything I write
with the threadbare art of my eye
seems a snapshot,
lurid, rapid, garish, grouped,
heightened from life,

yet paralyzed by fact.
All's misalliance.
Yet why not say what happened?
Pray for the grace of accuracy
Vermeer gave to the sun's illumination
stealing like the tide across a map
to his girl solid with yearning.
We are poor passing facts,
warned by that to give
each figure in the photograph
his living name.

29 December ✶ *from* Gawain and the Green Knight ✶ Anon., translated by Jessie Weston

One of the great texts in Middle English literature, *Gawain and the Green Knight* is an anonymous poem written at the end of the fourteenth century. An Arthurian romance, it opens at the court of Camelot, and sees the unexpected arrival of an enigmatic green knight riding a green horse. The knight challenges the crowd to a fight, and only Sir Gawain, King Arthur's nephew, accepts the challenge. The poem follows the tradition of the romance genre, which is not so much related to love as it is to a knight's quest. It is original in its style and use of language; the dialect – as well as some detailed landscape description – suggests that the author was from the North West, but the text is also rich in terms derived from Old Norse. Sir Gawain was written in the same period as Chaucer, although it is much harder for us to understand as our modern English evolved more directly from the latter. Luckily there are great translations on hand by the likes of J. R. R. Tolkien, Simon Armitage and this one by the medievalist Jessie Weston.

Look, Gawain, thou be swift to speed as thou hast said,
And seek, in all good faith, until thy search be sped,
E'en as thou here didst swear, in hearing of these knights –
To the Green Chapel come, I charge thee now aright,
The blow thou hast deserved, such as was dealt to-day,
E'en on the New Year's morn I pledge me to repay,
Full many know my name, *'Knight of the Chapel Green'*,
To find me, should'st thou seek, thou wilt not fail, I ween,
Therefore thou need'st must come, or be for recreant found!'
With fierce pull at the rein he turned his steed around,
His head within his hand, forth from the hall he rode,
Beneath his horse's hoofs the sparks they flew abroad.

30 December ✶ Mild is the Parting Year ✶ Walter Savage Landor

30 January 1775 – 17 September 1864

Walter Savage Landor is another one of those poets who, though not widely read today, helped inspire generations of writers. The lack of popular recognition no doubt partly stems from the fact that he often wrote in Latin! Landor once explained his preference by saying, 'I am sometimes at a loss for an English word, for a Latin never.' These Latin texts aside, Landor was known among his admirers for the range of his work, which spanned from biting little epigrams to delicate romance poetry, to imagined dialogues between various historical figures such as Elizabeth I, George Washington and Plato. Although clearly a very gifted man, Landor more than lived up to his middle name 'savage'. His stormy temperament dates back to his youth, when he was expelled from both his school and university, and he did not seem to mellow with age, continuously courting the ire of publishers and politicians, which did little to help his career. Still, he was much liked by fellow writers such as the Brownings, and Charles Dickens who based a character on Landor in *Bleak House*.

Mild is the parting year, and sweet
The odour of the falling spray;
Life passes on more rudely fleet,
And balmless is its closing day.

I wait its close, I court its gloom,
But mourn that never must there fall
Or on my breast or on my tomb
The tear that would have soothed it all.

31 December ✶ *from* The Land ✶
Vita Sackville-West

9 March 1892 – 2 June 1962

Vita Sackville-West, like Lord Alfred Douglas, is a writer better known for her romantic association with a literary celebrity – in this case Virginia Woolf. For ten years, she was the author's closest companion and partner, a muse, for the protagonist of the time-hopping historical novel *Orlando*. But Sackville-West was also a talented and successful writer, poet and journalist in her own right. Born to an aristocratic family, she grew up in a large country house called Knole as a rather solitary child, but one with immense literary gifts, penning eight novels as well as plays and poems before she turned eighteen. She married Harold Nicolson, and they lived at another ancestral property, Sissinghurst, where she created a garden of national renown. As a writer, Sackville-West is best known for her novel *The Edwardians*, and for her narrative poem *The Land*, a celebration of nature and rural life. This extract from the poem focuses on the seasonal changes of the passing of the year – a fitting final entry for our own poetic run through the calendar.

Now I have told the year from dawn to dusk,
Its morning and its evening and its noon;
Once round the sun our slanting orbit rolled,
Four times the seasons changed, thirteen the moon;
Corn grew from seed to husk,
The young spring grass to provender for herds;
Drought came, and earth was grateful for the rain;
The bees streamed in and out the summer hives;
Birds wildly sang; were silent; birds
With summer's passing fitfully sang again;
The loaded waggon crossed the field; the sea
Spread her great generous pasture as a robe
Whereon the slow ships, circling statelily,

Are patterned round the globe.
The ample busyness of life went by,
All the full busyness of lives
Unknown to fame, made lovely by no words:
The shepherd lonely in the winter fold;
The tiller following the eternal plough
Beneath a stormy or a gentle sky;
The sower with his gesture like a gift
Walking the furrowed hill from base to brow;
The reaper in the piety of thrift
Binding the sheaf against his slanted thigh.

Index of First Lines

Index of Poets and Translators

Acknowledgements

Thanks to
Gaby Morgan, Belinda Rasmussen, Jo Hardacre, Sarah Clarke, Sarah Plows, Alyx Price, Rachel Vale, Tracey Ridgewell, Charlie Castelletti, Amy Boxshall and Simran Sandhu at MCB, Nick de Somogyi, Clare Conville and the team at C&W, Georgina Moore and Hannah Bright at Midas PR, Zanna Goldhawk and Harry Goldhawk at Papio Press, Giles Andreae, Simon Russell Beale, Gina Bellman, Helena Bonham Carter, Beatie Edney, Dan Einav, Jane Epstein, Eliza Esiri, Jack Esiri, Mark Esiri, Rosie Esiri, Liam Etheridge, Jonathan Foreman, Juliet Garmoyle, Catarina Greco, Susannah Herbert, Arthur James, Emma Kay, Damian Lewis, Tif Loehnis, Michael Rosen, Samantha Weinberg and Samuel West.

The compiler and publisher would like to thank the following for permission to use their copyright material:

Achebe, Chinua: 'Pine Tree in Spring'. Copyright © Chinua Achebe; **Adcock, Fleur:** 'Nature Table' copyright © Fleur Adcock. Reproduced by permission of Bloodaxe Books (www.bloodaxebooks.com); **Agard, John:** 'Chilling Out Beside the Thames' from *Alternative Anthem: Selected Poems with Live DVD* (Bloodaxe Books, 2009). Reproduced by permission of Bloodaxe Books (www.bloodaxebooks.com); **Agbabi, Patience:** Excerpt from 'Telling Tales Prologue (Grime Mix)', copyright © Patience Agbabi; **Ahlberg, Allan:** 'Only Snow' from *Please Mrs Butler* (Puffin Books, 1983) copyright © Allan Ahlberg, 1983. Reproduced by permission of Penguin Books Limited; **Akhmatova, Anna:** 'Lot's Wife' by Anna Akhmatova; English translation from Poems of Akhmatova, Selected, Translated, and Introduced by Stanley Kunitz with Max Hayward (Mariner Books, an imprint of Houghton Mifflin Harcourt 1997). Copyright © 1967, 1968, 1972, 1973 by Stanley Kunitz and Max Hayward. All rights reserved. Used with permission; **Alexander, Kwame:** 'Busted' from *Booked* (Andersen Press, 2016). Copyright © Kwame Alexander. Used by permission of the publisher; **Alvi, Moniza:** 'I Would Like to be a Dot in a Painting by Miró' from *Six women Poets* (Oxford Publishing Limited, 1992) copyright © Moniza Alvi. Used with permission; **Andreae, Giles:** 'The End of the World' by Purple Ronnie. Reproduced by permission of Coolabi; **Angelou, Maya:** 'Still I Rise' from *The Complete Poetry* copyright © Maya Angelou 2015. Reprinted by permission of Virago, an imprint of Little, Brown Book Group; **Antrobus, Raymond:** 'Two Guns in the Sky for Daniel Harris' from *The Perseverance* (Penned in the Margins, 2018) copyright © Raymond Antrobus. Used by permission; **Armitage, Simon:** 'The Catch', copyright © Simon Armitage. Used with permission of Faber and Faber Ltd; **Arshi, Mona:** 'The Gold Bangles' from *Small Hands* (Liverpool University Press, 2015). Reproduced by permission of the Licensor through PLSclear; **Ashbery, John:** 'They Knew What They Wanted' from *They Knew What They Wanted*, 2018. Reproduced by permission of Carcanet Press, Manchester, UK; **Atwood, Margaret:** 'Siren Song', copyright © Margaret Atwood. Reproduced with permission of Curtis Brown Ltd, London, on behalf of the author; **Auden, W. H.:** 'O Tell me the Truth About Love' copyright © W. H. Auden. Reprinted by permission of Curtis Brown Ltd; **Ayres, Pam:** 'The Dog Who Bit the Ball' from *Pam Ayres on Animals* published by Ebury Press in 2021 © Pam Ayres 2021. Reproduced by permission of Sheil Land Associates Ltd**; Baldwin, James:** 'Le sporting-club de Monte Carlo (for Lena Horne)' from *Jimmy's Blues and Other Poems*, copyright © 1983, 1985 by James Baldwin. Reproduced by permission of Beacon Press, Boston Massachusetts; **Bellerby, Frances:** 'Ends Meet' from *Selected Poems* (Enitharmon, 1971). Reproduced by permission of David Higham Associates; **Belloc, Hilaire: '**Henry King' by Hilaire Belloc, copyright © Hilaire Belloc. Reprinted by permission of Peters Fraser & Dunlop (www.petersfraserdunlop.com) on behalf of the Estate of Hilaire Belloc; **Benson, Gerard:** Extract from 'Beowulf', translated by Gerard Benson. Copyright © Gerard Benson; **Bentley, Edmund Clerihew:** 'George the third and others' from *More Biography*, copyright © E. C. Bentley, 1929. Reproduced by permission of Curtis Brown Ltd, London, on behalf of the Estate of E. C. Bentley; **Berry, James:** 'People Equal' from *A Story I am In: Selected Poems* (Bloodaxe Books, 2011). Reproduced by permission of Bloodaxe Books (www.bloodaxebooks.com); **Berry, Wendell:** 'The Peace of Wild Things' Copyright © 2002 by Wendell Berry, from *New Collected Poems*. Reprinted by permission of Counterpoint Press; **Betjeman, John:** 'How to Get on In Society' copyright © John Betjeman. Reproduced by permission of John Murray Press, an imprint of Hodder and Stoughton Limited; **Bilston, Brian:** 'A Brief History of Modern Art in Poetry' Copyright © Brian Bilston. Reprinted by permission; **Bishop, Elizabeth:** 'One Art' from *Poems: The Centenary Edition by Elizabeth Bishop* (Chatto & Windus, 2011). Used by permission of Penguin Random House; **Bloom, Valerie:** 'Two Seasons' Copyright © Valerie Bloom 2000 from *Hot Like Fire* (Bloomsbury) reprinted by permission of Eddison Pearson Ltd on behalf of Valerie Bloom; **Boland, Eavan:** 'Becoming Anne Bradstreet' from *New Selected Poems* (Carcanet, 2005). Copyright © Eavan Boland. Used by permission of

Carcanet Press; **Brathwaite, Kamau:** 'Mmenson' from *The Arrivants: A New World Trilogy* (Oxford University Press, 1981). Copyright © Kamau Brathwaite Reproduced by permission of the Licensor through PLSclear; **Brecht, Bertolt:** 'The Burning of the Books', from *The Collected Poems of Bertolt Brecht*, translated by Tom Kuhn and David Constantine, Liveright, 2018, translation copyright © 2015, 2019 by Tom Kuhn and David Constantine. Reproduced by permission of Liveright Publishing Corporation; **Brooks, Gwendolyn:** 'We Real Cool', copyright © Gwendolyn Brooks. Reprinted by consent of Brooks Permission; **Brownlee, Liz:** 'Slithering Silver', copyright © Liz Brownlee. Used with permission of the author; **Bukowski, Charles:** 'My Cats' from *Come On In! by Charles Bukowski.* Copyright © 2006 by Linda Lee Bukowski. Used by permission of HarperCollins Publishers; **Camden, Steven:** 'Science Book Toilets' from *Everything All At Once* (Macmillan Children's Books, 2018) Copyright © Steven Camden. Used with permission; **Carter, James:** 'Love You More' from *Weird, Wild and Wonderful: The Poetry World of James Carter* (Otter-Barry Books, 2021). Copyright © James Carter. Used with permission of the publisher; **Carver, Raymond:** 'Happiness' from *All of Us: The Collected Poems* (Vintage, 1997). Reproduced by permission of The Random House Group Limited; **Causley, Charles:** 'I Am the Song' from *Collected Poems 1951-2000* (Picador, 2000). Copyright © Charles Causley. Used by permission of David Higham Associates on behalf of the estate of the author; **Cavafy, C. P.:** 'Ithaka' from *C. P. CAVAFY: Collected Poems,* Revised Edition translated by Edmund Keeley and Philip Sherrard, ed. by George Savidis. Translation copyright © 1975, 1992 by Edmund Keeley and Philip Sherrard. Reprinted by permission of Princeton University Press; **Chatterjee, Debjani:** 'Proverbial Logic' from *Animal Antics* (Pennine Pens, 2000). Copyright © Debjani Chatterjee. Used by permission of the author; **Clarke, Gillian:** 'Ode to Winter' by Gillian Clarke. Copyright © Gillian Clarke. Reproduced by permission of the author c/o Rogers, Coleridge & White Ltd., 20 Powis Mews, London W11 1JN; **Coelho, Joseph:** 'January' in *A Year of Nature Poems,* written by Joseph Coelho and illustrated by Kelly Louise Judd, published by Wide Eyed Editions, an imprint of The Quarto Group, copyright © 2019. Reproduced by permission of Quarto Publishing Plc; **Cohen, Leonard:** 'Anthem' by Leonard Cohen. Copyright © 1992, Leonard Cohen, used by permission of The Wylie Agency (UK) Limited; **Collins, Billy:** 'Bashō in Ireland' from *Rain in Portugal* (Picador, 2017). Copyright © Billy Collins. Reprinted by permission; **Cookson, Paul:** 'Let No One Steal Your Dreams' copyright © Paul Cookson. Reprinted by permission of author; **Cooper Clarke, John:** 'I Wanna Be Yours' Words and Music by John Cooper Clarke. Reproduced by permission of Sony Music Publishing, London W1F 3LP; **Cope, Wendy:** 'The Uncertainty of the Poet' from *Serious Concerns* (Faber & Faber, 2002), copyright © Wendy Cope. Used with permission of Faber and Faber Ltd; **Corbett, Pie:** 'City Jungle', copyright © Pie Corbett. Used by kind permission of the author; **Cornford, Frances:** 'Childhood' from *Selected Poems,* edited by Jane Dowson (Enitharmon Press, 2021). Used with permission; **Cummings, E. E.:** 'i carry your heart with me(i carry it in'. Copyright 1952, © 1980, 1991 by the Trustees for the E. E. Cummings Trust, from *Complete Poems: 1904-1962* by E. E. Cummings, edited by George J. Firmage. Used by permission of Liveright Publishing Corporation; **Dahl, Roald:** 'Where Art Thou, Mother Christmas?' from *The Roald Dahl Treasury* (Jonathan Cape and Penguin Books Ltd). Copyright © The Roald Dahl Story Company Limited. Used by permission of David Higham Associates on behalf of the estate of the author; **Day-Lewis, Cecil:** 'The Christmas Rose', copyright © Cecil Day-Lewis. Reproduced by permission of Penguin Books Limited; **de la Mare, Walter:** 'The Listeners' by Walter de la Mare. Permission granted by The Literary Trustees of Walter de la Mare and the Society of Authors as their Representative; **Dean, Jan:** 'It's Not What I'm Used To', copyright © Jan Dean. Used with kind permission of the author; **Dharker, Imtiaz:** 'Chaudhri Sher Mobarik Looks at the Loch' from *Luck is the Hook* (Bloodaxe Books, 2018). Reproduced by permission of Bloodaxe Books (www.bloodaxebooks.com); **Doolittle, H. D.:** 'Oread' from *Selected Poems* (Carcanet Press, 1997). Used with permission of Carcanet Press; **Donaldson, Julia:** 'The Mouse and the Lion' from *Crazy Mayonnaisy Mum* (Macmillan Children's Books, 2015). Used with permission; **Drake, Nick:** 'The Future' from *Out of*

Range (Bloodaxe Books, 2018). Reproduced by permission of Bloodaxe Books (www.bloodaxebooks.com); **Duffy, Carol Ann:** 'Mrs Icarus' from *The World's Wife* (Picador, 2017). Used with permission; **Dunmore, Helen:** 'Wild Strawberries' from *Counting Backwards: Poems 1975-2017* (Bloodaxe Books, 2019). Reproduced by permission of Bloodaxe Books (www.bloodaxebooks.com); **Dunsany, Lord:** 'And Were You Pleased?' copyright © Lord Dunsany, 1938. Reproduced by permission of Curtis Brown Ltd, London, on behalf of the Trustees of the Lord Dunsany Will Trust; **Dylan, Bob:** 'Boots Of Spanish Leather' Words and Music by Bob Dylan © 1964. Reproduced by permission of Special Rider Music / Sony Music Publishing Ltd, London W1F 9LD; **Eliot, T. S.:** 'Bustopher Jones: The Cat about Town' from *Old Possum's Book of Practical Cats* (Faber & Faber, 2014). Used with permission of Faber and Faber Ltd; **Ellams, Inua:** 'Shame Is the Cape I Wear' from *The Wire-Headed Heathen,* Akashic Books, 2015, copyright © Inua Ellams. Reproduced by permission of the author c/o Rogers, Coleridge & White Ltd., 20 Powis Mews, London W11 1JN; **Ewart, Gavin:** 'The Lover Writes a One-Word Poem', Copyright © Gavin Ewart. Reproduced by kind permission of the Estate of Gavin Ewart; **Fanthorpe, U. A.:** 'BC:AD' from *Christmas Poems* (Enitharmon Press, 2002). Used with permission; **Farjeon, Eleanor:** 'Poetry' from *Blackbird Has Spoken* (Macmillan Children's Books, 1999). Reproduced by permission of David Higham Associates; **Fenton, James:** 'Blood and Lead' copyright © James Fenton. Printed by permission of United Agents (www.unitedagents.co.uk) on behalf of the author; **Ferlinghetti, Lawrence:** 'The Sea is Calm Tonight' By Lawrence Ferlinghetti, from *These Are My Rivers,* copyright ©1993 by Lawrence Ferlinghetti. Reprinted by permission of New Directions Publishing Corp; **Frost, Robert:** 'My November Guest' from *The Collected Poems by Robert Frost* published by Vintage Classics. Copyright © 1969 by Holt, Rinehart and Winston Inc. Reprinted by permission of The Random House Group Limited; **Gaiman, Neil:** 'Dark Sonnet' copyright © 2005 by Neil Gaiman. Reprinted by permission of Writers House LLC acting as agent for the author; **Gill, Nikita:** 'Ancestors' copyright © Nikita Gill. Reproduced by permission of David Higham Associates; **Ginsberg, Allen:** 'Homework', copyright © 1956, 2021, Allen Ginsberg LLC. Reproduced by permission of The Wylie Agency (UK) Limited; **Giovanni, Nikki:** 'Ego Tripping (there may be a reason why)' from *The Collected Poetry of Nikki Giovanni.* Copyright compilation © 2003 by Nikki Giovanni. Used by permission of HarperCollins Publishers; **Gittins, Chrissie:** 'The Unseen Life of Trees', copyright © Chrissie Gittins. Used by kind permission of the author; **Glück, Louise:** 'All Hallows' from *The First Five Books of Poems* (Carcanet, 1997) copyright © Louise Glück. Used by permission of Carcanet Press Limited; **Goodfellow, Matt:** 'Puzzle' copyright © Matt Goodfellow. Used with kind permission of the author; **Graves, Robert:** 'Welsh Incident' from *Complete Poems in One Volume* (Carcanet, 2000) copyright © Robert Graves. Used with permission of Carcanet Press; **Gunn, Thom:** 'From the Wave', copyright © Thom Gunn. Used with permission of Faber and Faber Ltd; **Hardy-Dawson, Sue:** 'Old Foxy' copyright © Sue Hardy-Dawson. Used with permission of the author; **Harrold, A. F.:** 'Beowulf' copyright © A. F. Harrold. Used with permission of the author; **Hass, Robert:** 'Mosquito at my Ear' by Kobayashi Issa (translated by Robert Hass) from *The Essential Haiku: Versions of Basho, Buson and Issa* (Bloodaxe Books, 2013). Used with permission; **Heaney, Seamus:** Excerpt from 'The Cure of Troy', copyright © Seamus Heaney. Used with permission of Faber and Faber Ltd; **Hegley, John:** 'A Declaration of Need' copyright © John Hegley. Printed by permission of United Agents (www.unitedagents.co.uk) on behalf of the author; **Holub, Miroslav:** 'The Fly' from *Poems Before & After: Collected English Translations,* trans. Ian & jarmila Milner et al. (Bloodaxe Books, 2006). Reproduced by permission of Bloodaxe Books (www.bloodaxebooks.com); **Hughes, Ted:** 'Lobster' from *Collected Poems for Children.* Copyright © Ted Hughes. Used with permission of Faber and Faber Ltd; **Hughes, Langston:** 'Harlem' from *Collected Poems of Langston Hughes* (Alfred A Knopf Inc). Copyright © Langston Hughes. Reproduced by permission of David Higham Associates; **James, Clive:** 'The Book of My Enemy Has Been Remaindered' from *The Book of my Enemy has been Remaindered* (Picador, 2013). Used with permission; **Jennings, Elizabeth:** 'Friends' from *The Collected Poems* (Carcanet Press, 201212) Copyright ©

Elizabeth Jennings. Reproduced by permission of David Higham Associates; **Johnson, Linton Kwesi:** 'If I woz a Tap-Natch Poet,' copyright © Linton Kwesi Johnson. Reproduced by kind permission of LKJ Music Publishers Ltd; **Jones, Brian:** 'About Friends' from *The Spitfire on the Northern Line,* Chatto and Windus, 1975. Reproduced by permission of Shoestring Press on behalf of the Estate; **Joseph, Jenny:** 'Warning' from *Selected Poems,* Bloodaxe 1992, copyright © Jenny Joseph. Reproduced by permission of Johnson & Alcock Ltd; **Kay, Jackie:** 'Sassenachs' from *Darling: New & Selected Poems* (Bloodaxe Books, 2007). Reproduced by permission of the publisher; **Kline, A. S.:** Except from 'Satyricon' by Gaius Petronius Arbiter (author), A. S. Kline (translator) copyright © 2018, Excerpt from 'the Aeneid' by Virgil, and from the Odes by Quintus Horatius Flaccus Horace (author), A. S. Kline (translator), copyright © 2003. Used with permission; **Larkin, Philip:** 'Church Going' from *The Less Deceived,* Faber & Faber Ltd, 1966. Reproduced by permission of the publisher; **Lee, Laurie:** 'April Rise' Reproduced with permission of Curtis Brown Ltd, London, on behalf of the Estate of Laurie Lee. Copyright © The Estate of Laurie Lee 1940; **Leunig, Michael:** 'JOMO' Copyright © Michael Leunig. Used by permission of the author; **Levi, Primo:** 'If This Is A Man' from *Se questo è un uomo,* 1947; translated by Stuart Woolf in *If This Is A Man.* Copyright © 1958, 1963, 1971, 1973, 2005, 2012 Giulio Einaudi editore s.p.a., Torino. Reproduced by permission of Giulio Einaudi Editore S.p.A.; **Levin, Bernard:** 'On Quoting Shakespeare', copyright © Bernard Levin. Reproduced by permission of Curtis Brown Group Ltd, London, on behalf of the Estate of Bernard Levin; **Lochhead, Liz:** 'The Spaces Between' Copyright © Liz Lochhead. Used with permission; **Longley, Michael:** 'Persephone' copyright © Michael Longley. Reproduced by permission of Penguin Books Limited; **Lorca, Federico García:** 'Spring Song (28th March 1919)' translated by Martin Sorrel from *Selected Poems,* Oxford University Press, 2013. Reproduced by permission of the Licensor through PLSclear; **Lorde, Audre:** 'Now' from *The Collected Poems of Audre Lorde,* WW Norton, 2000. Reproduced by permission of Abner Stein; **Lowell, Robert:** 'Epilogue' from *Collected Poems* by Robert Lowell, copyright © 2003 by Harriet Lowell and Sheridan Lowell. Reproduced by permission of Farrar, Straus and Giroux. All rights reserved; **MacCaig, Norman:** 'An Ordinary Day' from *The Poems of Norman MacCaig,* PolyBirlinn, 2009. Reproduced by permission of the Licensor through PLSclear; **MacNeice, Louis:** 'Snow' from *Collected Poems* (Faber & Faber, 2016). Copyright © Louis MacNeice. Used with permission of Faber and Faber Ltd; **Mahon, Derek:** 'Everything is Going to Be All Right' from *The Poems (1961-2020).* Reproduced by kind permission of the author's Estate and The Gallery Press. www.gallerypress.com; **Maris, Hyllus:** 'Spiritual Song of the Aborigine' from *Spirit Song: A collection of Aboriginal poetry.* Reproduced by kind permission of the Estate for the author; **Masefield, John:** 'Sea Fever' by John Masefield. Permission granted by The Literary Trustees of Walter de la Mare and the Society of Authors as their Representative; **McGough, Roger:** 'A Good Poem' from *You Tell Me,* written by Roger McGough and Michael Rosen and illustrated by Korky Paul, published by Frances Lincoln Children's Books, an imprint of The Quarto Group, copyright © 2015. Reproduced by permission of Quarto Publishing Plc; **McNish, Hollie:** 'You Do Not Need a Chimney for Santa Claus to Come' by Hollie McNish © Hollie McNish, with permission of Johnson and Alcock; **Miller, Kei:** 'Roads' from *The Cartographer Tries to Map A Way to Zion* (Carcanet Press, 2014). Copyright © Kei Miller. Reproduced by permission of David Higham Associates; **Milligan, Spike:** 'You Must Never Bath in an Irish Stew' copyright © Spike Milligan. Used with permission of Spike Milligan Productions Limited; **Milne, A. A.:** 'Us Two' for *Now We Are Six* by A. A. Milne Copyright © Pooh Properties Trust 1927 Reproduced with permissions from Curtis Brown Group Ltd on behalf of The Pooh Properties Trust; **Mitchell, Adrian:** 'Celia Celia' copyright © Adrian Mitchell. Printed by permission of United Agents (www.unitedagents.co.uk) on behalf of the Estate of the Author; **Mitton, Tony:** 'St Brigid and the Baker' from Plum (scholastic, 1998). Copyright © Tony Mitton. Reproduced by permission of David Higham Associates; **Moore, Marianne:** 'I may, I might, I must' from *New Collected Poems of Marianne Moore* (Faber & Faber, 2017), copyright © Marianne Moore. Used with permission of Faber and Faber Ltd; **Morgan, Michaela:** 'Feeling Icky' copyright ©

Michaela Morgan. Used by permission of the author; **Moses, Brian:** 'A Feather from an Angel' from *Lost Magic: The Very Best of Brian Moses* (Macmillan, 2016), copyright © Brian Moses. Used with permission of the author; **Motion, Andrew:** 'Anne Frank Huis' from Selected Poems of Andrew Motion (Faber and Faber, 2002), copyright © Andrew Motion. Used with permission of Faber and Faber Ltd; **Mucha, Laura:** 'Dear Key Workers' from *Dear Ugly Sisters* (Otter-Barry Books, 2020), copyright © Laura Mucha. Reproduced by permission of David Higham Associates; **Muldoon, Paul:** 'Caedmon', translated by Paul Muldoon, copyright © Paul Muldoon. Used with permission of the author; **Nash, Ogden:** 'Song of the Open Road' from *Candy is Dandy* (Welbeck Publishing Group, 1994). Copyright © Ogden Nash. Used with permission; **Nichols, Grace:** 'Epilogue' from *Selected Poems*, copyright © Grace Nichols. Reproduced by permission of Curtis Brown Ltd, London, on behalf of the author; **Normal, Henry:** 'Three Lies and One Truth about the Moon'. Reproduced by permission of Independent Talent Group; **Noyes, Alfred:** 'Daddy Fell into the Pond' by Alfred Noyes. Permission granted by The Literary Trustees of Walter de la Mare and the Society of Authors as their Representative; **O'Hara, Frank:** 'Autobiographia Literaria' from *Selected Poems* (Carcanet, 2005). Copyright © Frank O'Hara. Reproduced with permission; **Oliver, Mary:** 'The Sweetness of Dogs' from *Dog Songs* by Mary Oliver - Published by The Penguin Press New York Copyright © 2013 by Mary Oliver. Reprinted by permission of The Charlotte Sheedy Literary Agency Inc; **Oswald, Alice:** 'A Short Story of Falling' copyright © Alice Oswald; **Owen, Gareth:** 'Bird' from *The Fox on the Roundabout* by Gareth Owen, Macmillan Publishers, copyright © Gareth Owen. Reproduced by permission of the author c/o Rogers, Coleridge & White Ltd., 20 Powis Mews, London W11 1JN; **Parker, Dorothy:** 'One Perfect Rose' copyright ©Dorothy Parker; **Patten, Brian:** 'Vanity' from *The Book of Upside Down Thinking* by Brian Patten. Copyright © Brian Patten. Reproduced by permission of the author c/o Rogers, Coleridge & White Ltd., 20 Powis Mews, London W11 1JN; **Pinter, Harold:** 'It Is Here', Copyright © Harold Pinter. Used with permission of Faber and Faber Ltd; **Plath, Sylvia:** 'Mad Girl's Love Song'. Copyright © The Estate of Sylvia Plath. Published by permission of Faber & Faber Ltd; **Pound, Ezra:** 'And the Days are Not Full Enough' By Ezra Pound, from *Personae*, copyright ©1926 by Ezra Pound. Reprinted by permission of New Directions Publishing Corp and Faber and Faber Ltd; **Prelutsky, Jack:** 'It's Halloween' from *It's Halloween!* by Jack Prelutsky Illustrated by Marylin Hafner. Used by permission of HarperCollins Publishers; **Pugh, Sheenagh:** 'What If This Road' from *Later Selected Poems,* Seren Books, 2009. Reproduced by permission of Seren Books; **Rankine, Claudia:** 'Don't Let Me Be Lonely [Mahalia Jackson is a genius]' from *Don't Let Me Be Lonely: An American Lyric*, copyright © 2004 by Claudia Rankine. Reproduced by permission of The Permissions Company, LLC on behalf of Graywolf Press, graywolfpress.org; **Rich, Adrienne:** 'What Kind of Times are These' from *Collected Poems: 1950-2012,* copyright © 2016 by The Adrienne Rich Literary Trust. Copyright © 1995 Adrienne Rich. Reproduced by permission of W. W. Norton & Company, Inc.; **Rieu, E.V.:** 'The Flattered Flying Fish' from *The Flattered Flying Fish*, Penguin, 1979. Reproduced by permission of Penguin Books Limited; **Robinson, Roger:** 'A Portable Paradise' from *A Portable Paradise,* Peepal Tree Press. Reproduced by permission of Peepal Tree Press; **Roethke, Theodore:** 'The Donkey' from The Collected Poems (Faber & Faber, 1985), copyright © Theodore Roethke. Published by permission of Faber & Faber Ltd; **Rooney, Rachel:** 'Seeker' copyright © Rachel Rooney. Used by permission of the author; **Rosen, Michael:** 'These Are the Hands' copyright © Michael Rosen. Used with permission; **Sackville-West, Vita:** Excerpt from 'The Land' from *The Land*. Reproduced with permission of Curtis Brown Ltd, London, on behalf of The Estate of Vita Sackville-West. Copyright 1926 © Vita Sackville-West; **Salkey, Andrew:** 'A Song for England' from https://poemsontheunderground.org/a-song-for-england. Reproduced by kind permission of the Estate of the author; **Sandburg, Carl:** 'Buffalo Dusk' from *The Complete Poems of Carl Sandburg*, copyright © Lillian Steichen Sandburg, 1969, 1970. Reproduced by permission of Houghton Mifflin Harcourt Publishing Company. All rights reserved; **Sassoon, Siegfried:** 'The General' copyright Siegfried Sassoon by kind permission of the Estate of George Sassoon;

Shire, Warsan: excerpt from 'what they did yesterday afternoon' by Warsan Shire, copyright 2014 ©. Used with permission of Rocking Chair Books Ltd; **Simic, Charles:** 'Watermelons' from *Selected Early Poems,* copyright © 1974 by Charles Simic. Reproduced by permission of George Braziller, Inc. (New York), www.georgebraziller.com. All rights reserved; **Sissay, Lemn:** 'Invisible Kisses' from http://blog.lemnsissay.com/2013/02/12/invisible-kisses/#sthash.PMUNdodt.dpbs, copyright © Lemn Sissay. Reproduced by permission of C&W Agency on behalf of the author; **Smith, Stevie:** 'Not Waving but Drowning' from *Collected Poems and Drawings by Stevie Smith* (Faber & Faber, 2015). Copyright © Stevie Smith. Used with permission of Faber and Faber Ltd; **Stevens, Wallace:** 'Thirteen Ways of Looking at a Blackbird', copyright © Wallace Stevens; **Tempest, Kae:** 'Icarus' from *Everything Speaks in its Own Way*, copyright © Kae Tempest. Reproduced by permission of Lewinsohn Literary Ltd; **The Poet, George (Mpanga, George):** 'The Benin Bronze', copyright © George the Poet. Used with permission of Brotherstone Creative Management on behalf of the author; **Thomas, Dylan:** 'Do Not Go Gentle into that Good Night' from *The Collected Poems of Dylan Thomas: The Centenary Edition* (Weidenfeld & Nicolson). Copyright The Dylan Thomas Trust. Reproduced by permission of David Higham Associates; **Tolkien, J. R. R.:** 'The Hoard' from *The Adventures of Tom Bombadil,* copyright © 1962 by J. R. R. Tolkien. Reproduced by permission of HarperCollins Publishers Ltd; **Vuong, Ocean:** 'Kissing in Vietnamese' copyright Ocean Vuong © 2021. Used with permission; **Wakeling, Kate:** 'Comet' from *Moon Juice* (The Emma Press, 2016). Copyright (c) Kate Wakeling. Used with permission of the author; **Walcott, Derek:** 'Map of the New World' from *The Poetry of Derek Walcott 1948-2013* (Faber & Faber, 2014). Copyright © Derek Walcott. Used by permission of Faber & Faber Ltd; **Walker, Alice:** 'Women' from *Revolutionary Petunias & Other Poems* by Alice Walker, copyright © 1970 and renewed © 1998 by Alice Walker. Reproduced by permission of David Higham Associates; **Williams, Imogen Russell:** 'Eurydice' by Imogen Russell Williams, published in *The Women Left Behind* (Dempsey & Windle, 2019). Copyright © Imogen Russell Williams. Used with permission of the author; **Williams, William Carlos:** 'Landscape with the Fall of Icarus' from *Collected Poems Volume 1 1909-1939* (Carcanet Press, 2018). Copyright © William Carlos Williams. Used with permission of Carcanet Press Limited;**Woodson, Jacqueline:** 'Reading', copyright © Jacqueline Woodson; **Yip, Wai-lim:** 'Wu-chüeh: 2 poems by Tu Fu,' in *Chinese Poetry, 2nd ed., Revised*, ed. and trans. Wai-lim Yip. Copyright © 1997, Duke University Press. All rights reserved. Republished by permission of the copyright holder. www.dukeupress.edu; **Zephaniah, Benjamin:** 'Talking Turkeys' from *Talking Turkeys* by Benjamin Zephaniah published by Puffin. Copyright © Talking Turkeys by Copyright © Benjamin Zephaniah 1994, published by Viking 1996, Puffin Books 1997, 2018. Reprinted by permission of Penguin Books Limited.

Every effort has been made to trace the copyright holders, but if any have been inadvertently overlooked the publisher will be pleased to make the necessary arrangements at the first opportunity.